Bruce

Murder on the Farm

Detective Inspector Skelgill Investigates

LUCiUS

SEE NO EVIL, HEAR NO EVIL, SPEAK NO EVIL

A REALITY DOCUMENTARY CREW is on the hunt for a victim. An unsolved murder from the 1970s that could leave the authorities red-faced. Celebrity criminologist Professor Simeon Freud plans to bask in the glory.

Posing as a researcher, DS Jones joins the production team, but Skelgill must work in the shadows. His instincts rebel – not least that his protégé is prey to a narcissist on the one hand and a killer on the other.

As evidence mounts, his unease grows: is there an altogether more sinister explanation, a cover-up that will not just embarrass the police force, but shake its very foundations? And will Skelgill get there first?

BRUCE BECKHAM is an award-winning author and copywriter. A resident of Great Britain, he has travelled and worked in over 60 countries. He is published in both fiction and non-fiction, and is a member of the UK Society of Authors.

His series 'Inspector Skelgill Investigates' features the recalcitrant Cumbrian detective Daniel Skelgill, and his loyal lieutenants, long-suffering Londoner DS Leyton and local high-flyer DS Emma Jones.

Set amidst the ancient landscapes of England's Lake District, this expanding series of stand-alone murder mysteries has won acclaim across five continents, with over 1 million copies downloaded, from Australia to Japan and India, and from Brazil to Canada and the United States of America.

"Great characters. Great atmospheric locale. Great plots. What's not to like?" Amazon reviewer, 5 stars

Kindle edition first published by Lucius 2023
Paperback edition first published by Lucius 2023
Hardcover edition first published by Lucius 2023

For more details and Rights enquiries contact:
Lucius-ebooks@live.com

Cover design by Moira Kay Nicol
United States editor Janet Colter

EDITOR'S NOTE

Murder on the Farm is a stand-alone mystery, the twenty-first in the series 'Detective Inspector Skelgill Investigates'. It is set in the English Lake District, and in some of the Cumbrian villages and towns on the northern and western flanks of the National Park.

Absolutely no AI (Artificial Intelligence) is used in the writing of the DI Skelgill novels.

THE DI SKELGILL SERIES

Murder in Adland

Murder in School

Murder on the Edge

Murder on the Lake

Murder by Magic

Murder in the Mind

Murder at the Wake

Murder in the Woods

Murder at the Flood

Murder at Dead Crags

Murder Mystery Weekend

Murder on the Run

Murder at Shake Holes

Murder at the Meet

Murder on the Moor

Murder Unseen

Murder in our Midst

Murder Unsolved

Murder in the Fells

Murder at the Bridge

Murder on the Farm

GLOSSARY

SOME of the Cumbrian dialect words, abbreviations, British slang and local usage appearing in *Murder on the Farm* are as follows:

Arl fella – father/old man/husband
Alreet/areet – alright (often a greeting)
Any road – anyway, besides
Bach – term of endearment (Welsh)
Bait – lunch/packed lunch
Bookie – bookmaker
Bottle – nerve (Cockney, bottle and glass)
Boyo – lad (Welsh)
Brass it out – call someone's bluff
Brassed off – exasperated
Callard and Bowsers – trousers (Cockney)
Cant – tip/spill
Chore – steal
Clarty – dirty
CPS – Crown Prosecution Service
Crack – chat/gossip
Cracked up to be – exaggerated prowess
Cuddy-wifter – left-handed
Dolly – easy (in cricket)
Double bubble – twice the normal rate of pay
DPP – Director of Public Prosecutions (USA = DA)
Dwam – trance, reverie
Eetsy peetsy – alternate goes
Estate – a car with a flatbed and rear door/s instead of a trunk
Fettle – health
Flannel – misleading statement
Gadgee – man
Gaff – place, dwelling
Gimmer – young female sheep
Ginnel – narrow alley between buildings
Girt – big/great

Gurn – pull a distorted face
Half-inch – pinch/steal (Cockney)
Happen – maybe
Howay – come on
Int' – in the/into
Jam Eater – local West Cumbrian insult
Karsey – toilet (Cockney)
Knock-off – stolen property
Laal – small
Mash – tea/make tea
Marra – mate (friend)
Mesen – myself
Mind – remember
Mithering – annoying
MO – modus operandi/method
Net – cricket practice (in netted area)
No-mark – worthless person
Nowt – nothing
Offcomer – outsider, alien
Off pat – rehearsed
Owt – anything
Owzat? – how's that? (cricketer's appeal)
Oxter – armpit
Pissed – inebriated
Reet – right
Saloon – a car with a hinged boot lid (enclosed trunk) – see also 'Estate'
Shooter – gun (Cockney)
Summat – something
T' – the (often silent)
Tapped – crazy
Tea leaf – thief (Cockney)
Thee/thew/thou – you, your
Theesen – yourself
Twang – local accent
Us – often used for me/my/our
Yon – that

NORTHWEST CUMBRIA

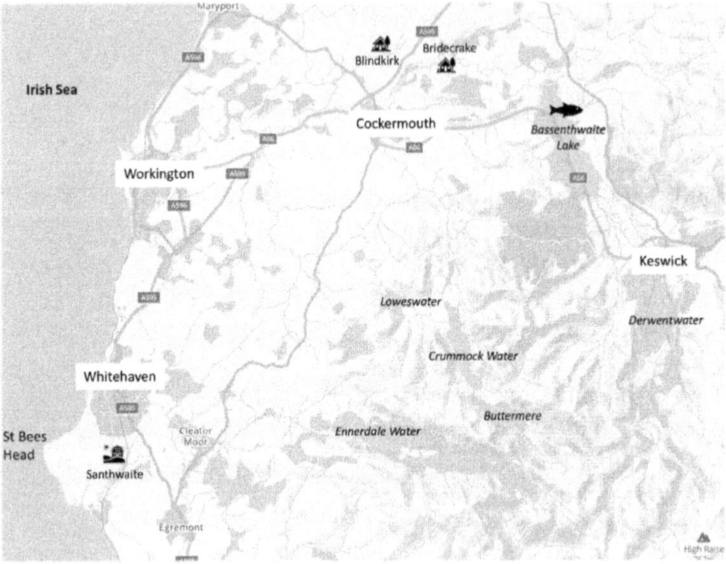

PROLOGUE

Article in THE WESTMORLAND GAZETTE by Kendall Minto

'MURDER ON THE FARM' NEW DOCUMENTARY & PODCAST

THE LONG, HOT SUMMER OF 1976 is remembered for its neatly symmetrical 76 days of unbroken sunshine, a season of Mediterranean proportions that has since to be eclipsed. But while the rest of the country sweltered beneath cloudless skies – while office workers went without their neckties; while Cadbury and Rowntree suspended production when chocolate would not set; while ladies lost high heels in melted tarmac – a cloud of a most sinister nature came to hang over the Lake District.

The callous shotgun murder of Will Featherston.

Aged just 17, the conscientious A-level pupil had recently passed his driving test. Saving for university, his summer job delivering for Whiting's of Whitehaven took him to villages and farmsteads between the Solway coast and the western fringe of the national park. The weekly visit from Whiting's distinctive ocean-blue-and-surf-white fish van was a lifeline for those lacking the means to travel to the larger population centres. And that summer, nobody wanted to carry home their Friday haddock on an overheated bus.

ROBBERY … AND MURDER

One such customer was Lady Fitzrovia, 40, of Caldblow Farm, near Santhwaite, just south of Whitehaven, widow of Lord Archie

Fitzrovia, a life peer appointed by Conservative Prime Minister Ted Heath, for his contribution to the arts. Having moved from London after her husband's death, she rented out the surrounding land to an adjoining farmer. Lady Fitzrovia enjoyed riding her hunter; accordingly the farmhouse was often left unattended and unlocked. It was Will Featherston's habit to knock and enter and deposit her Ladyship's order safely in the refrigerator.

On 13th August 1976, Will made his regular delivery.

It was to be his last.

No one knows exactly what took place, but what is certain is that Will inadvertently disturbed a robbery in progress. Police later found the house ransacked and valuable antiques missing. The stopper of a crystal decanter was found in bushes at the side of the property.

Will was discovered in the kitchen, slumped in an old armchair. We do not need to go into the gruesome details; it is believed he died instantly, blasted at point-blank range.

When news of Will's murder spread, fear gripped the entire county.

Fear, and anger. What kind of robber, armed and thus holding the upper hand, would commit such a despicable act? To take a young life; to destroy the lives of those nearest and dearest.

CUMBRIA'S BIGGEST EVER MANHUNT

While anxious families reined in or chaperoned their broods, Cumbria's police force was mobilised. More than 200 officers were drafted in from neighbouring counties and across the border in Scotland. Over 7,000 statements were taken. Hundreds of vehicles were stopped. Homes were searched. Forensic experts from Scotland Yard combed Caldblow Farm and its environs.

On the succeeding Friday, the police released a filmed reconstruction of what they believed were Will Featherston's last movements: his drive from his previous call at the Royal Oak pub in Santhwaite, leaving the hamlet to turn into the single-track lane that passed Caldblow Farm; turning again into the farm drive to park at the front of the property and enter by the kitchen door via a side gate.

But another week passed and there was no breakthrough.

The Gazette's archive captured an appeal from Chief Superintendent John Bromilow, speaking at his daily press briefing. "We have got a lot of good stuff, but it takes a little time to get through it all. It is not a black picture by any means. I am optimistic and my team is optimistic. We are seeking a chink of light to enable us to make a breakthrough." Indeed, it seems a pattern had begun to take shape, and that there were growing accounts of a vehicle parked at Caldblow Farm on the afternoon of Will Featherston's murder. Chief Superintendent Bromilow went on to make an appeal. "I am hoping that someone might identify a red car, possibly an estate, and provide a description of its occupants."

The police were hampered not just by the incessantly hot weather, but that it inevitably coincided with the peak of the tourist season. Throughout Britain schools were off and the Lake District was bursting at the seams. Lured by its shady wooded dales and cool freshwater meres, holidaymakers and day trippers alike had flooded into the national park, and fanned out to its breezy coastal towns for their beaches and ice cream stalls. Farmers and local countryfolk who might have noticed that which was out of the ordinary kept off the choked lanes during the middle of the day, moving only in early mornings and late evenings. Meanwhile sightseers who could have spotted something useful but would not appreciate its significance simply disappeared back to their homes elsewhere in the country, unaware that they may have taken with them the solution to the mystery.

KIRKSTILE FARM ROBBERY

And then, just as hopes were fading, five weeks after the murder at Caldblow Farm, came the breakthrough the police had been waiting for.

The robbers struck again.

Just 16 miles away at Kirkstile Farm, Brackenthwaite, near picturesque Loweswater, farmer Fred Fallowfield returned from inspecting his Swaledale lambs fattening on the intake pastures. Perhaps, to the shepherd's good fortune, his trusty dogs ran ahead of him – and set up a clamour. Another break-in was in progress.

A shotgun was discharged. It was a warning, fired into the air; no one was injured. Masked and empty-handed, the would-be burglars fled, almost driving down Mr Fallowfield in their battered van, a former Post Office vehicle that still displayed faded traces of its livery. This was an important clue. But they left something far more telling.

A fingerprint.

These might have been the days before the forensic tools we take for granted – DNA, CCTV, mobile phone tracking, even psychological profiling – but there was fingerprint analysis. And the clear impression of a uniquely scarred thumb left on a copper kettle that had been dropped by one of the robbers matched a print on file.

THE HARE TWINS

Joel Hare and his twin brother Jasper had served time in prison. By the age of 18 they had acquired a string of convictions in excess of their years. Starting with petty shoplifting offences as juveniles in their home town of Workington, they had moved on to breaking into sheds and outbuildings, unguarded warehouses and depots, before graduating to more brazen acts, carrying a sawn-off shotgun to threaten shop staff and hold at bay have-a-go-heroes, emptying cash from tills. But they had finally been foiled in January 1974. Making their escape having robbed the Safeway superstore at Maryport, their getaway car was pinned against a wall by an alert trucker, who with help of the store's forklift driver buried the vehicle in his delivery of toilet rolls. It was famously referred to in that week's Gazette as the "Busted Flush". Such black humour continued through the reporting of the Hares' trial, when detectives were praised for getting to the bottom of the matter, and the Hares' flimsy defence was described as a tissue of lies.

Fast forward to 1976, and the Hare twins were released on parole from youth custody. It seemed they reverted to type, now preying upon less conspicuous targets. The thumbprint was categorical. The twins were arrested on suspicion of committing the attempted larceny at Kirkstile Farm.

But the police were not finished.

Desperate for a breakthrough – under intense media scrutiny and unyielding public pressure – they drew associations between Kirkstile Farm and Will Featherston's murder at Caldblow Farm. The use of a shotgun. The daytime burglary of an isolated property left temporarily empty. The targeting of antiques. And the *red* Post Office van.

Yet, despite the clamour for news, all went quiet.

CONFESSION, CHARGE, CONVICTION

Police methods were different in those days – and perhaps the unrelenting heat played its part. Long interrogations followed. Eventually – after what seemed like an age but was only another seven days – a triumphant if perspiring Chief Superintendent John Bromilow came before the assembled media. The robbery at Kirkstile Farm and the killing at Caldblow Farm were connected. They had a confession. Two confessions.

Just five weeks after the event, the Hares were charged with the murder of Will Featherston and remanded into custody.

One year later, the case came before the bench at Carlisle Crown Court.

And there was a shock. A plea of not guilty.

The Hares had retracted their confessions and mutual accusations. The Defence averred that the first confession – by Joel Hare – had been obtained under extreme duress, and that the interrogating officers had used it to confuse and turn the sleep-deprived brothers against one another, each alleging that his sibling committed the crime. Neither Hare could read or write, and the Defence produced an expert witness, an internationally renowned professor of linguistics, who testified that the supposedly dictated statements did not match the Hares' vernacular language or limited vocabulary. The confessions could not have been spoken by them.

But twelve good folk of the jury found otherwise.

The Hares were convicted and sentenced to life, to serve a minimum of 25 years.

The remaining good folk of Cumbria breathed a collective sigh of relief.

ANOTHER KIND OF CONFESSION

Throughout their incarceration the Hares continued to plead their innocence. Their mother June Hare waged a tireless campaign on their behalf. She raised an unsuccessful appeal in 1982, but refused to give up.

In the end, however, it was a police whistleblower who dismantled the central plank of the Crown's case. On retirement, the anonymous detective had felt the weight of his conscience. He reported a fellow officer, a man known for his predilection for violence and contempt for the rule of law. In a separate test case in another regional force, it was proved beyond doubt that a confession had been both coerced and falsified.

The Court of Appeal deemed that in 11 other cases involving the bent copper, the confessions were to be considered unsound and should be struck from the evidence.

The murder at Caldblow Farm was one of those cases.

As the history books now tell us, after 12 years behind bars, in 1988 the Hares were acquitted and released as free men.

A MIXED REACTION

Cumbria Constabulary at the time disputed the outcome. Reluctant to accept the verdict of the Appeal Court, for many years the force remained in denial. One discredited confession did not make another so.

However, it was plain that there was no direct evidence to link the Hares to the Caldblow Farm murder. No forensics were produced to show they had been at the farm. No trace was ever found of the missing antiques (and the Hares were anything but sophisticated in the fencing of stolen goods in their previous offences). There was no verified sighting of the Hares at Caldblow

Farm. Only the vague connection between the "red estate car" and their second-hand Post Office van remained – and, as June Hare pointed out, a van is not an estate car, and only her boys were daft enough to commit burglaries in a distinctive postman's van.

Perhaps because the victims of their malpractice were inveterate criminals, the police did not receive the scrutiny that was due. Indeed, when the Hares had come up for sentencing and their lifetime catalogue of misdemeanours was read out in court, there was great public opprobrium. Despite their subsequent acquittal, among some observers there was a feeling that the 12 years wrongly served was the least the Hares deserved.

As one seasoned local put it, *"Flee wi' t' craws, get shot wi' t' craws"*.

And perhaps he was a fair representative of the vox pop at the time.

IF NOT THE HARES?

This, dear reader, is the question we at the Gazette hope to address. We have teamed up with Turnpike Media, makers of internationally acclaimed, award-winning investigative documentaries and podcasts.

Starting in this week's edition – under the banner of *Murder on the Farm* – there will be a regular news article, and a podcast that you may stream or download from our website. Yes – the Gazette takes one small step into the 21st Century! All of this will feed into a feature-length documentary, an investigation that will be led by renowned TV crime-buster, forensic psychologist Professor Simeon Freud, head of faculty at our very own University of Cumbria, and familiar to viewers nationwide through his recent hit documentary series for Channel 4, *Shrinking Crime.*

And this is where you might come in.

Yes, it was a long time ago – near enough half a century; two generations have passed. But some things can be seen more clearly from a distance. And hindsight can be a wonderful thing.

Perhaps an idea has already occurred to you, or maybe the podcast will jog a memory, long forgotten. The Gazette has set up a confidential telephone line and email address, and of course you can write to us by the traditional means. Any piece of information, however small, will be welcomed. Who knows – it could prove to be the key that finally turns the lock in this uncomfortable mystery.

Is this important?

Why, yes – together, we may be able to bring Will Featherston the justice he deserves.

1. ROOM 101

Top Floor, Police HQ – 10 a.m. Friday 16 July

'What do you reckon, Guv?'

Skelgill, standing at the window with his back to his colleagues, remains gazing at the view.

DS Leyton persists.

'It's not often the Chief praises anyone in advance, Guv.'

Skelgill makes what amounts to a snorting sound.

'Kiss of death, Leyton.'

He turns to look at DS Jones, as if to gauge her reaction; she appears a little conflicted, but she is supportive.

'She says it will be the most high-profile case in years.'

The suggestion is that Skelgill and his team ought to be honoured.

But Skelgill is reluctant to buy into the logic. He digs his fists into his pockets; it might almost be an unconscious act of rebellion. The fingers of his left hand tighten around a hank of baler twine.

'There's only one thing worse than getting the most high-profile case in years – and that's Smart getting it.'

DS Leyton emits an involuntary chuckle of approval. But he has other, more pressing things on his mind. While Skelgill has gravitated automatically to the row of windows that, from waist height, line two sides of the spacious corner room, on the top floor of the headquarters building, DS Leyton lumbers to inspect what lies beyond an internal door. He emits an exclamation of surprise.

'There's like a kitchen through here – and a flippin' karsey!'

DS Jones moves across to look.

'I had no idea this room even existed. But I did notice the door locked automatically behind us.'

She turns questioningly to Skelgill, but he does not reveal the status of his own knowledge. Certainly the room has the qualities of a self-contained suite. Centred towards one end is a long boardroom table that seats ten in upholstered chairs, and in the corner where the windows converge an arrangement of two sofas around a square coffee table. The main wall that houses the door through which they have entered is fitted with large pinboards and a wipe-clean whiteboard which doubles as a screen for a wireless projector hung from the ceiling. The only incongruity is an irregular stack of Bankers boxes that has been piled either side of the door to the kitchenette, about thirty in all, aged-looking and sagging, ready to burst in places.

But Skelgill's eye has been drawn by a neat array of three manila files, marked "Confidential" and each placed before a chair at the table, a red felt pen on one side and a yellow highlighter on the other. They are like three place settings. Each file bears the name of one of the detectives.

Rather uncannily, without instruction or mutual agreement, the trio take their places, Skelgill at the centre. They sit unmoving, like diners expecting a waiter to materialise in order to explain the etiquette. It is DS Leyton that breaks the silence.

'Blimey, Guv – it's like that Dungeon Escape up at Carlisle Castle. We took the nippers at Easter. They lock you in, and you have to crack the clues to find the combination for the lock before your time runs out.'

Skelgill appears vaguely interested.

'What happens if you don't?'

DS Leyton colours and squirms sheepishly.

'Thing is – we chose the kids' level of difficulty – so I didn't like to stick my oar in – being in the business, so to speak.'

But Skelgill now sees that DS Jones has already turned the cover of her file. The first page is a printout from the website of the Westmorland Gazette.

'Here's your chance to do it for real, Leyton.' He scowls unfavourably. 'Let's hope they've stocked that fridge.'

DS Jones murmurs – it seems she contains a laugh in her throat. But she has already read the first side and turns the page.

'1976. The Caldblow Farm murder.' She glances questioningly at Skelgill. 'Do you know of this?'

Skelgill opens his own file. He glares at the page. Almost imperceptibly, he seems to give a shake of his head.

'I've heard of it. Like I've heard of the Moors Murders and the Yorkshire Ripper.'

DS Jones reads on.

'Except the Caldblow Farm murder is unsolved.'

DS Leyton, now also perusing the article, gives a gasp of exasperation.

'Wait a minute – this has got next Friday's date on it. What's going on? Is the Chief up to some kind of trick?'

Skelgill merely glowers at the text that swims before his eyes.

'What did I just say, Leyton? Kiss of death.'

DS Jones is onto the next item. It is a densely typed report of several pages stapled together. She raises it, though they each have a copy.

'This is our brief. It's authored by the legal department.'

Her statement is sufficient to convince Skelgill that he has been sitting down long enough. He pushes back his chair and drifts again to the window. The elevation is a novelty, providing a fine view of the shallow vale where the rivers Eamont and Lowther converge, counterintuitively flowing eastwards towards the Pennines, prior to the confluence with the Eden and the eventual return of its trajectory westwards to the Solway. With trees in full leaf, the great flood plain has the look of Royal parkland, though populated by countless sheep that patiently crop the green sward, ruminating, converting cellulose into prime lamb and methane. Sleek black swallows shimmer as they hawk for dung flies.

'Shall I read aloud?'

DS Jones has some sympathy with Skelgill's inclination; it goes roughly along the lines that, if humans have been speaking and listening for the best part of a million years, what is so good about the modern obsession with writing and reading?

She takes the resigned shrug and lack of a rebuttal as an affirmative. Moreover, he drops onto a settee and hooks one leg over an arm.

DS Leyton is poised obediently, index finger on the first word.

DS Jones clears her throat.

'It begins with a list of protocols. All materials to be kept in the incident room. The code to the keypad is not to be shared beyond designated team members. There is to be no external publicity of police involvement and no mention within police circles. To all intents and purposes, this is not happening.'

She pauses and looks up and receives nods that she should continue.

'Next, a section headed "Chronology". I'll just read it verbatim.'

She scans for a moment, and turns a couple of pages to get her bearings.

13 August 1976 – CALDBLOW FARM MURDER
Caldblow Farm, near Santhwaite, 3 miles south of Whitehaven.
Killing of delivery boy, Will Featherston, 17; believed to have interrupted a burglary of antiques. Death caused by single shotgun blast to the temple. No prime suspect. Several persons of interest, including of note a local man, Percy Tuseling, 28. Sufficient evidence to investigate further.

20 September 1976 – KIRKSTILE FARM ROBBERY
Kirkstile Farm, Brackenthwaite, near Loweswater; 16 miles east of Caldblow Farm.
Unsuccessful antiques burglary. Shotgun discharged; no casualties. Fingerprint evidence and eyewitness testimony led to arrest of Joel and Jasper Hare of Workington, twins, aged 18.

27 September 1976 – MURDER CHARGE
Following confessions, Hare twins charged with robberies at Kirkstile Farm and Caldblow Farm, and murder of Will Featherston at Caldblow Farm.

12-16 September 1977 – HARES' TRIAL
Pleas entered of not guilty. Joel and Jasper Hare convicted of robberies, and murder of Will Featherston. Sentenced to life with a minimum tariff of 25 years.

4 October 1977 – BELLTOWER FARM MURDER

Belltower Farm, near Santhwaite.
Killing of farmer Colin Bell-Gibson, 60. Death caused by single shotgun blast to the temple.

DS Jones hesitates. Perhaps it is both the significance and the similarity of the incidents that gives her pause for thought. But she has also scanned ahead.

'What is it, girl?'

DS Leyton has followed doggedly, word for word; now he looks up expectantly, as though he must wait for the narrator.

She resumes.

Caldblow Farm and Belltower Farm share a field boundary. The land was jointly farmed from the latter. The perpetrator of the Belltower Farm killing – who handed himself in – was a local man who had permission to shoot birds on both farms. The man was Percy Tuseling.

She gives a shake of her head that might almost be a jolt of disbelief; the action dislodges a lock of fair hair and she pauses to brush it from her cheek.

20-24 March 1978 – TUSELING TRIAL
Pleas entered: guilty to manslaughter; not guilty to murder. Jury returned unanimous verdict of guilty to murder. Tuseling sentenced to life with minimum tariff of 18 years.

7-9 June 1982 – HARES' FIRST APPEAL
Unsuccessful.

10 February 1988 – HARES' SECOND APPEAL
Convictions for murder of Will Featherston at Caldblow Farm quashed on grounds of unsafe confessions. See commentary below.

5 October 1996 – TUSELING RELEASED
Percy Tuseling released on licence, having served full term of 18

years without remission or parole for murder of Colin Bell-Gibson at Belltower Farm.

The section ends and she looks at her colleagues to check for a reaction. The facts are largely new to them. But taken together with the press article the inference is clear. Indeed, DS Leyton homes in on this point.

'Where do we come in?'

His question is in part rhetorical, in that they all know as much as one another. DS Jones lays a palm on the papers before her.

'The next section is entitled "Commentary", okay?'

Skelgill is staring at her keenly – in fact so much so that he might almost be looking through her, beyond into some distant past, perhaps into those mists of childhood in which swirl incomplete fragments of adult news and pop songs of the time – then meaningless, but having left a lingering imprint, having evoked an emotion without accompanying explanation, like striking graffiti glimpsed from a speeding car, startling and salient, but lacking significance or relevance, be it artistic, territorial or political.

As DS Jones resumes her recitation, it is *political* that emerges as the watchword.

Records of strategic decisions at the time of the Caldblow Farm murder are not preserved, if any existed. This is unfortunate. It can be concluded, however, that the Hares' confessions shifted the entire focus of the inquiry. The wider investigation was wound down. In the context – the confessions themselves, the immense drain upon police resources, and intense public pressure and media scrutiny – this can be viewed with hindsight as an understandable if regrettable course of action.

Furthermore, Percy Tuseling's admission to the killing of Colin Bell-Gibson at Belltower Farm approximately one year later meant that a limited investigation took place: just sufficient to establish a degree of intent and premeditation in order to support a charge of murder. By that time, the Caldblow Farm case was closed, and the Hare brothers imprisoned.

Following a petition to the Home Office, the court bundle in the trial of Percy Tuseling was supplied to the solicitors representing the Hares. Information therein may have been influential in gaining leave to appeal in 1982. The appeal, however, was unsuccessful.

In 1987, further to revelations by a retired officer ("Officer X") of the West Pennines Constabulary, significant doubt was cast upon confessions obtained by a fellow officer ("Officer Y") in a number of cases over a period of 15 years. The Director of Public Prosecutions ruled that the evidence was sufficient that a test case should be reviewed by the Court of Appeal. The latter court accordingly found the conviction unsafe.

The corollary was a review of all such cases. During 1976, Officer Y had been briefly assigned to Cumbria Constabulary. It emerged that Officer Y played a lead role in obtaining confessions in the case of the Caldblow Farm murder. It should be noted that prior to their trial the Hare brothers had retracted their confessions and averred that they were made under duress; a position they maintained throughout their period of incarceration. Without reference to the facts of the case, in view of the primacy of the confessions in obtaining a guilty verdict, the Hares' convictions were ruled unsafe and quashed by the Court of Appeal in 1988.

DS Leyton exclaims and slaps the papers before him.

'So, it's a blot on the copybook, ain't it? The powers that be don't want us airing their dirty washing in public.'

He looks about at his colleagues. They nod; this seems to be the way of things. But DS Jones, the youngest and least-time-served of the trio is first to question this motive.

'Surely there's more to it? What would be the problem with admitting to procedural inadequacies and a rogue officer from a different force almost fifty years ago? There can't be anyone here now who was working then. Even the whistleblower – if it was to protect their identity – he or she must surely have passed away?'

There is a deliberative silence.

'Percy Tuseling.'

It is Skelgill that speaks.

His colleagues turn to look at him.

'He must be alive. And there must be evidence that says he did it.'

Skelgill jumps up and strides purposefully towards the stacks of boxes.

'What are you doing, Guv?'

'Time for a mash, Leyton – since no one else is offering.'

But his tone is sardonic – and the timing of the hiatus is clearly intentional. His colleagues exchange grins as they hear cupboards banging and crockery clinking, a metallic sound, running water. Skelgill is a queer fish when it comes to attention span. They know he can focus for hours upon end – they have both seen him in his boat, still and silent as a hungry crocodile – and other times he is more like the proverbial cat on a hot tin roof, unable to settle, in need of an off-ramp; when enough is enough and some form of digestion is called for.

There is the jangle of a teaspoon against china and a minute later he reappears with steaming mugs. He doles them out and now resumes a place at the main table, though he sits opposite and does not take his papers. DS Jones thoughtfully reaches to rotate the open file and slide it to within range.

She has read further ahead.

'Guv – you're right. He is alive. Listen to this. This is where the press article preview ties to – well – to us.'

She waves a hand over the document, as if to signify that she will summarise its contents.

'This TV production company – Turnpike Media.' She indicates to the press article. 'Here it just refers to the case in general – that's obviously the public position – for the purposes of the podcast and documentary they intend to record, *Murder on the Farm.* But in our brief it explains that Turnpike Media have reached a confidential agreement with Percy Tuseling.'

DS Leyton sits up.

'What – like they're paying him?'

DS Jones nods.

'It looks that way.' She finds a point on the page. 'Here – it says he has signed a contract for twenty hours of interviews. The premise is that he will act as a kind of chief witness. But since he was originally a suspect, the investigation will also provide an opportunity to remove any doubt about his possible involvement.'

She looks at her colleagues and taps the page.

'That sentence is italicised. I guess we're meant to read between the lines.'

DS Leyton exhales and combs the fingers of one hand through his mop of dark hair.

'What age is this Tuseling geezer?'

DS Jones peruses the document for a moment.

'He's seventy-five.' She glances at Skelgill. 'He's living at – *Blindkirk?*'

Her inflexion invites his input.

'It's about three miles due north of Cockermouth. Off the beaten track. Just the sort of place to hide if you've got a guilty secret.'

For a moment DS Jones holds his gaze; but she opts not to question his stance, though it is a little less than neutral.

DS Leyton sits back and folds his arms.

'Call me a doughnut – but what are we supposed to do?'

DS Jones again makes a brief reference to the papers before her.

'One of us is to join the production team – as a research assistant.'

'What – incognito, like?'

DS Jones nods.

'That's what it says.'

Skelgill shows a sudden interest. He cranes to see which page she is on, and pulls his own file towards him.

'At the foot of page six – beneath the sub-heading "Co-opting of Police Officer".'

Skelgill scowls at the document.

DS Jones begins to relate details from the section.

'Turnpike Media will gain unfettered access to Percy Tuseling. They will supply us with unedited copies of the recordings. We are to shadow them and follow up any leads. We also have the benefit of access to the case files – so we can guide the interviews to specific areas. It says we'll need to familiarise ourselves with the contents of the archive.'

Skelgill is glowering – and DS Leyton regarding him with a look of some alarm.

DS Jones continues.

'The suggestion is that I most fit the bill as a research assistant. They can substitute my photograph on their website for one of their existing employees.' She indicates to the page and looks up at Skelgill. 'Subject to your approval, Guv.'

DS Leyton releases a gasp of relief. It is settled as far as he is concerned.

Skelgill looks less willing to compromise.

He steals a sideways glance at the daunting stacks of precariously balanced Bankers boxes.

But he does not answer, and DS Leyton moves the debate forward.

'So, what's the idea – we ain't to put this Tuseling cove on guard?'

DS Jones is nodding; she seems sufficiently enamoured by the scheme.

'This kind of approach can be effective. There was a cold case in Australia recently – a thirty-year-old murder. The DPP had twice refused to indict the only suspect, despite two separate Coroners' recommendations. In the end, it was a long-running podcast that brought it to court. As the audience grew, witnesses began to come forward. It was a viral effect, way more far-reaching than a police investigation.'

DS Leyton, too, seems to see the positive side. He picks up the copy of the proposed news article. He rattles it illustratively.

'The Missus watches these things – that *Shrinking Crime* series – I saw some of it. He's a smart cookie, the prof what does it. You wouldn't want him on your trail. Mind you, I reckon the Missus liked it because she fancies the geezer.'

DS Jones watches for Skelgill's reaction – but he is frowning unblinking at the page. But when he might resort to a chip on the shoulder – that he has never yet brought down a crook with a degree certificate – he offers a more grounded caveat.

'How far can we trust someone who's being paid?'

There ensues a silence, for his concern deserves due consideration.

DS Jones sees that it falls to her to offer a counterpoint.

'Well, I suppose, if he had nothing to do with it, it's easy money – and fifteen minutes of fame. I imagine we'll work that out quite soon.'

DS Leyton prefers a more sinister prognosis.

'Or he thinks he's the clever clogs – he's fooled our lot once – he can do it again.'

2. RECCE – I

North and West Cumbria – Monday 19 July

BLINDKIRK, 11.45 a.m.

'There's another clump.'

'What's that, Leyton?'

DS Leyton, for a moment, seems surprised – as though he has spoken his thoughts out loud. 'On the left, Guv – that modern bungalow – what's it called, pampas grass, ain't it?'

Skelgill, in the passenger seat, just beginning to relax now that they have entered the obligatory speed constraints of the neat village, sits forward a little and looks to one side. He sees the object of his sergeant's interest. Indeed he catches a glimpse of a couple gardening – perhaps in their sixties, bronzed and scantily clad – the woman in a bikini and the man wearing the revealing briefs that have become known as budgie-smugglers. They look as though they have broken off from sunbathing to potter with hand-trowels amongst the well-tended borders.

DS Leyton interrupts his superior's reflections.

'That's the second one we've passed, Guv. The very first cottage at the edge of the village had some. I noticed 'cause we had a huge clump at the front when we moved in to our place. Flippin' nuisance – started to spread – I had to dig it up in the end. Shame in a way – I'm no gardener, and it was quite a feature. Folk used to slow down in their cars to admire it.'

But now he senses that Skelgill is staring at him. Both hands gripping the top of the steering wheel, he snatches a momentary glance to his left.

'What?'

Skelgill's features reveal a mixture of irony and disbelief, as when one person suspects the other is winding them up. But he answers evenly.

'I take it you know what they say about a house with pampas grass?'

DS Leyton, his eyes back on the twisting road ahead, makes a face of doubt.

'What, like – adds to the value, maybe? *Hah* – trust me to make a blooper. Thing is, where I grew up, the only grass you saw was weeds invading from your neighbour's window box.'

Skelgill is about to respond – but he changes tack.

'Howay – here's the King's Head. The house is opposite, according to the map. Pull into the pub car park and turn so we're facing out.'

The village hostelry has come upon them at short notice, and DS Leyton has to conduct the manoeuvre at greater speed than would be desirable for the purposes of their clandestine mission. There is a crunch of gravel and an accompanying cloud of dust drifts across the road on the gentle summer breeze. Skelgill is about to remark that there is nothing like keeping a low profile when his colleague interjects.

'Cor blimey – he's got some, an' all, Guv!'

Skelgill follows his sergeant's open-mouthed gaze.

And he is forced to admit, the sight is somewhat jaw-dropping – at very least incongruous in this village where most properties are modestly appointed, a blend of traditional farming cottages that line the road, interspersed with more modern but sympathetically designed bungalows, generally set back, all well maintained and proficiently gardened; there is the suggestion of a predominance of holiday lets and retirement homes; that Blindkirk is a dormitory village rather than the sort of active farming community that would be strewn with the broken-down and redundant paraphernalia of dealing with crops and animals.

'And the rest, Leyton.'

The bungalow directly in their sights is fronted by an open-plan garden of some thirty-five feet. An unfenced lawn extends from the pavement to the house. But what draws the eye is "the rest" to which Skelgill refers. Not one but three clumps of gently rippling pampas grass are interspersed by as many as twenty statuettes, some almost life size – of the sort that make bird baths and fountain ornaments – Greek nymphs and Roman goddesses – singles, and couples intertwined. There are naked female busts, and nude headless male torsos. At the centre what might be Aphrodite feeds a reclining Michelangelo's David-like figure from an overflowing cornucopia. The collective effect is of a branch meeting of Saturnalia, transported to this sun-kissed corner of Cumbria, and no little hint of lasciviousness.

DS Leyton appears to pick up such vibes.

'Bit rude, some of them – wouldn't you say, Guv?'

Skelgill does not answer; though he knows he can rely upon his partner to voice his own coarser sentiments. The theme, inadvertently raised by DS Leyton, is hard to avoid.

And DS Leyton has a further observation.

'He could charge admission for that, Guv. PG rated, mind you.'

Skelgill widens his eyes; a deliberate action.

'Cancel what I said about hiding away in a quiet village.'

'Right enough, Guv – he's doing the exact opposite, ain't he?'

Skelgill remains contemplative. Without thinking too much he is wondering precisely what messages are being expressed that underlie the more obvious, potentially prurient impression that the outlandish display seems intended to convey. Is his sergeant correct, that here is not so much an invitation but a challenge to all and sundry?

He reverts to an insight he has gained through some informal research of his own.

'I took George Appleby out in the boat on Saturday – just a couple of hours early doors on Derwentwater.'

DS Leyton might be puzzled by the apparent non sequitur, but he holds his peace – angling lectures usually arise only when there is the prospect of fishing before them. And he is proved correct in allowing Skelgill to continue in his own good time.

'George – he's not old enough to remember the Caldblow and Belltower Farm murders – but he does recall the campaign to free the Hare twins. Seems they set the record for a rooftop protest at Wormwood Scrubs. He reckons that Percy Tuseling's name would come up in the news.'

After a moment's cogitation, DS Leyton nods pensively.

'Yeah – it says in our brief, don't it – that the Hares' solicitors got the court bundle in Tuseling's murder trial? I ain't surprised if they made a connection. Even what we know already – two shotgun murders in cold blood – same MO – two farms that join one another – geezer that shoots on the land of both. Even I can see that, Guv.'

Skelgill grins ruefully. But his expression hardens a little; he does not want to jump the gun, so to speak.

And there is a significant caveat.

'Aye – except the Hares weren't released on the evidence. There was no new evidence presented on appeal – it was all about abuse of process. That said – by the sound of it – take away the rotten confession and there *was* no proper evidence.'

DS Leyton produces a harrumphing sound in his throat.

'The bad old days, eh, Guv?'

Skelgill looks at his sergeant a little askance – though he draws the line at contending the point, despite that on the tip of his tongue is the name of at least one of their contemporaries who would gladly turn a blind eye if truth stood in the path of glory.

'Look!'

DS Leyton's warning jolts him from his reflection.

A woman – perhaps in her late fifties, of medium build with long raven hair – has emerged from the front door and is wending her way towards them, following stepping stones set in the mown lawn. Her movement takes the form of an exaggerated sashay, and she wears a striking scarlet-and-black sarong dress that leaves a good amount of bronzed flesh exposed. She does not appear to notice them; she carries a woven straw beach bag and turns to her left, heading back the way they have come, presumably towards the village store. She disappears from sight around the bend.

'Think that's his Missus, Guv?'

Skelgill nods, though without conviction.

DS Leyton has facts available.

'Second wife, according to the records. The first one divorced him after he shot the farmer Bell-Gibson and knocked her about.'

Skelgill now regards his subordinate with a degree of alarm.

'I've been doing me homework, Guv.'

Skelgill has mainly fished over the weekend. Given the strict rules about materials being kept in situ, and the fact that not one iota of the Caldblow Farm murder case is digitised (and thus may not be remotely accessed), he concludes that DS Leyton must have spent some time at HQ.

'I knew I could rely on you, Leyton.'

'Oh – me and Emma had a bit of a party, Guv. That said – we only scratched the surface. Must be ten thousand documents. Still – it's surprising how much work you can get done when no one knows you're in the office and doesn't try to get hold of you.'

Skelgill has his own tactics for achieving this effect. Albeit 'work' for him takes a different, more esoteric form, over which he has less conscious control. And as yet it is too early in the day for his idiosyncrasies to make any useful progress.

But this general notion prompts him into action. The woman has gone and they should not hang around – Percy Tuseling may materialise to curate his menagerie and spot them. He looks a little longingly at the "Open All Day" sign that stands outside the front door of the King's Head. It is a welcoming sight, the building itself of pale locally hewn sandstone with window surrounds and quoins picked out in deeper ochre, quite unlike the hostelries of the fell villages, with their sharp, dark slate construction and steeply pitched alpine roofs and gables.

But Skelgill does not drink on duty and is ever too embarrassed to order tea in a pub, in case he is recognised.

'Reet – let's head west. Next stop Workington.'

DS Leyton seems puzzled.

'I thought it was near Whitehaven, Guv. Is Workington on our way?'

'Leyton, when there's a Haighs sausage roll in the offing, it's always on the way.'

FARMLAND BETWEEN SANTHWAITE & WHITEHAVEN, 12.35 p.m.

'See what you mean about these sausage rolls, Guv – just as well we bought extra for later.'

Skelgill, his mouth full, makes what is a mildly hysterical sound; DS Leyton can do a good line in irony.

Skelgill's lap is covered with crumbs. He elbows open the door and swings out his legs, knees together. With a lurch he manages to stand, and now brushes away the detritus. He reaches back in for his khaki army surplus rucksack and rests it upon the bonnet. He pulls out a large flask and two tin mugs, and beckons to his colleague that he should come and join him.

On Skelgill's instruction, without the use of maps, they have parked facing in a southerly direction on a modest rise in a layby overlooking the landscape ahead. The countryside hereabouts, though formally known as the West Cumbria Coastal Plain, is mildly rolling, and views are thus generally restricted. The urban settlements aside, it is characterised by its patchwork of ancient farmsteads, established between the 17th and 19th centuries; it is very much a working rural environment.

'Ah!'

'Aye?'

'That's it, ain't it – Caldblow Farm? I recognise it from the photographs in the case file.'

Skelgill is nodding with a small degree of satisfaction – that he has brought them to this vantage point. The property is quite clearly visible. Still surrounded by farmland – grazing pasture with sheep and cattle – it has, however, the look of a private residence. There is an ornamental garden where there were previously sheds, outhouses and barns clustered around. Parked in the tarmac driveway are two executive saloons suggestive of non-agricultural ownership.

'The main building ain't changed at all. Least – not on the outside.'

Skelgill is squinting into the midday sun, though his expression might also be critical. The property has an air of austerity, built of plain, old stone and disproportionately tall; it has the stoic, defensive look of a Scottish tower house.

'The hedges would have been taller, thicker.'

Those before them are trimmed in the modern fashion, for efficiency of land use, when once nature had a bigger share of England's acreage.

'So, what – the place would have been more hidden?'

'Aye.'

For a few moments they sip their teas in silence. Occasional vehicles pass, trailing eddies of roadside dust. Sheep bleat sporadically. A woodpigeon half-heartedly coos its five-note refrain from a leafy copse to their left, but otherwise birdsong is subdued. Occasional wafts of dung reach them on the balmy air.

Skelgill makes a sudden swat at a blowfly, scowling as he spills some of his drink.

'What was the story when the lad was shot?'

DS Leyton blinks several times, as if disturbed from his own reverie.

'Ah, well – timing wise, what happened was, the owner Lady Fitzrovia used to ride her horse round the two farms, pretty much regular as clockwork on a Friday, 3 p.m. for an hour. She didn't lock either the side door into the hall or the back kitchen door. They reckoned Will Featherston turned up between 3.30 p.m. and 4 p.m. – based on his last call at the pub in Santhwaite. It looks like he parked at the front and went into the kitchen as normal – because the thing is, the fish delivery was in the fridge. The Fitzrovia woman found him at ten past four – and that's when the 999 call was timed. He was slumped in an armchair. There were no signs of a struggle or defensive injuries. Looks like he'd either sat down or been made to sit down. Then he was blasted in the side of the head from close range.'

DS Leyton makes a pained face.

'It might be wishful thinking, Guv – but maybe he never knew it was coming.'

Skelgill nods, his gaze fixed unblinkingly on the old farmhouse before them.

DS Leyton continues.

'In all the witness statements there was no sighting of anyone. But there were reports of a vehicle. I reckon we should drive down by the front entrance, Guv.'

Skelgill knocks back the last of his tea by way of assent.

The surrounding vegetation and outbuildings may have changed, but the topographical aspects of Caldblow Farm – the building itself and its approach – remain unaltered. It is reached by a straight driveway of about fifty yards, perpendicular to the lane that forms the southern border of the original property. The lane, single track and C-classification, branches off from the wider but still modest B-road from which they have viewed the property. The C-road offers a shortcut in distance but not in time to a second converging B-road roughly a mile further on.

'Here we go.'

DS Leyton alerts his superior as they pass the entrance on their right and both glance across. While the upper part of the building is continuously visible above the low hedgerow that lines the verge, it comes into full view only briefly for the half-second it takes to pass the open gateway. DS Leyton continues for a hundred yards or so to a pull-in for a field gate, turns the car and makes a second pass. This time they crane to their left.

'You don't get much of a view from the driver's seat, Guv.'

Skelgill grunts. As passenger, he is having the reverse experience – now he sees more clearly.

'I doubt you'd even look, Leyton – unless you knew the place and were checking if anyone were there.'

'Or unless you saw someone turn in, Guv – and that's what one of the witnesses did.'

Having reconstructed what might be described as the 'witness manoeuvre', DS Leyton draws to a halt and now reverses level with the farm entrance, so that they can see the house. Skelgill notices a sign – it has been renamed, "Fitzrovia Hall" – the desire for change is understandable; and perhaps it remains in the ownership of the original family.

DS Leyton produces his notebook from the door pocket. He opens it to the first page; it is filled with detailed notes in his tiny neat hand – always a marvel to Skelgill. A skilled graphologist would never match the easy-going, ham-fisted Londoner with his dense penmanship.

'Since I knew we'd be doing this recce, I concentrated on the vehicle sightings. Prior to the Hares being fingered they stopped over seven hundred motorists in this area. There were about twenty claimed sightings between 3 p.m. and 4 p.m. of a vehicle in the driveway, parked up by the house. And likely it was already there when Will Featherston arrived – his fish van was parked a couple of cars' width to the left of the side gate – as if there had been something in the obvious spot.'

Skelgill waves a hand.

'What about this car seen turning in?'

DS Leyton nods – but he raises an index finger as he scrutinises his notes.

'Bear with us, Guv – let me go round the houses.'

Skelgill exhales – he prefers headlines to articles – but he steels himself; after all, his sergeant is the one to have put in the legwork over the weekend.

'Of these twenty-odd reports, more than half described a red car – and half of those that it was an estate. The rest were a mixture with no particular pattern – a couple of Land Rovers, and a couple that probably described the fish van. Lady Fitzrovia had a Land Rover, but she normally kept it in a barn round the back, which is where it was on the day of the murder. Quite possibly people describing it were actually remembering a different day. And, of course, that's the risk with any of the sightings.

'Now, the red colour – the fact that more than half the sightings were of red – that's why the police were focusing on it. And that's partly what did for the Hares, since they were using an old Post Office van.' DS Leyton pauses for a moment and runs his eye over his notes. 'However, not one report mentioned a van. There was a Vauxhall Viva, three Ford Cortinas, a Ford Granada, a Ford Escort, a Morris Marina, a Hillman Hunter and a Triumph Dolomite. The rest were not specified.'

Skelgill makes a gasp of exasperation. It is the policeman's frustration, that ten eyewitnesses to the same event will see ten different things.

'I know, Guv. It's plain from the statements that these are just what people thought the vehicle might have been. There's no reason to believe they were any better at identifying cars than folk are now. But *red car* came through, and so did that it was possibly an *estate*. I've checked and you could get a red estate in all of the models mentioned.

'But – to come to your point – this particular sighting. A sales rep who was considered the most credible eyewitness was taking the shortcut towards the farm entrance – the way we're facing – and he had to slow down while a car turned in. That was at about 3.50 p.m. – he knew because he was working to a journey plan with timed appointments, and he had to be in Whitehaven for a meeting at 4 p.m. and he was running a bit late. Interestingly, they also tested him on car ID and he was good – as you'd expect a rep to be. He said he saw a red Ford Corsair saloon, and the driver was a youngish bloke who seemed to be wearing some kind of uniform.'

Skelgill pushes back against the head restraint. There is suddenly a lot to unpack.

But DS Leyton has yet to deliver his punchline.

'Percy Tuseling owned a red Ford Corsair saloon.'

Skelgill remains still.

DS Leyton offers a qualification.

'Along with sixteen other people in the West Cumbria district – plus visitors.'

However, Skelgill can feel a small rush of adrenaline. It is like having to resist striking at a definite bite – the float momentarily disappearing, sufficient to conclude that the fish has the bait. But he refrains – and he too finds a caveat.

'A saloon's not an estate.'

But now DS Leyton shakes his head. He seems to have something up his sleeve.

'First of all, Guv – if you look at these cars – a Ford Corsair, you could probably mistake for something you thought you knew – a Cortina, Granada, whatever. It had quite subtle features, especially front-on. Now, I know it's not an estate – leastways, the one owned by Percy Tuseling wasn't – but what about if the boot lid was open?'

Skelgill turns his attention to the driveway leading towards the house; he tries to picture the scene as painted by his colleague. Certainly, a car parked facing them at a slight angle, with the boot up, the afternoon sun glinting off it, might well give the impression of being a longer-bodied vehicle.

DS Leyton has more to add.

'Some geezer was burgling the gaff, right? Quite likely he would have reversed up to that side gate and loaded gear brought out by the side entrance – we know that was left unlocked, and there were no signs of a break-in. The crystal decanter stopper was dropped in the bushes just inside the gate.

'What if Will Featherston was walking in with his parcel of haddock just as the burglar's coming out with the loot. The burglar sees the kid first – shoves his bag in the bushes – gives him some old flannel – gets him inside the house. If it's also correct that he was wearing some kind of uniform – not so much as a disguise but as an excuse for why he might visit a property – he might have pulled it off. He could have said he was there to read the gas meter – and did the lad know where it was? We know a uniform's a ruse as old as the hills.'

'Hold your horses, Leyton – you're solving the whole crime!'

But despite Skelgill's admonishment, there is a note of underlying approval in his voice. Accordingly, DS Leyton continues, albeit with some reservation.

'Thing is, Guv – I suppose what I'm saying is it's easy to see why they'd begun to home in on Tuseling. Emma has been concentrating on the historical statements – as preparation for meeting the documentary team to discuss the first interview with Tuseling. He was visited twice by detectives on the Caldblow murder case. The first time – it was just to eliminate him as an owner of a car that matched one of the sightings. He lived about five miles away. And he did have an alibi – they spoke to a co-worker who vouched for his presence. But about a month later there was a second interview. Now, I'm not sure what prompted it – maybe it was Lady Fitzrovia who provided names of people connected with Caldblow Farm – but in his first interview, he never mentioned that he knew the place. Yet they must surely have mentioned Caldblow Farm when they first saw him.'

Skelgill produces a scornful growl.

'Never mind that, Leyton – it would have been all over the news – tight-knit community like West Cumbria. According to George – his arl fella reckons it made the biggest splash since the Windscale fire.'

'Well – that's exactly it, Guv.' DS Leyton is encouraged. 'So – DS Jones fished out the transcript. It's just handwritten by the DC. They asked him why he hadn't mentioned that he shot on the land around Caldblow Farm. He replied that he sometimes worked part-time for Colin Bell-Gibson, who farmed the joint land under lease – and that he was scared he'd lose his main job if his employer found out he was working on the side.'

There is a small hiatus before DS Leyton adds a casual rider.

'Course – a year later he went on to shoot poor old Bell-Gibson.'

Skelgill makes a curious facial expression, one that most closely resembles the northern pastime of competitive gurning. It is difficult not to be tempted by the wildly bobbing float. But rather than speculate he puts a question to his colleague.

'What's wrong with having a second job?'

DS Leyton nods in a way that suggests he too has been considering this point.

'I know, Guv – it sounds like a lame excuse. Unless, of course, he was in the habit of moonlighting when he was supposed to be doing his day-job. Double bubble.'

Skelgill nods pensively. His colleague – knowingly, he presumes – makes a far more profound point than merely the issue of deceiving an employer. There is the possibility that Percy Tuseling was in the habit of visiting the farmland during normal daytime working hours.

'What was his day-job?'

DS Leyton has been expecting the question.

'TV engineer. Remember those whacking great cathode-ray jobs we all had as nippers – took up half the living room? Specially the size of our living room. Seems that back in the Sixties and Seventies they were made with valves and transistors. When the telly went wrong they didn't bin 'em like now – they sent for a repair man. Tuseling worked for Radio Rentals in Whitehaven. They had a high street showroom with a workshop behind. He was based there, and did calls to folk who couldn't take their set in. And sometimes he'd need to transport a set back to the shop to fix it.'

Skelgill folds his arms but does not comment.

'In a way, Guv, it's the ideal job for running your own little sideline. Plenty of callouts. In those days – no mobile phone or satellite tracker on the company motor.'

Skelgill gives a small wistful upward flicker of his eyebrows.

'What colour was the Radio Rentals van?'

DS Leyton nods. The point has not escaped him – nor did it his erstwhile colleagues, back in 1976. He taps the page of his jotter.

'Yeah – their vans were white with a green logo. Based on the Ford Escort.'

The fact seems a bit of a killer, but DS Leyton has a counterpoint.

'Two things about that, though, Guv. First off – Tuseling didn't take the van home at nights. It was kept at the back of the shop. So, if he had a late callout, he'd go in his own car, and return home from there. Second – when you think about it – if it's true what he said about being scared of being caught moonlighting, it's hardly likely he took the works van and left it parked where it could easily be spotted.'

Skelgill is nodding pensively.

'And definitely not on the kind of job we're talking about.'

'I agree, Guv. So you can see why he was in the frame. I mean – I get that the first interview was probably routine – after all, they took seven thousand statements. But for him to make the omission must have seemed suspicious. Like I said a minute ago – he knew the place. He used a shotgun on the land. Then it turns out he worked there part-time. And he later killed Bell-Gibson.'

Skelgill hisses and moves his hands either side of his head to suggest his brain is exploding.

But he does not embellish the mime.

'Admittedly, Guv – that last point – the second shooting – it's with hindsight. But it's like when you hear a judge instruct a jury to disregard the outcome of the accused's behaviour and only look at their intent. That never seems right to me.'

Skelgill inhales and exhales deeply a couple of times.

'There's still a lot to know, Leyton.'

DS Leyton relents. He closes his notebook on his lap and folds his disproportionately large hands over the cover.

'Yeah – I agree, Guv. It was the biggest investigation this force has ever conducted – and at the end of the day they came to a different conclusion. The Hares sang and the case was closed. If there ever was a proper review it never saw the light of day. There's no indication from the files. And all that material in Room 101 – it's pretty random – talk about needles and haystacks.'

Mention of haystacks within earshot of Skelgill and it is rather like calling out his name. He seems to start, and rouse himself, as though there is a constant peril of a descent into torpor.

'What is it, Guv?'

Skelgill scowls into nowhere in particular.

But then he jerks his head in the direction of the former farmhouse.

'What kind of person shoots a kid in cold blood?'

3. EPISODE 1: MURDERER

Incident Room 101 – 10.35 a.m. Thursday 22 July

"Percy, you're a murderer."

DS Jones feels the fine, invisible hairs stand up on her nape. This might be a recording, but she is reliving the emotion almost as powerfully. Professor Simeon Freud, seated casually at one end of the sofa in the chintzy parlour, a saucer in one hand and a cup of tea in the other, has launched his unexpected and devastating opening thrust. In their private briefing beforehand he had given no such warning, nor subsequently in the preamble any indication to Percy Tuseling that such a curveball was in flight. But the camera operator must have been primed, for she has Percy Tuseling's face full screen. And, just like in real time the previous afternoon, DS Jones finds herself transfixed by that cropped countenance, only the eyes, nose and mouth framed; the slightly bloated, oily skin with its distinctive dark pores; the small eyes a little too close together; the nose bulbous, a drinker's nose; the mouth narrow and the lips mean.

But it is the eyes that most fascinate her. In the second during which the insinuation hangs in the air, in which it resonates in ghostly fashion, out of all proportion to the ordinary surroundings, like an utterance in a chambered crypt, it seems those unblinking eyes set in the motionless face must inevitably – like those of the stereotypical vampire about to bare his fangs above the helpless maiden's throat – for one terrifying moment fill with crimson.

"I killed my best friend. He was like a father to me. I don't remember doing it. I did not dispute the evidence that I did it. I served my time for doing it. I have carried that burden all my life. I deeply regret the harm I caused."

The spell is broken. The tension is released. The sclerae of the eyes are white. The pale grey irises carry only a look of remorse. And the voice is now the distraction – an almost ridiculous falsetto, as a person might address a dog or a small child; yet it is strained and troubled by the painful recollection. And the eyes might have become watery. But the facial muscles stiffen and the skin in a band spanning the nose and cheeks reddens – and there is an underlying sense of contained anger.

DS Jones pauses the video.

Skelgill and DS Leyton exhale in tandem.

It is DS Leyton that expresses what may be their mutual take out.

'He went for the jugular, alright.'

Skelgill reaches for his mug of tea and takes a long draught.

DS Jones frowns over her notes of the interview. But for this particular juncture, she has nothing contemporaneous – other than that she had at some point written down the words.

"Percy, you're a murderer."

And now she appreciates the sublime skill of Professor Simeon Freud.

"Call me Sim. And – Detective Sergeant Jones – I had better call you Angela, since that is to be your alias."

This had been his response upon their introduction. His manner had been casual, just a hint disorganised, an impression consistent with his appearance: donnish, if trendily attired in cotton, corduroy and desert boots; tall, fair-skinned, a tousle of blondish hair that might be greying; and penetrating blue eyes, wideset under a prominent brow and above an aquiline nose and a strong jaw, full lips in a wide mouth. She noticed he demanded the admiration of the members of the production team, all females in their twenties like herself. She had put him in his mid-forties.

But the skill.

In that unequivocal phrase, "Percy, you're a murderer" were delivered nuances of many subtle shades. And not least there was the intonation. The sentiment conveyed was not the bald accusation and concomitant vilification that anyone reading from a transcript would hear in their mind's ear – but something altogether different. In that pithy utterance were a thousand more words of exposition. For a start, they were spoken with a smile. And the inflexion was not merely of surprise, but almost of amicable, mickey-taking disbelief. How can you, this genteel pensioner, seated here with afternoon tea and homemade scones, surrounded by a collection of ornaments and antiques, who has welcomed us so openly and profusely and with such politeness – and your good wife here – how can you, the archetypal law-abiding, respectable-beyond-all-reasonable-expectations type of chap, be a murderer?

It is almost as though the Professor has made a revelation of some extraordinary good fortune. To substitute the word millionaire for murderer would have sounded entirely congruent. "I am here to tell you about your recent entry into the national lottery – Percy, you're a millionaire!"

Now DS Jones, too, exhales.

She looks up, to see that Skelgill is staring at her.

'He gave no clue that he would open with that question. To neither the production team nor the Tuselings.'

The detectives share a moment's reflection, before DS Leyton speaks.

'The Tuseling geezer – sounded off pat, to me – like he's trotted out that line before.'

DS Jones glances at Skelgill; he seems preoccupied. For her part, she has had more time to acclimatise to Percy Tuseling's high-pitched voice and stilted demeanour.

'He has an odd way of speaking. He is a native of Whitehaven but seems to have mostly lost his accent. But there are occasional lapses – in accent and grammar. I don't think he's particularly well-educated or articulate.'

Skelgill enters the conversation with a request.

'Just go back to near the start. That bit where you arrive.'

DS Jones nods. They have watched approximately fifteen minutes of the rushes – the unedited footage of the documentary team's first formal encounter with Percy Tuseling and his second wife Maria. The camera has swept about to capture contextual clips, later to be cut and spliced – notably the statuettes in the front garden, a bath held aloft by the naked Three Graces (in which a pair of sparrows seem to be procreating) and similar artefacts and other impressions inside the bungalow – along with inadvertent shots of shuffling feet and blurred floors as progress was made towards the sitting room.

Of course, this meeting was to an extent staged. The production unit consists of interviewer ("Sim", self-proclaimed), producer/director (Jen), videographer (Kate), audiographer (Mel) and researcher ('Angela', aka DS Jones). The arrangement had been that they would record as they approached the house and that the Tuselings should answer the door as though their guests were expected.

This had not quite occurred as planned.

DS Jones restarts the recording.

The documentary team arrived at Blindkirk in a minibus, and had filmed from within, passing along winding lanes, leafy at this time of year, with occasional commentary from Simeon Freud in response to questions from producer Jen. The general gist to be conveyed was the background to the original Caldblow Farm murder of Will Featherston, and the possible double injustice – that the Hare twins were unsafely convicted, and that Percy Tuseling became considered as the after-the-fact prime suspect through his subsequent shotgun killing of Colin Bell-Gibson. There has been the reluctance of officialdom to re-open the case, leaving Percy Tuseling to bear the stigma long after the expiration of the punishment for his own heinous crime. Thus this documentary and podcast series may facilitate his exoneration. But Simeon Freud also goes on to comment on the nature of Percy Tuseling's actions at Belltower Farm. Some of the coincidences are remarkable, and ostensibly of his own making. But perhaps most perplexing is the brevity of the official record of the Belltower Farm murder. And so – says the renowned professor of criminology, his enigmatic gaze turning to transfix the viewer through the lens of the camera – for an aficionado of the human mind, and its more macabre depths, to interview a willing cold-blooded murderer is too good a chance to pass up.

Skelgill seems disinterested with this segment and fidgets impatiently.

The camera sweeps past the village sign.

It prompts DS Leyton.

'That's the same route we took, ain't it, Guv? I recognise that first house with the pampas grass. Just after it said Blindkirk.'

But Skelgill turns to DS Jones – she seems to understand his questioning look.

'They'll edit that out – they've agreed not to name the actual village. They're going to describe it as a small rural community in the northwest of Cumbria.'

Skelgill has his arms folded. He makes an acknowledgement with a small upward movement of his head, but he looks unconvinced by the idea that the location can remain a secret.

As the video runs, it becomes clear that the producer is phoning ahead to let the Tuselings know that their arrival is imminent and they should be ready to answer the door.

The camera homes in on the bungalow, with its extraordinary garden display.

It is Simeon Freud's first visit – he is heard to exclaim: "Look at this!"

The frame closes in on the front door; there is a nameplate, *Shangri-La*.

"He's coming out!"

There is animation in the professor's voice, as though he considers these observations to be of cumulative significance.

The camera responds, panning out a little – and there is revealed Percy Tuseling, attired in shirt and tie, moving purposefully to stand at the threshold of the garden and pavement; a couple of paces behind him follows his wife, also smartly dressed and distinctively made up, her coal-black hair piled extravagantly on the top of her head and her dark eyes glistening.

Simeon Freud seems keen to capitalise upon whatever it is that he reads into the situation; he scrambles from the minibus. Percy Tuseling is a shortish man, stocky and well-built, and in decent shape for his age. The professor is a good bit taller; he leans to shake hands. The camera operator and sound recordist close in to capture the coming together.

"Welcome to our humble home."

"Percy – may I call you Percy? Thank you for having us."

"I've heard a lot about you – and not all bad!"

Simeon Freud seems to hesitate for a moment – and before he can offer a rejoinder Percy Tuseling gives a disingenuous laugh, in the way that many a true word is said in jest.

"Well, yes – hopefully not all bad."

But the exchange prompts a strange moment of awkwardness. It is clearly now unscripted, when the intention was for the professor to advance stealthily, speculating along anthropological lines, creating anticipation for the moment when their quarry revealed himself.

It is left for Simeon Freud to regain the initiative.

"Shall we go inside – for a cup of tea, perhaps?"

"Tea? Yes of course – that'll be 50p!"

Again the quip, again the laugh – the person who is the joker in the pack, who supplies their own ready reaction of approval in case of a failure of sense of humour among those around them.

"Yes, certainly – well, I'm sure I've got that – yes, I'm sure I have 50p."

Once more, the professor has no ready reply – though it is apparent that he avoids banter which might seem competitive. The criminologist, despite his great experience and reputation, is a little disconcerted by the exchange.

Now Percy Tuseling begins to introduce his wife.

'Stop it there.'

It is Skelgill's order. DS Jones complies. She regards him expectantly. She can see he is both animated and concerned – but he seems either unable or unwilling to iterate his feelings.

'It's interesting, Guv – that you see that.' She does not elaborate upon the "that" exactly – but she casts a referencing hand over her notes. 'We didn't have long to discuss the interview afterwards – Sim had to get back to college for a meeting. But –' She hesitates – for she detects Skelgill's frown. 'But he did say – did we all notice how Percy Tuseling tried to take control – to get the upper hand against him – right from the first. How he came out, when we'd agreed we'd go to the door. Almost as if to supervise what we might say outside. And then those – well – kind of gauche putdowns. I've heard you're not all you're cracked up to be. This is my house – and you'll pay for tea. Jibes disguised as jokes.'

Skelgill is not quite sure if he is being praised for his sensitivity to the issue or patronised with the full explanation. But murmurs from DS Leyton at his side seem to be appreciative. Indeed, the latter offers his own comment.

'In a way, it showed that the Prof's got bottle – that he still opened with a humdinger of a question.'

But Skelgill seems more concerned with the clown than the performance of the ringmaster.

'Go back – I mean forward – to where we were before. The crocodile tears.'

DS Jones manipulates the slider on her laptop; a duplicate of what she does is projected wirelessly onto the large whiteboard across the room.

She arrives at a full-face shot – Percy Tuseling's tearful monologue, of which Skelgill is disparaging.

While the picture is still frozen, DS Leyton remarks.

'His face is all flushed, ain't it?'

DS Jones nods reflectively.

'It felt for a moment like he would explode. It's hard to characterise – but – it was like he was boiling up inside. I actually felt more with anger than remorse or embarrassment. He clearly still harbours a great sense of injustice for being suspected of killing Will Featherston. Though I think he has internalised it such that it feels like Percy Tuseling versus the world – entirely out of proportion to reality.'

Skelgill is scowling doubtfully, and it is DS Leyton who responds.

'Mind you, girl – it's not easy to feel sympathy – when you know what he actually did do to his farmer pal – and freely admitted it.'

Skelgill interjects.

'Let's have it from the horse's mouth.'

DS Jones restarts the action.

The seating arrangement must be strategic – the two

protagonists on the same sofa but at opposite ends – proximity with no barrier, but more space than would be natural. The main camera is hand-held and concentrates on Percy Tuseling. In the corner of the screen a second shot is inset, the stream from an SLR fixed upon a tripod, recording simultaneous video of Simeon Freud. Now there is a close-up of Percy Tuseling, as he listens, his small mouth with its lips compressed, the eyes furtive but fixed upon the questioner; eagerness seems to vie with distrust in the facial expression. But he begins to nod; it appears they now go by a pre-agreed script.

"Percy, at your trial, you offered no evidence in your defence – only that you had been drinking heavily – and thus you acted with diminished responsibility – which the jury did not accept."

There is a pause before the professor continues.

"You have maintained that stance – throughout your eighteen years of incarceration and several decades since. But are you ready to break your silence?"

Again the professor waits.

Percy Tuseling now looks more like a rabbit in the headlights. His blinking rate has accelerated. If his eyes had not teared up before, they do now. But still there is something unnatural about his demeanour.

"It was my twenty-eighth birthday. The fourth of October, 1977. My first wife Veronica and I had been invited round to Colin's for a celebration dinner cooked by Susan."

"That's Colin Bell-Gibson, a widower aged fifty-three, owner of Belltower Farm. And Susan was his daughter, in her late teens."

Percy Tuseling nods – accepting that his questioner is reading from his crib-sheet for the benefit of the listener or viewer. He seems to know to resume his narrative.

"Because it was my birthday I had already drunk some whisky before we arrived. I don't drink whisky now, in case it makes me nasty. And I drank more before dinner and wine with the meal. After the dinner we went through to the lounge and had more drinks."

Simeon Freud seems about to embellish – but it is evident that he restrains himself in order not to interrupt the flow.

"The drinks cabinet was in the dining room. Colin had gone to get more drinks. He called me through to give him a hand. He'd made drinks in cocktail glasses and he needed us to carry two each without spilling them."

Now it is Percy Tuseling that pauses. It seems he needs to reset, to steel himself.

"Colin had told me – he used to brag – when we were having a whisky from a hip flask at the back of the Land Rover after an afternoon's shooting – that he used to get together for dinner with some other farmers and their wives. At the end of the night he would make what he called 'Special Cocktails' that would get the women pissed. And they'd have a swap around."

His eyes flicker uncertainly about the crew off camera – and perhaps his wife who is in the room. But he makes no apology for his coarse language.

"I didn't think anything of it – he was a boastful sort, liked to one-up you – you didn't know whether to believe him about things. But I must have thought something of it." He hesitates, and quite deliberately raises a hand to touch one temple with the tip of an index finger – it seems in order to indicate that the notion had subconsciously embedded itself. "Because when we carried the drinks into the lounge where the ladies were sitting, Colin, he said in a big loud voice, *Veronica – I've made you a Special Cocktail!* And I cannot remember what happened next."

Percy Tuseling makes a referencing look at Simeon Freud. The professor, however, merely ushers him to continue with an upturned palm.

"Apparently, I took his gun from a door jamb in the hall, went to my car – got a hacksaw – cut the barrel off – I went in – and … then I went and shot him."

Though he raises the back of his hand to cover his mouth – a gesture of self-reproach, like a person who has unthinkingly cursed in polite company – there is something unconvincing about the action. The delivery, the intonation, has been in the same implausible falsetto – and the tone one of surprise that he can possibly be describing his own behaviour. He removes the hand to show his lips still compressed, the mouth now downturned; the skin across his cheeks and nose is once again flushed; the eyes appeal for belief.

In the hiatus that follows, Simeon Freud's voice seems almost disembodied.

"And you also attacked your wife, Veronica, and Mr Bell-Gibson's daughter, Susan."

Percy Tuseling looks doubly pained.

"I picked another gun up from another door jamb – put it in my car – I drove up the lane and saw an ambulance. One of the paramedics flagged me down with a torch. I stopped – *I stopped.*"

Suddenly he chuckles – as though this would be an improbable or even inadvisable thing to do. He shakes his head.

"I know." There is the suggestion that he feels his questioner is with him, in agreement. "It's all insane. I wound down the window – and I realised it was a chap I knew from the cricket club. He said, 'Percy – you'd better not go any further down the lane – there's a gunman on the loose.' I said, 'Terry – I think it's me.'"

Now he regards Simeon Freud in a rather hopeless fashion – yet to Skelgill's eye (and the idea of cricket conjured in his mind) it is little more than the blithe expression of apology of a fielder who has dropped a dolly catch – nothing more serious – there's always the next ball, when he might redeem himself. Yet the incongruity is stark – the next 'ball' would be the best part of two decades later, when Percy Tuseling had served his sentence.

DS Jones unilaterally pauses the recording.

She sees that her colleagues have their eyes glued to the screen – the full face of Percy Tuseling, an image reminiscent of Big Brother from Orwell's *Nineteen Eighty-Four.* Undoubtedly, at the first hearing – and even the second – there is something chilling and ineffably perplexing about the tortured yet cheerful delivery of the man's confession.

'I think it's instructive to consider some of the witness statements from the night.'

She waits until Skelgill looks at her. She reaches to extract a document from the papers she has tiled across the table at one side.

'I'll paraphrase – so we can get back to the footage. The ambulanceman to whom he referred – a Terry Thomson – he stated that he immediately recognised Percy Tuseling – and before he could respond, Tuseling handed him a shotgun, stock first, out of the window of his car. He could not recall the exact exchange, but he agreed to accompany Percy Tuseling to Belltower Farm – Percy Tuseling wanted to take him to the victim – at that point not knowing whether he was dead. Terry Thompson passed the shotgun to his colleague, who secured it in their vehicle, and he got into Percy Tuseling's car. The paramedics had been warned by radio not to approach the property, because of the risk of being shot – but now it seemed they had an explanation. In any event, at this point a police patrol arrived, and a small convoy led by Percy Tuseling drove back to Belltower Farm. There is a footnote – it sounds quite unreal – Belltower Farm was literally that, the old house had a belltower that formed part of the air-raid warning system during the last war. The bell was tolling.'

DS Jones pauses to select a second document.

'This is the statement made shortly afterwards by Susan Bell-Gibson. She said that her father had returned to the lounge with a tray of drinks and had placed them on the coffee table and resumed his seat on the settee. A few minutes later, as she put it – "All hell broke loose". Percy Tuseling entered and strode up to Colin Bell-Gibson and without a word of warning shot him in the side of the head at close range. She said she had not seen the gun and the first thing she knew was the ear-shattering bang. Her father had no chance to react or take evasive action. Veronica Tuseling sprang up and began to wrestle with her husband, but he beat her to her knees with the butt of the gun. Susan Bell-Gibson tried to intervene – but Percy Tuseling was a body-builder and she stood no chance. Veronica Tuseling broke away and he followed her. At this point Susan Bell-Gibson fled the room and ran upstairs – she locked herself into her father's bedroom where there was a telephone extension – and she rang 999. She said she could hear continued screams and banging taking place downstairs for what may have been another minute. But then it went quiet and she heard Percy Tuseling's car drive away. She came out and ascended to the belltower – and began ringing the bell. She said it was to attract help and act as a warning. That's how the police found her when they searched the property.'

DS Jones indicates to the big screen.

'What Percy Tuseling said there – he missed out a segment of about fifteen minutes – the timed interval between the 999 call and the ambulance crew and police meeting him. It appears that his wife Veronica escaped into the night from the back door of Belltower Farm – and that Percy Tuseling went looking for her in his car. She was picked up a mile away by a passing motorist. That was almost half an hour after the shooting. She must have fled across several fields – she was disoriented, scratched by thorns and caked in mud and blood. The driver took her straight to West Cumberland Hospital. So, Percy Tuseling must have been circling the lanes, and was driving back towards Belltower Farm when he met the ambulance crew waiting for police protection.'

DS Jones shuffles her papers.

'Then if we go back to the paramedic Terry Thompson's statement. He said that Percy Tuseling seemed entirely normal – other than he smelled strongly of alcohol. As they drove the short distance he asked him whether he had any more weapons in the car. Percy Tuseling said no – but that he had a live shotgun cartridge – which he produced and threw out of the car window. It was later recovered.' She pauses to look at her colleagues. 'It seems a small point, but it's worth noting – because a similarly discarded cartridge of the same make had been found in the verge a short distance from Caldblow Farm, when the lanes in the area were searched after the murder of Will Featherston a year earlier. A spent cartridge, in that instance.'

DS Jones leans back in her seat and exhales, as though the process has been draining.

DS Leyton takes the opportunity to present what is on his mind.

'His motive for the murder?' His tone is laced with doubt. He is about to embellish – but DS Jones interjects.

'Let me play the tape – that's exactly what Sim covered next.'

She sets the video back into motion.

It is Percy Tuseling, however, who speaks first.

"I just went bloody mad, didn't I – for a few minutes."

He strikes the same blithe note – of trivialising his actions, though straining to express remorse. It is a jarring combination.

Now Simeon Freud presses the point.

"Percy – you have just made a major confession, haven't you? A revelation."

Percy Tuseling nods – small movements of the head, but vigorous, his features pained and his eyes once again moist.

The professor continues.

"Because upon your arrest and during your trial you offered no evidence."

Percy Tuseling nods, tight-lipped.

"That's correct."

"But Percy – why did you not make the defence of provocation – that it was a crime of passion? You could have received a much shorter sentence."

The professor employs a tone that is somewhat pleading – despite that what he says is decades out of date for any useful purpose.

Percy Tuseling's lips are so compressed as to have disappeared. He seems to be making up his mind whether to say more.

"If I had revealed what I have just told you – and your listeners and your viewers –" He turns to stare into the lens of the camera, but only briefly as though it embarrasses him. "The gutter press would have had a field day with the lurid story – it would have ruined the reputations of the innocent ladies who were present that night."

The professor, cognisant of his wider role as arbiter of the investigation, quite subtly allows his gaze to drift to the static camera that films him. It is a long theatrical look that conveys unambiguously to the audience that here is a matter of some doubt. It is arguably the first indication he has given since his dramatic opening statement that exoneration of Percy Tuseling is not what drives his agenda. In the pursuit of truth he will be unbiased.

He turns back to Percy Tuseling.

"But you battered your wife and assaulted Susan Bell-Gibson."

Percy Tuseling shakes his head.

"I have absolutely no memory of what happened, from Colin

mentioning the Special Cocktail until I met Terry the ambulanceman."

The professor seems to debate with himself whether to contest the point further. There is the newly told rationale itself – whether it stands scrutiny – or even just the bizarre contradiction that it was to protect the very females whom he terrorised that night. But perhaps he senses that Percy Tuseling is in danger of withdrawing into his shell, and he changes tack.

"You were immediately remorseful – am I right?"

Percy Tuseling seems to be waiting for this cue.

"I showed Terry and the two police officers where Colin was. I wanted to say goodbye to him. They had to restrain me from hugging him."

DS Leyton is wanting to speak. He raises a hand and DS Jones pauses the video.

'Let me get this right, Emma – you've read all the Defence's case in the Belltower Farm murder. He's never mentioned this Special Cocktail business until now, right? I mean – literally – as he was recorded for this interview.'

DS Jones nods in affirmation.

'That's the way it seems. Jen, the producer, had an initial meeting with him – the proposition being that he could use the documentary to put his side of the story – to clear away any doubts about his involvement in Will Featherston's death. He has gone much further than anyone anticipated.'

Like the professor, DS Leyton seems discontented with the explanation.

'If that's true, why would he run a defence of – what – diminished responsibility? Plead guilty to manslaughter? I mean – he only went and sawed off the barrel before he shot the geezer! Without the provocation defence, that's first-degree murder every day of the week.'

Skelgill listens with eyes narrowed, though he makes no contribution to the debate.

DS Jones, however, has more to add on this specific point.

'In gathering evidence for the trial, the Prosecution had a firearms officer saw off the barrel of a similar shotgun with the same type of saw – it was just a junior hacksaw. It took five minutes.'

DS Leyton makes a hand gesture – that she proves his point. Though it a raises a query for her, that his experience might address.

'Why not just shoot Colin Bell-Gibson with the gun as it was?'

DS Leyton makes an exaggerated mime, part-opening his jacket with his left hand and reaching inside with his clenched right fist.

'Girl, there's only one reason a wrong 'un saws off the barrel – and that's to conceal the weapon. He must have wanted to take Bell-Gibson by surprise. Make no mistake. Give him no chance to get away or fight back.'

DS Jones nods pensively.

'Susan Bell-Gibson stated that she didn't see a gun until the shot was fired. And Colin Bell-Gibson was shot at close range in the side of the head whilst seated. There were no defensive injuries.'

There ensues what could be classed as a profound silence.

It falls to Skelgill to do it justice.

'Just like Will Featherston.'

DS Jones turns slowly to look at him. After a moment she indicates to her laptop.

'That's what comes next. Shall I?'

Skelgill is grim faced. He nods once.

They watch and listen with interest as Simeon Freud forms his next question. It is clear he chooses his words carefully and employs a tone that is designed to sound supportive.

"Percy – it has been suggested – cruelly alleged – that what Colin Bell-Gibson actually said related to the fact that you sometimes worked part-time for him, and shot on the Caldblow Farm land that he jointly managed from Belltower Farm. That he made some accusation against you – that you had an involvement in Will Featherston's murder – perhaps that he claimed he could even prove something."

Percy Tuseling listens, ultra-tight-lipped. He does not shake his head. If anything, he seems to be faintly nodding – as if he knows well this narrative, having had it put to him before. He does not speak.

"Percy, what do you say to people who advance that theory?"

But now his response is immediate, and decisive.

"That I had nothing to do with the murder of Will Featherston. Absolutely nothing. I was not at Caldblow Farm that day. I did not recognise Will Featherston. I did not shoot Will Featherston."

The professor does not respond.

There is a pin-drop silence.

What is clear is that Percy Tuseling intends to stare out his interrogator, despite that small movements in his features seem to reveal involuntary turmoil beneath the surface.

Then, after an age, it seems, comes a call of "And … *cut!*".

While the cameras keep rolling, the participants relax and stretch, blinking as if in the new light of day. The producer's voice comes again, "That's a good point to wrap".

There ensues some small talk as the cameras and sound equipment are moved away from the main actors. Percy Tuseling can be heard asking how did it go – and the professor replies with an encouraging platitude. Videographer Kate takes the opportunity to pan around the living room. She shoots an eclectic mix of antiques and statuettes and artworks that to some degree continue the theme that has followed them in from the front garden. Simeon Freud asks about a replica of the Venus de Milo – and Percy Tuseling replies that he made it – that he learned to sculpt while he was in prison. The professor remarks that he cannot tell it apart from the real thing, and Percy Tuseling replies that he won many external competitions for his art.

The main camera continues to record as the meeting breaks up; perhaps operator Kate takes on the mantle of editor at this juncture, and by intuition knows that something important may be captured once a subject's guard is down. From a distance, using her built-in microphone she captures an exchange between Percy Tuseling and producer Jen. The producer is explaining that they have enough material for the first podcast, and that it will be available to stream on Friday to coincide with the publication of the Westmorland Gazette. Also, that they will be in touch to schedule a second interview next week, possibly for Wednesday. Percy Tuseling's response is rather curious – although perhaps not out of character – for he quips, “So, I fooled the Professor’s lie-detector test, then?” and follows up with his trademark burst of faux laughter.

4. RECCE – II

West Cumbria Plain – Monday 26 July

BELLTOWER FARM – 10.50 A.M.

'Why didn't we come here last week, Guv?'

Skelgill slots his elbows a little gingerly between the jutting copings of the dry stone wall that separates the verge from the sheep-filled enclosure beyond. The lambs are making the best of the new grass, which has perked up after a band of rain passed over at the weekend. Skelgill stares ruefully – he might be witnessing a last supper, of sorts. Swallows dip and dive for the flies that thrive on the dung. Life is all about eating.

'I see it's still got its belltower.'

DS Leyton has moved on from his first question. And now the shift from an abstract question to a concrete observation seems to penetrate his superior's reflections.

Skelgill's eyes shift from the foreground fauna to the farm building some two hundred yards beyond; partly surrounded by sycamores it is a substantial pale sandstone affair, lacking symmetry, with steep gables and white-painted bargeboards, and a central tower capped by an audaciously pointed spire that once housed the bell, and perhaps still does. It makes an extravagant contrast to its austere near neighbour, Caldblow Farm. Gothic plays ascetic.

'No point getting us knickers in a twist.'

'Come again? Oh, I see what you mean.'

DS Leyton realises that Skelgill has responded to his opening query.

'Not a good idea, trying to get your head round two unrelated crime scenes on the same day.'

DS Leyton gazes a little wanly across the field. He rather doubts that 'getting one's head round something' is a method that

Skelgill favours – but as a figure of speech it makes sense of a sort. However, there is the underlying meaning.

'Are you saying you think they're unconnected?'

Skelgill, too, gazes with a degree of abstraction. He has a fine dry straw of wild oats between his front teeth; the panicle quivers in the way an angler's float reveals unseen activity beneath the water surface.

'They were a year apart. There's no evidence yet that any of the same folk were involved.'

DS Leyton frowns. Is Skelgill taking a particularly severe line? Perhaps a double dose of devil's advocacy because – and it was not difficult to read between the lines – Professor Simeon Freud is clearly on a mission to expose Percy Tuseling as a two-time killer? There are ways to steal his thunder.

But there are the prima facie facts.

'Like the Prof pointed out, Guv – the basic coincidences are remarkable. The only two shotgun murders in the entire county in a five-year period – and they're on adjoining farms. What are the odds of that?'

Skelgill does not answer. DS Leyton employs a tried-and-trusted tactic to elicit a response.

'How many farms – farmhouses – are there in Cumbria?'

Skelgill's straw betrays increased cogitation. His expression, however, does not offer any discrimination between recall or assessment.

But his answer when it comes is definitive.

'Above five thousand.'

DS Leyton emits an exclamation of surprise. He closes one eye piratically. Then he clicks his tongue with a sound of satisfaction.

'There you go, Guv. One in twenty-five million!'

Skelgill turns sharply to regard his colleague.

'Come off it, Leyton – how do you get that?'

DS Leyton seems amused – despite the accusative tone, he knows he is on firm ground.

'Just square the number, Guv – it's basic accumulator betting.'

Skelgill makes a face of some scorn. He turns back to the meadow.

'Aye, but this is human behaviour. We're not talking horseracing.'

DS Leyton does not try to contest the assertion – but he has a way of furthering his point.

'True enough, Guv. But if it were, and you started factoring in what else we already know, the odds would be compelling.'

Skelgill reluctantly concedes some ground.

'Such as?'

'Well – the similar nature of the shootings, to start with. Both victims blasted at point-blank range whilst seated, seemingly taken by surprise. That might indicate a predator repeating a previously successful method – or a geezer that don't want to look his victims in the eye. Either way – bring the odds into it. How many random murders would you need to investigate before you found your next one with an identical MO?'

It is obviously a rhetorical question, and he continues.

'Let's be generous and say it's a hundred. Then there's the red motor. A red car was definitely at Caldblow Farm on the afternoon of Will Featherston's murder – and a reliable eyewitness identified it as a Ford Corsair. Percy Tuseling owned a red Ford Corsair. Again – what are the odds of that? It was an uncommon model – at a conservative estimate, one in a thousand.'

Now there is a pause while the long-time-London-bookie's nephew completes the necessary mental somersaults.

'Twelve zeros.' DS Leyton hems and haws for a moment longer. 'Yeah, that's right – one in two-point-five trillion.'

Skelgill spits out his straw.

'You've invented a new way of solving crime, Leyton! Happen we should patent it and I can go fishing.'

A little sheepishly, DS Leyton hunches his broad shoulders. But, like a stout English yeoman at the barricades, he declines to yield.

'Maybe it should be done more often, Guv. No one bats an eyelid when some boffin stands up in court and says the DNA evidence is one in four billion. The accused is bang to rights – the only bloke on the planet. Compared to that, we're already in outer space with our numbers. A trillion's a thousand billion.'

Skelgill is tempted to retort that in outer space is exactly how they would be regarded were they to advance his sergeant's statistical theory. But he holds back. He senses that more coincidences lie in their path.

DS Leyton determines he need not over-egg this particular pudding.

'What did you make of Percy Tuseling's performance, Guv?'

Skelgill nods slowly; he seems to approve of his colleague's question.

'Aye – it looked that way.'

The answer, overheard by an eavesdropper, might seem vague – but DS Leyton does mean 'performance' and Skelgill has taken him literally. DS Leyton is encouraged to elaborate.

'Even allowing for his weird manner – I just don't buy that excuse. First off, like I said to Emma – why run a defence of manslaughter when you've gone outside and sawed off the barrel. Drunk or not, you have to know what you're doing. Provocation would have been a much safer bet. A jury would give a geezer a bit of leeway if he were looking out for his missus.'

Skelgill is pensive. He watches with a certain detachment as lambs butt off against one another.

'His excuse, Leyton – as you put it. Freud gave him an easy ride. He didn't challenge the basic idea.'

DS Leyton now rotates his shoulders as if he is suffering from some stiffness in the muscles.

'I looked up the pampas grass malarkey, Guv.' He pauses apprehensively, but Skelgill merely waits for him to continue. 'Cor blimey, it's all over the flippin' internet! Mind you – it says it was a fad in the 1970s.'

Skelgill gives a small snort of disdain.

'Some of these Lakeland villages think they're still in the 1970s.'

It seems to DS Leyton that his superior does not dismiss the idea.

'Thing is, Guv – there's an obvious contradiction, right?'

Skelgill is unperturbed.

'I like contradictions, Leyton – they stop you getting carried away.'

DS Leyton delays his response for a couple of seconds – perhaps in due deference to Skelgill's words … before ignoring them.

'I reckon the logic goes like this. If the Tuselings are into the swinging scene nowadays – then fair chance Percy Tuseling was involved back then – at the time he shot Colin Bell-Gibson. If so, that makes a mockery of his admission – that he took umbrage at the mention of the Special Cocktails.'

Skelgill shows no sign that he negates the proposition.

'I was thinking we could stake out the Tuseling's place – see what really goes on in that village.'

Skelgill turns in alarm.

'You volunteering to be struck blind, like Peeping Tom? You'd be better off signing up on the local wife-swapping website.'

Now it is DS Leyton's turn to express consternation.

'Struth! If I did that, Guv – it wouldn't be two shotgun murders you'd have on your plate, but three!'

Skelgill grins phlegmatically. There is an obvious route in the interim, which he now iterates.

'What did the statements say? The two females?'

DS Leyton raises a hand to speak – but he is drowned out by the sudden roar of RAF jets. The pair watch for a minute as a dog fight of sorts ensues. It would be hard to know if it is combat training or gratuitous skylarking. The rumble recedes and a solitary line of birdsong is switched back on – a blackbird in a spinney at their rear; so well into summer it is languid, lacking its spring gusto.

DS Leyton resumes.

'Trouble is, Guv – obviously no one asked them that specific question. Why would anyone think of it? All the cops wanted from the women was that they witnessed the shooting – they weren't especially interested in the motive. The only statement taken from Tuseling's first wife Veronica was while she was in hospital, the next morning. It was brief, and she declined to give further evidence against him in court. That was before they changed the law, obviously – but it didn't matter, since he was putting his hand up for the murder. Susan Bell-Gibson – she was interviewed on the night of the shooting, and again later. But she basically said it came like a bolt from the blue – there had been nothing between Percy Tuseling and Colin Bell-Gibson to suggest any animosity or simmering feud or whatever. After all – it was a birthday dinner for Tuseling.'

There is a short silence before Skelgill speaks.

'Can we find them?'

DS Leyton nods eagerly.

'DC Watson's on the case. So far, we know Veronica Tuseling obtained a divorce and remarried. It seems Susan Bell-Gibson left the district soon after. Assuming they're still alive, Veronica Tuseling would be seventy and Susan Bell-Gibson sixty-four.'

And, again, a pause while they each reflect on these facts. In time, DS Leyton moves on.

'What did you reckon to Percy Tuseling's answer to the Prof's parting shot – that Colin Bell-Gibson said something about the murder of Will Featherston?'

Skelgill looks like he will answer in an obtuse manner, and he does not disappoint.

'Have you read up on the Hares' case?'

'A good bit, Guv.'

'Was there any evidence that either of them knew Will Featherston? They wouldn't have been much older.'

'That's right – they'd have been in the year above him – *hah* – if they'd been at school.' But now DS Leyton shakes his head. 'But they were from Workington – already career tea leaves, a proper pair of no-marks. Will Featherston was from Whitehaven – decent background, studying for university. No indication that the circles they moved in overlapped.'

Skelgill has homed in upon the critical point, albeit in a roundabout way.

'The fishmonger the lad delivered for. Where was that?'

DS Leyton produces his pocketbook. He already has copious notes, and a rudimentary indexing system. He flicks to and fro.

'Back Harbour Lane – Whitehaven.'

Skelgill once again seems distracted by the fate of the lambs. But his succeeding question shows he is paying attention.

'What about Radio Rentals?'

'Where Percy Tuseling was based?'

'Aye.'

DS Leyton makes a vibrating sound with his malleable lips as he peruses his records – and then a more startled exclamation.

'Stone the crows. There go the odds again. *Back Harbour Lane* – Whitehaven.'

Skelgill does not immediately react. Then he turns to his colleague. His expression is severe, but there is a distinctive gleam of triumph in his eyes.

'You know what else is in Back Harbour Lane?'

'Search me, Guv.'

'The other branch of Haighs.'

WHITEHAVEN TOWN CENTRE – NOON

Though in many respects a twin to near neighbour Workington – each settlement at around 25,000 souls and their outer suburbs just five miles apart, and sharing in rugby league one of the fiercest rivalries of local derbies in all forms of English sport – Whitehaven is the sibling that got the good looks, at least as far as its town centre architecture is concerned. Both grew from medieval fishing villages to become by the 19th century mercantile powerhouses, shipping vast tonnages of locally hewn coal and smelting world-class iron; "Workington rails circle the globe" was a saying. Precipitous decline during the Thatcherite reorientation of British industry saw the West Cumbrian economy cast adrift to flounder among the sharks of the free market. Recovery has been slow, and is far from complete. Workington, a victim of 1960s planning, could not be described as easy on the eye. But Whitehaven survived unscathed, and its Georgian grid pattern behind the extensive port (the latter fortified against the Americans, who last attacked in 1778) is reputed to be the template for the street plan of the Big Apple, no less.

DS Leyton, ever a fish out of water in Cumbria's wide-open spaces, is not quite sure what to make of the place. It might be bumping along the bottom in economic terms, but as a creature of London's East End, he feels a curious affinity with this urban microcosm. He notices that strangers say hello, and ask after one's fettle – whatever that might be – it feels welcoming; something commonplace that is characteristic of a stable indigenous community: you chat for five minutes and find you're related.

The main shopping street is busy with Monday folk, catching up on supplies and weekend gossip, and now that it is midday small queues are beginning to form outside sandwich bars and inside cafés.

'Leyton.'

Skelgill's insistent tone rouses him. His boss seems to be craning his neck to observe a large seagull that ornaments the apex of a gable end. And then he sees it.

'Oh – yeah – look at that. It says *Whiting's*, don't it?'

Skelgill does not answer, though he squints up into the sun to where faded lettering tells of a long-defunct retail establishment.

'Kind of like a ghostly reminder, Guv – a message to us from beyond the grave.'

Skelgill regards his colleague reprovingly.

'Leyton – you've got low blood sugar. You need summat to eat.'

DS Leyton subconsciously puts a hand to his stomach; low blood sugar is not something one is likely to suffer working with Skelgill. Though it is a mixed blessing; there are the perennial complaints about having to get his suit trousers let out.

Notwithstanding, he takes a moment to consult his notebook.

'It was a family business, Guv. Closed down when the owner died in 1980. He was the last Whiting in the line.'

And now DS Leyton takes on a more proactive role.

'So this must be number 36 – yeah – that's right, look – that cobbler's number 38. Radio Rentals where Tuseling was based was at 84. Must be further down, on this side.'

They continue along the narrow pedestrianised thoroughfare, crossing an intersection busy with traffic, and DS Leyton counting and readjusting where he spies a number – there being the curious phenomenon of commercial premises, which often exhibit erratic enumeration.

But when they reach 84 it is clearly marked. It is a nail and brow bar. From behind the glass a woman, multidimensionally enhanced and thus of indeterminate age, stares out at them disconcertingly.

'Try the ginnel.'

The phrase is another unintelligible to DS Leyton, but Skelgill disappears into a narrow, covered alley that divides the beautician's from its neighbour, a second-hand shop that rather unsatisfactorily aspires to antiques. The passageway is dark, until a dogleg carries them blinking into a bright yard. Stone steps run back up to a door marked 84B, on what is the first floor – a domestic residence, it seems, a flat.

'That must have been the workshop.'

DS Leyton nods pensively.

Standing in the heat, beginning to perspire, he knows he must share his superior's thoughts of the fateful summer of 1976, when Will Featherston and Percy Tuseling both worked in this street. Certainly, had Whiting's and Radio Rentals been adjacent, they would surely have met in this yard. The lad might have loaded fish while the man heaved a television set. And Percy Tuseling would have left his distinctive red Ford Corsair here during the working day.

But in actuality the shops were well apart – and further divided by the perpendicular road. Their back lanes had separate means of access. At best their liveried vans might have simultaneously turned out of their respective junctions, neither driver paying particular attention to the other, among the hundreds of vehicles abroad. And for Will Featherston it had been a summer job – he could only have worked for a few weeks at best.

'Think it's a red herring, Guv?'

Skelgill produces the sort of look that is knowing, yet wary – like he suspects there is a pun or a punch line to follow. But his sergeant appears in earnest.

'Howay, Leyton.'

Skelgill turns and leads them back into the alleyway; it seems that he might agree.

Yet his shoulders do not sag and his step is jaunty. Could it be his theory of intuition: that going somewhere, however superfluous it may seem at the time, adds an ineffable quality to one's understanding.

Or, more likely, that there is always serendipity of sorts.

Directly opposite the entrance of the alley is the famed butcher's shop, established circa 1880.

Skelgill does not break stride.

DS Leyton follows, rather more judiciously sidestepping pedestrians, who would in his judgement have right of way.

Thus arriving a couple of seconds behind, at the counter for baked goods he cannot help noticing that Skelgill is greeted with an extra dose of familiarity. Of course, his boss can do the accent, and probably in appearance blends in (when in sartorially refined company his attire might raise an eyebrow) – but there is some banter that suggests this emporium is a more frequent port of call than Skelgill has been prepared hitherto to admit.

Indeed, Skelgill has exchanged phrases incomprehensible to DS Leyton's southern ear, and makes some arrangement that the quite elderly and very diminutive lady behind the counter seems to approve of. He turns empty handed, however.

'We'll sit in the window, Leyton – watch the world and his wife.'

The shop is quite large; through an archway is the cold butchery from where emanate chops and clunks and occasional chatter; it has its own entrance to the street, while at their end is a small café area, and a bar along the window, with stools. Skelgill encounters a little trouble in fitting in his legs; DS Leyton's challenge is the ungainly hop needed to attain his seat. Evidently their order will be delivered – indeed Skelgill explains his rationale.

'They've got a batch just coming out of the oven.'

While they wait, DS Leyton wonders if Skelgill will raise the subject – back to statistical probability – of Will Featherston and Percy Tuseling crossing paths sufficiently for recognition to have played some role in the former's fate. It is surely the only feasible motive. A robbery was in progress and the delivery boy stumbled upon it.

DS Leyton's mind drifts; he finds his gaze attracted by the window display of the second-hand shop. Down the years, he has done his share of inspecting such places for stolen goods – with mixed success – but always, when some sought-after item was unearthed, to the ingenuous astonishment of the storekeeper. This particular outlet strikes him as bona fide. Behind dusty glass there is a confection of old and not so old. He can make out an army greatcoat, a mangle, and upon a worn leather trunk a table lamp with a faded red velvet shade. These are not the currency of today's cat burglars. Then he notices that the base of the lamp seems to be a naked statuette.

He starts, and turns to Skelgill.

'Guv – we really ought to look into Percy Tuseling's work history.'

Skelgill, presently engrossed in his own musings, takes a moment to reply.

'I thought you were doing it?'

DS Leyton shakes his head like a horse that is trying to displace flies; he has not explained himself.

'What I mean – it was a burglary taking place at Caldblow Farm – that's surely what got Will Featherston shot, right?'

He waits until Skelgill deigns to nod.

'Odds on it wasn't the burglar's first go.'

Skelgill nods again, playing along.

'Tuseling's job would have taken him to isolated properties hereabouts. Okay – it seems he kept his nose clean – at least as far as his employer knew. There's no mention of disciplinary issues.' Now DS Leyton raises a hand, and indicates in the direction of the would-be antiques shop and its adjacent ginnel, just as a man in an overall and toting a tool bag turns out of the latter and disappears into the flow of human traffic. 'But imagine if we could match up housebreakings with customers of Radio Rentals – especially if they'd previously called out the TV repair man. Ideal job for casing a joint.'

Skelgill looks sharply at DS Leyton. His expression is such – could it be competitive – that for a moment his colleague might fear he is going to claim the point. But instead he falls in alongside him.

'When did Radio Rentals go bust?'

DS Leyton picks up his notebook. He begins to speak as he

seeks the fact.

'Well – as I recall, they didn't exactly go bust – more like taken over and merged into something else. Obviously the technology changed – cheap flatscreens started to come in from the Far East – renting fell by the wayside. Fixing tellies was replaced by taking them to the dump. Here it is – the year 2000.'

In the time it has taken DS Leyton to reply, Skelgill has become distracted by activity at the counter. A small queue of patrons who have been patiently waiting for the piping hot batch of sausage rolls are being served. But Skelgill's anxiety is assuaged by a reassuring wink from the elderly assistant, her grey head bobbing busily as she packs and dispatches the orders with practised aplomb.

DS Leyton brings him back to the subject in question.

'I'll need to put someone onto it, Guv. I'd be surprised if we can get anything from the remnants of Radio Rentals – but at least there'll be crime records of housebreakings.'

But now DS Leyton sighs.

'What is it?'

'More manual records to comb through, that's all. Barnacle-encrusted files.' DS Leyton shrugs resignedly. 'But, since I've suggested it –'

Skelgill gives him a wry look.

'It's not such a bad shout. We can get Jones to find out from Tuseling what area his patch covered. That's part of the idea of her being incognito, isn't it?'

DS Leyton glances sideways at his boss; there is a distinct note of cynicism in his voice, perhaps erring on the astringent.

And now Skelgill seems agitated – but it could be the tantalising aroma and the continued absence of substance. He casts about distractedly. There is a small pile of well-thumbed newspapers at the end of their window shelf. On top is the Westmorland Gazette. He pulls it closer. It has been left folded at Kendall Minto's new article, summarising the first podcast under the dramatic headline, "INTERVIEW WITH A MURDERER."

But suddenly he is galvanised by the arrival of their order, a tray of steaming mugs of tea and plates each with two substantial sausage rolls, and plastic squeezy bottles of red and brown sauce, personally delivered by the lady with whom he has been in cahoots.

The detectives each lean sideways to allow her to reach between them.

'Margaret – you're not old enough to have worked here in the 1970s.'

DS Leyton regards his colleague a little wide-eyed. Skelgill's remark comes entirely out of the blue. And he is on first-name terms.

The woman slaps his forearm for his insouciance – but she is plainly flattered.

'Garn with yer – I started in 1969! Fifteen, I were.'

Skelgill grins knowingly, as though he does not believe her, but is prepared to park the argument. He jerks his head in the direction across the street.

'Did you know Percy Tuseling – worked at Radio Rentals?'

For a second the woman might just harbour a glint of suspicion in her deep-set grey eyes; but the sentiment passes, as inquisitiveness gains the upper hand.

'Him as was jailed for shooting yon farmer? Aye. I knew of him. He came in sometimes. We had more young lasses then – a couple of them used to fancy him. A bit of a ladies' man, he would be called.'

She says this in a way to suggest such interest would therefore have been beneath her. Although perhaps there is an underlying hint of bruised pride being recalled.

Skelgill brings the newspaper to the fore.

'Have you seen this?'

The woman recoils a little hyperopically. But she nods, all the same.

'Aye – it's got folk talking. After all these years. Summat about the murder of young Will Featherston.' She frowns portentously, looking from Skelgill to DS Leyton, and back to Skelgill. 'They say they're meckin one o' them there pot casts.'

Skelgill nods; through a slightly pained expression he appears to be trying to convey something like commiseration.

'Aye – you'll probably get them in here, asking questions.'

The woman inhales sharply, and then hesitates, as if what she is about to add ought to wait for an alternative audience – her moment in the spotlight, perhaps.

She glances around at the counter – as if this has some role in her unspoken narrative – but she notices the queue that is re-forming, and a female colleague singlehandedly struggling against the odds. She takes half a step away – before leaning in conspiratorially.

'Back int' day, one of t' young lasses as worked here – she were a Margaret, an' all – laal Meg, we used to call her. Meg Boycott, she were, afore she were wed. She had a brother as knocked about wi' t' same crowd as Will Featherston. Her kid reckoned they knew Percy Tuseling because he lived in t' same road. They used to play football or cricket or summat.'

Skelgill ostensibly listens casually.

'Will Featherston could have known Percy Tuseling?'

Skelgill's words are unhurried – but DS Leyton can see that his grey-green irises are focused laser-like upon their subject.

'It were just hearsay.' She reaches to tap the newspaper that Skelgill holds. 'They got them Jam Eater twins for the murder of Will Featherston, didn't they?'

DS Leyton is glancing anxiously from Skelgill to the woman. Perhaps the latter's memory – or knowledge – is incomplete. Evidently Skelgill decides not to press for a correction.

'Aye, they did, Margaret – they did that.'

Now the woman receives a plaintive request – an urgent call for help from the counter. She makes an apologetic face to Skelgill and backs away.

'I've put your take-out order int' hot cabinet.'

Skelgill gives her a thumbs up.

Left to their own devices, Skelgill swivels to face the window and immediately tucks into the first of his sausage rolls. DS Leyton, after a moment watching him, and waiting in vain for some comment (all he gets is a raised eyebrow), follows suit.

It is a good two minutes before Skelgill has consumed sufficient of his lunch to pay attention.

By this time DS Leyton has again interrogated his notebook.

'Guv, Will Featherston resided in the same house for his entire life. If she's right and Percy Tuseling lived in the same street – that must have been near the Featherston family address – not the other way round.'

Skelgill nods; he has reached the same conclusion. He does not seem surprised. He starts on his second sausage roll.

DS Leyton peruses his notes, his brow furrowed.

'At the time he shot Bell-Gibson, Tuseling must have been at his next address long enough not to have raised a red flag. I suppose, what with the Hares being collared so soon, the investigating team hadn't yet probed that deeply into Tuseling's background. They had a score of suspects and thousands of statements. I doubt they could see the wood for the trees. No wonder they dumped all their chips on the Hares.'

Skelgill has finished eating. He washes down his lunch with the last of his tea and rubs flakes of pastry from his facial stubble. He slips off his stool and brushes crumbs from his thighs.

'Two ticks.'

DS Leyton watches a little helplessly as he makes for the counter and inserts himself between two waiting customers to gain the attention of the elderly woman. A short confab now takes place, before Skelgill is handed up a folded brown paper bag that already bears grease stains as witness to its contents.

He gives a wave and turns towards his colleague. He raises the bag unapologetically.

'One for the road.'

DS Leyton gingerly lowers himself from his stool. He grins stolidly.

'You seem to have a way with her, Guv.'

'Leyton – her maiden name's Graham.'

WOODHOUSE ESTATE, WHITEHAVEN – 1.00 P.M.

'This must be it, Guv. Kirkstile Avenue starts here.'

'Another one for your accumulator, Leyton.'

'What's that, Guv?'

'Where was the place where the Hares bungled their raid?'

'Cor, yeah – that's right – Kirkstile Farm, wasn't it?'

DS Leyton furrows his brow.

'Mind you – that is a genuine coincidence – I mean, there's no significant connection – is there?'

Skelgill, in the passenger seat of his colleague's car, leans back and folds his arms. Though his sentiment is unspoken, it is clear he takes a small pleasure in the timely reminder – that all coincidences should be treated with caution.

He sniffs, and casts about as DS Leyton drives more judiciously as they approach their destination. They have been navigating a sprawling post-war estate, built by the local corporation as council housing, but partially sold off into private ownership in the 1980s under Mrs Thatcher's 'Right to Buy' policy, when tenants were able to claim title for a song, as little as a half of market value.

They have reached a point where the avenue forks, and between the western and eastern branches opens up a public green area. But where it might provide a breath of fresh air after row upon row of near-identical grey-harled semi-detacheds, Skelgill merely sighs. The treeless, bushless, herbless green is surrounded by protective railings, but lacks any features other than a couple of dog bins – and one man on a mobility scooter who exercises an unsteady hip-heavy Alsatian across at the far side. For an outdoorsman such as he, the estate is rendered all the more depressing for the lip service paid to the wellbeing of its denizens.

'Number fifty-three, wasn't it, Guv?'

DS Leyton's question comes as a relief from his dismay. Skelgill turns to scrutinise the houses they pass on the left.

'Aye – Avenue West, that's what she reckoned. The one with pampas grass.'

'Really?'

DS Leyton is surprised – but then he spies Skelgill's grin.

'Ah – very droll, Guv.'

But he nods knowingly – understanding that Skelgill is doubling down on his point, that happenstances are to be handled with care.

That said, in following Skelgill's nose they have made not insignificant progress – despite that his superior has played it down. Skelgill's insistence is that the whole town was probably a hive of gossip and conjecture – a deafening clamour when Will

Featherston was murdered – reaching a second crescendo when the Hares were tried and convicted a year later. When Percy Tuseling shot Colin Bell-Gibson a few weeks after that – folk naturally jumped to their own conclusions. Not least if the Hares went down kicking and screaming, protesting their innocence – and the police were seen to jam their fingers in their ears.

'Here.'

Skelgill has spotted a broken number – the three is missing but its algal silhouette is adequate.

They lurch to a halt. DS Leyton sounds cheerful.

'No pampas – but plenty of grass, Guv.'

He refers to knee-deep hay, formerly a small front lawn, enclosed by a decaying paling fence.

On approach, Skelgill leans to peer into a window. At the angle he can just see a section of a widescreen TV that is showing cricket on a cable channel.

There is no bell but his knock on the door is answered by the cockcrow howl of an irascible terrier.

A man's face briefly appears at the window – he is balding, unshaven, somewhat overweight and wearing a vest; he looks to be in his mid-sixties. He makes an expression of disapproval.

The door opens to more barking and now television commentary, and jubilant crowd noises as a six is hit and repeatedly replayed. The man insinuates himself between the edge of the door and the jamb. It seems the dog must be in the back kitchen.

'Mr Boycott?'

Skelgill does not wait for an answer and makes a succinct presentation of their credentials. DS Leyton notices he employs maximum use of the vernacular.

Their subject remains suspicious. He glowers at the warrant card. He holds the door against his body. He wears disreputable grey tracksuit bottoms and women's fluffy carpet slippers.

Skelgill elaborates upon his opening question.

'Jeff Boycott – who's got an older sister, Margaret – known as Meg?'

At this, the man seems to move on from the issue of his own identity.

'What's up wi' her?'

'Nowt that we know.' Skelgill pauses only briefly. 'She used to work in Haighs with a relative of mine in the 1970s. Margaret Graham, she were, back then.'

The mention of the Graham name prompts a second, inquisitive glance at Skelgill – that this police officer is connected to the illustrious clan.

Skelgill produces the newspaper. He displays the article.

'We're looking into this. Are you aware of it?'

The man squints, and scowls. He remains tight-lipped. But he shows some interest. He takes the offered periodical. It would seem the answer is *unaware*. He checks the date of publication before handing it back.

'I thought it were long dead and buried. Who'd want to rake that up?'

Skelgill looks like he wishes he could agree.

'It's a free country. There's a documentary being filmed. They're calling it *Murder on the Farm*. We're the piggy in the middle.'

It is possible to take from Skelgill's manner that he shares the man's cynicism, and that they are in this together.

Jeff Boycott looks alarmed. And belligerent.

'You won't get us ont' telly.'

This is an admission upon which Skelgill swiftly capitalises.

'Just say you've told the police all you know and have no further comment.'

The man seems to realise that he has walked into a little trap – but Skelgill does not give him time to backtrack. He motions to the newspaper. Centrepiece is a photographic montage: Percy Tuseling, Will Featherston, and the Hare twins.

'It's been said that Percy Tuseling was known to the bairns hereabouts. Something to do with football or cricket. Happen he was a youth coach or summat?'

The man sucks at his teeth, and shakes his head slowly. But just when it seems he will gainsay the suggestion, he surprises them.

'It were cricket – but he weren't a coach.'

For a moment he seems unwilling to offer more – but then he steps down and pulls the door to behind him. He glances about, bemused, as though he has not seen his garden for some time. Then he lifts his head and gazes somewhat wistfully across the green. Two small boys have appeared, kicking a football. The grass is well overdue for a cut, and they cannot get any lift on their passes.

'This time o' year – place used to be packed. It's all computer games now, int it?'

A pause ensues. They wait for him to speak again.

'We had timeless tests – reet through t' school holidays. All t' lads as lived hereabouts. We had regular sides – West v East – any stragglers just joined in, eetsy peetsy.' The man seems distinctly misty-eyed. 'There must have been half a dozen blokes. Some as played when they got home from work. Some were on strike or laid off – from t' steelworks and t' pits. Percy Tuseling – you'd hope he'd come when it were your side's turn to get the next player. He were a club cricketer – opening bat. Didn't care if it were a bairn bowling at him – he'd slog 'em out of t' ground.'

Skelgill takes his time.

'Did he play often?'

'More occasional, like. He weren't one of them as were laid off. Half the country were on strike in the 1970s. Didn't bother us bairns.'

'But you definitely remember him?'

'Oh, aye – he lived across yonder – Avenue East. Then he moved away.'

'What year are we talking?'

The man contemplates, still rheumy-eyed; perhaps it is just his condition.

'I reckon we packed it in by the time we were fourteen, going on fifteen.' Now he flashes a knowing look, unashamed that it is salacious. 'Other interests took over.'

Skelgill is gently persistent.

'But what about Percy Tuseling?'

The man makes a face of strained concentration, staring out over the green as if seeing into bygone years and the faded memories of everlasting cricket matches.

'He might have been gone a couple of year before we packed it in. That were '74, I reckon.'

'When you stopped?'

'Aye.'

Skelgill waits for a moment – then he shows the newspaper once more.

'Margaret mentioned you knew Will Featherston.'

He does not clarify which Margaret. But the man replies.

'We were int' same year at school. Can't say as I was his marra, like. He were int' swots' class. He lived along Avenue East, an' all. His folks stayed there until they died – must be above ten year ago, now – see where t' England flag is.'

Skelgill, however, gestures more generally to the green.

'So – Will – he were involved in the cricket?'

'Aye. He were good. A bowler. He were a left-arm spinner. Quick, orthodox. The blokes used to call him Deadly.'

The man directs an unexpectedly challenging look at Skelgill.

Skelgill calls his bluff.

'Underwood.'

DS Leyton looks quizzically at Skelgill – but this is one game that is up his superior's street.

Indeed, Jeff Boycott grunts his approval.

'Aye, Underwood. Didn't think you'd have heard of him – your age. Took eight for fifty-one against Pakistan on a wet turner at Lords. Greatest spell of spin bowling I've seen. That would've bin about that time. *Hah* – they can keep their Warnes and their Muralis.'

Skelgill is conscious of the potential for becoming sidetracked – but he wrests the helm away from his own inclination to do so.

'Will Featherston would have played at the same time as Percy Tuseling.'

That it is a statement and not a question seems to have the desired effect. The man stiffens, and looks now at his inquisitors in turn, as if he is reminding himself of the gravity of the matter, and that these are police detectives.

'Aye he would. For a while, any road.'

There is a sense of more to be said, but now he waits for Skelgill to say it.

'They could have known who one another were.'

The man nods slowly. It takes him a few moments to reply.

'I reckon Will Featherston would have known who Percy Tuseling was. You knew all the blokes – like you knew older kids at school – but you paid no attention t' bairns.'

'Are you saying it might not have been mutual?'

Now the man shrugs.

'No way of knowing. Time you're talking about – we would have been twelve or thirteen. There were older lads that would have had the banter wi' t' blokes.'

'You say Will Featherston got himself a nickname from them – from the adults.'

The man seems unconvinced.

'We had long hair as youngsters. Everyone looked like Noddy Holder from Slade. Later on, Will Featherston started knocking about with punk rockers. I didn't recognise him mesen when they had his picture on t' police posters.'

Skelgill, however, brushes past such obstacles.

'But that were the crack, reet?'

Jeff Boycott seems to understand Skelgill's question. It is, after all, the logical corollary of their abridged debate.

'You're saying –' He pauses, and indicates to the newspaper. 'They got the wrong 'uns for Will Featherston. Seeing as Percy Tuseling went and shot that farmer.'

Skelgill now responds with surprising indifference.

'By all accounts, that were fairly common knowledge.'

Again the man seems reluctant to go quite so far.

'It's hard to mind. Aye – it were mentioned. But your lot –' And now he looks a little guardedly at the detectives. There is the suggestion that he would like to use the term "bad lot" for the police of the time, and perhaps still harbours such distrust. 'They had no doubt it were them Hare twins. But I doubt folk were all that fussed. If they banged up t' Hares for t' wrong murder – good riddance. And if it were Percy Tuseling – well, he were int' clink, any road – weren't he?'

*

'What's a timeless test, Guv?'

Skelgill is occupied by timeless taste. They are each consuming their 'one for the road'. DS Leyton has parked in Thwaite Road, outside the address that official records show was Percy Tuseling's place of residency at the time he shot farmer Colin Bell-Gibson. It is nine-tenths of a mile from Kirkstile Avenue, and though sharing many characteristics, the district feels marginally more salubrious, a rung up the social ladder. The hiatus in their conversation has allowed DS Leyton to mull over the more peripheral aspects of their interview.

Snacking interruption or not, Skelgill cannot resist showing off his knowledge.

'It were a pre-war thing – the test matches were played to a finish. It stopped one team shutting up shop. The longest one on record lasted nearly a fortnight, including rest days. Nowadays it's restricted to five consecutive days.'

DS Leyton murmurs his approval.

'Sounds like a good idea. I can't stand it in football that they decide it on penalties. Sudden death. In the end, some poor cove has to miss – and you can bet your bottom dollar they'll be wearing an England shirt.'

Skelgill nods reluctantly.

'It's all about advertising, Leyton. Cash is king.'

DS Leyton covers his mouth to speak as he munches.

'That stuff about the kid's nickname – *Deadly?*'

Skelgill again needs no prompting. Moreover, as a club cricketer himself and a left-hander to boot, he is a student of those of the sinister ilk.

'In first-class cricket, when it rains they cover the wicket. Back in the day, they didn't. Track gets wet – the ball bites into the damp surface. Derek Underwood were a left-arm spinner who bowled at the same pace as a seamer. On a sticky wicket he could turn it sideways. At his speed he were unplayable.'

Skelgill's tone is wistful, but DS Leyton wants to get to the bottom of the facts.

'I thought the wicket was the name for the stumps?'

Now Skelgill smirks.

'Aye – it can be the stumps. Or it can be the track. Or it can be when you get someone out – that's a wicket, an' all.'

DS Leyton makes a sound of exasperation.

'Cor blimey, Guv – no wonder I stick to footie. All you have to worry about is the offside rule.'

Skelgill is a little scornful.

'At the end of the day, Leyton, cricket's just one bloke chucking a ball at another bloke.'

A small pause ensues.

'Or woman.'

'Aye.'

And now a longer silence; perhaps both men have appreciated the diversion, beating about the bush before the unspoken agreement that they ought to dive back into it. DS Leyton makes the first move.

'By the sound of it, Guv – at the very least, Will Featherston would surely have recognised Percy Tuseling.'

Skelgill is nodding – but he is also cautious.

'Leyton – do the kids in your street recognise you?'

DS Leyton inhales – and holds the breath – in the way that indicates Skelgill has made a good point.

'I doubt it. Maybe a couple that ours knock about with. But if I'm honest – the ones you see walking past to school or kicking a ball around – I don't pay 'em much attention, and I reckon they ignore me. Be a different kettle of fish if I were in uniform, mind you.'

Skelgill accepts the explanation.

'And there's nowt in the files about this?'

DS Leyton raises his hands, a delaying gesture.

'I wouldn't go so far as to say that, Guv. All those flippin' boxes – we've only explored the tip of the iceberg.'

Skelgill remains pensive. He looks now at the house outside which they are parked. But he makes no complaint – he knows it is a thankless task that he could not contemplate.

'I reckon it's one for Jones.'

DS Leyton notes he does not say it is one for the professor.

5. EPISODE 2.1: PLACES OF INTEREST

Incident Room 101 – 12.15 p.m. Wednesday 28 July

Drone photography is all the rage these days; it is de rigueur for any self-respecting documentary. Turnpike Media are no exception to this rule, and DS Jones, having logged in to the secure portal for interrogating the rushes, and fast-forwarded through footage that comprises mainly aerial landscapes of the West Cumbria Coastal Plain, settles to normal playing speed for a segment that begins with a vertiginous bird's-eye view of what is recognisably the Gothic rooftops of Belltower Farm, and as it descends a small cluster of antlike characters in a paved area at the front of the property becomes the documentary crew. It is apparent that some additional person must be operating the drone, perhaps subcontracted for this day's work with its emphasis upon location shots.

The weather is still and sunny and warm, and the airborne camera's microphone picks up almost no sound until it hovers just a few feet from the bell tower – although if there is still a bell it is too dark within the narrow, arched slits see it. There is now the chirruping of house martins that breed under the eaves; the adults flirt with the drone as though it is another bird – on reflection perhaps they think it is a kestrel or a sparrowhawk, for the young retract their heads into their shingled mud-cup nests in response to their parents' warnings. The drone continues to descend, all the way to ground level, where in a border of purple Michaelmas daises tortoiseshell butterflies flick and flutter and jostle with bumbling bees. Watching, somewhat entranced, Skelgill realises he is never going to shed the small residual schoolboy urge to capture them.

'Looks like they've spliced some takes already.'

It is DS Jones's voice that springs Skelgill from his flight aboard the tiny aircraft. Though he continues to watch placidly as the filming cuts to a handheld camera. Now a Steadicam is being used, and its progress towards its human subjects – Professor Simeon Freud and Percy Tuseling – has a floating, dreamlike quality. DS Jones again inserts a few words of commentary.

'The owners of Belltower Farm only consented to us filming on the front driveway.'

The professor is giving a short summary of the previous interview – that here is the place where Percy Tuseling almost inexplicably shot dead the farmer he regarded as one of his best friends. Finally, he turns to their subject, and the camera operator seems to know to zoom in upon the man's discomfited features.

"How does it feel, Percy? This must be the first time you have been back?"

Despite its seeming innocence, it is a potentially loaded question – what if he has been back – would that mean as a voyeur, to relive those moments, or gloat at the scene of his crime?

"Yes, it is."

The small eyes are once again watery and strained – yet to Skelgill they convey a doubtful sincerity. Percy Tuseling seems to know to embellish the effect.

"I feel very upset for what I apparently did."

"Has the place changed?"

Percy Tuseling looks about pointedly, as if it has taken the question for him to think about this aspect.

"Not that I can see. There is better upkeep. Colin was lazy. That's why he had work for me."

"What kind of work did you do?"

"It could have been anything on the farm. Loading hay bales. Mucking out the stable. Mending fences. Putting out feed. Whatever was happening at that season."

"So you have been here many times?"

"Hundreds. And I was his chauffeur, his gardener – all sorts of things."

"And you shot on the land – was that for pleasure?"

Percy Tuseling displays just a hint of irritation – as if the professor has diverged from a pre-agreed script.

"No – to keep down the vermin. Pigeons and crows. Occasionally rabbits."

"Did you shoot alone?"

"That was part of my job – vermin take stealth."

"But also sometimes with Mr Bell-Gibson? I think you mentioned it."

"I sometimes acted as driver or beater. Or we went to get a couple of pheasants, for the pot."

"And did you bring your own gun?"

"I didn't have a shotgun. I would borrow Colin's spare."

Skelgill's attentive ear picks up a prompt from one of the crew – perhaps he does so because the voice is familiar. The professor evidently takes his cue.

"In one of your interviews with the police you told them you had a shotgun, did you not?"

The impression of suspicion in the man's eyes intensifies. Here is the battle of wills with the professor that he has been expecting. He does not trust the academic's motive.

"I told them I had *sold* a shotgun. A year before. I told them who I had sold it to and they went and checked."

From off camera the professor has been handed a note – indeed there is a glimpse of DS Jones as she retreats from the shot. He scrutinises its content before resuming his questioning.

"Let me see – yes – that was a year before the murder of Will Featherston?"

"That's right."

"So, *two* years before you shot Colin Bell-Gibson – with one of his own shotguns, the one you sawed off?"

"Yes."

Percy Tuseling is tight-lipped. He is not relishing the exchange. His questioner has the upper hand, and his features are reddening. To Skelgill's mind there is a sense of the surreal – that two men can be standing in such ordinary circumstances conversing about guns and murder.

"And what about Caldblow Farm – you shot there, as well?"

"Colin farmed the land of both farms. It's continuous."

The professor has a characteristic of bringing his right hand up to his chin. While it is perhaps affected, to convey concentration, it suggests the man's mind has moved elsewhere, and in wishing to conceal the fact he inadvertently reveals it. However, on this occasion he restates his question.

"So, just to clarify – you shot on Caldblow Farm land as well?"

"Sometimes."

Simeon Freud looks long and hard at Percy Tuseling – it may be for the benefit of the camera, and the audience beyond.

"Percy – you can see why you brought suspicion on yourself. When you were first interviewed after Will Featherston had been murdered. And you didn't mention your connection to these farms."

The professor's observations are made somewhat languidly; in contrast, Percy Tuseling's response is immediate; it comes in short, staccato bursts.

"The police didn't ask me if I knew the farms. They were obviously in a hurry. I answered all their questions. They wanted to know if I owned a red Ford Corsair, and where I was on the afternoon that the boy was killed."

Now he stares defiantly at the professor.

"But, Percy – there was great hue and cry – it was all over the news." That the professor was not even born at the time does not deter him from speaking as though from personal experience. Though his words are critical, he maintains a tone that verges upon amicable disbelief. "A murder at a farm that you knew well. Surely it would have been the most natural thing to mention your connection?"

"Like I say, I answered all the questions. There were hundreds of things about myself that I could have told them. Look, I'm wearing pink socks – I've just done a poo in the toilet."

He seems for a second as though he will produce his faux laugh – but instead he lets the slightly offensive remark take effect, like a chamber pot emptied upon one who assails his fortification.

But perhaps he misinterprets the professor's expression of distaste as one of undermined credence – for unexpectedly he offers an alternative explanation.

"Plus, I didn't want to lose my job. If my employer found out I was working here, I could have been sacked."

The professor does not respond directly to this seemingly new information. Instead he doubles down on his more general thesis.

"Well, there is an argument that if you had nothing to do with it, you would have no reason not to mention it. Not doing so created greater suspicion – and indeed it did when the police later linked you to both farms and interviewed you again."

DS Jones pauses the recording.

She places a hand on the papers at her side and turns to her colleagues.

'I retrieved the records. This is the brief I prepared for Sim.'

She hands out copies.

'Remember we speculated about what led the detectives to go back to him? It wasn't Lady Fitzrovia – at least, she wasn't the only source. Percy Tuseling was first interviewed at home on Wednesday 18th August 1976, five days after the shooting of Will Featherston. They went soon after to verify his alibi – that he was at work. It checked out, and it seems he was dropped down the list of suspects. But on Wednesday 15th September the police station at Cleator Moor received an anonymous call naming him as a person who shot at Caldblow Farm. It was made from a public telephone box and the number wasn't traceable. The caller's voice was described as male, and disguised by some sort of muffling. This information was relayed verbally to the main incident room and transcribed. That note is in the file. It would seem to be what prompted the second visit to Percy Tuseling. That interview took place at his work address in Whitehaven on Friday 17th September. But on Monday 20th September the Hares unsuccessfully tried to rob Kirkstile Farm armed with a shotgun and the entire focus of the investigation shifted.'

She turns the page of her document. She looks up to see that DS Leyton is following diligently; Skelgill considerably less so.

'The transcript of the second interview opens with the question:

"Mr Tuseling, what is your connection to Caldblow Farm?" He replied that he worked there part-time. There is no qualitative indication of how he reacted. He explained that he feared Radio Rentals might sack him if it was discovered he was doing another job. He is also recorded as stating that, of course, he would be in trouble with the taxman.'

DS Leyton emits a choked exclamation of disgust.

'As if it ain't bad enough that he put himself first – oh, and by the way, I'm committing tax fraud – but we're all men of the world, aren't we? A kid's been killed – but, so what!'

DS Jones regards her fellow sergeant's outburst with a hint of alarm – but she shifts her gaze to Skelgill to see that he is observing their colleague intently.

'It's probably best if you both watch how it plays out.'

The action resumes with a belligerent Percy Tuseling.

"When the police asked me about working at the farms, I told them exactly."

"How did the police react – that you hadn't informed them previously?"

"They understood. Besides – they'd already checked my alibi. I couldn't have been at Caldblow Farm when Will Featherston was shot."

A perceptive onlooker would detect a small collective frisson in Room 101 – it is the use by Percy Tuseling of the word *alibi* that raises the hackles of those present – that he regarded himself to be in possession of such a thing, that slippery eel which secretes itself amongst the rocks of the criminal mind, the obscure but pervasive consciousness of guilt.

The two protagonists are standing somewhat awkwardly. As in the first episode, with the abnormal distancing on the sofa, it is apparent that the professor is not wanting to convey accusation through aggressive posturing. Percy Tuseling rocks uncomfortably from one foot to the other, his feet planted unnaturally far apart. The discontinuity poses a challenge for videographer Kate to get them both in shot, and it adds to the air of unease.

"Percy, when did you first hear of Will Featherston's murder?"

The camera homes in on his face. What a moment – if the

answer is "When I shot him".

"I was at work. No – wait – my wife told me when she got home, didn't she? She'd heard it on the local radio in her car."

The man's answer is even, and terse – but nothing more.

"What did you think?"

"Well – *bloody hell.*"

The professor nods, his expression reflective.

"The shock of a murder aside – surely that you knew Caldblow Farm so well – didn't it make you want to do something? The police released an immediate appeal for witnesses."

The furtive eyes fix upon the professor. And now the falsetto note in his voice becomes heightened.

"But I wasn't a witness. I wasn't involved. I would have been a distraction for them."

The camera pulls out. The professor turns a little circle – there is something Holmesian about his movements, his slow pacing, the exaggerated curvature of his spine. He emerges as if through an invisible curtain a more brooding character, and perhaps Percy Tuseling ought to expect the unexpected.

"Percy – if you could speak to Will Featherston now – what would you say to him?"

The camera shifts back to Percy Tuseling, but rather than frame his face it keeps him at full length. He pivots by forty-five degrees to face the camera, and turns out his palms, his arms a little away from his sides. His expression switches to the mode that is strained remorse, his face flushed and his small eyes glistening. He, too, has the melodramatic manner of an actor about to address his audience.

And, indeed, his tone wistful, he launches into a soliloquy.

"Well, Will, many years ago, because of two horrific murder cases, that happened in this vicinity, your name and mine became intrinsically joined." He sighs. "How I wish we could have been fused together under different and happier circumstances. Through the power of silent prayer, I have spoken to, and prayed for you, Will, many times. This, Will, is what I say to you. God bless you."

He freezes, his arms extended a little further – it is almost as though he is remaining in character until he hears the word "cut". It does not come – though he acts as though it has – and he drops his arms and turns in clear expectation of the professor's approbation.

DS Jones seems to know she should pause the recording once more.

DS Leyton immediately pronounces.

'He's off his flamin' rocker!'

DS Jones regards her colleague sympathetically.

Yet there is a case for the sympathy to flow in the other direction – and it seems DS Leyton realises this.

'What's he like – what's it like for you, girl – being so close to him?'

DS Jones places her hands together on the table and considers the question. They have all – even she, with her more limited experience and her colleagues a decade older – met their share of unbalanced individuals. But the norm is a relationship of pursuer versus fugitive, or of accuser versus suspect. Here, it is more complex. Percy Tuseling has a role like that of an aging celebrity being chaperoned by a film crew to investigate his roots – an ancestral trail on which he stops to express shock and pathos when confronted by the antics of his forbears – when in fact it was he who was at the centre of this gruesome history.

DS Jones nods pensively.

'He's not particularly intelligent – he's sly and streetwise. I think he's well aware that he's in a game of cat and mouse. Sim calls his manipulative behaviour 'duping delight' – when it fails you sense there are moments when he's about to erupt. I think in many circumstances he would resort to violence.' She gestures to the papers that have been processed into marked piles at one end of the long table. 'I read an account of a fellow inmate from the time he was at North Sea Camp, towards the end of his sentence. The account's another story that we should probably come back to – but the prisoner said Percy Tuseling was always in the gym, he described him as "massive" – and that the other cons were terrified of him.'

DS Leyton is shaking his head.

'He says, "Two horrific murders" – cor blimey, he just happened to commit one of 'em!'

DS Jones is nodding.

'He keeps saying things like, "apparently I did this" and "they say I did that" – you've heard some of it already. Then he will state that he regrets what happened and that he paid the price to society. He conveys an air of remorse – but it seems overbaked, to me. At times it's almost as though there are two people, separating right before your eyes – like you're getting double-vision.'

'Wolf in sheep's clothing.'

It is Skelgill who interjects.

The others look at him. He makes a face of indeterminate displeasure, but adds no further commentary.

After a pause, DS Jones restarts the video.

The professor seems to sense that a few moments' silence is the appropriate rejoinder to Percy Tuseling's message to the afterlife – he leaves the man looking at him rather helplessly, and now tongue-tied, as if embarrassed for what he has just said, and wishing that Simeon Freud would respond with "Amen" in order to provide closure.

But the professor steps back from the esoteric.

"Percy – it has been said that the similarity of the shootings – almost exact circumstances and on adjacent farms – is an extraordinary coincidence. How come Colin Bell-Gibson ends up dead in exactly the same way as Will Featherston?"

Percy Tuseling quickly regathers his wits. His tone becomes just a touch impatient, as though he might feel betrayed for revealing his inner feelings, and yet now they are back to the inquisition.

"I don't know – I don't know about that. Circumstances or – what do you call it – coincidence, or whatever. But apparently he did."

The professor steps closer, confidingly.

"That must strike you as eerie?"

Percy Tuseling now nods willingly.

"Eerie – yes, yes. The police said to me, it's exactly the same as Will died. Exactly the same."

The professor brings his hand to his chin and frowns pensively. Then he swings away and casts an arm along the direction of the driveway.

"When you came to work on the farms, did you park here or at Caldblow Farm?"

"Oh, no – always here – Colin was my employer."

"What do you say to the sightings of a red car like yours at Caldblow Farm on the afternoon of the murder of Will Featherston? Indeed one witness who identified a car turning in as a red Ford Corsair driven by a man wearing some kind of uniform."

Beneath the remorseful shell, agitation is growing. It is possible to imagine DS Jones's characterisation of the dual personality that is splitting asunder.

Percy Tuseling's words come more sharply.

"That it could not have been me. People were coming to these farms all the time. Feed salesmen came, the vet came. The doctor came. I knew the grocer's van came. I knew somebody delivered fish – but not who."

For the second time there is just the hint of a collective reaction in Room 101 – all three detectives make the slightest of movements. But there is no comment and the recording rolls on. The professor, however, does not pick up on the rider that has arrested them. He is preoccupied with his own line of questioning.

"Percy – why do you think Will Featherston was killed?"

Percy Tuseling digs his hands into his trouser pockets; he looks away.

"Well, I can only go on what the police said. It was a robbery and he got disturbed."

"Robbers don't normally shoot defenceless teenagers."

"No – neither do law-abiding electricians, thank you very much."

"Law-abiding electricians don't normally shoot their best friends."

"And law-abiding electricians, Simeon, don't go on armed robberies in their work uniform to places where they are very well known."

The quickfire exchange, of increasing vehemence, reveals much of what has been bubbling under the surface. The professor has launched a planned attack, and Percy Tuseling, rather than keep his cool, has punched back.

"For me, Percy, he was shot because he could identify his killer."

"I know what you're thinking, but let me just make this perfectly clear, I would not have, under any circumstances, come on an armed robbery to a farm where I thought people were in, and where I was known and I knew someone delivered fish now."

"Maybe you weren't doing an armed robbery?" Simeon Freud has dropped any pretence of there being a third party. "You could have been doing anything. You spotted something when you were in the house – you could have been taking things to sell on. And Will Featherston, because the back door was open, was used to walking in because he would put the fish in the fridge if no one was about. And he walks in and he encounters somebody, and he goes, 'Oh, hello, Mr Tuseling'."

"Yeah? That's a theory of yours, is it?"

"No – it's actually a theory that's in a lot of –"

"It's a police theory – do you believe the police?" Percy Tuseling looks suddenly smug, like he has pulled an ace from his sleeve. "The lies they've told, and you still believe them?"

It seems he refers to the Hares' infamous and ultimately unsafe confessions. But the professor treats the question as rhetorical – and now he moves to lower the temperature. He changes tone altogether, his body language conciliatory, his arms hanging loosely by his sides.

"I think Will was shot because he could identify the person or people who were breaking in."

Percy Tuseling still has his guard raised. But it is clear he wants the off-ramp.

"Well, that's feasible."

"Is that feasible?"

"It's feasible – I have no argument against that. But who were they or he?"

"Ye-es?"

"It certainly wasn't me."

The professor nods, accepting the point.

Percy Tuseling continues.

"The two who were arrested for it, I believed had done it. I don't know – I *believed* they did."

"And do you still believe they did?"

Percy Tuseling bows decisively.

"Yes, I do."

There is a longer pause – and then producer Jen calls "cut" – it seems she senses that the round is over, the bell has rung – perhaps a sound effect to be added, the tolling of the quarter from the belltower.

The camera keeps rolling, however, and quite noticeably the protagonists visibly relax, as though they have indeed been engaged in some staged contest. Jen's voice can be heard commending them for a good scene. And now the microphone picks up an aside from the professor.

"Percy – we have to do this devil's advocacy to have any credibility with our audience. If I don't ask the questions that they will be screaming at their televisions, they will simply switch channel."

The digital file ends and the screen displays a menu of options. But DS Jones seems to understand that there are tangles they should unpick. She switches off, so that there is no distraction.

She makes the first point.

'Notice how he dealt with the suggestion of being recognised. He didn't contest the idea – it just made him angrier.'

Skelgill is nodding, though DS Leyton wants clarification.

'That was before you took him to the housing estate, right?'

'Yes. We should have that footage later today – it's probably worth waiting until we get the rushes, so you can see his reaction then.'

DS Leyton raises and lowers his shoulders and sighs heavily.

'I reckon that there Prof's got him showing his true colours. I mean – all that about armed robbery. What kind of answer's that? It's like he was saying he *would* commit an armed robbery, but only if he knew he could get away with it. Why wouldn't you just say –

robbery, shooting – that's *never* the kind of thing I would do?'

'Because it is.'

It is another of Skelgill's pithy interventions.

'Guv?' DS Leyton remains puzzled.

'He shot his marra, didn't he? It's *exactly* the kind of thing he would do. He's not got a leg to stand on, with that argument.'

'Yeah – good point.' DS Leyton now rubs at his thick dark hair in frustration, leaving it in suitable disarray. 'But it's still a criminal's excuse, in my book.'

Skelgill looks at DS Jones.

'What's his previous?'

She reaches to extract a page from her tiled arrangement of papers.

'This was presented after the conclusion of his trial – and it was included in the bundle that was sent to the Hares' solicitors in relation to their appeal. He was convicted of two cases of wilful damage at Whitehaven and Millom Juvenile Court at the age of nine – of larceny when he was ten, for which he spent a month in a remand home – and of office-breaking and larceny when he was nineteen, for which he was fined £25. The definition of larceny was changed to theft in 1968.'

DS Leyton stares somewhat wide-eyed.

'So – he had burgled before.'

There ensue a few moments of collective reflection. To break into someone's property is outside the scope of the regular citizen's moral compass. And these were just the offences for which Percy Tuseling had been caught.

A text alert on DS Jones's mobile phone interrupts the silence. She checks it – and suppresses a giggle.

'Who is it?'

It is Skelgill's inquiry.

'Oh – it's about the next batch of rushes. They're saying after three o'clock.'

Skelgill is scowling. But DS Jones does not give him time to dwell upon whatever thought perturbs him.

'Should we break for lunch? I've booked the video call with Ballistics for two – and that's for an hour.'

Skelgill does not exhibit his customary enthusiasm, despite that shepherd's pie and date pudding are today's specials in the canteen.

6. GUNS & ROSE

Incident Room 101 – 2.00 p.m. Wednesday 28 July

'Are we sitting comfortably?'

'All present and correct – can you hear us okay?'

'Aye – loud and clear. But, Emma – maybe if you move your laptop a bit further away, I'll be able to see the lot of you.'

DS Jones does as requested. She watches the wall-mounted screen until both of her colleagues appear in the inset.

'How's that? It's DI Skelgill beside me, and DS Leyton.'

'Perfect. Fellas – in case you didnae ken, I'm Mike Rose, originally a firearms examiner with Strathclyde Police – nowadays I run a private forensic ballistics consultancy that's licensed by the Home Office.'

DS Jones's colleagues each raise a polite hand. The man on the screen seems affable, somewhere in his fifties, balding, rosy-cheeked (Rose by name, they might be thinking), and the bearer of a distinct west-coast Scots accent.

DS Jones picks up the narrative.

'Well, thanks for doing this, Mike – at such short notice – there was a lot to absorb.'

'Och – it was just a paper exercise. No great skill needed.' He reaches to one side, out of shot, and there is the sound of his hand patting what might be a pile of documents. Now he taps the top of his head. 'I should state at the outset – Ah'm nae gonnae solve yer case for ye.'

That the man lapses into a stronger vernacular seems to prompt Skelgill to speak – he leans forward, but then holds back, deciding against it. In fact he has formed the impression from the outset that guns per se are unlikely to provide many answers; the case might have been mishandled, but shotgun murders are notorious for their impenetrability.

DS Jones responds reassuringly.

'Mike – we just felt it would be useful for a firearms expert to review the specific evidence – the original investigation seems to have become overwhelmed with information.'

'Aye – I reckon they did get their knickers in a twist, if you'll pardon my Glaswegian.'

There are nods of agreement. DS Jones is keen to move ahead.

'How would you like to proceed?'

'I've looked at it in chronological order – how's that?'

'Sounds perfect.'

'Right, then. Bear with me – there'll be a wee bit of repetition of facts that you already know.'

The man slides some notes in front of him and dips his face into a pair of narrow-lensed reading glasses.

'The first incident was the murder of Will Featherston at Caldblow Farm on Friday 13th August 1976. He was shot at a distance of under three feet with a 12-bore shotgun. At that range it's impossible to tell if the barrel was sawn off. There was no gun or cartridge cases at the scene. The lead shot was size 5 and of Eley make. A recently fired cartridge case that was found just beyond a roadside hedge about 300 yards from the entrance to the farm was also an Eley size 5.'

Despite the man's introduction in which he lowered expectations, this short account creates immediate interest. DS Leyton is first to voice his thoughts.

'So that could have been the cartridge used to shoot the kid?'

'Aye, it could. But Eley size 5 was – and still is – the most popular type of ammo. They sold almost ten million of them in 1976.'

His caveat is the cause of some silent reflection. Skelgill glances at DS Leyton to see his lips are moving; perhaps he is adjusting his accumulator with this new statistic.

Mike Rose continues.

'Next, there's the robbery – attempted robbery – at Kirkstile Farm. That was on Monday 20th September 1976, just over five weeks later. A sawn-off shotgun was brandished and fired, and it was later recovered.' He cross-checks with a note to one side, leaning momentarily out of shot. 'According to the files, the Hares led the police to where they kept it buried. There were a dozen unused cartridges with it. They were Eley size 3.'

He pauses and looks up, as if anticipating a question. DS Leyton obliges.

'Not the same ammo that killed Will Featherston?'

'That's right.'

'What's the difference?'

'The number refers to the size of the shot – the little ball bearings that get stuck in your teeth when you eat game pie. It's like fish hooks – the lower the number the bigger it is.'

Skelgill inhales – but once again checks himself.

'Size 5 is what you'd typically use for pigeons or crows – there's more pellets, so you get a wider spread. For bigger targets like pheasant or large ducks or geese you might want size 3 – it takes a heftier slug to bring them down.' But now the man chuckles sardonically. 'This is completely academic, of course, when it comes to armed robberies.'

'But it might indicate what the gun was mainly used for.'

It is Skelgill that has intervened.

'Quite right, Inspector – Will Featherston was killed by size 5 shot. Pigeon, crow … rabbit maybe.'

DS Leyton now jumps back in.

'Mike – could the Hares' gun have fired the size 5 cartridge?'

'It could.' But it is plain there is another qualification coming. The man looks up over the rim of his spectacles like a doctor about to deliver an unwelcome prognosis. 'But it didnae.'

He waits for a moment in order for his words to sink in – but not so long that one of them feels obliged to ask for clarification.

'You cannae tell from lead shot which gun it was fired from. Shotguns are not like rifles or sidearms in which the rifling on the barrel leaves a unique pattern on the projectile. But you can tell something from the cartridge case. Every firing pin leaves a distinctive mark – a signature, if you like – on the brass head of the cartridge, and there may be additional impressions, such as the breech face and the ejector mark.'

He leaves another pause – this time it seems out of politeness to allow his audience to process the terminology.

And then the killer fact.

'The size 5 cartridge found near Caldblow Farm – the lead shot from which *could* have killed Will Featherston – was not fired by the Hares' gun. It was fired by another gun altogether – and that gun appears nowhere in the investigation.'

Skelgill now speaks with the authority of an outdoorsman.

'Anyone shooting could have ejected that shell. Wander about the countryside with your eyes down, and soon enough you'll find a cartridge case.

'That's correct.'

DS Jones, however, is clearly well-versed in the details of the investigation, and she has a small counterpoint.

'There was a strident appeal – for anyone who had shot in the area – so they could eliminate that cartridge. Nobody came forward.'

There is, of course, the unspoken appreciation among police officers that witnesses, however innocent, often do not present themselves. It is a circumstance likely to be amplified where private land, guns and murder are involved.

Allowing a suitable gap for reflection, Mike Rose determines he may continue.

'After that, it's all a bit more straightforward. Just over a year later, on 4th October 1977, Percy Tuseling killed Colin Bell-Gibson with a 12-bore shotgun that was owned by the farmer himself. He sawed off the barrel and fired, also from close range. The cartridge was an Eley size 5 – as was the live cartridge that he later threw from the car. The sawn-off shotgun was recovered from the murder scene with the spent cartridge still in the chamber. The second shotgun – not sawn off, and also owned by the farmer – the one that Tuseling had in the car when he surrendered, was single-barrelled and was loaded with an Eley size 5.'

Skelgill's mind is working quickly.

'You said that neither of Colin Bell-Gibson's guns fired the cartridge that was found near Caldblow Farm?'

'Aye, I did, Inspector. The ballistic tests were categorical – and I've checked the photographs and the forensic reports.' He reaches sideways to pat his pile of documents once again. 'The signatures of those two guns were entirely different. Though of course we don't know if that cartridge was used to kill Will Featherston.'

DS Leyton has been making detailed notes. Now he looks up and leans in to the camera on DS Jones's laptop.

'So – Mike – just to get me head straight. The Hares' gun could have been used to kill Will Featherston, but not the ammo they had in their possession – and it didn't fire the Eley size 5 cartridge from the lane. And Colin Bell-Gibson's guns didn't fire the cartridge from the lane – but one of them could have been used to shoot Will Featherston.' He is about to withdraw – but adds a rider. 'And the murder weapon could have been either a sawn-off or a full-barrelled shotgun.'

The man listens intently, peering into his screen over the rim of his glasses.

'Aye – that's about the long and short of it.' He removes the spectacles and folds them away into the breast pocket of his shirt. 'Like I said – I'm afraid I'm not going to solve your murder. Anyone could have shot that poor lad.'

*

The video conference over, Skelgill rises and walks across to the window to stretch out his recalcitrant spine. Beyond the glass unfolds another fine summer's day, and his compressed features reveal a wish to be out there, perhaps dabbing a fly speculatively upon one of the meandering rivers. But he suddenly realises that DS Jones is at his side, and starts. She too is staring out.

'What is it, lass?'

She turns, surprised that he has detected her discomfort.

Now she casts about the makeshift incident room.

'When we first came in here – and read the brief.' It is apparent that her thoughts come disjointedly. 'And we were wondering why – what's this all about – why is it so hush-hush?'

'Aye?'

She points across to the papers on the long boardroom table.

'I've been reading the transcript of the Hares' trial. As far as I can establish, the size 5 cartridge found in the lane near Caldblow Farm was not presented as evidence. Nor was there any discussion of the size 3 cartridges that the Hares had been using.'

She pauses. DS Leyton, listening from his seat, now joins the dots.

'You mean they didn't want to cast doubt on the Hares as the killers of Will Featherston?'

She stares at her colleague and then at Skelgill.

'It looks that way, doesn't it? It was convenient for the Prosecution that the Hares were armed – but not the discrepancy between the types of ammunition – it would have been a gift to the Defence, to cast doubt in the jurors' minds.' Now she waves a hand loosely in the direction of the big screen on the wall. 'As we've just heard – anyone could have shot Will Featherston – and there's certainly no proof that points to the Hares.'

The detectives reflect once more in silence. Quite likely it was enough to proclaim in court simply that the Hares brandished a sawn-off shotgun – a weapon that has such sinister and emotive criminal connotations.

'Whoever shot Will Featherston could just have used one of Bell-Gibson's guns.'

It is Skelgill that speaks with terse pragmatism, his features retaining the critical grimace with which he has been scrutinising the presently unattainable outdoors.

He leaves the statement hanging in the air, for his colleagues to work through the logic. They each come round to regard him rather like nodding dogs. Amidst all the permutations of shotguns, sawn-off or otherwise, cartridges, size 3 or size 5, firing pin and breech markings, it is easy to overlook the obvious facts at the core of this mystery: that Percy Tuseling regularly shot at Caldblow Farm using a gun borrowed from Belltower Farm.

It is DS Leyton that picks up the thread.

'What you're saying, Guv, is that provided no cartridge case was left in the kitchen at Caldblow Farm, there was no way of linking those Belltower Farm guns to the killing.'

Skelgill does not answer. Instead he looks inquiringly to DS Jones. Perhaps understanding he seeks something other than agreement she offers an alternative explanation.

'There is the possibility that Percy Tuseling had another gun – one of his own – it could have been the weapon that was used – the one that fired the discarded size 5 cartridge.'

'He had a shotgun licence, aye?'

DS Jones moves across to her arrangement of documents. She quickly locates the item she seeks.

'That's right. And a detective followed up his claim that he had sold his shotgun a year before the murder of Will Featherston. That checked out.'

DS Leyton emits a sound that is a mixture of frustration and scorn.

'He still could have had a gun. I've looked into this before – couple of historical bank jobs when I was in the Met. Back then the licensing system was bits of triplicate paper and handwritten log books kept by the local force. Nothing like today, where we've got every serial number on the system. Guns went walkabout all the time and nobody would notice.'

DS Jones slowly combs back her fair shoulder-length hair with the fingers of both hands to reveal she is wearing diamond stud earrings that sparkle as she tilts her head to one side, indicating the case papers. She speaks with a sobriety that belies her natural allure.

'They lost valuable time, didn't they? I mean – the fact of the antiques robbery and the red car seen at Caldblow Farm. They treated it as a kind of hit-and-run. They were immediately looking over the horizon. It was five days before they even interviewed Percy Tuseling and that was solely about his Ford Corsair. It was a month later that the anonymous call was made. If he'd come forward on the day, they would have been crawling all over Belltower Farm. At the very least they would have been able to establish if either of the guns had been fired that day, and by whom. And, if not, was there another gun? Had Percy Tuseling been found to have been out shooting on the day of Will Featherston's murder – well –' She looks at her colleagues in turn. 'I don't suppose we'd be cooped up in here today.'

It seems in her final words she intuits something of Skelgill's frustration. She adds a rider.

'Colin Bell-Gibson was at a masonic social event on the afternoon of Will Featherston's shooting. It was a race day at Cartmel – a good hour away, and the last race was at 5 p.m. There's a note that refers to unimpeachable corroboration of his whereabouts. But, get this – he stated that he generally didn't lock up the farmhouse – that his dogs were a sufficient deterrent to strangers. His guns were examined a week later and showed signs of use, but he was unable to specify when – he admitted he took pot shots at passing crows most days.'

Skelgill is grimacing.

'I'd have been more suspicious if the guns had been cleaned.'

DS Leyton hits the heel of his hand off the table surface.

'I know we can't tie the ammo to the murder – but Tuseling chucking that live cartridge out of the moving car. Why didn't he just hand it over? I can't help feeling it's too much like a habit.' He turns to Skelgill. 'Tell me to change the record, Guv – but this case is riddled with coincidences.'

Skelgill produces an exclamation somewhere between a sardonic laugh and a scoff of disdain.

'What are your odds up to now, Leyton?'

'There ain't enough noughts on me calculator, Guv.'

DS Jones has received an email alert – she is momentarily diverted by her laptop.

'Ah – that's the next batch of rushes being uploaded to Turnpike Media's server – it's saying just over ten minutes.'

'Time for a mash.'

It is Skelgill's proclamation, but DS Leyton suddenly raises a finger in a way that wins his colleagues' attention.

'That reminds me – I've got some cake.' He rises and rather unsteadily shambles over to where his briefcase rests on a cabinet. 'Old girl who lives next door – she's always coming round with home-baked biscuits and whatnot. The Missus didn't want the nippers high on sugar, so she's packed it off with me.' He hesitates reflectively, seeing some private irony in this act. 'Borrowdale chocolate shortbread, it's called. Do you know that one, Guv?'

'Aye – you won't like it, Leyton.'

7. EPISODE 2.2: KIRKSTILE & JOAN

Incident Room 101 – 3.00 p.m. Wednesday 28 July

Drone footage provides an overhead shot of a silver vehicle moving slowly along a suburban street that divides into two lanes around a lozenge of green, where a tiny human figure drifts slowly amidst a cluster of shifting dark shapes that must be a small pack of dogs. In some back gardens there are worn-out patches of lawn and in others blue trampolines. Vegetation in the form of trees or shrubs is sparse and there is a collective ramshackle of sheds. Relatively few cars populate the roadsides. There must be a slight breeze, for a flag of St George that has been hung from an upstairs window sill occasionally flaps so as to be partially visible from above.

The screen goes blank for several seconds – and DS Jones reaches to make an adjustment – but before she can the action resumes. Now inside the minibus Professor Simeon Freud is seated beside Percy Tuseling in the back row of seats. Kate is filming them from a couple of rows forward, diagonally opposite. The rest of the crew must be out of picture, towards the front of the vehicle.

Percy Tuseling is looking out of the near-side window with obvious discomfort.

"Percy, I asked our driver to come this way in order to clarify the point we were discussing a little earlier."

"Yes."

The man's voice is strained – it is an attempt at co-operative interest, but there is no hiding the underlying note of alarm. He does not ask what is the said point that requires clarification.

"You would know this area, of course, Percy."

"Of course I would know it – I grew up in Whitehaven – I lived in the town all my life until –"

He produces his stock laugh, but it lacks conviction – logically, the words would have been "until I spent time at Her Majesty's pleasure".

"But this particular area, Percy – Kirkstone Avenue East – you would know better than most parts."

"I don't see why I should."

The professor leans away from Percy Tuseling but keeps his eyes fixed on the man. It is an exaggerated expression of surprise and disbelief. But Percy Tuseling remains tight-lipped, his head turned to the glass and his eyes on the passing houses.

Simeon Freud relaxes his pose.

"Well – for a start, Percy – Kirkstone Avenue East – this is the street where Will Featherston lived – his parents' house was number twenty-two."

"Right."

"But you also lived here."

"I lived in Thwaite Road. I lived a mile away."

"Yes – you lived in Thwaite Road at the time of Will Featherston's murder – but you previously lived here, didn't you? At one time you were a near neighbour of the Featherstons."

"I have no knowledge of being a neighbour of that family. You must have that wrong."

It is a weak denial – the man's body language suggests growing inner tension, and his narrow lips compress to the point of disappearance.

"Percy, we have done our homework."

The professor stares at his subject for a couple of seconds, and then he breaks out of acting mode and rearranges his hair – as if knowing the segment will be cut – and he turns to consult the crew.

"Angie – remind me, please – what does the council register state?"

It seems he has already made a familiar diminutive of DS Jones's alias, Angela.

Skelgill glances sideways at his colleague – but her attention remains fixed on the screen. It seems she is about to have a small cameo – albeit one that would presumably be edited out of the final production. But the camera does not pan around to find her – Kate seems to know that now is the time to zoom right in on Percy Tuseling's face.

"A Percival and Veronica Tuseling rented a council house at 14, Kirkstile Avenue East from March 1970 to September 1972."

DS Jones's voice comes clear and steady; her soft Cumbrian brogue entirely non-accusatory in its tone.

The contrast in Percy Tuseling's features could not be more extreme.

Just as when Simeon Freud had uttered his opening line in their first interview, "Percy, you're a murderer", eliciting a reflex of pure vitriol, once more a sudden boiling venom burns in the man's eyes. It is plainly reserved entirely for DS Jones. It is like the devil himself has possessed him.

And all hell breaks loose.

There is a great clatter.

It is not on the recording – in the minibus – but in Room 101.

With a snarled and unprintable oath, Skelgill clears the table, scattering papers with his boots.

He springs to the wall and head-butts the screen.

It falls to the floor.

Skelgill staggers back, turns, and lurches into the kitchenette, slamming the door behind him.

Literally open mouthed, his two sergeants stare at one another.

Neither speaks – until DS Leyton, who shrugs and tilts his head towards the space on the wall, makes a resigned declaration.

'Want to give us a hand to get that level?'

They reinstate the screen, and do their best to tidy the disrupted documents.

From the kitchenette comes the splash of running water and other miscellaneous sounds; snorting and excessive clearing of the throat.

When the door opens, Skelgill emerges upon a largely restored situation; his colleagues are in their seats.

His hair is damp and has obviously been slicked back.

There is the semblance of a flush on his prominent cheekbones

– but he grins quite shamelessly.

'Just as well there weren't a loaded shotgun in there, eh?'

He need not elaborate – they get his allusion to Belltower Farm.

DS Leyton merely folds his arms and smiles broadly; it is plain he revels in his superior's temporary loss of self-restraint.

The somewhat misted look in DS Jones's hazel eyes is more contemplative. Skelgill sees this, and briefly raises his eyebrows; it might be an admission of some sort.

He returns to his place. He gestures to the screen with its frozen image of Percy Tuseling.

'Carry on, then.'

DS Jones shakes her head, and restarts the video.

The action resumed, recognising that Percy Tuseling is on the back foot, the professor wastes no time in pressing home his advantage.

"Veronica – your first wife. You and she lived just four doors down from the Featherstons – for over two years. Percy – you must have known them."

Percy Tuseling's threat to erupt has subsided. For a second he seems panicked – but clearly he recognises the futility of denial. His self-control is impressive, and now he sighs, and makes experimental movements with his lips, as though he reluctantly dons the heavy mantle of the reasonable man.

"Simeon, I keep myself to myself. I'm not a person that has much to do with neighbours. In those days with my two jobs and my sports I was much too busy to get to know people."

The professor merely scrutinises the man with a look of doubt – it is an effective curb and Percy Tuseling's rather limp rejoinder withers in the ensuing silence.

The minibus is travelling from the opposite direction that Skelgill and DS Leyton took, and passing slowly along what would have been the far side of the green. As they reach the properties in question the professor points them out in turn, 22 and then 14, highlighting their proximity.

"But Percy – you must have seen them, if only in passing, mowing the front lawn, washing the car – and Will Featherston would have walked by every day on his way to school – and played out with his friends on the green."

"That would have been many years before Will Featherston was shot."

"Just under four years."

The professor's intonation is designed to play down the scale of the interval.

"He would have been a young boy – I didn't recognise him."

There is another of the now familiar collective shifts in the audience that watches this private preview in Room 101 – but as before, Simeon Freud seems to be travelling aboard his own predetermined train of thought. Skelgill glances at DS Jones – it is a brief look, but one that decries the academic's seeming inability to recognise a small gift horse in the passing.

"Percy – we have it on good authority that you would play cricket here in the late afternoons with the teenagers. That you and some others of the adults would join in with their game after work. And that Will Featherston was a promising cricketer – he stood out. You must have noticed him."

"If any boy stood out, I didn't notice him. I only played cricket here when I had a club game that evening – I would treat it like a net. It was many years before."

Percy Tuseling's voice is terse and determined. He is undoubtedly peeved, but he endures the questioning like he must have suffered police interrogations in years gone by. As a free man now, he could walk away – decline to engage with the subject – but perhaps there is a subservience to authority that became ingrained during his long years of incarceration. There is also the implicit aim of the process in clearing his name, not to mention the matter of his fee that sustains him.

Rather curiously, the professor seems to have little to add. He has executed their ambush and flushed out their subject's reaction. He gives one of his long neutral and therefore suggestive looks to the camera – it seems to say to the viewer, now you be the judge of what you have just witnessed.

Percy Tuseling has detected this small retreat, and moves to test the air.

"I thought we were supposed to be going to look at where I did live?"

"We can do that – of course, we can do that, Percy."

"Well, then – I have little surprise for you."

"What's that, Percy?"

There appears a sly glint in Percy Tuseling's eye – perhaps that he has wrested back a little control.

"You'll see – it's on the way – just before we get there. Carry on, driver!"

The sequence ends with another look to camera from Simeon Freud – but this time it seems more one of affected intrigue, an effort to demonstrate that he is not unbalanced by his opponent's counter thrust.

*

Following what must have been only a short break in filming, the environs do not appear greatly different – perhaps a tighter-knit neighbourhood, with more trees and houses individually decorated.

"Percy – are we almost there? This is Thwaite Road, isn't it? I think I just saw the sign."

Percy Tuseling is peering ahead; he calls out to the driver.

"Can we pull over – a bit further along on the left – by the pillar box?"

The professor is clearly bemused.

"What is this, Percy? You're not posting a letter, are you?"

"You'll see. You just wait."

The minibus draws to a halt. The visual and sound become a little disjointed as the production team scrambles like a news crew on the tail of an evasive politician. By the time they have their act together Percy Tuseling has led the way through the gate of a neatly appointed semi-detached; he marches up to the front door.

He speaks, half to himself, half as assumed narrator. His voice is excitable, his tone erring towards that of his strange high-pitched falsely affable baby-talk.

"It's all in good order. Oh, she's got a doorbell camera. *Hello camera!*"

He gives a kind of twee wave, before he pokes a stubby finger at the button on the device.

Kate the video camera operator is frantically trying to take in shots that may later be valuable. She has kept hard on Percy Tuseling's heels, but now she swings back round to reveal Simeon Freud and DS Jones in close confab, having hung back at the garden gate, the taller man with one hand on the young woman's upper arm and leaning close, confidingly – though it is evident that it is she who is performing the briefing. He is nodding – and he quickly pulls away to catch up with Percy Tuseling before the door is answered. He seems possessed of renewed vigour, and delivers a condescending nod into the camera; naturally, he is in the know.

The crew is ready when the door opens and there now ensues an uncomfortable cameo. It is like a gotcha moment: *Candid Camera*; or *This Is Your Life*. Blinking like a fieldmouse prematurely roused from its hibernation a small, slender, grey-haired woman in her early sixties emerges onto the threshold. Her small mouth forms the shape of an 'o' and her button nose is a little turned up, the nostrils flared; hairless brows are raised and brown eyes widened; an ensemble that may always take this appearance, but more likely is startled. Skelgill and DS Leyton watch her closely – she is dressed tidily and shod like she might have just readied herself to go out – but there is no sign whatsoever that she is expecting the sight with which she is confronted, which plainly she finds impossible to take in.

And, despite what might be a reasonable expectation, it appears she does not even recognise Percy Tuseling. Undeterred, he takes a stride forward and stretches out his arms in a way that invites – demands, even – an embrace.

"Joan – it's me, *Percy!*"

Whether the woman feels there is no choice, or it is now a genuine reaction, she steps down and allows him to hug her – although she barely reciprocates, placing her hands only tentatively against his ample loins. But now perhaps the voice sinks in – as if, less prone to the attrition that time and tide take as their toll on the flesh, it strikes a chord.

"Ooh. Ooh."

She is bamboozled, overawed, press-ganged – but perhaps there is a genuine hint too in these sounds that she experiences a small tremor of both recognition and thus excitement.

"Joan – they're making a documentary about me. After all these years."

He steps back.

"This is the famous criminologist, Professor Freud – you must have seen him on the telly? Professor, this is Joan – she is my former colleague."

Swiftly and smoothly the professor plays the card that has been slipped to him by DS Jones.

"Yes – yes – well, it's a great pleasure to meet you, Joan." He leans down to shake her by the hand. "You must be the Joan Arkwright who worked with Percy in the 1970s at Radio Rentals."

There is just the slightest of reactions – a sideways glance from Percy Tuseling – but it seems this is one gift horse the professor is not going to overlook.

"Joan, would you be able to spare us a little time – could we come in and film for a few minutes?"

The woman still appears to be mildly if not unpleasantly shocked – perhaps the combination of the infamous and the famous, equally unexpected – she is undoubtedly starstruck and accedes shyly – though on reflection there is perhaps a look at Percy Tuseling that seeks any objection.

A little more confusion follows – footage that will not make the final cut – she is uncertain whether to stand at the threshold to welcome them in one by one, when there is not really space in the narrow entrance and hall. The professor urges her to lead the way to the best room to fit them, and sound and picture become increasingly disjointed. The professor can be heard complimenting her on keeping such a nice place – and Percy Tuseling's voice, "She was always very neat and tidy in her work – never made a single mistake with the invoicing and the books. Little Miss Perfect, we used to call you – didn't we, Joan?" The woman coos ingenuously at these various blandishments.

For ten seconds or so a blank screen punctuates scenes, and the action reopens upon what is an unexpectedly organised set.

Though it is a nondescript sitting room, salient is the

arrangement of the subjects facing the camera – not least that Percy Tuseling nestles to the right of Joan Arkwright on a cramped, two-seater sofa, her right hand clasped in both of his and held almost upon his left thigh. This being their first sight, again Skelgill and DS Leyton are unusually attentive – and there is something slightly bizarre about the scene; it has the quality of a soap opera, or perhaps it smacks of the old-fashioned first date at a picture house – made more curious by the presence of the professor, seated at angles on a dining chair that has obviously been placed to get all three of them in shot, and looking for all the world like an Alan Whicker character prepared to interview them about their experience hitherto.

Certainly the take out is that Joan Arkwright is nervous and Percy Tuseling has the role of reassuring chaperone – a seasoned intermediary with this crew of strangers and its celebrity head.

Indeed he speaks past the camera – presumably to producer Jen.

"How do we look? A rose between two thorns!" He produces his faux laugh. He seems pleased to have bracketed the professor, some thirty years his junior, with himself.

There is an answer of approval, and indeed producer Jen calls action.

The professor leans forward, resting his forearms on the thighs of his corduroys, and regards Joan Arkwright studiously.

"Joan, how long is it since you last saw Percy?"

She immediately looks at Percy Tuseling – there is the sense that she wants to know what is the correct response – and he interjects before she can answer.

"It's nearly fifty years, isn't it, Joan? And she doesn't look a day older."

The professor raises his hand to his chin – he is perhaps having to do more work on the hoof than he would like, this meeting being entirely unexpected and therefore unscripted.

"Joan – I'm afraid there's no easy way of saying this – Percy must have just disappeared from your life one day – when he was arrested for what happened at Belltower Farm."

"*Surrendered.* I wasn't arrested. I voluntarily surrendered. I had a mental aberration and I handed myself in." Percy Tuseling speaks to neither Joan Arkwright nor Simeon Freud, but directly across the room into the lens of the camera, as though it is to the wider audience that it is necessary to reiterate this point.

The professor folds his arms and sits upright, plainly a little frustrated by the added challenge of Percy Tuseling's interventions. But he keeps his focus upon the woman.

"Joan – you must have been shocked when you heard what happened – to Colin Bell-Gibson?"

This time Percy Tuseling does not interrupt. The woman nods, though rather uncertainly.

"Very shocked, yes. Percy loved his work there. He often used to talk about it – tell us the things he did – the turkeys at Christmas and the lambs in spring. His friendship with Mr Bell-Gibson."

The three detectives are attending minutely – even DS Jones, for whom the scene is not new, but perhaps now a chance to scrutinise more closely the nuances in the reactions of the actors. DS Leyton sits motionless, a little open-mouthed; a pose merited by what are, after all, quite bizarre circumstances. Anyone observing Skelgill, however, might detect a sudden narrowing of his grey-green eyes.

"And you've not had contact since – our visit today, this is out of the blue?"

Percy Tuseling again jumps in. He is like the traditional dominant husband, head of the household, entitled to speak first whenever he chooses. The woman sits meekly and does not demur.

"I was far away, eventually in an open prison in Lincolnshire, where I did community work. Initially I lived in that area. When after a long time I moved back to Cumbria, I decided it wasn't for me to get in touch with people I'd known."

The professor appears to accept this explanation at face value. Among the watching detectives, however, there is a brief exchange of glances. At the very least, Percy Tuseling must have had some foreknowledge of this woman's continued existence, and that she was residing at this address.

Meanwhile, the professor has formed his next question. To his credit he is striving to probe in a way that makes it more difficult for Percy Tuseling to take over.

"Joan – so how does it feel – to see Percy again?"

It might be imagined that she is some kind of hostage, like a citizen of an authoritarian state, knowing there is a party line to be toed. And still she seems largely overawed.

"Well, it's lovely to see him."

The response wins Percy Tuseling's approval – there might almost be a gloating look cast at the professor – that here is some vindication of the sort he seeks.

The professor nods encouragingly to the woman.

"Well, Joan – Percy has agreed to help us – we're filming a documentary – and there is a weekly podcast" (the woman nods in a way that could suggest she knows about the latter) "reviewing the evidence in the murder of Will Featherston at Caldblow Farm back in 1976."

There is a tensing in the frames of both of those seated on the couch – perhaps Percy Tuseling has squeezed the woman's hand, unseen. But when the professor could reiterate some detail of the case, and indeed reveal what he knows about her involvement, he takes an unexpected tack.

"I wouldn't ever like to ask a lady her age – but I'm guessing you must have been a contemporary of Will Featherston?"

She seems relieved by the closed question – and, when she could simply agree, she gives a more elaborate reply.

"I was sixteen at the time – I'd been at the same school – he was a year ahead of me. But in those days you could leave at fifteen – and that's what I did, got a job as a clerkess – my parents wanted some money coming in for my board."

"Did you know Will Featherston?"

She shakes her head.

"It were a big comprehensive."

"All the same, it must have been a terrible shock – the talk of the town, I should think?"

The woman is nodding.

"And then you were drawn into it – in a manner of speaking. The police interviewed you in relation to Percy – that must have given you just as much of a fright, as such a young girl?"

She looks at Percy Tuseling. Again there is the impression of the submissive wife seeking her husband's consent. But he seems content that she should continue.

"I didn't really have time to think about it. They said they had to check on lots of people who'd got cars matching descriptions – that it was just routine. You know – how they have to eliminate people? I think hundreds."

The professor has been treading carefully, but as he has shown before, he is not afraid to make progress.

"But didn't you think it odd that Percy had a connection to the farm where Will Featherston was killed?"

Now Joan Arkwright seems confused.

"I don't think I did – I mean –" She turns to look at Percy Tuseling – and now, for the first time properly, addresses him directly, her language and accent shifting noticeably towards the vernacular. "That were a different farm where you worked for Mr Bell-Gibson, weren't it?"

Percy Tuseling looks a little apprehensive. But there is also an underlying gleam of triumph in the small grey eyes – there is the impression that he walks a perilous tightrope, and seems increasingly confident of making it to the other side of the ravine.

"None of that mattered, though, did it, Joan?"

Despite that he has controlled much of the dialogue, now he seems not to want explicitly to put words into her mouth.

The professor provides a more specific prompt.

"What were you able to tell the police, then, Joan?"

The woman hesitates. Perhaps she has now grasped that she is there to put Percy in the clear – but that she too walks the tightrope – and perhaps she is struggling to remember and is worried she will make a misstep.

She looks at Percy Tuseling.

He bows his head.

"He took me for a drink."

Her words are blurted, compared to her tentative answers hitherto – and for a split second Percy Tuseling seems alarmed, as if this is not what he has anticipated.

But the professor is quickly on the case.

"And you were sixteen – you were young to go for a drink?"

"Ooh – it weren't to a pub – it were to St Bees Head."

"St Bees Head?"

If the professor feigns his surprise it is well acted – he turns to look at his team, as if this is indeed a significant piece of news. Percy Tuseling is watching his reaction, and the hint of a smirk forms at the corners of his mouth.

The professor turns back to the woman.

"So – do I understand correctly – you took the afternoon off work and went to St Bees Head?"

She shakes her head.

"No, it weren't that – it were straight after work. Percy phoned through from the workshop – he said he'd just won money on a horse and wanted a drink to celebrate – and it were such a hot day – and he said there'd be a lovely cool breeze on the cliffs and a view of the Isle of Man across the sea. And it weren't far out of the way."

She regards Percy Tuseling with an expression that might almost be a little wistful – but it could equally be to check that her response is satisfactory.

Whichever it is, Percy Tuseling evidently feels that some elaboration is in order.

"You see – Joan lived here, with her parents. I lived just along the street. So, on afternoons when I was in the workshop I would offer her a lift home." He gives her hand a small shake. "It saved you two buses, didn't it, Joan?"

"And a bit of a walk."

The professor appears to be musing, contemplative. When he finally speaks his question is intriguingly oblique.

"The win on the horses, Percy – that's not something we knew about – that you liked a flutter?"

"I didn't." His voice is suddenly strained and the reply curt. Indeed, he seems to realise it is unduly so, and softens his tone. "At least – not often – not gambling. Colin was a follower of the turf, and he would pass me the occasional tip. Mostly I ignored them – but in the workshop I'd have to run televisions to set them up properly and check they were fixed. I'd use the test card for the static picture and colour, but then it was best to play action and sound – and they showed horse racing in the afternoons. Sometimes Colin would have given me a bet for a live race. As it was that day."

The professor now joins in the conspiracy.

"Ah, I see. So, you were in the workshop that afternoon – you won on a horse – and it was hot and you felt like a celebratory drink."

"And Joan would have been travelling back with me, so I rang through to ask if she would join me. It's only fifteen minutes to St Bees Head – it's not like we went off on a tour of the Lakes."

"And you remember that well, Joan?"

"I do."

"And that's how you were able to satisfy the police – to corroborate Percy's alibi. It ruled him out of the Caldblow Farm murder case – so you were instrumental in clearing Percy?"

There is perhaps something about the quasi-legalese of the professor's analysis that unnerves the woman – for suddenly she appears to doubt her own words, that too much responsibility rests upon her shoulders alone – as if she has never before considered this to be the case.

"But it were – them –"

To the watching detectives, she is presumably about to name the Hares – but in struggling to recall such, she leaves a hiatus that the professor fills with what might on the face of it be an attempt to alleviate her discomfort. He leans over to give her the slightest touch on the knee.

"Joan, I bet you can remember the name of the horse."

Joan Arkwright looks surprised – and she turns questioningly to Percy Tuseling.

For his part, there is now a well-formed smirk that permeates the entirely of his rather turgid countenance.

"Were it Red Rum?"

Percy Tuseling chuckles. He seems delighted.

"*Not Red Rum* – it was called Dancing Queen – remember, and Abba were number one about then?"

"Ooh, yes – I remember Dancing Queen."

Whether she now means the winning horse or the chart-topping glam rock hit it is not apparent – but it is enough for Percy Tuseling. He leers triumphantly at the professor.

"There you go, Simeon – you'd better put that in your pipe and smoke it."

*

'Thing is, Emma – how come you knew who she was?'

DS Jones pauses over her mug. They have retired to the easy chairs in the corner by the windows. DS Leyton has produced a portion of his neighbour's chocolate shortbread which it would appear he had earlier held back.

DS Jones has laid out some selected papers – two documents in particular, of the pro forma type, filled in by untidy hand – of different handwriting and colour of ink, one blue, one black.

'It was when I went through all the elimination reports – owners of cars that might have matched, and other people who were potential suspects for some reason or other – known housebreakers, antiques dealers, licensed gun owners and so on. As I mentioned, they interviewed Percy Tuseling because of his red Ford Corsair. They followed up his claim to be at work – and that's where her details appear. She supplied the same address as today – she must have inherited her parents' house.'

She reaches for one of the stapled reports.

'This is it.'

She turns the first page over and hands it to Skelgill. He gives it a cursory glance, and passes it to DS Leyton.

'As you can see, it says very little, other than Joan Arkwright confirmed that Percy Tuseling was at work at Radio Rentals on the afternoon that Will Featherston was murdered – a reminder, the time of which was approximately between 3.30 p.m. and 4 p.m. – and that he gave her a lift home at closing time, five o'clock.'

DS Leyton is scowling at the page.

'It don't mention their jaunt to Beachy Head.'

Skelgill splutters into his tea.

DS Leyton looks moderately hurt.

'What? What did I say?'

'St Bees Head, Leyton.'

DS Leyton looks puzzled, as though he believes this is what he said. But he shrugs, and continues.

'You think she'd have told them that.'

Skelgill and DS Jones exchange brief glances. Skelgill takes on the reply.

'Tuseling was married, Leyton – happen she didn't want to ruffle any feathers.'

DS Leyton turns out his rubbery lower lip; but it is a gesture of acknowledgement rather than vexation.

'Your aunt – her in the butcher's shop – she said he was a bit of a ladies' man – that was the phrase she used, wasn't it?'

Skelgill nods mildly.

'I suppose, Guv – if you add that to what we might suspect of him.' Now DS Leyton pinches the end of his nose. 'Reckon she just covered for him?'

Skelgill is looking at DS Jones, without giving away what it is he attempts to divine. He shifts his focus back to DS Leyton.

'You've seen it yourself, Leyton – it's hardly above ten minutes' drive from Caldblow Farm to where Radio Rentals was. The workshop had its own separate access and entrance.'

DS Jones now chips in.

'Realistically, he could have phoned her from anywhere.'

There is little need for members of the trio to elaborate for one another's benefit. All detectives become hard-wired in the knack of finding loopholes in alibis.

But DS Jones does probe one aspect.

'What do you think about the horse racing story?'

It is recognised as a question for DS Leyton.

'I can check that out, easy enough.' He gestures with a dismissive hand at the documents. 'The old police records may not be up to scratch – but every horse race ever run has been logged, right down to what make of Callard and Bowsers the jockeys were wearing.' He looks up to see his colleagues are regarding him with mild bewilderment. 'Form you see – and horses for courses.

That's what it all comes down to.'

Now he gives a click of his thumb.

'Yeah – I can find out if there was a Dancing Queen and when she ran. But there's no proof that he put on a bet or watched the race. It could have just been a cock-and-bull story to soft soap the girl with.'

DS Jones is nodding.

'And – or – an embellishment to his alibi.'

There is a silence while they each apparently consider this aspect – until DS Leyton gives an ironic laugh that seems inwardly directed.

'You going to tell us, Leyton?'

DS Leyton does not respond for a second – and then he starts, realising he has been questioned.

'Oh – it's just horses' names, Guv. It's quite a palaver to get a name approved. The British Horseracing Authority has to vet them – obviously, you don't want two nags with the same name in a race. Although it can happen with a horse from overseas. I reckon there's a Dancing Queen doing the rounds at the moment – probably there's been a few down the years. And some owners think it's clever to give the commentator a tongue-twister – or try to slip through something rude.'

Skelgill is now interested.

'What like?'

DS Leyton glances a little apprehensively at DS Jones – there is the suggestion that he is running possibilities past an internal censor.

'Well – for instance, one that got through was a filly called Nicholas Mistress.' He frowns, self-censoriously, but his colleagues appear amused. 'Course, when you see it written down you see a geezer's name – and the owner was called Charlie Nicholas, so they didn't think anything of it.'

There is now a collective silence, as if they each might be trying to make something up.

But DS Leyton moves the subject on.

'Funny – she mentioned Red Rum.'

Skelgill seems to detect some nuance in his sergeant's musing.

'Why funny?'

'Well – in a way – she would say Red Rum.' DS Leyton looks at his colleagues in turn. 'I even expect *you've* heard of Red Rum – greatest chaser to set foot on the turf. Won the National in '73 and '74, second in '75 and '76 – won again in '77. They've got a bronze statue at Southport, where he was trained on the sands.'

Though Skelgill looks moderately impressed by his colleague's knowledge, he is clearly dissatisfied with his response. DS Leyton reads his expression.

'Yeah – well – funny, Guv – because Red Rum spells *murder* backwards.'

DS Leyton makes a po-face.

Then he shakes his head ruefully.

'I've always wondered about that.'

There is the suggestion in his manner that this relates to some other, long-past conspiracy.

But Skelgill is having none of it.

'You can add it to your accumulator, Leyton.'

DS Leyton chuckles.

'I think I'll pass on that one, Guv.'

DS Jones is not entirely familiar with her colleagues' ongoing banter concerning coincidences and the law of probability, but she does inadvertently touch upon the theme in raising what is one of the core and as yet undiscussed issues of the material they have viewed.

'What did you make of Percy Tuseling being confronted about living close to the Featherstons?'

In many respects, the footage speaks for itself – Percy Tuseling was patently discomfited – and perhaps because of this success, Skelgill responds somewhat capriciously.

'I notice the prof was claiming the credit for it.'

DS Jones looks momentarily dismayed – as though she either is disappointed in Skelgill's reaction, or is sorry that she has had a hand in feeding Simeon Freud's vainglory. Perhaps it is more the latter, for she puts a positive spin on the matter.

'But we know Sim is following our lead – and if it weren't for you finding out about Kirkstone Avenue, I'm not sure Percy

Tuseling would have taken us to meet Joan Arkwright.'

It is an inarguable point, but Skelgill glowers, nonetheless. It seems he is in a battle with his professional pride – if not one more complicated than that.

Now DS Leyton pitches in on the side of optimism.

'Think we should pay her a call, Guv? She might tell us something useful – now she's had her memory jogged.'

Skelgill regards his sergeant pensively, but he does not answer the question. He is not quite ready to admit that his colleagues have logic on their side.

'He missed a couple of tricks.' His response garners nods of encouragement. 'Tuseling was over-egging his excuses. And she dropped a couple of clangers, don't you reckon?'

Now his subordinates regard him with anticipation.

But he rises and turns to the window. It is almost as if he is wanting to sniff the air, but for safety reasons the glass units are sealed and the room artificially ventilated. He places his left palm flat on the pane, leaving an ephemeral handprint when he draws it away.

'Anyone fancy a trip to Beachy Head tonight?'

It seems as though the malapropism is deliberate, a replay of DS Leyton's earlier slip.

'Cor blimey – chance'd be a fine thing. I've got gymnastics and beavers and the supermarket in between.'

Now Skelgill turns to regard DS Jones – his expression is quizzical rather than presumptive, but she plainly finds herself on the horns of a dilemma.

She brushes at what may be a loose strand of invisible fair hair that has slipped across one eyebrow.

'I've committed to attending a post-production meeting at six-thirty with the Turnpike Media team. It's to do a final sense-check on Friday's podcast before it's sent for digital mastering. I'm not sure what time we'll finish – they were talking about getting pizza delivered.'

8. BITTER SHANDY

King's Head, Blindkirk – 10.00 p.m. Wednesday 28 July

Skelgill has returned inland, twenty miles from St Bees Head. Having teetered within the hour upon the great vertiginous cliff, he can appreciate the subliminal error made by DS Leyton, in transposing the names. Four hundred miles south, at the very limit of the leafy county of East Sussex, Beachy Head has a dark reputation; it is a site with fatal attraction, one of the most notorious suicide spots in the world; it conjures up the lovers' pact.

Despite his derring-do at the Cumbrian precipice nothing has piqued his imagination – but maybe it will come later. Pennies rarely drop to order. But he remains unsettled by Joan Arkwright's ostensibly innocent account of a cool, celebratory drink on one of the hottest days of the year, in what his elders insist was the hottest summer England has experienced – "the sun were crackin' the cobbles for nigh on three month" according to George Appleby, who can hardly be old enough to remember, but claims to have been there, all the same.

"Aye, Skelly lad – by night crickets were chirping all round Bass Lake. When have you ever heard that?"

Truth be told, he has never heard one. The grasshopper is his familiar, and it fiddles from the long grass only in the heat of the day; crickets are what folk speak of after their first holiday to Europe.

The cricket, named like the cuckoo and the crow for its onomatopoeic quality. The thought diverts him, bringing to mind the homonym, the cricket of whites and cucumber sandwiches. Now it is the etymology that occupies his musings: there were crickets long before there was cricket; was the name of the game appropriated for the snick of leather on willow? Not unless there were crickets in England of yore. Catch 22.

He is stumped.

He realises his pint glass is empty.

He frowns.

He is drinking bitter shandy. It is not entirely satisfactory, although – and here is cricket again – when he played regularly it was his stock first order – a pint that wouldn't touch the sides, a sugar boost and rehydration after an afternoon standing half the time at deep long leg, one of the more ignominious fielding positions, but justified by the skipper on the grounds that it gave him a breather between overs – "Plus you've the best arm in the side."

And Percy Tuseling was a cricketer.

Cricket, the team game that accommodates the lone wolf like few other sports. Football, rugby, hockey – it is all about collective shape, tactics, passing and movement; no player can function without their teammates. Cricket is not like that. When you're facing the bowler, or vice versa, it is every man for himself. So much is this a truism, that to do something "off your own bat" is implanted in the English language (though he reflects ruefully there is no such equivalent that recognises the toil of the bowler).

Percy Tuseling – thus far met solely on camera, true – but maybe it takes one lone wolf to know another. Tuseling is clearly a man who has kept his own counsel. The best part of fifty years, his debt to society paid, and he has still not admitted why he really killed Colin Bell-Gibson – for Skelgill is unconvinced by the Special Cocktail.

And the best part of fifty years and he has still not confessed to the murder of Will Featherston.

Whoa! Steady on. A conjecture alert.

He reaches for his glass and is about to rise when he notices the flicker of a light out of the corner of his eye.

He hisses in self-reproach.

It is remiss of him, staring at the glass – crystal ball gazing – when he should be on watch.

Someone is coming out.

His station is a table beside a small window in an alcove at the front of the King's Head, Blindkirk. Challenged, his presence here he would assert to be down to his predatory instinct. It is why he has been to St Bees Head. It's what hunters do. They speculate, yes – but it is informed speculation. Even when he is fishing, he does not randomly row and cast. There is always a reason for his choice. A wind lane where drowned invertebrates collect, a field drain supplying edible detritus, a leafy overhang where larvae may lose their grip. A bay where he has caught before. A reedbed where he has seen his quarry.

Across the road, Percy Tuseling's bungalow.

But not exactly a bungalow. Like most such properties these days, its roof space is converted and dormer windows form mini-gables – at all four points of the compass, by the look of it.

And, as dusk has advanced, he has learned there may be an open-plan attic room, a single large space, judging by occasional shifting shapes and shadows, and movements in the light – there might almost be a torch in use, or a camera-mounted beam such as the professionals employ.

But now the loft is in darkness and a porch light has come on.

Skelgill watches.

It is a party leaving. That is – two couples – in the growing gloom it is hard to discern their appearance, let alone identity – it is a warm evening and the men are in short sleeves and the women in loose summer frocks that bare their shoulders. All seem tanned and hale and hearty. They are jaunty, excited. Age-wise they look around the sixty mark, maybe a decade younger than Percy Tuseling – who is now at one side of the front door, pressing it open, while his raven-haired wife stands beside him, the pair silhouetted against the light of the hallway. Strange that Skelgill has visited vicariously, through the eye of the lens – he recalls a particular lewd statuette – what do visitors think of that?

But the impression is of the familiar break up of a dinner party. Friends well known to one another. Finishing off conversations – reminded of things unsaid – and insisting our turn next.

Of course, Skelgill can hear none of this – it may be inane chatter or it may be of some greater salience to his presence.

But one thing is peculiar.

Both of the males carry holdalls – of the sports bag kind – black and quite substantial, and reasonably heavy looking, going by the way they each tote them, after a while changing hands to rest the arm muscles.

Eventually the four turn together and give farewell waves.

The Tuselings watch them part-way and then withdraw.

The foursome pauses briefly to bestow critical acclaim upon some noteworthy garden sculpture. A joke must be made, for one of the females feigns a reproving slap upon the cheek of her partner.

There are no cars outside the bungalow – Skelgill's guess is that they will have used the King's Head's car park.

But, no. They turn left onto the pavement and walk, chatting and joking, two-by-two, the men ahead swinging their bags, the women bringing up the rear.

They move out of the limited sight afforded by Skelgill's small window.

He picks up his pint glass.

He steps through to the bar. No one is there. He sets his glass on the counter.

But he does not break stride and leaves by the front door, taking care to deaden any click of the latch.

Cooler night air has crept into the village. He experiences the thrill of fishing when the dewpoint is reached and stillness becomes all-pervasive; the sun has set, dusk is done with, stars twinkle; night birds for company; no crickets. But there is the just-audible bass squeak of a noctule bat; a soprano pipistrelle he last heard as a teenager – was that when senescence began to set in?

A black cat slinks across the road, and then a dog fox.

'Howay, tod.'

He has on rubber-soled walking boots. At something between a jog and a run he gains the first bend and then the second. A Wednesday night – most of the village seems already to be sleeping, though in some houses close to the road he detects the violet flicker of a television.

He has rounded three turns before he hears a voice, a woman's laugh. It is drawn out, with a note of salacious surprise, as if a risqué comment has been passed. The foursome had not looked drunk – but quite likely they have been drinking; it would be unusual otherwise.

Gaining the next bend he has to dart into the cover of a driveway and peer around a neatly manicured yew hedge. There must be honeysuckle climbing nearby; the heady night scent is cloying in his nostrils.

They are much closer. They have stopped.

The reason, though, becomes immediately clear – for one couple have reached their home.

They are saying their goodnights.

Now their voices are hushed – perhaps in consideration of neighbours trying to get to sleep. He picks up only a murmur and not the words. To compound his difficulty, he could swear there is mix of accents: Scots, Welsh, Northern Irish and local English; a full house of home nations.

They exchange hugs, quite long and affectionate, he thinks.

The pair disappears; there is the diminishing crunch of feet upon gravel.

The others turn and continue.

He waits for the first to enter and close their front door.

He halts for a moment at the end of the driveway.

The remaining couple moves more quickly now. They pass the odd comment, harmonious, it seems.

Indeed, they each put an arm around the other – perhaps, with the longest walk, they are feeling the night chill in their summer's day attire.

Skelgill follows at a distance – they turn into the driveway of a bungalow at the edge of the village. He watches them pass out of sight behind abundant foliage. Again he dwells for a minute.

He returns pensively the quarter of a mile back to the King's Head.

He checks his watch – he is in time for last orders. There is a seasonal summer ale on tap that he wouldn't mind trying, unadulterated by lemonade. A hoppy thirst-quencher, and at only 3.3 percent, a pint poses no risk to his driving licence.

He peers into the small window that had been his lookout.

His spot has been taken.

A couple are holding hands across the table, leaning in and gazing longingly at one another. Their drinks, ringfenced by their arms, are untouched. The man has a straw-coloured pint. The woman has a pink cocktail.

Skelgill marches to his car.

He has left his phone in its holder; but he hesitates before roughly poking it into life.

No message.

He exhales, having held the breath.

After a moment, he reaches with a grunt to the glovebox – and extracts a half-packet of chocolate digestives.

9. RUMOURS

Police HQ – 8.15 a.m. Thursday 29 July

'What do you reckon they were up to, Guv – is it what we think it is? And Tuseling's the ringleader? It could explain how he cooked up his excuse for shooting the Bell-Gibson cove. The leopard ain't changed his spots.'

Skelgill, cutlery poised in praying mantis fashion over his canteen fry-up, regards his colleague uncertainly. When his sergeant might have berated or, more likely, mocked him for usurping the very tactic that he had ridiculed – the staking out of Percy Tuseling's bungalow – instead he has listened with enthusiasm to Skelgill's account of the previous night. Now he is wide-eyed at the revelation of first the mysterious attic soirée and second that the Tuselings' guests had retired into those very homes that had caught his drive-by attention … for their prominent clumps of pampas grass.

But DS Leyton's logic is not entirely watertight. Would Percy Tuseling risk drawing attention to his present-day peccadillo – let alone if he had been involved in Colin Bell-Gibson's swinging scene back in the Seventies? And there is more. It falls to Skelgill to crash-test the proposition.

'Don't you reckon he's pushing it, for that kind of thing? He's what – seventy-five?'

DS Leyton saws enthusiastically at a substantial Cumberland sausage. His expression, however, suggests that he does not have a ready yardstick.

'Dunno, Guv – I mean – what about that Italian politician – him and his, what were they called, *bongo-bongo* parties?'

Skelgill frowns dubiously. But the two detectives seem to share now a certain unspoken reluctance – that this is about as far as they wish to venture into such conjecture.

DS Leyton offers an alternative angle of attack.

'What do you reckon they had in their bags, Guv? Costumes?' He gives a little *ahem* cough. 'Accessories?'

Skelgill scowls again but this time offers a comment.

'You don't usually take your sports kit to a dinner party.'

'And if you take a gift – like wine or chocolates – you leave it.'

A pause ensues while they each catch up on some eating.

DS Leyton is first to speak.

'Maybe this Joan Arkwright will shed some light on it.'

'She were just a young lass, Leyton.'

'I know, Guv – but there's enough straws in the wind. At least we can ask her – in a roundabout way. And I reckon the Prof's probably softened her up a bit.'

Skelgill is still looking doubtful.

'Have you got her contact details?'

'Emma gave me her mobile phone number and address. But anyway she's in the phone book. Which means Tuseling could have just looked her up.'

Skelgill nods in a satisfied way – his sergeant means that Percy Tuseling need not have contacted the woman to know she was there.

'But I thought we'd just rock up, Guv – in case they are in cahoots.'

Skelgill, chewing again, nods in approval.

'Howay, Skelly lad! Why am I surprised to find thee here?'

The friendly local brogue that interrupts them belongs to desk sergeant George Appleby. He has arrived at pace and squats at the end of their table, showing admirable flexibility of joints for a fellow in his late middle age. He gives a friendly wink to DS Leyton.

A laid-back character, he spends a good deal of each day wielding wit and satire to parry the weird and wonderful accusations hurled over the front desk by eccentric members of the public, sorting the wheat of genuine need from the great chaff of time-wasters and grudge-bearers. But right now his manner is urgent, his eyes lit by a glint of excitement and his distinctive bald head coated in a fine patina of perspiration that seems excessive, even in the current warm weather.

'Skelly – about this *Murder on the Farm* business.'

Skelgill and DS Leyton duck simultaneously, as if an airburst has gone off overhead.

Skelgill is not about to lie to his good friend and fellow angler. But his voice comes at a warning low.

'How do you know about that?'

The desk sergeant taps the side of his nose with an index finger, and glances about furtively.

Skelgill is nonetheless alarmed.

'George – someone'll be for the high jump if the Chief hears word's got about. I can't have her thinking it's one of us that's leaked.'

'It's alreet, marra – your secret's safe with us. Besides – I've got you a lead. Happen it were just as well he phoned the front desk.'

'Who?'

'Gadgee by the name of Jack Dixon. Retired police officer – uniform. Worked at the time of the Will Featherston murder. He said he read about it int' Gazette. He said do we know about the card?'

'The card?'

'Aye – a piece of card that was handed in. Like an anonymous message. Purporting to point the finger for the killing at someone else.'

Skelgill glances at DS Leyton.

DS Leyton looks blank. This does not sound like a promising development. Many investigations receive crank letters. A case as notorious as the Caldblow Farm murder was no exception. He cocks his head skywards.

'You should see the mountain of documents up there, George.'

However, the desk sergeant leans forward conspiratorially.

'Thing is, lads – *happen it were handed in by Percy Tuseling.'*

There ensues a freeze-frame moment in which nobody moves.

But now Skelgill issues a warning from the side of his mouth.

'Hey up.'

He has noticed that DI Smart has spotted them – he is standing with a tray, his pinched features furtive like a fox that has infiltrated a hen coop unnoticed and which is now assessing the field to select a victim; no doubt the little confab that has been taking place at Skelgill and DS Leyton's table has its attractions. He begins to weave casually in their direction. George Appleby gets it. He slips a small memo note to Skelgill.

'There's his details. He lives at Bridecrake.'

'Bridecrake? Definitely Bridecrake?'

'Aye.'

The desk sergeant stands with a groan.

'I shouldn't let the grass grow under your feet – the arl fella's pushing ninety.'

But DI Smart is fast approaching and he takes his leave. Skelgill slips the note into his shirt pocket.

'Alright, cock?'

DI Smart ignores DS Leyton and casts his eyes over Skelgill's attire, as though he is pricing each item.

Skelgill nods in a curt fashion.

'Word is you're running psyops from a suite on the top floor. All in the line of duty, eh, Skel?'

DI Smart gives a sarcastic cackle.

While specifically he misses the mark – perhaps intentionally so – there is a not-so-hidden implication in the Mancunian's choice of words that knocks Skelgill off balance. Momentarily dizzied, and before he can construct a casual rebuttal, DI Smart lands a sucker punch.

'I hear Emma's been spotted with some documentary crew – digging up old bones.'

'Sounds like you know as much as I do, Smart.'

But Skelgill's terse reply is insufficient when pitted against the wiles of his scheming associate.

'In that case I might have a word with her – warn her, as a friend, like.'

'Warn her about what?'

DS Leyton, a silent spectator, stares with some alarm at the hold Skelgill has upon his knife, the handle gripped tight in a clenched left fist and the blade pointing vertically.

But DI Smart seems not to notice the reaction he is eliciting.

He leans a little confidingly towards Skelgill and lowers his voice.

'Simeon Freud – they say he'll only work with an *all-female* crew. That's probably all you'll need to know, Skel.'

'And all you need to know, Smart – is that she can look after herself. In fact – as I recall, you already do.'

Perhaps there is just enough in Skelgill's rejoinder – that he touches a raw nerve, that there is veracity in the statement – or perhaps it is simply a steely stare that triggers a flight instinct. DI Smart begins to back away. But he remains outwardly smug, exhibiting no shame in his blindsiding.

'Can't be too careful – that's all I'm saying, know what I mean, cock?'

They watch him as he turns and moves off, already seeking his next target. When he is out of earshot, DS Leyton gives a somewhat apprehensive chuckle.

'I thought we were working up to another white screen moment there, Guv.'

But Skelgill seems unwilling to enjoin with his sergeant's attempt to lighten the atmosphere. He is glowering darkly across at where DI Smart has pulled rank and invited himself to the table of a young female trainee. It takes Skelgill a moment to re-engage with his colleague. He flashes an unconvincing grin and rather savagely digs his fork into the last of his sausage.

DS Leyton looks a little relieved.

'Do you know what they're doing this morning, Guv – are they filming with Percy Tuseling?'

Skelgill perhaps gives a shrug – but the fact is, he does not know; he has not heard. But by the time he has finished his mouthful he can avoid the question.

'I was planning for you and me to see Joan Arkwright.' He releases his knife and pats his breast pocket. 'But I reckon we'll divide and conquer.'

10. JOAN REVISITED

Whitehaven – 10.20 a.m. Thursday 29 July

DS Leyton is experiencing a strange sense of déjà vu. The sitcom-like setting of a sofa with its occupants facing out into the middle of the room is one that now confronts him. The difference being that just Joan Arkwright is seated opposite him – though still to one side, the right as he looks, and the cushion that Percy Tuseling's ample rear must surely have indented has been plumped. For his part, DS Leyton has an armchair that was pushed aside for the purpose of filming, while a coffee table is now reinstated between them. A large and somewhat faded print of J.H. Lynch's smouldering *Tina*, which producer Jen must have decided would be too distracting is now back in its place on the wall behind the couch. Joan Arkwright has been baking, and has provided tea to go with a plate of almond biscuits.

On the face of it, his job is simply to dig beneath the surface of the filmed interview watched yesterday. He has discussed with Skelgill several anomalies, along with loose ends that the professor either did not notice or declined to pick up. Arguably, it is just a matter of asking the right questions in the right way – to elicit answers rather than evasion. He should take heart that Skelgill must consider him the better equipped for this task.

Of nagging concern, however, is his superior's offhand directive. "Make sure she don't blab to Tuseling." To the extent that it is feasible, they must keep under wraps that behind the overt documentary there is a covert inquiry. If Percy Tuseling suspects a shadow police operation, quite likely he will pull in his horns.

DS Leyton's first tactic has been to skip any detailed preamble.

Coming hot on the heels of the dramatic appearance of a documentary crew, the event fresh in her mind, he capitalises upon such momentum. Thus far she has acquiesced to his unscheduled visit.

Now, however, he must open up. They can make no progress without facts. He will cross the bridge of blowing their cover when he reaches it.

No great aficionado of the almond, he makes nevertheless sounds of approval as he finishes his biscuit and washes it down with tea.

'We're trying to help – to put the record straight, you see, madam – and one of the things that's puzzling us is that the report at the time missed out your little trip to St Bees Head.' He is encouraged that Joan Arkwright is nodding compliantly. 'We're wondering why they didn't record that, because it would have been a more convincing part of Mr Tuseling's alibi. When you think about it – it's not very likely a chap would shoot a schoolboy one minute, and then the next take a young girl on a romantic picnic.'

She does not baulk at his use of the word romantic, nor even the more general assertion of it being of an intimate nature. She folds her hands in the lap of her apron, and blinks mildly – though she holds his gaze.

'Aye – well – I think – you see, Percy had asked me not to mention that.'

DS Leyton raises his hands, palms upward.

'Ah – that would explain it, madam – but why?'

When before – on the screen, he was sure – there had been a wistful look in her eyes, now he reads it as worldliness, perhaps even contrition.

'Well – he were married, weren't he?'

DS Leyton again gestures in a way to suggest he has rather naïvely overlooked this obvious reason. But here it is – he has evinced what they had already suspected.

'So – did he say, don't tell the police?'

'Ooh, no – just that if *anyone* asked – it would be better to say that he'd given me a lift home. Because that were true, an' all.'

'Was it a regular thing – taking a detour?'

'A few times. Once or twice we had a walk round the harbour after work. Got an ice cream. Maybe up onto the cliffs over by Haig pit.'

DS Leyton nods amenably.

'Why did you think it was okay to mention this now?'

Perhaps a flicker of anxiety crosses the woman's benign features.

'I thought that's what he must have wanted. That was the extra bit that hadn't been told. Like you say, Sergeant Leyton, it seems more convincing, don't it? Besides – she divorced him, his wife – long past. So I didn't suppose it would matter, her knowing now – if she's even alive.'

DS Leyton listens earnestly. Her take on what passed is reasonable – not least given Percy Tuseling's closing taunt aimed at the professor. It did seem to be what he was angling for.

'Did you know he was coming round – with the film crew?'

'Ooh – no. It were a complete surprise. I hadn't seen him since – well – since before the incident.'

DS Leyton makes a brief note.

'Can I ask – you were just a young girl – sixteen and impressionable. He would have been twenty-eight. Did you feel like you were his girlfriend?'

Now perhaps the woman does appear just a touch abashed.

'Well – I probably did think that a little bit. Not that we were dating, like – and nothing ever happened. Any road, after that, I saw him chatting and walking out with other girls – during my lunch hour, sometimes.'

'By all accounts he was an attractive man.'

'Well, he were very fit and muscular – a sporty chap – and he were quite good-looking back then.' She smiles ruefully. 'We were all better looking, back then.'

For a second DS Leyton wonders if she fishes for a compliment, but it seems not in her nature. Instead he returns to the clifftop tryst.

'What do you remember about going to St Bees Head? I'm told it was very hot in the summer of 1976.'

She nods thoughtfully.

'Aye, it were. Sunshine, day after day. And we were sweltering int' shop, with all the display TV sets switched on. We didn't have so much as a fan.'

'So it was cooler at the coast. And you took cold drinks.'

But now she appears a little conflicted, bemused by some memory, it seems. She lowers her gaze and gives a small shake of the head.

'Funny thing were – it were a bottle of red wine that Percy had. I think he said something about it being a special vintage. It were all dusty, like. And he didn't have a corkscrew. I remember he pushed in the cork with his thumb and then pulled it out with his shoelace.'

'His shoelace?'

She looks up. 'Aye – he were pleased with that – showing me. And then he had actual crystal glasses that made it seem all the more mad. And I'd never had wine – and I can't say I liked it. It weren't cool at all – I only drank half a glass.'

DS Leyton feels rather like he is trying to discern the scene through the peephole of a kaleidoscope, such is the strangely fragmented tale that she relates. Accordingly, he clings to the basics.

'What about Mr Tuseling – he had some wine, right?'

'He drank the lot.'

She regards DS Leyton seemingly without alarm.

'And then drove?'

'Aye. But they didn't bother much about drink driving in them days.' She murmurs, nostalgically it would appear. 'There were lots of things folk didn't have to bother with – like seatbelts, and speed limits, and crash helmets – and smoking indoors.'

DS Leyton eschews any diversion into debate: what has the nanny state ever done for us? Instead, there is a question he has brought, courtesy of Skelgill's perspicacity during the filmed interview. If not exactly burning, it has been smouldering at the back of his mind. Now he raises it as casually as he can.

'And Mr Tuseling's job at the farm, I believe he would talk about that sometimes?'

'That's right. He had some good stories. Or he might bring in a dozen eggs or a bag of taters. A rabbit once.'

'So – it wasn't a problem, that he had a second job – the boss didn't mind?'

Joan Arkwright seems a little surprised – but not guarded. She shakes her head artlessly.

'Plenty of folk had second jobs. I used to work Saturdays in a café up by the harbour. It's up to you, what you do in your own time, isn't it?'

From a philosophical standpoint DS Leyton would be inclined to agree, much as it flies in the face of his personal experience. He treats the statement as rhetorical.

'And he liked his work there – got on well with Mr Bell-Gibson?'

'Ooh, aye – that's why it were such a shock when I heard what had happened. I thought it must have been some terrible accident, while they were out shooting.'

'How did you hear about it?'

She takes a moment to reply. Her gaze shifts to a cabinet against the wall to her left. Though its top is covered in brass ornaments, DS Leyton recognises it as a traditional radiogram, that will have a turntable beneath its hinged lid.

'I think I was here. The next day were a Wednesday – that were half-day closing – and Percy hadn't come in to work that morning. Then it were on the radio about the shooting at Belltower Farm – but the police said they weren't looking for anyone. I can't rightly remember when they announced it were Percy they'd arrested.'

She looks back at DS Leyton with a small frown creasing her brow. Her grey hair is short and straight and she has a slightly uneven fringe. Her brown eyes seem a little watery, as if recalling the revelation has disturbed her. DS Leyton bows his head sympathetically. For a credulous teenage girl to have discovered that her erstwhile suitor was a shotgun killer must indeed have come as a shock.

'It was a long time ago, madam. You've done very well to remember what you can. If you were to ask my Missus, she'd tell you I can't even remember the family birthdays.'

'Ooh!'

For a second DS Leyton thinks she has reacted rather reproachfully to his admission – but he realises a chord has in fact been struck. He leans forward and eyes her receptively.

'It were my birthday – the sixth of October – that's right – when the detectives came to the shop the second time – asking for the job book from the year before.'

DS Leyton experiences a small raising of his pulse rate. *The police came back?* He endeavours to sound interested without seeming unduly fascinated. He selects the mundane aspect of what she has just revealed.

'The job book?'

She nods evenly.

'Well, it weren't actually a book. It were a loose-leaf file, with twelve dividers, one for each month. I booked in all the jobs – the repairs – and put them in date order.'

'What, like it was used to organise Mr Tuseling's work schedule?'

'That's right. He'd pop into the office each morning. He'd take a batch of job-sheets and deal with them, first come, first served. He'd bring them back with his time filled in and what parts were replaced – valves and transistors, you see – and I would price them up and send the invoices at the end of the month.'

DS Leyton is nodding, though he fears his racing thoughts might be revealed by his outward demeanour. For safety, he continues to focus upon the small practical aspects.

'What about repairs that required a call-out?'

'They were int' folder, just the same. I'm not sure how Percy organised when to fit them in – it were left to him to decide. I suppose he would look for jobs near one another, where possible.'

'And you were in the office?'

'Aye – int' shop, a little cubbyhole at the back of the showroom.'

'So, you were quite separate from Mr Tuseling?'

'Aye. To get to the workshop you had to go out the front and down the ginnel. It were in a different building int' yard at back. That's why there was a phone. Sometimes even Percy needed to call for a hand to get one of them big sets down the steps and into the van.'

DS Leyton is conscious that a decision is upon him. Right now he could inquire how certain she was that Percy Tuseling was at Radio Rentals for the entire afternoon on which Will Featherston was murdered. But, of course, she was asked this at the time, and she answered in the affirmative. He has seen the report of her interview. True, it was not a signed statement – but the investigating officers were sufficiently persuaded to cross off Percy Tuseling from their list of warm suspects. And even when the anonymous caller pointed a finger at him, this most persuasive aspect of his alibi was not undermined.

And, yet, immediately following the murder of Colin Bell-Gibson, detectives returned to inspect the job book – the nearest thing to timesheets. And not the timesheets of 1977 – but those of 1976. Yet so far neither he nor DS Jones has come across any record of this visit.

Perhaps judiciously – and certainly he will be telling Skelgill it was such – he asks a different question altogether.

'What did the police have to say – when they examined the job book?'

Joan Arkwright wrinkles her small, upturned nose as if it is an aid to recall.

'Well – that were the funny thing. They took it out to their car and looked at it – and when they came back they said what they needed was missing.'

'What was missing?'

'I think it was some of the job sheets.'

'They didn't tell you exactly?'

Now she looks a little pained.

'I can't rightly remember. They said they thought their colleagues must have taken them the first time – when they came to ask me about Percy's car and him giving me a lift home.'

DS Leyton regards her earnestly.

'By all accounts you were well organised. Wouldn't you have noticed if documents were gone?'

She seems mildly flattered and momentarily lowers her eyes. But still she shakes her head.

'Not if they were from the month before. Once I'd priced the jobs at the end of the month – we had a separate invoice folder to chase up payments.'

DS Leyton nods pensively. But he has a fallback. He thumbs to the chronology in his notebook.

'According to our records, the police called at Radio Rentals to speak to yourself and Mr Tuseling on Friday 17th September, 1976. So I think what you're saying is that if they'd taken the job sheets from August 1976 or before that, you might not have noticed.'

She has listened carefully.

'Aye, that's right. Unless there were some claim – if a set went wrong again – there'd be no cause to refer back to the job sheets. And the guarantee would only last twelve months. After that, there was no need even to keep them.'

DS Leyton does not want to draw excessive attention to the matter. But he has a final question.

'Where did you store these files? Were they locked away?'

She seems mildly amused.

'Just in a cupboard. I don't think anyone would have stolen papers – not when there were all those brand-new TV sets int' front window.'

DS Leyton grins affably.

'You'd be surprised – some of the daft burglars we come across, madam.'

The woman chuckles, and now rises with the offer of mashing him another mug of tea. But DS Leyton takes the opportunity to thank her for her help and hospitality. He feels he should not overstay his welcome. His impression is that she has taken his visit in her stride, and is not at all suspicious or even protective on the part of Percy Tuseling. So, get out while he is ahead. As he is chaperoned to the front door, however, he suffers a small pang of doubt.

'Madam, I'm going to sound a bit like Mr Tuseling all those years ago – except I am the police – but would you mind not mentioning this – that you've had a call from a detective today?'

To his relief, she exhibits no dissent.

'Ooh, yes – that's just what they told me before.'

'The police told you that?'
'Aye.'
'When they came about the job sheets?'
'That's right, yes.'

11. JACK DIXON

Bridecrake – 11.45 a.m. Thursday 29 July

Bridecrake, as the crow flies, is hardly two miles from Blindkirk. It is a fact of topography that had contributed to Skelgill's double take when George Appleby had made mention of the former hamlet. Then there is the seemingly familial nomenclature, which must have confounded many a postie. More than once, perusing maps, striving to read between the lines of name origins, Skelgill has wondered if some mischievous local transposed the prefixes when Norman clerks came calling, compiling the Domesday Book a millennium ago. For Blindkirk boasts a small but spectacular parish church that is popular with to-be-weds, and Bridecrake a more bucolic aspect where the lesser-spotted corncrake surely once skulked in wild field margins.

It is to a former farm labourer's dwelling that he has come. He draws up his shooting brake behind a small white Mini. Set on the edge of the village the single storey cottage was once well tended but is now being overrun by its flora. Sprawling wisteria and rambler roses are taking over the building, shrouding the small windows. Shrubs have run riot and borders have been invaded by rose-bay willowherb and nettles. Though to Skelgill's non-horticultural eye the natural effect is perfectly pleasing.

He clambers out a little tentatively to stretch his spine. It is another hot day to recall the legend of 1976. A dome of clear blue crystal covers Cumbria. The air is still and birdsong subdued. There is the pebble-chatter of sparrows. The lament of a collared dove. Hungry stub-tailed juvenile swallows wait on a telegraph wire while their more elegant parents perform aerobatics in pursuit of flies, calling *zinc-zinc*. Pay attention, children, this is how you use the microwave.

There is a distant murmur of a radio, which might be coming

from the rear of the property.

Skelgill glances at the Mini as he passes. There is an NHS card displayed on the dashboard. The front gate is open, trapped so by weeds, and the paved path of interest to a bryologist.

He approaches the latticed porch, intending to follow the path to the left and around the side of the cottage.

The front door opens.

A woman emerges – striking and incongruous. The incongruity quickly passes, however, for he connects a nurse's tunic with the calling card. However, the strikingness grows: she could have walked fresh from the cover of a glossy magazine.

She must be about his own age, perhaps a little less, and not far below his height. The outfit, for workwear, is remarkably well tailored; white and immaculate, it enhances an hour-glass figure. A lanyard with an ID draws his eye to its natural resting place. Her black hair is tightly drawn back and secured by some means.

He meets her gaze to find it severe, the eyes a cool shade of blue.

'Mr Dixon contacted us through a former colleague. You obviously weren't expecting *me*.'

He finds himself showing his warrant card. His words feel blurted and he ends with an involuntary emphasis of self-deprecation.

The woman does not immediately reply. It is possible that a faint blush appears upon her prominent cheekbones, though it may be subtle make up.

She is holding in one hand a small medicine bottle and in the other her car key fob.

'He sits at the garden.'

Her voice is light, the accent Slavic.

To terminate an awkward silence Skelgill pushes off his right foot.

'Don't fret, lass – I'll find him.'

As he rounds the corner he inhales the heady scent of jasmine that spills from its overgrown trellis; it seems to raise his heartbeat.

The rear garden has similarly run to disorder; beyond clumps of brambles it gives on to grazing populated by a scattering of blackface gimmers, mainly in repose. Skelgill dwells for a moment on the greater vista, picking out the familiar silhouette of Skiddaw for the purposes of orientation.

It takes him a moment to focus upon the immediate setting, an irregular patch of mown lawn where a frail-looking old man in a floppy wide-brimmed sun hat and loose khaki trousers and shirt reposes on a wooden bench, facing into the noonday sun. Beneath the shadow of the hat he seems to have his eyes closed. A traditional portable wireless and a mug rest upon a half-rotten slatted wooden side table. From the radio emanate the voices of commentary, background cheers and applause.

Skelgill rounds into view and crouches a little.

'Mr Dixon? I'm DI Skelgill. You rang Penrith HQ. You spoke to George Appleby.'

The eyes, after all, are open and alert.

'Aye, lad – 'bout time. Sit theesen down.'

He pats the bench.

Then he reaches the other way, quite easily, and lowers the volume.

'That's the Aussies four wickets down afore lunch. They'll be regretting not putting England in. Happen it were a good toss to lose. Happen we would've batted.'

Skelgill has already determined that the man is listening to the first morning of the latest Ashes test, taking place not so far away at Old Trafford.

Skelgill takes a seat and looks about.

'I shouldn't have fancied bowling in this weather.'

The man turns to regard him with interest.

'They're saying there's a bit of green int' wicket.'

'I suppose it helps when you're the ones paying the groundsman's wages.'

Now Jack Dixon chuckles.

'We need every little help we can get, after that tannin' we took at Lords.' He shakes his head ruefully. 'Mind, when do we ever beat the Aussies at Lords?'

They share in some silent reflection. Skelgill is reminded of his colleague's advice, not to let the grass grow under his feet. But if

George Appleby was referring to what might be the old man's transient recall, his mind has been put at ease. Jack Dixon, despite his fragile appearance, seems mentally as sharp as a tack.

'How long is it since you retired, Jack?'

'Nigh on thirty year. I don't suppose there's many left – as when I were int' force.'

Skelgill nods broodingly. There may be few even left alive.

Jack Dixon's attention drifts to settle upon a sprawling buddleia, its cascading purple racemes laden with several dozen vanessid butterflies; following his gaze, Skelgill becomes aware of the delicate fragrance that has drawn them from far afield.

He decides not to beat about the bush.

'Did you work on the Caldblow Farm case?'

'Nay, lad – but I did have me fifteen minutes of fame. Or I should've. It never came to owt.'

Skelgill remains optimistic.

'George Appleby said summat about a card – an anonymous message?'

The man nods pensively.

'I read int' Gazette – they're asking for information. But it were second nature for me to contact the police. Besides, the press would make a meal of the coincidence.'

There is that word again – although Skelgill has at least been primed by George Appleby to expect it.

'Sounds like it were more than a coincidence.'

Jack Dixon turns to look at Skelgill with a twinkle in his eye.

'Aye – you couldn't have made it up.'

'Because it involved Percy Tuseling?'

'Aye.'

The man settles back against the bench and folds his arms. Skelgill waits for him to continue.

'I were duty officer at Mirehouse – south side of Whitehaven – you know Mirehouse?'

'Aye.'

'They closed the station years ago. But I were on the desk this night – a month or so after the murder of the Featherston lad. It were about ten-thirty, and these two chaps come in. One said he were Percy Tuseling and the other his brother-in-law, who lived in Mirehouse. They'd got this piece of corrugated card – torn from a cardboard box, about six inches by eight. On it were written a message to Percy Tuseling.'

Jack Dixon pauses, as though to give Skelgill a moment to digest this first course of facts.

But Skelgill is hungry for more.

'Can you remember what it said?'

'Not exactly. It were really badly written – big uneven capital letters – and like in twang – as if by someone half-illiterate. "PERCY – 'IM 'OO SHOOTS ONT' FARM – 'E SCARES THE FITZROVIA WOMAN." Summat like that. The gist of it were a warning to Percy Tuseling – of an unnamed bloke who supposedly shot on the farmland, and that he had a red van – I remember it said a J-reg. And it mentioned the Caldblow Farm murder – young Will Featherston.'

Skelgill gives an involuntary shake of his head. His thoughts – were he to give them free rein – might just stampede to all points of the compass, like a firecracker has been let off in their midst. He bites abstractedly at the corner of a thumbnail. Jack Dixon seems mildly amused by the inadequately concealed reaction.

'There's more, lad. Like I say, I weren't involved in the investigation. They'd drafted in an army of offcomers. But I knew all about the case. It was all you heard – we must find the lad's killer. I didn't know then that Percy Tuseling had been a person of interest – but I did know Percy Tuseling. Not well, like – but I knew him by sight. Then when I took his details I realised his name – Percy – was the same as on the card. So I thought he was telling me it had been posted through his door – but then why was he in Mirehouse? And then he tells me they'd been for a drink at the Miners' Welfare – and walking back to his brother-in-law's they'd picked up this piece of card int' street.'

'What – like it had been left for him to find? Not pinned up, or owt?'

'Aye – ridiculous, weren't it? Percy Tuseling didn't even live in the area. And there's a message for him, lying ont' pavement int' dark. What are the odds of that?'

Skelgill finds himself nodding reflectively. DS Leyton is going to love this one.

'What did you do?'

'I put it in an evidence bag and when I finished my shift I drove to Whitehaven Central – that's where the main incident room was based. I handed it in with the statement I'd took.'

He regards Skelgill somewhat fatefully. In the shade beneath the hat there is perhaps a tinge of regret in his eyes.

'That were t' last I heard of it. There were above a dozen teams of detectives – and no computer. They reckoned the incident room were swamped. A few days later, they'd picked up them Hare twins. There were a big fanfare.'

Skelgill gazes, unseeing now, across fields to the distant line of the Cumbrian fells.

'Did you think he were just an attention-seeker?'

The man shrugs uncertainly.

'It were tempting – but I can't say I did. You'd think he would have gone to the papers if he were. Thing is – like I say – at the time I didn't know he'd been a person of interest. He came across like a good citizen doing his public duty.'

Skelgill nods understandingly.

'You did as much as you could.'

'Aye – except the next thing – Percy Tuseling's arrested for the murder at Belltower Farm.'

Jack Dixon sounds contrite; Skelgill responds with more ambivalence.

'It were a year later. Did you do owt then?'

'Aye – I mentioned it to my superior. But the Belltower Farm murder were an open and shut case – and by then the Hares had been sent down for killing Will Featherston at Caldblow Farm. What was there to do? It were all tied up. Besides, it were well above my pay grade.'

Skelgill gives a resigned expiration of air.

The man's inference has set a little alarm bell ringing. Perhaps viewing from the distance of his rickety retirement seat, Jack Dixon discerns a bigger picture, albeit lying before him a landscape blurred by the passage of time.

'The Hares' convictions were overturned – the confessions were deemed unsafe.'

The old man nods.

'Aye, I mind. Some bent copper from West Pennines Constabulary. Is that what you're looking into?'

Skelgill rubs a knuckle against the stubble of his chin.

Such ideas are mere shifting shapes and shadows, like the oversized pike he sometimes dreams of that stalk his boat, never quite willing to show itself, or to take a dangled bait. However, Skelgill sticks to the more tangible line of inquiry.

'Truth be told, Jack – all roads are leading to Percy Tuseling.' He gives a short ironic laugh. 'And you've just tarmacked another one.'

The man raises leathery hands in apology.

'You said you knew him?'

It takes Jack Dixon a moment to compose his response.

'Aye – by sight, like I say. I kept wicket for the Whitehaven police eleven. I must have played against him a few times afore I packed it in. You know how you get to know faces? And his girt backside. But it were more than that.'

'Aye?'

'I saw him again. This were well after the card incident. Must have been the summer of 1977. It were the Mirehouse gala day – on the big green they've got there. And he had a stall. I noticed him because he were in his whites. He must have come from a match.'

Skelgill is interested.

'What kind of stall?'

'It were bric-a-brac – second-hand stuff – maybe some antiques.'

'Do you think that were a regular thing?'

'I couldn't tell thee, lad. But there were another bloke running t' show with him – and that were the brother-in-law that'd come into the station on the night of the card.'

Skelgill narrows his eyes. He watches the butterflies as they jostle for nectar. Once again faintly roused is his boyhood instinct of pursuit, capture, collection. But he sees them barely subliminally. He has learned several important facts – but it is the abstract that most absorbs him.

Then comes a sudden burst of sound, cheers and applause and excited commentary from the otherwise quietened radio. England have their fifth wicket of the pre-lunch session. He turns to share in the good fortune with Jack Dixon – but he sees the wide-brimmed hat has nodded forward and the man is asleep.

Skelgill rises gingerly, and treads softly when he reaches the gravel of the path that skirts the cottage. At the side of the house, watching his step and ducking beneath trailing jasmine tendrils, he almost collides with the nurse coming the other way.

Instinctively, he raises a hand, and forms a thumb pointing back over his shoulder. He speaks in a whisper.

'He's fallen asleep.'

The woman seems a little breathless. There is something different about her, that Skelgill cannot exactly discern. Perhaps she has been doing some housework – changing the bed perhaps – her long dark hair is cascading over her shoulders and the first two buttons of her tunic are unfastened. She stares at Skelgill; the cool blue eyes seem to have lost their earlier guardedness.

'When you come – I –' She does not complete the sentence. 'Mr Dixon – his bathroom shower – he not work. You fix for me.'

Her manner is somewhere between expectant and persuasive.

'Not the shower.' Skelgill has muttered the words under his breath before he knows it.

'I am sorry?'

She is standing half a pace closer than might be considered customary. There seems to be another fragrance, more musky, heady, that mingles with the scent of the jasmine. He leans back a little, as if inviting inspection.

'Madam, can you tell me – do I look like a plumber, or something?'

12. REVIEW

Incident Room 101 – 11.00 a.m. Friday 30 July

'That's the second podcast just gone live.' DS Jones is checking the app on her mobile phone. 'Do you want me to play it, now?'

Skelgill gestures towards DS Leyton and then in a circular motion to include the three of them, ensconced in the corner seats.

'Let's get us ducks in a row. It's not like we don't know what's in it.'

DS Jones nods compliantly – she understands that her colleagues have been out prospecting, and there is the suggestion of nuggets to share. But she adds an observation.

'I think this one will draw a bigger audience. Turnpike have produced radio ads – soundbites from Episode One. They're quite provocative. I'm not sure Percy Tuseling will approve. But Jen told me he's getting a royalty on top of his fee – so it's in his interest to maximise awareness.'

Skelgill makes a scoffing sound, his face in his mug.

'You sound like one of those marketing types.'

'Absolutely. Yesterday we took a deep dive into the case – there was an awful lot to unpack. But I think we identified the low-hanging fruit – and I'll do my best to keep you across developments.'

DS Leyton bursts out laughing, and even Skelgill does not try too hard to suppress a grin. DS Jones's received pronunciation is impressive. Clearly, she does not take offence.

But now she makes a point in favour of the cliché.

'They could teach our publicity department a lesson or two.' She smiles benignly. 'But let's see whether it generates any leads.'

'In the meantime, we'll do Freud's legwork.'

It is Skelgill's jibe. The moment of levity has evidently not assuaged his underlying belief that they are wearing out all the shoe leather and the professor is winning all the kudos. But perhaps, too, there is some deeper resentment.

DS Jones regards him sympathetically.

'They are appreciative of your work behind the scenes. But I do think they perform a valuable role – they can say what they like, knowing they'll never have to prove it. It gives them a lot more leeway to make insinuations that we could never stand up in court.'

It is plain that Skelgill is not entirely sold on the argument – but he gestures to DS Leyton, that he is to go first.

'Righto, Guv.'

DS Leyton has his trusty pocket notebook. He taps the open page with an index finger.

'Oh, yeah – first off. I got a text this morning. A nag called Dancing Queen came in at 13/2 in the 2.10 at Newmarket on Friday 13th August 1976.' He looks up at DS Jones. 'What was that – an hour and a half before Will Featherston was murdered?'

DS Jones nods.

DS Leyton addresses Skelgill.

'That part of his story could have been bona fide. Or not. Yes – there could have been a winning bet and a celebratory drink. But I've got some not.'

Skelgill seems to understand his sergeant's turn of phrase, and nods for him to continue.

DS Leyton folds over the page.

'Joan Arkwright.'

He inhales as if to make an announcement, when something distracts him and he looks inquiringly at Skelgill.

'Guv – you ever heard of pulling out a cork with a shoelace?'

Skelgill seems a little disdainful – perhaps that there would be any doubt that he might be ignorant of such a practical feat.

'Aye – you tie a knot in it. You need to drop it below the cork.' He makes a disparaging face. 'It's a bit of a last resort – dipping a clarty bootlace in your wine. Not that I drink the stuff.'

DS Leyton looks like he in two minds – there is scope to digress. He nods pensively, and returns his scrutiny to his notes. Again, he taps the page.

'Seems that's what Tuseling did when he took Joan Arkwright to St Bees Head. Maybe that's why it stuck in her mind. He didn't have a corkscrew – but he produced a dusty bottle of what he claimed was vintage red wine – and a pair of crystal glasses.'

'Stolen?'

Both male heads turn to look in surprise at their female colleague. For once, it seems, she has permitted herself an injudicious exclamation.

But quickly, she adds a rider.

'Remember – they found the stopper of a crystal decanter in the bushes beside the gate – when they searched the grounds at Caldblow Farm?'

DS Leyton gives a growl of realisation.

'Stone the crows – I'd forgotten that.' He glances at each of his colleagues in turn. 'I mean – I thought it was queer enough – what was a working-class bloke doing producing a bottle of vintage claret and crystal glasses? But, now you mention it, Emma – *phew.*'

Skelgill is less excitable.

'Have we found the inventory of items stolen from Caldblow Farm?'

He addresses the remark to DS Jones – though it is reasonably a question for either of his subordinates. They indeed exchange hopeful glances – but plainly here is another needle to be sought amidst the haystack of documents piled precariously against the far wall.

DS Jones replies on their joint behalf.

'So far, just what's in the summary report – a reference to a miscellany of small items. The suggestion being that it was one person working alone, filling a holdall or a suitcase.'

A moment's silence washes about them.

'Better put a pin in that one.'

Now DS Jones laughs. Skelgill attempts to glower – but she has rumbled his little attempt at sarcasm – that he too has employed the jargon of management speak.

DS Leyton, meantime, is just eager to speak.

'Ok – so, about the jaunt to St Bees Head.' He waggles a finger at Skelgill to signify that he has used the correct name for the cape.

'Just as we were previously discussing – Tuseling didn't want his missus to know he was canoodling with a young girl.'

'Canoodling?'

DS Leyton rows back a little.

'Well, not exactly – she said nothing ever went on – but she did consider that she was kind of like his platonic girlfriend – and that she'd seen him flirting with other young females around the town. So she agreed to say that he'd just given her a lift home.'

His colleagues have sombre expressions etched upon their faces, and the effect seems to prompt DS Leyton to come to the defence of Joan Arkwright.

'She didn't know she was alibiing him. And in a way – as far as the picnic was concerned – she wasn't. It was well after the fact. More consequential was that she made a statement that he was at the workshop all afternoon – when she couldn't have known that for certain. But I reckon he did a good job of making it seem like he was there. Maybe told her he'd put on a bet at lunchtime – and that he'd bought the booze when he nipped out to collect his winnings. Phoned through to her a couple of times. Took her at five.'

There seems to be no great dispute that this could be a possible scenario; they have already considered the ease with which Percy Tuseling may have visited Caldblow Farm, his absence undetected, and made a phone call from some other location.

'Another pin, Guv?'

DS Leyton plies Skelgill with a look of optimism.

'Another pin.'

DS Leyton nods with satisfaction.

'And the next one. About Percy Tuseling working at the farm.' Now he regards Skelgill earnestly. 'You were dead right, Guv. Seems like he would talk freely about it. The gaffer at Radio Rentals knew he'd got a second job and didn't give a fig. So Tuseling lied.'

'Are we surprised?'

Skelgill's tone is acerbic – but he sees that DS Jones is looking somewhat conflicted.

'Jones.'

'Well – of course – his argument is that he didn't lie. In the first police interview they only asked him about the car and his whereabouts. He agreed he had a red Ford Corsair, and told them he was at the workshop. In the second interview, when asked directly about his connection to Caldblow Farm, he admitted it.'

DS Leyton, however, is less equivocal.

'Except he's now let slip that he kept quiet about working on the farms for a reason that wasn't true.'

Skelgill makes a cynical expiration of air.

'He still got away with it.'

But DS Leyton has something to add in this regard.

'There's one more thing – I'm not sure our boys did entirely buy his excuses. Seems they went back to Radio Rentals directly after Tuseling was arrested for topping Colin Bell-Gibson. They asked to see his job sheets for the time of the Will Featherston murder. They'd only do that if they hadn't completely written him off as the killer.'

Skelgill is frowning.

'They went back a year later?'

'That's right, Guv – 6th October, 1977 – Joan Arkwright's birthday. And here's the thing – the pages were missing. Tuseling's timesheets. Gone.'

'Covering the date of Will Featherston's murder?'

DS Leyton turns out his notebook as if to indicate he has it in black and white. Though he responds with a caveat.

'We're relying on Joan Arkwright's memory. But she reckoned the officers took the job book out to their car. They came back in a bit later – saying the sheets for August 1976 were gone – and that their colleagues must have taken them at the time, the year before. Seems they were a bit red-faced – they asked her to keep mum.'

Skelgill's consternation appears to have deepened, and he hauls himself up by the arm of the sofa and rests his elbows on the window sill. He gazes out across the leafy yet arid summer landscape, but his eyes find no fixed point of interest. And when he turns, and settles, when his colleagues might expect some pontification, he surprises them with praise for DS Leyton.

'Well done, Leyton – I knew you had a way with the ladies.'

Before DS Leyton can respond, Skelgill follows up.

'Want to hear how I got on?'

It seems Skelgill is sticking a third pin in DS Leyton's findings. Perhaps he has joined dots but is unwilling to consider their pattern.

His colleagues regard him obediently; he turns to DS Jones.

'You heard about this card – a retired officer phoned in to George?'

DS Jones shakes her head once, though it is enough to dislodge a blonde tress that she absently draws back.

'Just the top line.'

Skelgill recounts Jack Dixon's story of Percy Tuseling and his brother-in-law, handing in the scrap of cardboard, and its cryptic and barely literate missive. His subordinates listen with widening eyes. But when Skelgill reaches the point where he explains that the card – seemingly a personal message to Percy Tuseling – was picked up from the pavement over a mile from where he lived at ten-thirty of a night, DS Leyton cannot suppress a small explosion of disbelief.

'An' I'm a flippin' monkey's uncle.'

Skelgill looks inquiringly at DS Jones, as if to invite an inventive idiom of her own.

But she is prosaically literal.

'He surely must have written it.'

Her response merely endorses what is a state of general agreement. But now Skelgill folds his arms and leans back into the settee.

'Why didn't we know about this?'

When his words might be interpreted as a reproach of those present, his tone clearly aims the criticism at the omnipotent powers that be, the authorities, the 'they' who have gone before and have landed them in the midst of this thorny conundrum.

DS Jones indicates with a palm over her shoulder; she refers to the document hoard.

'It could still be in there. And those job sheets.'

They eye the inner wall of perilously perched boxes with some trepidation. In an idle moment, DS Leyton has estimated that the unstable structure comprises over a quarter of a million individual pages.

Skelgill is looking like he thinks either the task is impossible, or that it would in any event be a futile search. DS Leyton combs splayed fingers through his mop of dark hair. DS Jones appears to have turned her mind to a chart on the coffee table before her, on which she has laid out a chronology.

She seems to suffer a little jolt.

'Jones.'

Skelgill has detected her reaction.

She regards him intently.

'Did you say when Percy Tuseling handed in the card?'

Skelgill did not, but he can remember George Dixon's account, if not the exact dates.

'It were the Saturday before the Hares were picked up.'

DS Jones runs an index finger over her list.

'That would have been the day after he was interviewed at the workshop. After the anonymous phone call. And after he'd been forced to admit he shot at both farms.'

'He must have panicked!' It is DS Leyton who ventures this suggestion. 'Laid a false trail. And I bet it was him that half-inched the August job sheets – to cover his tracks. Belt and flamin' braces.'

The two sergeants regard Skelgill eagerly, as though seeking his endorsement for their collective deduction. But when he might reasonably agree, and with justified enthusiasm, instead he remains implacable.

Yet, after a few moments of deliberation, he shares an unexpected adjunct.

'There's an antiques connection.'

They are all ears.

'We know Tuseling played cricket. So did Jack Dixon. He'd have been a good bit older – but they crossed paths. That's how he knew him by sight when he handed in the card. He reckons the following summer – 1977 we're talking now – he saw Tuseling and the brother-in-law running a bric-a-brac stall at the Mirehouse gala.' After a pause he adds a rider. 'He didn't know if it were a one-off or a regular sideline.'

DS Jones is making rapid shorthand notes on her pad. She holds it up to her colleagues, despite that it has no meaning to them. There is a flush of excitement blooming about her cheekbones.

'I think this has to be the next episode – the next location shoot. We could take Percy Tuseling to Mirehouse – and challenge him about the card – and the stall. Sim will be delighted.' She speaks the last phrase almost to herself – and then realises that she has shifted into her counterpart role as Turnpike Media researcher.

'I mean – we were discussing on Wednesday night – the importance of momentum – of new revelations. These are beyond expectations. It will bring home why they need us.'

DS Leyton seems perfectly content with such praise, but Skelgill is plainly dissatisfied with DS Jones's attempt to compensate. Undeterred, she taps her pen firmly upon the notepad.

'But I had better message them – this morning they've been making arrangements for Monday.' She reaches for her mobile. 'Then I'll make tea.'

She types quickly, two-thumbed, and lays down the phone on her pad when she is finished. She gathers their empty mugs and disappears into the kitchenette.

DS Leyton rises with a prolonged groan, and stretches randomly as he ambles across to stare at the artificial edifice that is the irregular arrangement of Bankers boxes. He stands, arms akimbo.

'It's like Hadrian's flamin' Wall, Guv. What do you reckon the odds are of me pulling out that card, lucky dip?'

But Skelgill does not answer.

Were DS Leyton to turn at this juncture, he would find his superior seemingly interrogating DS Jones's handset – indeed he appears to tap in a message, and swipe a couple of times before swiftly replacing it. While DS Leyton bends and crouches and cranes his head sideways to read scrawled legends on the box ends, Skelgill stares at the phone. When, after about thirty seconds the screen locks, he responds to his sergeant.

'What was that, Leyton?'

'Nah, Guv – don't worry. I reckon we've got the gist of what was on that card – and Jack Dixon sounds like a trusty witness. I shall be interested to hear what excuse Tuseling comes up with.'

Skelgill nods pensively. But now DS Jones emerges, and he implements his maxim never to compete with the tea lady. Though he casts about forlornly, that they have no suitable accompaniment.

DS Jones deposits the freshly filled mugs and walks across to the screen that doubles as a wipe-clean workboard. She selects a marker pen and turns to Skelgill.

'Should I make an action list?'

Skelgill nods. He understands her penchant for such a thing, to see the written word – she is the visual sort, where he would be classed as kinaesthetic.

She immediately writes a heading "TURNPIKE" and beneath it "Mirehouse – card & antiques stall".

Then a new heading, "LOCATE" and beneath it "Mirehouse card" and "Radio Rentals visit report 6/10/77".

'Job sheets? August 1976.' It is DS Leyton's suggestion. DS Jones adds the item.

There is a pause before Skelgill speaks.

'Persons of interest.'

DS Jones creates a new column.

Skelgill seems to wait to see if anyone will oblige – but perhaps they reciprocate, knowing he must have someone in mind. He reacts a little impatiently.

'Come on. Tuseling's first wife.'

DS Jones writes "Veronica Tuseling" – but she speaks as she does so. 'DC Watson is on the case – but still no advance on her having disappeared off the radar shortly after Percy Tuseling was jailed and she divorced him.'

Skelgill responds with a second name – or, at least, a descriptor.

'Tuseling's brother-in-law.'

DS Leyton now chips in.

'I wonder if he were the wife's brother, or her sister's husband.'

DS Jones again narrates as she scribbles.

'I think more likely the latter. We've been trawling council records and old phone books. Veronica Tuseling's maiden name was Collinson – and no other Collinson has come up so far.'

She turns to look at Skelgill, but he does not dwell upon the point.

'Bell-Gibson's daughter.'

DS Jones swivels back to the screen. In her loose summer dress that cannot conceal the toned physique, to Skelgill's eye she could be a young teacher – like the probationers he remembers, his form scenting blood and giving them hell. Were DS Jones that probationer, the fifteen-year-old class wag would have been hauled out unceremoniously. His hand drifts to his ear, as though he suffers a small psychosomatic episode. He grins wryly. They never had one quite this good looking.

DS Jones has remembered the woman's first name, "Susan Bell-Gibson".

She turns to look at Skelgill – he starts, as though she has caught him daydreaming inappropriately. After a second she indicates to the screen.

'At least these are uncommon names.'

Skelgill and DS Leyton nod like obedient pupils.

DS Leyton even raises a hand as a precursor to speaking.

'Could we include an appeal in the podcast? For anyone who knows their whereabouts to get in contact.'

But Skelgill baulks at the suggestion.

'We don't want to put the wind up Tuseling – he's edgy enough.'

DS Jones offers some mitigation.

'Maybe wait and see what today's episode flushes out. If the ads have done the trick.'

DS Leyton nods; he is willing to concede the point.

'Right enough, the proof'll be in the pudding.'

'Eating.'

It is Skelgill's interjection.

'Come again, Guv?'

'The proof's in the eating, Leyton.'

DS Leyton looks confused – as though he is not entirely sure what correction Skelgill is advancing.

'I thought that was cake, Guv – having your cake and eating it.'

Now Skelgill scoffs disdainfully – but his expression dissolves into something of a pained grimace, as he is reminded of the dearth of any such sweetmeats.

'Chance'd be a fine thing.'

But DS Leyton suddenly raises an index finger. It can be the precursor to an irrelevant random thought, or an incisive practical insight.

He leans around the side of the sofa and drags up his capacious briefcase.

'That reminds me, Guv. Yesterday after I'd seen Joan Arkwright – I passed the Whitehaven branch of Haighs. I cleared them out of sausage rolls.'

Skelgill's reaction is reminiscent of a dog that sees its owner's hand move towards the treats pocket. His tone is jubilant.

'About time, Leyton. You're finally getting the hang of this policing malarkey.'

13. PRESS GANG

Mountain Café, Keswick – 11.00 a.m. Saturday 31 July

'Oh – it's you.'

'Don't mither yourself – I've bought you some coconut shortbread.'

'Well – that's very generous of you, Inspector.'

Kendall Minto is somewhat breathless. The attic café is situated in a hanging mezzanine on what is the fourth storey of the outdoor gear store, and perhaps expecting what he believes might be a more receptive audience he has put on a little sprint for the final flight; head down, he has been watched by Skelgill from his eyrie overlooking the balcony.

'I could have sworn that the meeting request came from Emma's phone.' He sweeps back his hair with the fingers of both hands and smiles artlessly at Skelgill. 'Perhaps she couldn't make it?'

Skelgill glares; there is the suggestion that the use of the familiar might have offended him.

'I reckon if you checked DS Jones's phone you'd find no text.'

Kendall Minto's gaze falters under Skelgill's steely stare. He has not been invited to sit, but now he gasps as though he is sweltering and swings his trademark leather jacket onto the back of the free chair opposite the police inspector. He tugs his mobile phone from his hip pocket and places it upon the table.

'In fact this meeting's not even taking place.'

Before Kendall Minto can react, Skelgill reaches across, snatches up the handset and tosses it over the banister rail.

'Aargh!'

The young reporter lurches to look – just in time to follow its trajectory as it lands fifteen feet below in a large dump bin of cut-price fleece tops.

'Collect it on your way out.'

Kendall Minto regards Skelgill pleadingly.

'I – er – I wasn't recording.'

'Now I don't need to wonder if you were.'

Kendall Minto seems entirely disoriented. Rather giddily he takes his seat. He has been outflanked. Not least that Skelgill has apparently used his subordinate's mobile phone to lure him to a clandestine rendezvous. And Skelgill's choice of seat commanding the approach – that he flung the handset without even looking – suggests more than a modicum of malice aforethought.

But the cub reporter is astute. He rather suspects that had he transgressed in some way – perhaps in relation to DS Emma Jones – he would already be nursing a black eye. The eccentric detective has summoned him for a reason – and if it is not about his female colleague, it must be business. And he must want something. Ergo, his own position cannot be so disadvantaged – he surely holds a half-decent hand of cards.

He reaches a little gingerly for the coffee that stands with the shortbread on its side plate.

'Thanks.'

Skelgill acknowledges with a faint nod.

And, now, a little curiously, he seems reluctant to begin.

A combination of nerves and the irrepressible journalist in Kendall Minto comes to the fore.

'Is this about our joint venture with Turnpike Media?'

'Got it in one.'

Kendall Minto grins ingenuously, but there is no change in Skelgill's manner; he remains severe and unforthcoming. Kendall Minto pats his pockets a little ostentatiously, as if to demonstrate he is out of something.

'Do I need to take notes?'

Skelgill seems not to hear. After a few moments more he speaks.

'How much do you know?'

Kendall Minto understands that he should reply with the greatest degree of intelligence he can muster. On top of the burden he bears in being a contemporary and unashamed admirer of the man's female subordinate, Detective Inspector Daniel Skelgill does not suffer fools gladly, nor tolerate prevarication.

'Inspector – naturally I have read all the historical reporting in the Gazette's archives. All three cases – the Caldblow Farm murder of Will Featherston in August 1976, the Hare twins' robbery of Kirkstile Farm a month later, and Percy Tuseling's shooting of Colin Bell-Gibson at Belltower Farm in October 1977. Take the Hares out of the equation and it's not difficult to draw the conclusion that Percy Tuseling was the real killer of Will Featherston. The police succumbed to the great public outcry – the Hares were suitable scapegoats. It strikes me that Professor Simeon Freud's agenda is to hex Percy Tuseling into making a confession.'

Skelgill has listened implacably. He certainly cannot chastise Kendall Minto for pulling his punches.

'What about my agenda?'

'I assume it has befallen you to find a diplomatic explanation.'

'Aye, me and diplomacy.'

Kendall Minto cannot tell if Skelgill is being sarcastic and self-deprecating, or threatening. He wonders if he has ever seen the inspector smile. Skelgill remains tight-lipped – though he takes the last remaining bite of his cake. It might be a good sign.

'What I mean, Inspector – the police at the time made a perfectly understandable mistake – compounded by one corrupt officer drafted from another force. One bad apple. The mistake was to set out their stall for the Hares – and why not? They rob a nearby farm of antiques and let off a shotgun. The investigators were floundering in a sea of datapoints in an age before electronic data were invented. Tossed by such a storm, the Hares shone like a beacon of salvation. Moreover, the Hares were no angels – and ostensibly confessed.'

The inspector may be nodding.

Hitherto untrammelled, Kendall Minto feels a growing sense of excitement. Perhaps here is another angle entirely – not only that the Gazette might help to flush out Percy Tuseling – but also the prospect of a second, more magnificent feather in his cap, to uncover historical malpractice by the authorities.

He speaks with growing confidence.

'Inspector – you'll have analysed the reports of Percy Tuseling's trial?'

Skelgill has not.

'We're going through everything with a fine-toothed comb.'

Kendall Minto nods eagerly.

'The striking thing is how little peripheral evidence was brought. How few witnesses testified.'

'He put his hand up for it. He pled guilty.'

'To manslaughter, yes – but the Prosecution wanted to prove intent. They wanted him for murder.'

'They got him for murder.'

'After much deliberation by the jury. The judge eventually accepted a majority verdict.'

Skelgill seems to realise he has been drawn into a quickfire interchange against an adversary in full possession of the facts; he reverts to taciturnity.

'So, what are you saying?'

'Merely that here was a trial that was a potential embarrassment to the police – a political hot potato. There was very little media coverage. Why was that? More so back in the day, the press relied on the police giving briefings. There was no great fanfare when Colin Bell-Gibson's killing occurred and Percy Tuseling was taken into custody. Normally the police are quick to trumpet their triumphs. Moreover, several of the leading officers, who also investigated Will Featherston's murder, were not called to testify. What should we read into that?'

Skelgill slides his elbows onto the table and rests his chin upon the tips of his long fingers.

'You tell me.'

Kendall Minto mirrors Skelgill's move, leaning forwards himself.

'I would say to avoid them being exposed to cross-examination. Imagine if evidence had surfaced that linked Percy Tuseling with the murder of Will Featherston. The "Hares Are Innocent" campaign would have pounced upon it like hungry tigers.'

Skelgill sits back and folds his arms.

They are fast approaching unplumbed depths of which he himself is unsure. Yet the reporter's instinct seems to lie congruent with his own. That the Hares' conviction was overturned on the grounds of flawed process rather than new evidence has long given the police a political lifeline. Despite that Skelgill has received no formal briefing to the effect, the implied corollary of his team's assignment can only be to expose the glistening and rarely glimpsed spring tide mud of police corruption.

'Would you agree, Inspector?'

Jolted from his brown study, Skelgill stares violently.

'Find out who was the officer in overall charge.'

Kendall Minto is nonplussed.

'What – you mean, who was Chief of Police?'

'Whatever.'

He remains bewildered.

'But – surely – you can get that information far more easily than I?'

Skelgill bangs his left fist down on the table. He makes Kendall Minto jump, the crockery jump, and even patrons across the café jump.

Kendall Minto sways back, raising his palms in appeasement.

'Sorry – my mistake – that's why I'm here. You can't do that – alarm bells would ring. Got you.'

The reporter grins endearingly, but Skelgill does not seem amused.

He tries another tack, and meets the older man's stare with a look that is worldly-wise, if patently manufactured.

'I take it it's not just a name that you're looking for?'

'Use your imagination.'

Kendall Minto nods vigorously.

'I shall – I shall. Don't worry, I get it. I'm good with imagination.'

There now ensues a longer hiatus than the several awkward silences thus far. It seems to Kendall Minto that the interview is concluded. He looks about, and then indicates somewhat limply with a hand over the banister rail.

'Er – how shall I contact you?'

Skelgill taps the tabletop.

'Week today. Same time, same place. Anything urgent, phone the front desk and ask for DS Appleby.'

Kendall Minto rises and pulls his jacket from the back of the chair. He peers over the balcony – down below a scowling woman browses, lifting one fleece after another from the dump bin, taking no care in replacing them. He makes to move away – but then hesitates.

'Emma's doing a great job – she's really getting into the weeds. She more or less ran the last joint planning meeting. I take it I can't discuss this with her?'

'Get out while you're ahead.'

He begins to muster an apology, but Skelgill pre-empts him.

'Were you followed here?'

Kendall Minto is taken aback.

'Well – I never thought –'

'There's a staff exit on the lower ground floor. Turn right into the ginnel. Then go through the arcade in the direction of the lake. Don't hang about.'

With a look of alarm gripping his features, the young reporter gives a bow of his head and backs away.

Skelgill monitors his progress, first dispassionately as he delves for and finds his phone, and then with a widening grin as Kendall Minto turns up his collar and makes a self-conscious retreat, glancing nervously about.

When he is out of sight, Skelgill considers the table before him. Kendall Minto's coffee is half-drunk; the coconut shortbread is untouched.

He shrugs and pulls the plate towards him.

14. EPISODE 3: THE CARD

Incident Room 101 – 10.45 a.m. Tuesday 3 August

'Seatbelts fastened?'

'Very funny, Jones.'

DS Leyton chuckles; he gets that his colleague's remark is aimed teasingly at Skelgill and refers to the previous podcast episode, when their superior came off worse in an altercation with the projection screen.

DS Jones hovers over her laptop, narrowing her eyes.

'I'll fast-forward to a significant point. These rushes are completely unedited – but Jen was keen we had them asap, in view of the leads we've been generating.'

DS Leyton snaps his fingers.

'There you go, Guv – someone appreciates our efforts.'

Skelgill looks unconvinced – but his attention is drawn as the video starts rolling. It opens upon a continuous sequence that describes the scene, initially a row of properties of 1960s construction, red brick and plain with small windows. Of three storeys the upper two are residential, flats with small shops at ground level and a wide tarmacked pavement where pedestrians in summer clothes are going about their business or stopping to chat. A couple of kids whizz about on scooters. The camera pans across a hairdresser's advertising its beauty and sunbed services. A convenience store. A pharmacy. A Chinese takeaway. Another convenience store. A chippy. The suburban complement found in little clusters around towns throughout the United Kingdom, perhaps just lacking a bookmaker. Then comes a public green area, quite extensive if uninspiring, with a scattering of buildings. First a café, the Copper Kettle, converted from what looks like it might have been a small stand-alone single storey municipal office of some kind (or possibly public toilets); second a contemporary redbrick church that has a Dutch look about it; third a modern care home – subtly hedged in, also single storey; then, always to Skelgill's eye incongruous in England, a high-fenced basketball court, as proof to his scepticism being used by a group of youths playing football. There are empty park benches. Finally Kate zooms in on a pair of jackdaws picking over the remnants of a chip wrapper among lines of pale grass-cuttings, left in situ to compost inadequately but cheaply.

The scene cuts to Percy Tuseling and Professor Simeon Freud. They are taking up their stances at the edge of the green against the backdrop of the café some thirty yards beyond, across the road. Adjusting his outfit, the former is plainly self-conscious. He wears brown corduroys that are belted too high in the absence of any functional waist. His smartly-pressed grey check shirt is rather tight over his portly form, and the buttoned collar looks positively choking. The professor by contrast wears a loose outdoor shirt outside beige chinos, and his trademark desert boots. He moves casually, as if aware of gawping onlookers, and affectedly brushes at his subtly disorganised hair. He takes a last glance at his crib sheets and then hands them away to producer Jen. She backs off, and calls action.

Before the professor can speak, however, he is pre-empted by Percy Tuseling.

"There's a hairdresser's over there – they might be able to tidy up that mop."

It is the cocky, slightly belligerent persona of the very first passage of the opening episode – indeed there ensues the false laughter that fills the unamused void and simultaneously demands that the joke be acknowledged.

"Yes, well, Percy – I might just take you up on that suggestion."

For a moment Simeon Freud is wrong-footed. The detectives are becoming familiar with the nature of such interchanges. Clearly the professor likes to control the narrative, and he seems disconcerted by Percy Tuseling's put-down. Such joshing banter is not his forte – certainly, when he is the target. But he does have experience and technology on his side. He knows that any awkward moment or imperfect exchange of dialogue can simply be re-recorded, and the original discarded. Accordingly, he waits for a moment, and then begins as if the taunt was never uttered.

"Percy, I've no doubt you'll recognise this area."

Percy Tuseling licks his lips but before he can answer the professor continues.

"We've had an immense response to our podcast – and there is feedback I should put to you. Firstly, one particularly attentive listener has identified a contradiction."

The professor delivers this introduction in a collaborative tone of voice, as though the issue is one that they all share.

"You said that you never mentioned your connection with Caldblow Farm – or Belltower Farm – because it would jeopardise your job with Radio Rentals. You didn't want your boss to know that you also worked at the farms."

Percy Tuseling, despite the professor's best efforts, is immediately guarded.

"Yes."

"And yet – as this person has pointed out – your former colleague Joan Arkwright stated that you often spoke of how you enjoyed working at the farms, and of your friendship with Mr Bell-Gibson."

Simeon Freud waits.

Percy Tuseling's small eyes flick from side to side, reminiscent of a schoolboy apprehended for some misdemeanour, looking for the best direction in which to run.

Just when the professor might be about to prompt him, he responds.

"That was just Joan that knew that. And I never said I worked there. I just said I shot there – as a hobby. She might have assumed I told others, but I never did."

The professor is regarding his subject like a parent knowing their small child is being creative with the truth. There is a faint smile of amusement and a condescending nodding of the head.

"Yes I see, Percy."

Percy Tuseling appears to relax, but it is a false dawn.

"Because, of course, Percy, the inference that could be drawn is that your reason for not telling the police originally about your work at Caldblow Farm was not because of the risk to your job, but because of the risk of being associated with the murder of Will Featherston."

"I thought we'd been over this. Finished with it."

Percy Tuseling's response is terse and irate; the professor seems to detect some incipient hostility, for he leans slightly away.

"Well, yes – of course – we have, Percy – but an important aspect of this project is to let our listeners have input. That will help us produce a rounded product for the final documentary. And there will be people with new information. Memories that are jogged. Which leads me on to why we have come here to Mirehouse today. Even though it is some way from where you lived – and from where Will Featherston lived – about a mile from each location, I understand?"

"Yes."

The question, and that the professor has backed off from the accusatory matter, at least re-engages Percy Tuseling.

"Another listener has been in touch, with a fascinating fragment of information, you might say."

Skelgill folds his arms; it is a reaction of irked vindication. DS Leyton is less restrained, he blurts out an oath and is obliged to apologise to present company. What is about to ensue stems not from the podcast but former Sergeant Jack Dixon's reading of the Westmorland Gazette. No credit where credit is due.

"Percy, this was about an anonymous message on a torn piece of card – do you remember that?"

Simeon Freud has provided only limited information; it is death by a thousand cuts.

Percy Tuseling might have fended off one attack, but now he is cornered.

There are the familiar telltale signs of the repression of a welling up of emotion: the tightening of the narrow lips, a deeper flush across the already ruddy complexion, and the rapid eye movements.

He does not speak.

"Yes, Percy – it was a handwritten note that suggested there was a man who shot on the farm – Caldblow Farm – and who apparently frightened the resident, Lady Fitzrovia. And that this man owned a red vehicle."

"There were hundreds of false reports made to the police."

Now Simeon Freud looms over the shorter man; here comes the coup de grace.

"But only one handed in by you, Percy."

Kate has zoomed right in on Percy Tuseling's beetroot countenance; the close-up enhances the impression that unless the tight collar is unfastened his head will soon explode.

"Surely you remember that, Percy?"

Percy Tuseling growls through gritted teeth, his voice taking on the panicked falsetto.

"That came to nothing."

But the protest is inadequate.

"Percy, let me get this straight. Our listener is a retired police officer – he was on duty at the time. Late at night, you walked into the local police station –" The camera pans out, and Simeon Freud half turns and indicates with an outstretched arm to the creatively named Copper Kettle. "Right behind us, now a community café. And you handed in the note, stating that you had just picked it up in the street. And yet you didn't live around here."

Percy Tuseling shifts stiffly from one foot to the other; he has declined to follow the professor's invitation to look at the small building.

"Come on, Percy. A scrap of cardboard randomly lying on the pavement – addressed to you and referring to the Caldblow Farm murder. And you find it! What are the odds of that? One in a million, surely?"

"It was addressed to me – and it suggested a person *who wasn't me* was the murderer."

Percy Tuseling seems to have moved on from denial.

"Exactly! Of course it did – it pointed to another suspect!"

The professor sounds suddenly warm – that they have reached, albeit painfully, a conclusion that is – after all – of a benefit to Percy Tuseling. It would not seem out of keeping were he to clap the man on the back.

"As a matter of interest, Percy, did the police ever ask for a sample of your handwriting?"

No matter that it is innocently posed, his question rings of duplicity.

"No, they did not."

The professor inserts a long pause, he rubs his chin pensively, all the time looking at Percy Tuseling as though some previously unnoticed feature might reveal a new insight.

"Percy, you can see what I'm trying to clear up, can't you?"

"I can see what you're insinuating – and you're very wrong, I can tell you."

The professor speaks soothingly.

"Percy – as I have mentioned before, I have to pose the obvious questions that our audience will ask." He spreads his arms theatrically and half turns towards the camera. "Unless we drive away these gathering storm clouds, we cannot ascend the sunlit uplands of innocence to reach the shining pinnacle of truth."

Percy Tuseling appears both offended by the content of the abridged soliloquy and affronted by its Shakespearean delivery – it is such an obviously rehearsed line.

But suddenly he is forthcoming, his tone disparaging.

"There is an explanation you've obviously not thought of."

"What's that, Percy?"

Percy Tuseling seems to gather himself. Pulling back his shoulders he seeks out the camera and steps towards it – it is a replay of his eccentric habit to address the unseen viewer, the jury.

"I was with my brother-in-law. Harry Robertson. You can check that out. He could have done it."

Simeon Freud exhibits exaggerated interest.

"What do you mean by that?"

He intones in a coaxing manner – trying too hard, in fact – but Percy Tuseling responds, nevertheless.

"He could have written the message."

"But why would he have done that?"

Percy Tuseling stares for a moment at the professor, and then smirks, as if he thinks he has gained some advantage.

"To put me in the clear."

The professor hesitates.

"Wouldn't you have known that, Percy?"

"He could have dropped it without my seeing, on the way to the club."

"But you found it – in the dark. What would make anyone pick up a piece of litter like that?"

"He could have drawn my attention to it."

"You mean, he did?"

"I can't remember – why would I remember that? But, anyway – I'm a tidy, public-spirited person. I would pick up a piece of litter and put it in a bin."

"Surely, if this Harry Robertson concocted the message – doesn't that imply he suspected you of having some involvement in Will Featherston's murder?"

"Not at all."

The professor narrows his eyes and regards Percy Tuseling doubtfully. But he does not speak and in due course the silence forces his opponent to elaborate.

"Of course he knew that I matched details that had been made public. I had a red Ford Corsair. I worked and shot at the farm."

The professor is nodding pensively.

"But Percy – he misguidedly drew attention to you – don't you think? By doing something that surely even the most dim-witted of detectives would deduce was such an impossible coincidence – that it had to be you. You had panicked because you had been interviewed for a second time and were trying desperately to invent some non-existent scapegoat."

The professor looks and sounds as if he is taking Percy Tuseling's side, that he sympathises with his predicament – but it is a form of passive aggression – for his words are barbed.

Percy Tuseling seems unable to speak.

"You see that, Percy – don't you? It would have been counter-productive."

Percy Tuseling manages a choked, high-pitched rejoinder; he merely repeats himself.

"Well – it came to nothing, didn't it?"

The professor gazes skywards, contemplating this answer.

"Well, so it seems. Was your brother-in-law asked? Did you ask him?"

"I did not. I've no idea if the police asked him."

"Can we ask him?"

In Percy Tuseling's eyes there is a sudden flicker of smugness.

"You can certainly try. Go down to Low Road and see how you get on. Take a clairvoyant with you."

He emits a burst of his faux laughter.

The professor responds cautiously.

"Are you saying he has passed away?"

Percy Tuseling chuckles again, now triumphantly.

"Where's your famous research? Low Road's the cemetery!"

This time Simeon Freud does not appear disconcerted by the gleeful jibe.

"Harry Robertson – he would have been the husband of your first wife Veronica's sister?"

Percy Tuseling is suddenly respectful; he lowers his gaze.

"Cynthia. Also passed away."

The professor is nodding thoughtfully – but it is plain that he steals a glance at the producer, off camera, and it seems a signal is passed to Kate, for the shot closes in to frame Percy Tuseling's face.

"You also had a little sideline with Harry Robertson – together you ran a second-hand goods stall?"

The professor's tone is inquiring, almost apologetic – but it generates an instant retort from Percy Tuseling.

"I did not."

"Oh."

The professor is plainly knocked off his stride, such is the vehemence of the denial. For a moment he looks a little angered – but he turns to the crew to raise his hands in a gesture that indicates he expects this footage to hit the cutting room floor.

"Ange – do you have the notes?"

Skelgill folds his arms, but does not comment.

DS Jones – her alias now further shortened – appears in shot, and hands a sheaf of papers to Simeon Freud. He looks a little confused, and she has to lean closer to point out what he seeks.

Then he gives a nod of satisfaction and presses a palm on her shoulder as he returns the crib sheets. DS Jones reverses out of sight. The professor indicates he is ready to begin.

"Percy – you say not – but the same former policer officer to whom you handed the card identified you with Mr Robertson manning a stall at the Mirehouse gala the following summer. You were wearing your cricket whites."

Beyond his customary look of discomfort and ire, Percy Tuseling gives little away.

"That was a one-off charity fete, for the local community centre."

The professor regards him earnestly.

"Well, perhaps that was something else about your brother-in-law that you didn't know about."

"I don't think so."

"You can see, Percy, why this might be significant?"

"I don't see what it's got to do with anything."

"Well – if we go back to what led up to Will Featherston's killing – and you previously agreed with this – he disturbed a burglary at Caldblow Farm. Antiques were stolen."

"That's what would be stolen. That was the business the Hare twins were in. You didn't steal electric kettles and pots and pans."

"But it's another to add to the list of coincidences. You had a connection to a man who may have dealt in antiques – unofficially so, with no fixed place of business, who would be hard to trace – and you were connected to a farm where such a theft took place."

The ire has gained the upper hand, and Percy Tuseling steps closer to the professor, his tone menacing.

"This is yet another one of your ridiculous insinuations, Simeon. If it's all so obvious, why didn't the police work it out at the time and do something about it?"

"Well, some might say the Hares inadvertently rode to the rescue of Will Featherston's real killer. It was just a few days after you handed in the anonymous card that they robbed Kirkstile Farm and were arrested. In short order they were charged for Will Featherston's murder."

The inference is plain – not that it has been, or is ever, far beneath the surface of the professor's baldly disingenuous probing.

Skelgill shifts uncomfortably in his seat. Kendall Minto's view of Simeon Freud's agenda seems right enough – although Percy Tuseling appears to be far from a confession. He is tongue-tied, but pugnacious and still firmly in the fight.

The camera pans out and the professor seems to know to ply the viewer with one of his trademark looks, an invitation to feast upon the evidence he has so expertly unearthed for their delectation.

Percy Tuseling, meanwhile, storms out of shot.

The video sequence concludes.

'Cor blimey – he really winds him up, don't he?'

It is DS Leyton's observation.

'He's enough to wind anyone up.'

Skelgill's tone is dispassionate.

'I'm surprised Tuseling ain't swung for him, Guv.'

Skelgill appears to share the sentiment. But he turns to address DS Jones.

'What happened after that?'

She shakes her head.

'Actually – he came around quite quickly. He knows which side his bread's buttered. And he thinks he performs better than he does. He may not realise until they air the documentary that it's such a car crash. Or that he comes across as so intimidating. You could well believe he's a killer.'

Skelgill stares at her.

'He is.'

'Ah – yes – but, you know?'

Skelgill nods.

'Will Featherston.'

There is a short silence before DS Leyton makes an observation.

'He's got no scruples, has he – the Prof? He's claiming all the credit. I should think your pal Minto's well brassed off.'

DS Jones glances briefly at Skelgill before she replies.

'Well, I suppose at least he can make something of it in his next article. There's probably not much overlap between the audiences for the different media.'

Skelgill casts a hand towards the blank screen.

'How come Minto's not on the scene? Seeing as the Gazette's a big part of this.'

It takes her a moment to compose an answer.

'Sim doesn't want the set overcrowded – he feels it will inhibit Percy Tuseling.'

DS Jones looks like she realises this is an incomplete answer. But just as she is about to improvise, a message alert causes her to glance at her mobile telephone.

She picks up the handset.

'Ah. This is interesting.' She opens the message and frowns as she reflects upon its evident import. 'It's from Jen – confidential – I mean, she hasn't mentioned it to Sim.'

She looks up with some urgency, first at DS Leyton – who is open mouthed – and Skelgill – who is grave.

'It's a lead – a listener to last Friday's podcast – Episode Two.'

DS Leyton asks the question.

'Who is it?'

'A Mrs Veronica Smith, née Collinson. Percy Tuseling's first wife.'

15. VERONICA

Carlisle – 2.20 p.m. Tuesday 3 August

'So, Mrs Smith – what made you decide to get in touch?'

Despite that there has been a lengthy preamble, including the detectives' admission and introduction, and the procurement of a pot of tea and a plate of digestive biscuits – a process that, due to the elderly lady's infirmity, DS Leyton and Skelgill have assisted – the woman seems short of an answer to this vital question.

Skelgill in fact is not even seated. He stands behind the settee on which his colleague sits and is facing out of the large, low window, which he realises is designed with a disability in mind. Veronica Smith does not use a wheelchair, but she has made unnecessary apologies for the rheumatoid arthritis that inhibits free movement. The modern ground-floor apartment is well appointed and clean and tidy, and contrary to Skelgill's expectations – being part of a three-storey development of sheltered housing – is really no different to any ordinary modern flat – the window height being an exception, along with similar foresight in the placement of plug sockets, light switches, door handles and suchlike.

Beyond the pane and just across a playing field curls a great meander of the River Eden. In finding the location, Skelgill a few minutes earlier misdirected his colleague past the property and ultimately into a dead-end parking area shaded by shimmering poplars. Before DS Leyton could engage reverse gear, Skelgill had baled out, muttering that he had "best just check the level", and had proceeded on foot where he had stationed himself at the centre of the century-old steel cantilever construction that is Carlisle's memorial footbridge dedicated to lives tragically lost in the Great War.

He had returned a few minutes later, merely with the cryptic phrase, "Confluence of the Petteril", and landing in the passenger seat had jerked a thumb over his shoulder. "It's back the way, Leyton."

Veronica Smith née Collinson formerly Tuseling they now know to be seventy years old, and a widow of four years – the death of her husband John Smith having precipitated her move into assisted living, where janitorial services are available around the clock and limited communal facilities provide the opportunity for company, and social events with other residents. The detectives' arrival coincided with a delivery for Mrs Smith of frozen ready-meals – indeed, she had first mistaken DS Leyton – bearing the large, heavy box – for the courier. It had been a convenient ice-breaker, however, and while tea was mashed DS Leyton simultaneously stacked the freezer and made a suitable exposition. The small hurdle – the contradiction – that she had rung the podcast hotline and yet here are the police, he overcame via the double-glazing salesperson's pitch of "being in the area" and their wish to respond promptly to her call while Turnpike Media are filming elsewhere in the county; and that in any event they are working in close cooperation. This explanation was accepted without consternation, and perhaps – Skelgill has detected – even a small degree of relief.

He has been reticent to join in, though it is not out of character. His colleague has superior skills in ingratiation and small talk, and the patience of a parent when it comes to – to put it bluntly – the more trusting of folk. Skelgill is better equipped when their target approaches his own levels of cunning. He has been waiting for the initial brouhaha to die down. He gazes benignly, weighing in his left hand a tiny brass ornament that he has picked up from the windowsill. Though he is hardly aware he has it, its intrinsic heaviness for an object so small both satisfies and fascinates him. It is hardly one inch by two, yet his guess is a good five ounces. He opens his palm and regards the item – part polished, part tarnished where rubbing cannot reach, it is a rendition of the Three Wise Monkeys. He allows himself a rueful grin – there is one not dissimilar on the mantelpiece in his mother's Buttermere cottage; as a child he would inspect it and ponder its surely hypocritical ethos.

See no evil, hear no evil, speak no evil.

And now the delay in the woman's reply to DS Leyton's question prompts him to turn and regard her properly for the first time. He thinks she looks older than her age, though her curling hair is black and appears naturally so. She is broad of face and beam, with small wideset blue eyes that are watery and somehow troubled; indeed her default expression in response to a question – as now – is a grimace that reveals irregular teeth; it the sort of face pulled when a person is asked to do something beyond their office or comfort zone, an expression of unspoken qualms typically accompanied by a sharp intake of breath.

And yet, despite this habit, she has responded candidly to DS Leyton's conversational if fact-finding enquiries that have filled in the broad gaps in her background, including a brief tour of photographs ranged upon a dresser that portray her in her younger days with the late John Smith, and their children – a girl and a boy – and grandchildren – two families whom she says "live down south".

And again, now, despite the precursor of the grimace that suggests a negation of each question, she is once more forthcoming. Perhaps the reaction simply reflects the physical discomfort with which she is sadly afflicted and bears otherwise with stoicism. Perhaps even small movements cause her pain.

'I thought it were about time I told my side of the story.'

Skelgill takes a last lingering look at the ornament and replaces it. He rounds the sofa and takes a seat, and picks up the cup that has been filled for him, and a biscuit, which he immediately dunks and swallows whole without any reference to those around. The woman watches but does not seem perturbed.

There is a lot to unpack in her answer.

DS Leyton is wise to this, and waits to see if Skelgill will make the first move. But he just takes a second biscuit.

DS Leyton makes a couple of short notes.

Skelgill leans slightly and squints at what his colleague has written. "About time." And "My side".

Evidently more pins being put in – for his subordinate resumes on a somewhat different tack, which interests Skelgill.

'Mrs Smith, are you hoping to be interviewed – for the documentary?'

Again there is the grimace that bares the teeth, the corners of the mouth downturned.

'What if he found out where I live?'

'You mean, Mr Tuseling?'

'Aye. And he'd be able to recognise us.'

DS Leyton shoots a glance of alarm at Skelgill. The implications of what she has said, aside, there is a requirement to improvise. Skelgill leaves him to it.

'Madam, you must have seen programmes where a witness appears as a dark silhouette, perhaps against a window – and their voice is changed. That's easily done.'

Skelgill shifts a little uncomfortably in his seat. At just this moment they are on shaky ground. They may have been imprecise about their function, but DS Leyton is straying into territory that is the exclusive province of Turnpike Media. And yet their decision that Veronica Smith is too important a potential witness to give first dibs to Simeon Freud (interestingly, a view evidently shared by producer Jen), feels already to be correct – despite that she is still to furnish them with anything of import.

She gurns once more; the impression is that now confronted with the reality of interviews and interrogation she is having second thoughts.

Skelgill intervenes.

'Mrs Smith. You can just speak to us.'

He leaves it at that – he does not try to confuse her with elaboration.

The woman nods, perhaps reassured – but then offers an unexpected retort.

'He's making a pretty packet – so Ada reckons.' She lifts a hand to indicate the dividing wall. 'She's in t' next flat.'

DS Leyton probes tentatively.

'Madam – what do you think about that?'

She shakes her head vehemently.

'It'd be a bit like blood money, wouldn't it? I shouldn't want owt like that.'

DS Leyton's hulking shoulders might just relax a little.

'You don't think Mr Tuseling should profit from what he's doing?'

There is the face again – but they are now getting used to the fact that she will apparently disagree before agreeing.

'It int' right, is it? After what he did. To Mr Bell-Gibson, and Susan – and to me.'

When Skelgill might nudge his colleague, DS Leyton is alert to the opening – and keen to make progress.

'Mrs Smith, the first podcast episode was about Mr Tuseling and the shooting of Colin Bell-Gibson. Roughly a year after the murder of Will Featherston.'

This time the facial contortion is accompanied by a distinct shudder.

'Aye – I were there. For Colin.'

DS Leyton waits for a moment.

'How well did you know Mr Bell-Gibson?'

'Not all that well. We'd been round a few times.'

'But Mr Tuseling knew him well?'

'Aye. He were there often. Regular part-time working – and shooting.'

She seems to baulk at the mention of shooting.

'I've blanked it mostly from me mind – like I dreamt it. It were like a dream – a bad dream. I had nightmares for a long time after.'

'I can see you're upset, madam – even now – it must have been a terrifying ordeal. And we've read your original statement, and the other statements and reports. There's no need to go over any of those events again.'

Despite DS Leyton's reassurance, she continues in a matter-of-fact manner.

'I thought he were going to kill us – and Susan – and then probably turn the gun on himself. I'd seen him angry, he had a short fuse, but that night he were possessed by the devil.'

DS Leyton takes a drink of his tea. He makes brief eye contact with Skelgill; they have seen glimpses of the inner demon.

'Was he a violent man?'

She shakes her head slowly.

'Never towards me. He might punch a wall or a door. I heard he'd been in a few fights when he were younger. He did body-building at the sports club. Once he did threaten a drunk who was pestering me in a bar – put the fear of God into him.'

DS Leyton again adapts to a useful cue.

'Mr Tuseling at his trial, and ever after – in parole hearings, for example – he declined to give a plain reason for why he shot Mr Bell-Gibson. He claimed it was a moment of madness brought on by drinking too much. But of course the jury didn't accept that – largely because he took a gun outside and sawed off the barrel – which proved premeditation.'

The woman is nodding.

'But in the first podcast he finally gave a reason. And, if I can put it delicately, madam – he is now suggesting that he was protecting your honour. That Mr Bell-Gibson had made a lewd suggestion, to which Mr Tuseling took extreme umbrage.'

Having listened earnestly, Veronica Smith surprises the detectives with a scoff of disparagement.

'And now he's parading his fancy women! St Bees Head – that's where he used to take me when we were courting.'

DS Leyton opts for the diversion.

'Are you referring to the lady, Joan Arkwright, who appeared in the second podcast?'

'Aye – and the rest.'

'Do you mean that Mr Tuseling had several girlfriends, and that you knew about it?'

'I didn't know – but I suspected.'

She regards them in turn with a look of apprehension, as though she feels they might not approve of such feminine intuition when it is applied to a congenital flaw in the male race.

DS Leyton reverts to the main thrust of his inquiry.

'Thinking about Mr Tuseling's explanation – that he took offence when Mr Bell-Gibson apparently suggested – not to put too fine a point on it – some sort of group sexual activity – you don't believe that?'

It takes her a moment to respond; her lips are compressed and she frowns. After a moment she shakes her head.

DS Leyton proceeds, a little disjointedly now.

'Can I ask – was that something – that you – as a couple – ever engaged in?'

'Certainly not. Not me.'

'What about Mr Tuseling?'

'Not that I knew of. But I didn't know about the floozies, neither. He said he were shooting or summat. How was I to know if he weren't?'

There is a pause, and before DS Leyton can speak Skelgill interjects.

'Mrs Smith – what about Mr Bell-Gibson? Since he apparently suggested it?'

She meets Skelgill's gaze a little uncertainly.

'Like I say – I only met him a few times. Maybe three or four.' Veronica Smith squeezes the fingers of one hand with those of the other. She furrows her brow pensively. 'I mean – he had a roving eye. And wandering hands, especially after he'd had a drink. But that were just normal back in them days.'

DS Leyton, however, is looking a little alarmed. He voices his concern.

'Do you think he could have made the suggestion that Mr Tuseling claims?'

But the woman eyes him with dismay.

'That were his *daughter* there with us. It were just the four of us. And he were much older – the age me father would have been. I were only twenty-four in 1977.'

DS Leyton raises a hand; she makes a compelling argument.

'Mrs Smith, you weren't asked to testify at Mr Tuseling's trial, and the statement you made from hospital just described the sequence of events that you witnessed. I appreciate you would want to forget about such a dreadful experience – but you must have wondered, if it wasn't for the reason we've just discussed – and if it wasn't a drunken fit, which the jury didn't accept – *why did Mr Tuseling shoot Mr Bell-Gibson?*'

She is shaking her head before DS Leyton has finished his question, and despite the rising emphasis in his voice.

'Aye, I know. But, God's honour, I really don't know. It were just out't blue. One minute we were sitting there – the next Percy came back in and all hell broke loose.'

DS Leyton nods understandingly.

'There's been speculation – and it's been suggested in the podcast – that Mr Bell-Gibson had some evidence that Mr Tuseling was involved in the murder of Will Featherston, a year before. And on that night he said something that caused Mr Tuseling to decide to silence him.'

'And a lot of good that did him.'

Her answer is the pragmatic retort – the overarching flaw in the logic of committing one blatant murder to cover up another. The mitigation of a lesser sentence for manslaughter hardly seems a calculation that would be made in the heat of the moment. A more likely explanation would simply be that the act was the product of an unstable personality and an irrational, illogical mind.

But DS Leyton seems to detect that she is not entirely satisfied.

'Madam?'

She makes the habitual grimace.

'There were some things. I don't mean about what Colin might have known. I mean – well – coincidences.' She hesitates. 'Things that weren't right. Happen I didn't put two and two together at the time.'

DS Leyton is quick to reassure her.

'Madam, you'll know from the podcast – there's a whole string of coincidences that cast events in a new light. You'd be far from alone in thinking that.'

She nods pensively.

'When I got home he were acting all strange.'

DS Leyton noticeably under-reacts and Skelgill is sitting perfectly still. It seems she has taken the plunge.

'Do you mean when the news came out – on the day of Will Featherston's murder?'

'Aye.'

'In what way strange?'

DS Leyton's voice is relaxed, almost conversational.

'When I got in from work, he were in t' back garden. He'd hung his work trousers on the line. He never did any washing.

And he were agitated. I could see through the window, his body language.'

She hesitates, narrowing her eyes as she recalls the scene.

'I did notice – but I didn't notice. It were a long time after that I wondered about it. I were distracted, you see? I'd heard on the radio that there'd been a shooting at Caldblow Farm. I knew Percy worked there – shot there – but his car were in t' driveway when I got back.'

'That was a relief?'

'Aye. I thought it might have been him that was shot. An accident.'

'Did he appear to know about it?'

She scowls and shakes her head – but her expression is inconclusive.

'He said he weren't feeling well – I must have thought that was something to do with the trousers.'

DS Leyton waits, but when she does not elaborate, he moves on.

'Did you ask him if he had been at Caldblow Farm that day?'

'Aye. I did. I did ask him that. He said he'd been at his work.'

'Did you have any suspicions?'

'Not then. They'd said on t' news it were a robbery – and that the criminals had fled the scene. I didn't associate that with Percy. Maybe I did have a worry a bit later.'

'In what way?'

'Percy had gone to bed early. Like I say – he were in bad fettle. It came on News At Ten that it were a boy that had been shot – they named him – Will Featherston. And I remembered we used to live near a family called Featherston.'

DS Leyton nods encouragingly.

'I must have panicked a bit when I heard that. I ran up to Percy – he were still awake, like. I shook his arm and said please to God you've had nowt to do with it.'

'How did he react?'

'He were like – don't be ridiculous. That he'd been at work. But then he kind of sat up – all serious like – and he said he'd have to get rid of his gun.'

'He owned a gun – a shotgun?'

'Aye.'

DS Leyton is finding it difficult not to look at Skelgill; but Skelgill has sunk back into his seat and is literally maintaining a low profile.

'Why would he have to get rid of it?'

'He said the police would find out he shot there – he said, don't you think they'll be after me – it's on my patch. Then he said he were in the toilets for a long a time – if someone at his work had been looking for him, they might have thought he weren't there.'

'Did that make you more suspicious?'

The grimace. But this time her reply is largely in the negative.

'When someone's your husband – you want to believe them – for better or worse. He were older than me – I'd always looked up to him – like an authority figure. I trusted him. And I suppose I didn't want to ask questions against him.'

DS Leyton is nodding.

'You say that when you heard the name Featherston it shocked you.'

The grimace.

'I mean – I didn't work owt out – not like that professor's said – that the boy were shot because he recognised the burglar. I were just shocked because we knew who the family were. It brought it home – that it weren't just another story you hear on the news.'

DS Leyton waits, but Veronica Smith is finished.

'You said there were some things – is there more?'

She has been looking with a frown at her clasped hands, as though she perhaps suffers some seller's remorse in relating her memories.

'It were me sister, Cynthia. She told me summat.'

There is a longer pause, and now it takes a prompt from DS Leyton.

'Is this also in connection to Will Featherston?'

She gives a half shake of her head.

'She said she'd seen Percy go into her Harry's toolshed with a bag.'

'At the time of the murder?'

'It were later she mentioned it – a few weeks later. So she didn't know when exactly – just it were one afternoon before her Harry got back from work. She remembered it were a hot day – but they were all hot days that year.'

'Did she investigate the bag?'

'No – but, afterwards, Harry told her that Percy had brought him some antiques for his stall – and he'd made Percy take them away again because he thought they were stolen.'

Now the detectives do exchange a brief glance. They seem to know to wait until the woman continues.

'But that were a queer thing. You see – Harry – Harry Robertson his name was – he's dead now and so is Cynthia – he had this little antiques business on the side – and truth be told he wouldn't have asked too many questions about where stuff came from. He were a good-hearted fellow but it weren't easy to make ends meet in the Seventies – what with all the strikes and the Three-Day Week. He were laid off a lot. Folk would do what they could.'

'Have you any idea what the items were?'

'None at all. Just it were a bag – like a carpet bag. She noticed that – it looked expensive, like. She said it were a fancy pattern – they were all the rage in the Sixties.'

'So it wasn't Mr Tuseling's bag – or one that he'd borrowed from you?'

'Nay.'

'Did you speak of it with Mr Tuseling?'

Veronica Smith looks rather guiltily at DS Leyton. Her tone is regretful.

'No, I never did. Like I say – I didn't want to think about the bad side of it. There were these connections – but he was my husband. I couldn't believe he'd be involved in summat like that.'

DS Leyton nods sympathetically.

'Did he often supply antiques to Mr Robertson? Were they in partnership?'

She makes her regular face.

'He did from time to time. Because Percy's job took him about the county, he would pick things up cheap at markets and second-hand shops and house clearance auctions. He'd occasionally help Harry – but mainly Harry did his stall in summer at fetes and galas and Percy would be playing his cricket.'

Skelgill watches while DS Leyton catches up with a few notes, writing with slow determination in his neat condensed script.

Veronica Tuseling seems to wait until he has dotted I's and crossed T's.

'But he were interested in antiques – specially old tools and weapons. And he'd sometimes buy and sell a shotgun, because he had a licence – and he did shooting anyway. But then they caught them Hares – and they'd got a gun – and that seemed to settle it. It were a relief, truth be told.'

Skelgill now makes one of his limited interventions.

'The Hare twins were sentenced shortly before the incident at Belltower Farm. Were you aware of that?'

'Aye, folk were always talking about it. First, who killed Will Featherston. Then it were the Hares. Then they were claiming innocence – but they were found guilty. Then a campaign started.'

Skelgill persists.

'What about on the actual night Mr Tuseling shot Mr Bell-Gibson?'

'I can't rightly remember, but – like I say – it were never far from the surface. I'd be surprised if we didn't mention it. Colin seemed to like controversy, as you might say. He would start political arguments and that. He were always slagging off the strikers, calling them reds under the bed. He sometimes made you feel uncomfortable – but he seemed to enjoy that, too.'

Skelgill nods but has no more to add.

DS Leyton has turned back to the opening page of his notes. He marks a small neat tick against the phrase "My side".

'Mrs Smith, you said it was about time you spoke out. What is it now, that's made you feel like that?'

She wrings her hands and seems to suffer a jolt of pain – as if it is a small penance for her conduct.

'He's forced my hand – this publicity in the papers and the podcast – and they're making a programme.'

Again DS Leyton casts a glance at Skelgill. This is a slightly contradictory way of putting it. Her explanation thus far covers a spectrum of motives ranging from resentment to injustice.

But perhaps she, too, senses this inadequacy. Though she is finding it difficult to put into words. It takes her a few moments more to elaborate – perhaps she is even working out for herself for the first time what it means to her.

'When it happened – and I were in hospital – and I were in shock – and I was repulsed by the thought of what he'd done – and of ever seeing him again. The last memory of him hitting me with the butt of the gun.'

She pauses, but the detectives understand to be patient.

'The police were very considerate – they said I needn't have anything to do with him. I needn't go into court. I didn't have to see him or speak to him.'

She looks now a little urgently from one detective to the other.

'In fact they said they would be more likely to get a conviction if I didn't. That that was probably what I wanted, wasn't it? Then he were tried and convicted and sentenced – eighteen years – it *were* a relief. I wanted to blank it from my mind and I didn't want folk coming up and sympathising. They call it PTSD nowadays, don't they? I got a divorce and I applied for a job up here in Carlisle under my maiden name. That's where I met John – at Shaddon Mill, where we both worked. And I just started a new life here.'

To sign off her monologue she gestures to indicate the photographs on the dresser. DS Leyton turns obligingly to look. They know Percy Tuseling had no children. So here is the simple explanation for his first wife's disappearance from public view – something she engineered for entirely understandable reasons. Why be tarred with the brush of a cold-blooded killer? Never mind the trauma she underwent that night at Belltower Farm. Sweep it under the rug and forget all about it. A new identity and – as she says – a new life.

But long-buried sentiments have been exhumed, exposed by the glare of media revelation. Percy Tuseling has risen zombie-like, seeking vindication for his deeds and exoneration of public slurs. So now she needs to talk, to unburden herself – such that she might lay the ghost that was never truly exorcised.

DS Leyton turns his gaze to the woman; she seems to understand what he is thinking.

'Mrs Smith – I expect your family don't know about this, do they?'

She gives a jerk of her head that is ambiguous.

'Now the world and his wife's finding out about it.'

'You could have stayed silent. But you felt there was something wrong about that.'

His words are designed as a comforting statement rather than a question, and she nods in agreement, though still somewhat pained by the idea.

DS Leyton turns to look at Skelgill.

To his surprise, his superior appears entirely disengaged.

Skelgill is staring across the room, at nothing in particular – they face a cream-painted plasterboard wall. But his expression is such that he might be looking at an alarming sight. Indeed – in this, the land of the grimace – he contrives a facial contortion to rival anything that Veronica Smith has achieved.

'Guv?'

Skelgill snaps out of his dwam.

Directly, he addresses Veronica Smith.

'You've told us a lot more than you know.'

The woman blinks several times under Skelgill's solemn gaze. It is apparent he will not elaborate – but, all the same, she is empowered to pose what must be for her the burning question.

'Will you be re-opening the investigation into the murder of Will Featherston?'

Skelgill responds with a question of his own.

'Do you think Mr Tuseling was involved in that murder?'

Just when they might think she will jump at the chance to agree, there comes the grimace – the more extreme version that is a harbinger of doubt. Her eyes seem more tearful than before – and perhaps a small battle takes place behind them, a contest between once-betrothed loyalty and the trauma of ill-treatment.

'I think he knows more than he's admitting to.'

16. APPLES AND ORANGES

Blindkirk – 9.45 p.m. Wednesday 4 August

'They've been in there a good hour, now, Guv.'

Skelgill does not react, though his gaze shifts to his quarter-full glass, as though it were a form of sand-timer. He wonders if he has ever eked out a pint to last quite so long. Though working outside of normal hours, they are technically on duty, and his no-alcohol rule is one he rarely breaks. There are other options, but by this time of a day he is tea'd out – and DS Leyton, manfully drinking mineral water, is driving.

Now he cranes to see the sky.

'Give it five more minutes. It's clouding over.'

He expects his subordinate to understand the corollary.

'What time did they wrap up last week?'

'Well after dark.'

DS Leyton nods and sips, the small glass pathetic in his large hands.

'Them having a regular night, Guv – makes it seem like something organised is going on. If Tuseling is up to his tricks – *still* up to his tricks, I mean. The more I think about this case, the more I reckon it hinges on his motive for shooting Colin Bell-Gibson.'

Skelgill eyes his colleague suspiciously. But he does not demur. He moves to take a drink, but has second thoughts, as if there might only be one swig left and now is not quite the moment.

'Don't you agree, Guv?'

Skelgill takes a long time to answer.

'Happen that's what we're doing here, Leyton.'

He does not sound entirely convincing. In Skelgill's parlance, *happen* lives on a fairly broad spectrum, a scale that ranges from the indefinite to the certain.

It is left for DS Leyton to speculate.

'I wondered, Guv. Veronica Smith. I mean – she seemed pretty candid – but this swinging malarkey – I can see why she might not have wanted to admit that to us. It's a bit embarrassing, ain't it? As it is, she's worried that her identity's going to come out.'

Here Skelgill more plainly disagrees.

'I reckon she wants her family to know, Leyton – at least, that she was married to Tuseling. Now her arl fella's gone. She wants the monkey off her back.'

He suffers a jolt – it is the memory of the small but mighty brass ornament. The conjoined trio that shuns controversy.

DS Leyton curtails his boss's musings.

'But maybe not about any shenanigans, Guv. Folk were more prudish back in those days. She even called it courting. I reckon sex was a bit of a dirty word.'

But Skelgill only glowers.

'Leyton – they called it the Swinging Seventies.'

DS Leyton looks somewhat perplexed.

'I thought that was the Sixties, Guv?'

'It's all the same to me, Leyton.'

DS Leyton alternately raises his shoulders.

'From what we've been hearing, it sounds more like it was the Striking Seventies.'

Skelgill frowns at this. It does not take a political historian to share the folk memory that haunts Cumbria – and much of the North – a decade of strikes in the 1970s ushered in a decade of closures and mass unemployment in the 1980s, read by many as right-wing retribution wreaked upon the recalcitrant workers.

The notion of the attendant hardship prompts a segue that may not be obvious to his deputy.

'Where are we with the burglaries – and the Caldblow Farm inventory?'

DS Leyton exhales a little frustratedly.

'I've been promised something for tomorrow on the rural thefts. We've had to get IT to crunch the numbers – make sure any result is statistically significant. DC Watson's still working on the inventory. If it's there, she'll find it – she's like a dog with a bone – but it's a heck of a bone and a very small dog. Well – smallish.' DC Watson is a member of the rugby team.

Skelgill again looks at his pint, and again resists a drink.

He leans close to the window. The darker it gets outside, the harder it is becoming to see past their own reflections. He can just discern the illuminated attic of the bungalow across the road. But still he sits tight.

'I thought that was pretty compelling, Guv – the carpet bag full of swag.'

Skelgill nods.

'Pity she couldn't tell us when – or what was in it.'

DS Leyton, too, is nodding.

'He'd be more or less bang to rights if we could pin the robbery on him, Guv. I wonder what he did with it.'

'Happen he'll tell us.'

At this DS Leyton looks shocked.

'Are you planning on calling his bluff, Guv?'

However, Skelgill scowls and looks away. So pressed, he seems some way from being confident about the strength of their hand.

But DS Leyton plays another of the cards won from Veronica Smith.

'And he had a shotgun that he didn't admit to.'

Skelgill seems even less animated by this revelation.

'There was no shortage of guns, Leyton. You said it yourself.'

'I get that, Guv – but there's a pattern of behaviour. He did everything he could to distance himself from the two farms. And he had no qualms about misleading the police.'

Skelgill nods, but his demeanour is still lacklustre.

DS Leyton, however, is getting into his stride.

'And why was he washing his trousers?'

Skelgill replies in what might be described as locker-room language.

'I know, Guv – sounds like that's what his missus thought – but it could have been blood.'

Skelgill now makes eye contact with his subordinate.

'Why just the trousers? Will Featherston was killed at point-blank range. The shot was fired chest-high.'

DS Leyton has to accept the point.

He makes a summing-up gesture with his two hands.

'What she did have to say, Guv – imagine if they'd not copped the Hares and had interviewed her instead. Tuseling would have been right back in the frame for Will Featherston's killing. And he admitted to her – he wasn't even in his workshop all the time.'

Skelgill grimaces; it is an action replay of the woman's default expression.

'I reckon she lived in fear of him.'

DS Leyton reluctantly concurs.

'Right enough – she probably would have clammed up – or at least toed his line. But I tell you what – I believe that story about the swag – and that the brother-in-law made Tuseling get shot of it. What do you say to him being the mystery caller?'

Skelgill appears surprised by this – though there is at least a gleam in his eye.

'Why would he cant on family?'

DS Leyton shrugs.

'He was no blood relation to Tuseling, was he? Maybe there was no love lost. The fact is – he rejected the antiques, whatever. If Tuseling told him they were from Caldblow Farm – it wouldn't take a genius to deduce who shot Will Featherston. Fencing's one thing, Guv – but accessory to murder – that's beyond the pale.'

Skelgill regards DS Leyton pensively. His own sentiments extend somewhat further. Never mind being tarred with the brush of Percy Tuseling's felony – there is, after all, the moral imperative.

But he remains silent.

'Do you reckon we should get the Prof to put these points to him? We kind of left it with Veronica Smith that we wouldn't blow her cover.'

Skelgill seems indifferent to this argument.

'It doesn't have to blow her cover. It's just easier for Tuseling to deny, when it's presented as hearsay.'

'I reckon they'll want to get her on camera, Guv.'

Skelgill is nodding, though his features are grim.

'It may not come to that.'

He peers out once more, his face close to the small window. Now he drains his glass and rises.

'Howay, Leyton. Burke and Hare strike again.'

'I thought they were grave robbers, Guv?'

'And the rest.'

DS Leyton considers the last of his mineral water before leaving it untouched.

Skelgill first walks as if he is heading to their car – but seeing they are unobserved he strides past the vehicle and beyond the cone of downlight cast by a streetlamp affixed to a telegraph pole.

The bungalow adjacent to the Tuselings' is a holiday home called "Nooky Corner" and is clearly unoccupied. It shows no lights, nor is there any car in the driveway. Skelgill ducks into the darkness afforded by the dividing hedge of dense holly and moves almost silently over the gravel. DS Leyton, in his wake, less so.

Though there has been no exertion yet, DS Leyton is a little wheezy. There is the impending thrill of action – and he has no idea of what is his superior's plan. He assumes their route is to avoid the security light over the Tuseling's front door.

The prickly barrier of holly is impenetrable. Has Skelgill done a recce? Perhaps so – for at the very end, where the boundary line forms a T-junction with the hawthorn hedgerow that borders fields, what otherwise would be a gap between the two gardens is filled by a single six-foot larch-lap fencing panel.

Without reference to his less nimble and shorter colleague, using the horizontal strut halfway up Skelgill scales it in Spider-Man fashion and drops noiselessly to the other side.

By the time DS Leyton has performed a less graceful version of the manoeuvre Skelgill has retraced their parallel tracks into the deeper shadows at the side of the Tuselings' bungalow.

'Guv?'

DS Leyton's appeal is hissed.

Skelgill makes a kind of *psst* to reveal his location.

Now panting, DS Leyton heaves alongside.

Skelgill is surveying the eaves, which descend to about eight feet above the ground. Reaching up, he can just wrap his fingertips around the plastic gutter, but it would never bear his weight. The tiled roof inclines at forty-five degrees to one of the four dormer windows of the attic room.

'You can't go up the roof, Guv.'

DS Leyton's whisper conveys his alarm.

Skelgill casts about, straining to see in the semi-darkness; an ambient glow from the loft above gives a vague outline of their surroundings. They are hemmed in between the cottage and the holly hedge, a passageway with lawn underfoot of about ten feet in width. Halfway between, an ancient apple tree, rising almost to the height of the apex of the roof overarches them. It has no low boughs. But at its base there is what may be a coal bunker or log store, a dark felt-covered cube of about four feet in all dimensions with a sloping hinged lid.

'There, Leyton. Get on – and give us a bunk up.'

'I don't reckon I'll balance, Guv.'

There is consternation in his sergeant's voice.

Skelgill ignores him – and begins to step across when suddenly an internal light comes on just feet from where they stand. Instinctively they simultaneously duck and scramble behind the bin.

It is the kitchen. Peering over the top of the bunker they can see washing-up liquid and a potted Christmas cactus on the inner sill. Skelgill rises higher and DS Leyton apes his movement.

'They can't see out.'

By *they* he means the man and woman – not the Tuselings – who are getting refills for drinks. The man holds a tray of glasses while the woman tops them up with a ginger-coloured liquid from a large glass jug, presumably taken from the refrigerator. Skelgill recognises them.

'That's the couple from the house by the village sign.'

'Lumme.'

DS Leyton's retort is explained by his rider.

'It's a toga party, Guv.'

Indeed, he is surely right.

Beyond the couple's semi-naked appearance, what next catches the eye is their attire – perhaps makeshift, but convincing-looking outfits of white robes (bedsheets?), knotted on one shoulder and baring the other, rope belted at the waist. Each of the pair is crowned by a gold-leaf headband that must originate from a costume accessories website.

DS Leyton's animation rises further.

'Guv – they're having a flamin' Roman orgy!'

The man and woman move away and the light is extinguished.

DS Leyton exhales sharply – the sound a mixture of excitement and relief.

'Maybe we've seen enough. It might be a bit embarrassing.'

Skelgill tuts.

'Leyton – we've come this far – it's you that wants to bottom it.'

'That could be an unfortunate phrase, Guv.'

'Howay – I'm not about to take photos.'

Skelgill springs up onto the bunker, first on all fours, testing the lid for his weight. He leans out to haul up his colleague, DS Leyton protesting under his breath.

Skelgill can now reach a bough of sufficient substance – gripping with both hands he could swing sloth-like – but DS Leyton seems to understand his role is to get his ample shoulders beneath his superior's soles. Skelgill disappears up into the canopy.

'What can you see, Guv?'

It takes Skelgill a moment to respond to the hissed entreaty. Several grunts precede his answer.

'I need to get higher – and further out – there's too much foliage.'

Further sounds of exertion ensue, and tremors that vibrate through the tracery.

'Any joy, Guv?'

Movement has ceased – and that Skelgill does not reply suggests he is watching something.

Then.

Crack!

Whump!

Splatter!

The real-life Marvel Comic sound effects are respectively the *crack* of a branch, the *whump* of a body landing on the roof tiles and the *splatter* of apples that shower DS Leyton and drum upon the hollow bunker.

Skelgill rolls from the roof and lands catlike but winded upon the turf.

There is a brief moment of silence and then the loft window flies up.

'Who goes there!'

There is no mistaking Percy Tuseling's agitated falsetto.

The detectives crouch.

They are below the line of sight from the dormer window, even were a torch to be shone.

But now comes the sound of the front door opening – the security light illuminates.

And then the back door – and a second external light.

Their escape routes are cut off.

Skelgill rises and yanks up the lid of the bunker.

'Get in.'

His command is hissed, a mere whisper.

'Guv?'

'Do it!'

DS Leyton obeys – when logic is telling him they should just brass it out – they have warrant cards – they could say they are assigned to keep clandestine watch upon Percy Tuseling for his own safety.

But there is no time for such discourse.

He makes hard work of clambering in – Skelgill peremptorily tip-tackles him to complete the job.

Skelgill ignores the muffled complaint as his colleague face-plants.

He springs in alongside him and lowers the lid.

Inside, darkness is total.

They breathe through gritted teeth, hearts pounding in their ears.

Perhaps someone is moving close by – perhaps they have a flashlight.

Then a Welsh male voice, sing-song.

'Percy – someone's been scrumping your apples, bach.'

There is a faint oath in response – Percy Tuseling must still be up at the open window.

Then another man's voice – also more distant – it would seem from the front.

'Nae harm done – they've nae taken any souvenirs.'

This time the Scots accent. It seems he refers to the garden ornaments.

Percy Tuseling responds from above.

"Bloody kids – I'll murder them".

His controversial choice of words jars with the crouching detectives.

'Back to work, boyos!'

It is the Welsh voice that calls out.

Skelgill and DS Leyton strain to hear: the rear door closes, and then the front.

Skelgill wastes no time.

He pushes up the lid two-handed and leaps out, mauls his flailing colleague and silently closes the bin.

'Quick, Leyton – while the front light's still on.'

His plan seems counterintuitive – but to trigger it again would be more obtrusive. With a headlong dash they make it back to the sanctuary of DS Leyton's car.

DS Leyton is breathing heavily.

He lets his feelings be known.

'Jeez, Guv – never mind Burke and Hare. That was like being in a flippin' coffin!'

Skelgill slumps back and folds his arms. He seems unperturbed by their adventure – but preoccupied, all the same.

Across at the property there are signs of movement in the attic, shadows and fluctuations in the light.

Now DS Leyton inhales deeply; he has gathered his wits.

'So, Guv – what did you see?'

His question is loaded – his tone expectant – of the lurid, the salacious, the scandalous.

Skelgill takes a moment to answer. His gaze remains fixed upon the Tuselings' bungalow. His expression reveals perhaps just a hint of having been thwarted.

'Sculpture.'

'Sculpture?'

Skelgill now turns to his associate.

'They're having a sculpture class.'

'What?'

'A sculpture class – in clay. Remember, Leyton – it's what Tuseling got up to in prison. He won awards. He's giving the others a lesson. It must be what they do each week. That explains the heavy bags. They're taking turns to pose as models.'

The penny has dropped. DS Leyton curses in self-reproach.

'The garden ornaments. And those ones in the house. The Roman outfits. Maybe Greek.'

They sit for some seconds in silence.

'Was that a waste of time, Guv?'

Skelgill regards him sharply. 'Not necessarily, Leyton.' He digs into the side pocket of his climbing trousers. 'Here.'

DS Leyton cannot suppress a laugh – Skelgill has produced two apples.

He is not a man for salad, but there is something comradely in the moment, and he takes the proffered fruit and bites into it.

'I suppose it answers our question, Guv.'

Skelgill is weighing his own apple like it were a cricket ball.

'And raises plenty.'

'How do you mean, Guv?'

Skelgill inspects the fruit as though it is a specimen of evidence.

'Are we trying to add apples and oranges, Leyton?'

The question is baffling to DS Leyton – not least because one half of the metaphysical equation is before his eyes.

'In what way, Guv?'

Skelgill takes a bite of his apple and ponders while he chews.

'Leyton – you know what fly fishing is?'

'Er – ain't that when you thrash it back and forward.'

Skelgill gives his colleague a sideways look.

'You might do, Leyton. But – right enough – you're actively casting. When it's flat calm you look for a rise – that's a fish coming up to take an insect from the surface film.' He inserts a pause that may be illustrative of his point. 'You can wait for ages – nothing. Then, splash – splash – splash – splash – splash.' He dabs the apple randomly towards points across an imaginary lake. 'They all come up together – too far apart for it to be coordinated.'

DS Leyton is looking increasingly perplexed.

'Where do the oranges come in, Guv?'

Skelgill scowls. He realises he is tangling metaphors like the wind knots on a bad day for fishing.

He gives a growl in his throat.

'We're setting a lot of store by coincidences, Leyton. Conflating the two murders.'

DS Leyton regards his superior pensively.

'It has been the theme of this case, Guv – there's no denying it.' He gives a nod towards the Tuseling property. 'Tonight – sculpture class – it's the first thing that's not quite fitted the pattern.'

Skelgill stares long and hard at his colleague.

Paradoxically, it seems he endures some inner conflict over this assertion – as though, despite his somewhat fatalistic stance and devil's advocacy, there is an underlying instinct that recognises what, in fact, they have learned; it is just not revealed to him.

He sighs, as if to say, "I'll think about it tomorrow."

'Tell you what, Leyton.'

'Guv?'

'You'd better wipe your face before you get home – you look like you've been down Haig pit.'

17. FLOATING IDEAS

Bassenthwaite Lake – 7.15 a.m. Thursday 5 August

'Why *do* they rise in concert, do you think?'

Skelgill produces an exaggerated frown, his tanned forearms resting upon his knees, his shirtsleeves rolled up around his paler biceps – an arrangement he had effected before rowing them through the dawn mist from Peel Wyke to their present mooring in Scarness Bay. He squats on the stern thwart facing his female companion, her slight form a better fit on the forward thwart.

'I was thinking you'd know.'

'Daniel, ask me about the law, by all means – but there is an expert angler in this boat, and it is not I.'

Skelgill finds himself caught between the compliment and his duty in deference to the lady's own humility. Alice Wright-Fotheringham might be a retired barrister and judge, but she displays the deftest control of a fishing rod that he has witnessed.

He accepts the cue.

'It's hard to imagine they communicate. And it's not as if brownies feed in shoals – they patrol singly. You can watch them in the Derwent – they're territorial, aggressive.'

The woman gives the hint of a smile; she turns her head to look across the water and shades her eyes with a slender hand.

'I suppose it would confuse a predator – an osprey, for example.'

'It confuses me.'

'There you are, then – a survival mechanism.'

Skelgill remains perplexed.

'I'd just like to know how they do it.'

'Perhaps the sound – the vibrations – travels through the water. The stimulus from one fish triggers half a dozen others. If we can hear it above the surface, why would not a fish below?'

Skelgill is nodding. Though he is unconvinced. The logic is sound as far as the laws of physics go – but it fails the test of biology: if they are talking natural selection, where is the fish that can suppress the instinct to be first to a floundering mayfly? That is not his experience. But he won't argue the case.

Beneath his well-worn Tilley hat his grey-green eyes now survey an arc, one hundred and eighty degrees from port around to starboard. They have a rod out at each of three points of the compass, the stern excepted.

The morning is still early and only the occasional zephyr disturbs the ice-like surface of Bassenthwaite Lake, as though some invisible winged creature quarters the expansive mere, revealing itself in ripples that distort the near-perfect reflection of Skiddaw each time it twists and turns. There is plenty of insect life in evidence – sedges and midges and daddies; hatches, matches and despatches. And the occasional lazy plop of a trout – yet no exuberant salvo, as per the subject of their discussion.

Perhaps Alice Wright-Fotheringham detects his chagrin at this.

'Can we expect the pike to move in concert?'

Now Skelgill scowls more deeply. The last outing a blank, he has promised her a monster specimen – a different method this time, one that "never fails". Less demanding on the elderly lady's wrists than his favoured plugging, they are float fishing with deadbaits.

'Move would be a start.'

She regards him sympathetically, as a teacher to a talented pupil frustrated by his uncharacteristic failing.

Accordingly, she does not chide him for his indignant retort.

'Daniel, what is the striking protocol?'

Perhaps he senses the grump that has descended upon him; he makes an effort to shift into advisory mode.

'A pike's not like a brownie that'll spit the fly the instant it tastes metal. When you see the jewellery that some of the arl warriors are wearing, you wonder they can feel owt.'

'So you get, what – a few seconds? *Happy birthday to you* – something like that?'

Skelgill seems briefly reluctant to commit to an answer, though he grins at her ditty.

'Give or take. Depends what the float does. If it sets off like its motorised, don't hang about.'

'Stay vigilant, therefore.'

'Aye.'

Alice Wright-Fotheringham nods rather imperiously; she was formidable on the bench, and despite her advancing years the vital pale-blue eyes convey an undiminished perspicacity.

'While we wait, I assume you want to ask me about the Percy Tuseling case.'

'How do you know we're involved in that?'

'I have been listening avidly to the podcasts. *Murder on the Farm.* I briefly heard the voice of your delightful assistant. What with reading between the lines of the reports in the Gazette, I put two and two together. And I still have my contacts.'

'I promised I'd get you this pike.'

Now she is grinning.

'Two birds with one stone – never fear.'

Skelgill realises it would be futile to attempt to pull any wool over her eyes. He shakes his head; an admission of mea culpa.

'What do you make of it so far?'

'The eminent professor is circling for the kill, no?'

Skelgill shows his approval; her tone carries just the right amount of sarcasm and disparagement to reveal where her favour lies.

'He's hiding behind the argument that he needs to clear Percy Tuseling before they can move on to the truth.'

She interjects.

'I think if one were to ask Mr Tuseling he would say the case is being built relentlessly against him. Certainly, speaking as a neutral bystander, that is how it is coming across.'

Skelgill, however, now seems to waver. It prompts her to probe.

'You have a certain professional empathy?'

'With the professor?'

'Yes.'

Skelgill grimaces, though he is plainly a little conflicted.

'I can see why he's tempted – why he's going down that road. My oppo reckons no bookie in the land would lay odds against it being Percy Tuseling that shot Will Featherston.'

'Is there DNA evidence?'

Skelgill shakes his head.

'No smoking gun?'

Now he glances at her, eyebrows raised inquiringly – but the idiom seems innocently chosen. He growls.

'Just more coincidences than you can shake a stick at.'

Alice Wright-Fotheringham regards her surrogate pupil musingly. She reaches down into her rucksack and brings out a sketch pad and pencil.

'Back in the day, when I reviewed a case for the CPS we used a scoring system. If it met the points threshold we would prosecute. Often there would be no single incontrovertible item of evidence, a killer fact. But we regarded our process rather like the manufacture of a rope. A rope comprises many individual strands, each of which alone would not bear weight. But skilfully wound together they possess a combined strength beyond their individual sum – ample to hang a man.'

Skelgill is listening intently.

'Want to hear?'

She smiles again.

'As much as you want to tell me.'

Skelgill lets his gaze shift from one float to another and then to the third. The prominent nose, the craggy features, the sharp eyes in shadow; he turns his head like a peregrine on its ledge.

He speaks quietly.

'You'll know some of them, from what's been broadcast. Take as the start point Percy Tuseling admitting the murder of Colin Bell-Gibson at Belltower Farm. A shooting at point-blank range with one of the farmer's own guns. A ruthless execution – a violent, barely provoked reaction – the victim taken unawares. Then rewind a year. Compare it to the death of Will Featherston at

Caldblow Farm – the circumstances, the MO – it's like a copycat killing.'

He pauses while Alice Wright-Fotheringham makes a couple of notes, mere flourishes of the pencil. He cannot see what she has written, but her brevity calls to mind DS Jones's shorthand.

She signals with a nod for him to continue.

'Tuseling worked part-time and shot at both farms. He could easily have been at Caldblow Farm at the time of Will Featherston's murder. Several witnesses identified a car there that matched his red Ford Corsair. He had an alibi – but it's got holes in it. He had a girlfriend on the side at Radio Rentals where he worked – he may have taken advantage of her, to cover for him.'

Another quick scribble; she almost might be ticking items off a list she prepared earlier.

'Tuseling previously lived a few doors down from the Featherston family. He almost certainly knew Will Featherston by sight – and vice versa. The blokes used to play cricket on the green with the local lads after work. Tuseling was into cricket and Will Featherston was a budding left-arm spinner – he'd stand out.'

'A scarce commodity in England.' The lady knows her cricket. 'Almost as rare as a left-arm quickie.' She grins knowingly.

Skelgill is tempted by the aside, but he contrives to stay on track.

'You've heard the accusation – that Tuseling was committing a burglary at Caldblow Farm and in walked Will Featherston, delivering fish. He recognised Tuseling and that's why he died. Shortly after the murder, Tuseling tried to palm off a carpet bag full of antiques to his brother-in-law who ran a second-hall stall. The brother-in-law knew Tuseling was interviewed as a suspect – he didn't want anything to do with the swag. There's no proof that it came from the farm, but on the day of Will Featherston's shooting, perhaps to reinforce his alibi, Tuseling took his girlfriend from work to St Bees Head for a drink – a picnic – as a detour from giving her a lift home. He produced crystal glasses and a bottle of vintage red wine covered in dust. When Caldblow Farm was searched they found the stopper of a crystal decanter under a bush near the side gate, where Tuseling would have parked.'

Alice Wright-Fotheringham adds more short notes.

'Tuseling's wife has now come forward. That's how we heard about the carpet bag. She states that he was behaving strangely when she arrived home. He was claiming to feel sick. He'd washed his trousers and hung them on the line. The news was all over the radio and the TV. She asked him if he'd been at the farm and he denied it. He said he'd been at work – but he'd been ill and wasn't in his workshop the whole time. Later that night he told her he'd need to sell his shotgun – because the police would link him to the farm.'

'And frame him?'

With a shrug Skelgill conveys a reluctant sympathy with the argument; the police certainly did a good job of fitting up the Hares.

'He was originally eliminated as a suspect because of his alibi. But it was five weeks before they arrested the Hares. Shortly before that, someone – an anonymous caller, male – phoned to say Tuseling was involved with Caldblow Farm – and possibly the murder. So they reinterviewed him, and his connections to the two farms came up.'

'Which he had previously withheld?'

'Aye. He claimed he only answered the questions that were put to him. Never mind that he shot there and knew the kid. Or that he still owned a shotgun.'

'So he was probably sweating.'

'Exactly. A couple of days later he walked into Mirehouse police station claiming to have found a message lying in the street. This is a mile or so from where he lived. He'd been for a drink with the same brother-in-law. It was on a scrap of card – but addressed to him – describing a bloke who drove a red van and shot on the land – who scared the landowner, Lady Fitzrovia – half-garbled nonsense.'

'Did they test the handwriting?'

Skelgill tuts scornfully.

'Looks like it disappeared into the mountain of evidence. The investigation was chaotic. There were multiple teams of detectives and no computers, no proper coordination. You have to question the leadership.'

His eyes make a round of the floats and settle back upon his companion; she is staring at him intently. He concludes the narrative.

'A couple of days later the Hares robbed Kirkstile Farm with a shotgun – the rest is history.'

'A travesty. If your name was Hare.'

Skelgill's view is not entirely congruent with this assessment.

'What they served – it was about the time they were due, for everything they'd got off with scot-free.'

Alice Wright-Fotheringham wags her pencil at him.

'But that is not justice, Daniel.'

He rows back a tad.

'I'm just passing on the word on the street.'

'Village justice has its limitations.'

'Aye, reet enough.'

There is a silence; he eyes her sketch pad optimistically.

She resists, however.

'I could do with one more significant fact.'

Hitherto forthcoming, Skelgill seems suddenly discomfited. Beneath the hat, perhaps his prominent cheekbones take on a flush.

'A couple of small points. For one, armed robbers rarely shoot schoolkids. For two, when Tuseling was arrested at Belltower Farm, he tossed a cartridge out of the car – like it was a habit. They'd found a fresh cartridge case in the roadside verge near Caldblow Farm.'

'Noted. But is there something else?'

He performs another quick scan of the floats, and then gnaws at the corner of his thumbnail. But now he overturns his reluctance.

'So, the Hares were jailed for the murder of Will Featherston – about a year after the event. A few days later, Tuseling shot Colin Bell-Gibson. There was no manhunt – he surrendered on the night. There was a limited investigation and a quick prosecution. They kept it simple – he pled guilty and was banking on a verdict of manslaughter. The jury didn't buy it, because he took the gun outside and sawed off the barrel.'

'Yes. I am familiar with that.'

She knows there is more to his account than superficial detail. A stern gaze produces the desired effect, and Skelgill continues.

'It looks like they – the police – *some* of the police – revisited the possibility of Tuseling being the Caldblow Farm killer. His girlfriend at Radio Rentals told us they came looking for his timesheets from the day of Will Featherston's murder.'

'They came a year later?'

'Aye. And they were gone. The pages for August 1976 were missing.'

'Had the police taken them originally?'

She is quick to make the deduction.

'If they did, we can't find them.'

Again, her mind moves with alacrity.

'The more tempting explanation being that Percy Tuseling had made them disappear, to cover his tracks.'

Skelgill nods.

'He could have done that – because by then it was September – the accounts girl only used them for the current month. So no one would have noticed they were gone.'

'And this coincided with his production of the bogus cardboard message?'

'Aye – you got it.'

Alice Wright-Fotheringham makes a final flourish on her pad. She regards it at arm's length, and seems satisfied by her work.

Skelgill waits for a moment, but it appears she wants him to ask for her verdict.

'I take it you've come out with the same result as my oppo?'

Now she rotates the pad to display her work.

Skelgill's eyes widen.

She has played a game of hangman.

The scaffold is complete and the stick figure is complete. Hung.

He cannot suppress a laugh.

'Is that what they get up to in the CPS office!'

Alice Wright-Fotheringham smiles demurely.

'It was my own private system. I have to say, it was almost

foolproof. It's not exactly that the strands wind together to make an unbreakable rope, but it has a certain graphic consonance, I'm sure you will agree. It customarily takes ten wrong guesses to lose at hangman. I made it that your Percy Tuseling lost by thirteen. Unlucky for some.'

Skelgill lets out an ironic hiss.

'And I doubt I've remembered everything.'

'Small wonder your sergeant believes the odds are stacked against the suspect.'

Skelgill nods.

They each sink into a pensive silence; the calm surface of the lake seems to expand to infinity to allow speculation to travel unhindered.

Then a shadow passes overhead – not a cloud, the sky is cloudless – but a bird of prey, an osprey, the subtle curvature of its more slender wings distinguishing it from the commoner buzzard. As Skelgill tracks its progress, wondering if it will catch a fish before they do, his companion floats a suggestion.

'But, Daniel – you have another idea altogether, don't you?'

Skelgill starts. Now he seems suddenly cornered. Certainly in a small boat, there are few options available.

But she lets him partially off the hook.

'Not for you the easy path.'

He scowls; it is an admission of sorts, duty driven.

'Look where it got them last time.'

'You mean the wrongful conviction of the Hares?'

'Aye, I suppose so.'

'As I understand it, the official line has never wavered. The Hares were guilty but escaped on a technicality.'

Skelgill nods broodingly.

'That's right.'

'Have you been told otherwise?'

Another grimace as Skelgill looks out over the lake.

'Not in so many words. Not in any words.'

'But there is an implication?'

Now he shrugs.

'The fact that we're on this case – and it's hush-hush. We've got a private incident room on the top floor. Read into that what you like. If there's an official line now – about what we're up to – it's so that Percy Tuseling doesn't know we're on his tail.'

Now Alice Wright-Fotheringham nods, too – slowly, with consideration.

'It sounds like your Chief wants the record set straight, diplomatically.'

An ironic growl rises in Skelgill's throat.

'She's picked the right man, then.'

The lady once more wags her pencil, a reproof handed down from the bench.

'Daniel, you undersell yourself. But that aside, a left-handed perspective, shall we say – new light cast on the matter – it is exactly what this case needs.'

He glances up. She is grinning. And she holds the pencil illustratively – here speaks a fellow cuddy wifter, in the vernacular.

But he sighs.

'I'm still in the dark – twilight, at best.'

She gives a kind of *ahem.*

'You have asked my counsel but you have not yet picked my brains.'

He regards her more intently.

'Do you remember owt about it?'

'Because of my extreme age?'

'Howay, lass!'

It is his turn to reproach.

'Daniel, there is no denying the march of time.'

'Well, you're doing a good job, Alice.'

The lady cannot hide a small indulgence at the compliment. She gazes abstractedly across the water, but only briefly, and re-engages, her tone practical.

'I was in London, at the bar, during the time of the two farm murders. Of course, hailing from hereabouts, I paid attention to reports. Although it was limited, the national press coverage. I did know of Lady Fitzrovia, of course.'

'Aye?'

Her matter-of-fact mention is in contrast to Skelgill's inflexion.

Here it seems is something she knows that he clearly does not.

'You are unfamiliar with her story?'

Skelgill looks puzzled.

'I know she was a widow. Aged around forty at the time. Leased her land to Colin Bell-Gibson. Returned from a hack to find the farmhouse had been burgled and the body of Will Featherston in her kitchen. As best I can gather she attracted little reference.'

'That might be considered out of character. One could certainly say she attracted controversy.'

Skelgill shakes his head, his bottom lip turned out. It is an invitation for her to continue.

'She was an *It Girl* of the late Sixties. A London socialite. Curiously attractive – not a classic beauty. But she rose from apparent obscurity on the back of her marriage to Lord Fitzrovia. He was rather a loose cannon – a reputation as a playboy. He died in somewhat uncertain circumstances around 1970. She was left to ply her trade with impunity.'

There is something about the way that Alice Wright-Fotheringham says this that prompts Skelgill to repeat her words.

'Ply her trade?'

'Oh – don't get me wrong – as I recall there were just rumours. I was a Junior Counsel, striving to climb the legal ladder towards silk. I had my head in books and case files the whole time. I didn't pay much attention to the news, let alone the gossip columns. But since Lord Fitzrovia had his Cumbrian connection through the ancestral estate, I suppose the name always caught my eye. The long and short of it was that she frittered away what money she had inherited, and turned to – well – what were described then as immoral practices. There was talk of a house of ill repute. I suspect she had lawyer friends in high places – and perhaps *by* other places – *ha-hah* – but notwithstanding it ended in bankruptcy. The Knightsbridge townhouse had to go – the West End lifestyle. But she faded away without too much of a fanfare. I believe Fitzrovia's will gave her a liferent on Caldblow Farm – it would have been in the family trust. I suppose the leasing out of the land would have given her a modest income – but not to the manner to which she had grown accustomed.'

Skelgill is listening intently.

'When would this have been?'

'I would say late 1973 or early 1974 that she moved out of London. I presume she lived here thereafter.'

Skelgill nods.

'We've been trying to find out what happened to her.'

'It would not have been like her to live the quiet life. I imagine she left a paper trail. She was certainly newsworthy. But I take it she is no longer alive?'

'We think not. But she's not been traced. There's no death registered in the name of a Lady Fitzrovia.'

'What about the Bell-Gibson daughter – she was present on the night her father was murdered. Surely she will still be alive?'

Skelgill seems a little frustrated by the idea.

'Not traced, either. She'd be in her mid-sixties, now. It seems that the folk who were wrapped up in this wanted to leave it all behind. You've heard some of what Joan Arkwright had to say. And Tuseling's first wife more or less took on a new identity.' He tuts. 'It's easier rattling for worms.'

The lady chuckles.

'I can see your dilemma. I take it that behind the scenes you are charged with finding fodder for Simeon Freud and his avaricious audience.'

Skelgill does not go beyond a nod in explanation.

'It strikes me, Daniel, that Percy Tuseling is taking something of a risk, raising his head above the parapet.'

Skelgill gives a half shrug.

'He's so mad he's convinced of his own innocence.'

Alice Wright-Fotheringham might ask Skelgill to distinguish between insanity and anger – though quite likely he would have used the word *tapped* had he intended the former. And even the casual listener to the podcast can be in no doubt of the persistent ire that smoulders within Percy Tuseling.

But now Skelgill raises a technical issue.

'Put your judge's hat on for a minute.'

'Not the black cap, I hope – not quite yet.'

Skelgill glances at her sketch pad – but he does not contest her point.

'If he'd been found guilty back then – for both murders – what would have happened?'

'You mean in terms of sentencing?'

'Aye.'

She nods and purses her lips; she knows what he is getting at.

'Yes – quite an irony, I suspect. Almost certainly the two sentences would have been handed down to be served concurrently.'

'What about now?'

'He would get a brand new term – he would probably never again see the light of day.'

Skelgill narrows his eyes and gazes across the lake to the starboard side. Why, as Alice Wright-Fotheringham says, would Percy Tuseling take such a risk? Is it because his hubris knows no bounds – that he revels in his battle with his intellectual adversary, the TV celebrity and great brain Professor Simeon Freud?

He inhales to speak – but events overtake him.

'Strike! Alice – *strike!*'

Without hesitation, the lady does as bidden.

She drops her pad and pencil and snatches up the rod that is her charge.

She begins to lift but can only get the rod to the perpendicular before it threatens to have her over the side.

'Monster.'

Skelgill hisses the word through gritted teeth – but otherwise hides his alarm as his lightweight companion is caught off balance. He lurches forward and straddles the centre thwart, simultaneously hooking his right arm round her narrow waist and leaning as far as he can to port; otherwise *The Doghouse* would be in danger of capsizing.

But when a person might now be panicking, Alice Wright-Fotheringham curses defiantly.

Skelgill begins to chortle.

'You can take the lass out of Cumbria!'

And she does not merely protest loudly, but she understands

the principle of leverage – quickly she braces her left sole against the gunwale and her right the middle thwart. Cautiously, Skelgill lets loose his grip.

'Just let it run, there's plenty of line.'

They are in open water, so there is little danger of a snag unless the fish runs at the boat. Skelgill moves to clear the other two lines.

'I'll get these in –'

And now it is his turn to resort to intemperate language – as first the float beyond the bow and almost instantaneously the one to port dip from view – and stay dipped.

Skelgill strikes, a rod in each hand. The reels' anti-reverse mechanisms are on, but he has no means of retrieving; meanwhile Alice Wright-Fotheringham is straining with all her might to contain her own fish.

Skelgill takes a moment to steady the situation; he stands and raises both rods vertically and lifts the butts to head height. The bow fish leaps – he sees that it is a modest-sized jack – and it makes up his mind.

Alice Wright-Fotheringham has now realised his predicament – but she hardly dare take her eyes off the water.

'Daniel – what will you do?'

He glances sideways at her – her knuckles are white and she is straining the sinews of her wrists and probably many more elsewhere.

'You just hold tight – take line if it runs our way.'

'I shall.'

She gasps out the response, but there is no doubting the determination in her voice. And now she risks a look at Skelgill.

Extraordinarily, he performs a pirouette – a full three-sixty-degree turn, the effect of which is to twist together the lines that extend from the two rods. He stoops and drops the rod on which the jack pike is hooked and now, as if there is only one fish, begins to retrieve with the remaining rod.

For there is method in his madness. The point of intersection quickly runs down the doubled line until the two fish are drawn to converge.

And now – set against the irony that three pike seem to have synchronised their hunt (despite the distance between the baits, and Skelgill's scepticism of possible collaboration) – there is the convenient truth that the duo brought into temporary union fail any such intelligence test, and attempt to swim in different directions.

Skelgill has them alongside the boat in thirty seconds, and released in thirty more.

'Howay, lass – it's in your hands.'

His words are apposite, for Alice Wright-Fotheringham certainly has a fight on her hands. But though she might almost be mismatched, she makes up for the disparity through artistry. A skilled angler, she senses when to give line to the fish and when to take it. And while it yet shows no sign of tiring, never mind making an appearance at the surface, slowly but surely she gains the upper hand.

'Can I trust the knots?'

Skelgill permits himself a grin.

'Tucked blood knots – my speciality.'

It is not just the querying of his craftsmanship that amuses him – for he sees that she is digging in. The fish will come home.

And now a great swirl to starboard. A greenish shape. The impression of an alligator.

Skelgill is driven to a further oath.

'Pardon my French.'

'I thought that was Anglo-Saxon?'

He passes.

'That's a decent fish, Alice.' It is as near as Skelgill gets to hyperbole.

She is breathless, and the creature is still giving a good account of itself – but she flashes him another glance.

'No more than you promised.'

'Howay. It's twice the size of my pair put together. And then some.'

She lets out a laugh of triumph.

Skelgill reaches for his net. He frowns; he has a bigger one, but to have brought it felt like a bad omen.

'We'll skip the net.'

She takes a moment to respond – the fish has put on another spurt.

'Daniel, can you do it without?'

'Swap sides.'

He shifts to the starboard gunwale while Alice Wright-Fotheringham shuffles as best she can to port.

'Shall I try it?'

'Aye, go on – nice and slow.'

Skelgill, his eyes laser focused, his left arm crooked like the neck of a heron stalking frogs, leans over the side.

She continues to reel – and now with a groan of effort she lifts the rod.

A glistening prehistoric head breaks the surface; slime-green and dappled gold; great jaws arrayed with irregular battle-scarred teeth; coal-black pupils with the stare of a remorseless killer.

In what must seem an act of madness – akin to putting one's head into the lion's mouth – Skelgill's arm snakes out.

He emits a cry that is somewhere between foolhardiness and audacity – but in reality it is just the sheer effort – his aim is true and he straightens, the fish half out of the water, gripped firmly between gill plate and gills, and effectively immobilised.

'She must be close on the record.'

The huge fish eyes them coldly, unmoved by such acclaim.

'What is the record?'

'For Bass Lake? Thirty-seven pound.'

'By whom is it held?'

Skelgill glances at her; sheepishly would be an understatement.

'Want me to land it?'

She shakes her head urgently.

'No, no – no need – and it's far better for the fish, yes?'

Skelgill regards her wryly.

'Sure?'

'Daniel – I shall thrive on the angler's tale.'

She refers to the catch that puts on a pound each time the story is told.

He hesitates for a moment.

Then with his free right hand he pulls sturdy forceps from his thigh pocket and deftly removes the hook.

'You had it right in the scissors. Not a scratch.'

'Happy birthday to me.'

He glances again – it is a moment of curiosity.

But she indicates with a nod.

'You had better release it before your arm gives out.'

They each take a last lingering look – then Skelgill lowers the pike beneath the surface until he feels the fish achieve buoyancy. Slowly, perhaps rather casually, he withdraws his hand.

A second great eddy on the surface is its signature sign off.

Alice Wright-Fotheringham hands Skelgill her rod and sinks back into the bow.

'That was spiffing.'

He reaches for a high five – though he groans in the act.

'Did you pull a muscle – under the strain?'

Skelgill scowls.

'Last night – I had a disagreement with a roof.'

'All in the line of duty, I hope?'

'Kind of.'

She accepts his explanation, and now reaches back into her rucksack; she produces a circular sky-blue cake-tin.

'Daniel, do you have your Kelly kettle?'

'What is it they say about the bear and the woods?'

'Well, then – I have gingerbread. My own concoction – last time was the Grasmere recipe. Today, something different is called for.'

She pulls of the lid and holds out the tin.

'Here – smell – double the amount of ginger.'

Skelgill takes it two-handed and dips his nose into the tin.

'What do you think?'

He looks up, frowning.

'Smells of fish.'

He passes back the tin with a grin and reaches for the anchor rope.

18. EPISODE 4: ST BEES HEAD

Incident Room 101 – 9.00 a.m. Friday 6 August

'The rushes first? Guv?'

Skelgill starts. He looks at DS Jones as if for a moment briefly unseeing. Then he blinks, as though alarmed that he has spoken his private thoughts aloud. While DS Jones and DS Leyton have been setting up the AV equipment – and while, in the corner by the window DC Watson assiduously works her way through yet another Bankers box of injuriously disarrayed papers – his mind has drifted, almost literally, to yesterday's early-morning paddle about Bassenthwaite Lake, as it has done so intermittently in the intervening hours. A miscellany of flashbacks disturbs his equilibrium, much like the fantastic winged beast over the water, fleeting and unpredictable. There is the facile but incontrovertible hangman sketch; the notion of a twenty-something Alice in early 1970s London; the exploits of *It Girl* Lady Fitzrovia; and – not least – and the particular chimera from which he is roused, the matter of most personal salience, that he is still smarting from Alice Wright-Fotheringham's extraordinary philanthropic refusal to weigh her pike. Then there was the ginger cake.

'Hangman.'

Not for the first time this century, a Skelgill retort baffles his colleagues.

DS Jones's question refers to the fact the DS Leyton also has a short presentation this morning.

'You mean start with Percy Tuseling, Guv?'

Skelgill looks surprised that he has not been understood.

'Aye. Tuseling. Fire away.'

Just as DS Jones sets the video running, DC Watson in the

corner makes a snorting noise; most likely a sneeze suppressed in an effort not to disturb them. They do not pay particular heed when she gets up to leave the room; in passing she unobtrusively lays a slim manila folder beside DS Leyton.

DS Jones adds some commentary to the opening sequence.

'This was recorded yesterday morning at St Bees Head. Since Percy Tuseling had admitted going there, the logic was that we could pick up a thread that he could not deny, and then introduce some of the new material you obtained from Veronica Smith.'

Skelgill's expression is revealing. Scepticism lurks in the peripheral shadows of his mind. These initial location shots will have no place in the podcast. They are all about the award-winning documentary. Where the podcast is disjointed and exploratory in nature, no doubt the final showpiece will present a polished production, a laser-focused mission. How the sly and scheming Percy Tuseling is tripped up by the nimble artistry and superior intellect of the great criminologist Professor Simeon Freud: a triumphal Ali towering over a questionably fallen Liston.

But the familiar scenes begin to drive away his scowl; it is the precise spot he went to nine evenings ago, albeit to little direct avail. He sees the same rough-coated beef cattle graze short sparse grass; he is reminded of his concern that clumps of bright-yellow poisonous ragwort populate the meadow, and then again that its bitter taste when fresh is normally sufficient a deterrent – else they would have chomped it already. The seabirds are off their ledges by now; plenty sail on the updraft, inquisitive beady-eyed fulmars, so buoyant on their starched wings that they could be suspended on invisible elastic, bobbing above the line of the clifftop turf. The Isle of Man, distant in the smoky haze, seems to inch like a great stretched bulk-carrier along the western horizon, the summits of Beinn y Phott and Snaefell its bridge and funnel respectively.

Without introduction the film cuts directly to the professor and Percy Tuseling seated upon a wooden bench. At their backs is a lime-mortared wall of about five feet and, beyond at a little distance, the upper section of St Bees lighthouse, brilliant white in the sunshine, its latticed glass glinting on the south side, and indicating the time of day to Skelgill. He takes pride in Cumbrian firsts – England's ten highest peaks, and all the natural lakes worth mentioning – and here is the country's highest lighthouse at 335 feet, visible for eighteen nautical miles (worth another fifteen percent as land miles). He notices the arrow of the weather vane reveals a northeasterly drift – though there is no extraneous sound; the wind muffs on the microphones must be doing their job.

"And … *action.*"

Also familiar, the voice of producer Jen; does he now detect a West Country twang?

But the professor begins to speak, and Skelgill's speculation is supplanted.

"So, Percy – it must be close to here that you had your picnic with Joan Arkwright. Perhaps you spread out a rug against this wall – it is so secluded and yet offers such a magnificent view. I imagine little has changed."

It is clear that Percy Tuseling has been bracing himself for his perceived adversary's first line of attack, and he seems unwilling to engage in what is arguably a reasonably conversational opening.

"There's not much that could change, is there?"

The professor treats the retort as rhetorical.

"It's the perfect spot for a secret liaison. Did you entertain other young girls here – your wife when you were dating?"

The question is peppered with controversy, and Percy Tuseling is immediately irked. But now it seems he might have prepared a line of his own.

"I'm not the one surrounding myself with attractive women that are half my age."

"Percy – I'm not being paid to be interviewed."

Percy Tuseling responds with a version of his facetious laugh, this time setting the tone for what he is about to say.

"Simeon, don't tell me you don't go round making a fortune out of other people's *misfortune.*"

"Well, Percy –"

Simeon Freud is discomfited. Once again, he shows himself to be lacking when it comes to such unscripted cut and thrust – but he realises he has been drawn into an unbecoming exchange. And – again – he knows he is master of the scissors – he will decide what ends up on the cutting room floor. Accordingly, he simply waits, adjusting his hair and clothing without explanation, as though he was merely rehearsing and is now getting ready for a considered take.

It seems they have each contrived to put a shot across the other's bows. And, for once, Percy Tuseling has pierced his adversary's sails.

The professor resumes.

"Percy – on the day that Will Featherston was murdered, we now have confirmation that you left work with Joan Arkwright and came here for a drink to celebrate your win on the horses. This lovely scenic viewpoint therefore figures prominently in your alibi."

Despite the professor's superficially amenable proposition, it is plain that Percy Tuseling is stung by its submerged tentacles. If he needs an early reminder not to trust the man's generosity, this is it.

And he is proved right.

"But that trip did raise other questions, Percy. We had a follow-up conversation with Joan Arkwright – just to check one or two facts before we go to press, so to speak. She told us that when you came for your little after-work drink that you produced a bottle of vintage red wine and crystal glasses. I would have thought a couple of cans of chilled lager would have been more the thing for a scorching afternoon in the summer of 1976? And perhaps a bottle of dandelion and burdock for a sixteen-year-old girl."

Videographer Kate has closed in, watching for Percy Tuseling's reaction. But the tone has already been set and the familiar belligerence is in evidence; the small eyes watery, the narrow lips tightly compressed, the complexion blotchy and reddening. A simmering anger.

But he does respond.

"She must be thinking of a different time. Or someone else. She never did have much of a memory."

Several avenues are offered here – but the professor is astute in the one he selects.

"And I thought you complimented her for her diligence – Little Miss Perfect, wasn't it?"

"I was talking about her bookkeeping."

The professor again chooses the offered diversion.

"Well, that's also strange, Percy – because she mentioned the discovery, over a year later, that your timesheets – job sheets, I believe they were referred to as – had gone missing for the month of August 1976. The period covering the shooting of Will Featherston."

There is a subtly different look now in Percy Tuseling's eyes; it is tempting to see it as the hunted animal, the cornered rat that berates itself for having turned into a cul-de-sac.

"Well – if she got rid of them for my benefit – then she made a big mistake. They would have shown exactly where I was and what I was doing."

DS Jones makes a sudden movement; she reaches to pause the replay. She addresses her colleagues.

'I thought it was telling that he skipped any denial or preamble – he showed he understood exactly the significance of the timesheets. And also interesting that he assumes it was Joan Arkwright.'

'Or pretends to assume.'

It is Skelgill's qualification.

DS Jones looks at him for a moment, taking in his point before she restarts the recording.

"It's another one of the many strange coincidences, Percy. Of all the timesheets that might have been missing, it was those which could have proved your innocence."

The professor seems to have reverted to a stance that is supportive.

"I didn't need anything to prove my innocence."

"Nevertheless, Percy – I'm surprised you didn't bring them to the attention of the police, when they came to interview you at Radio Rentals – when you told them about your connections to Belltower Farm and Caldblow Farm."

Percy Tuseling's voice becomes more strained, his tone terse with impatience.

"I've told you. I answered accurately the questions that I was asked. I didn't tell them what colour underpants I was wearing or when I last went to the toilet."

Once more the professor is alert to an opening.

"You were in the toilet rather a lot that day, weren't you?"

Percy Tuseling snaps back.

"What day? What the hell are you talking about?"

In the mode of a prosecuting counsel confident of his position, Simeon Freud ignores any suggestion that he should explain himself, and presses home the attack.

"You had an upset stomach – you were away from your workshop for long periods."

"If Joan Arkwright is saying this – like I say, she's got a memory problem. She's obviously not right in the head."

But the professor is on a roll.

"You even washed your clothes. On the day Will Featherston was blasted at close range with a shotgun. There would have been blood spatter."

Percy Tuseling's voice rises to its highest falsetto.

"Have you got this from Veronica?"

"Veronica? You refer to the woman who became your first wife?"

"Who else would I refer to?"

His features compressed, anger barely controlled, now bitterness has infected Percy Tuseling's manner.

The professor leans away, affecting affront at such an unreasonable reaction.

"Percy – the podcasts and the press coverage are gaining momentum. Our audience is growing. We all agreed, that is what we wanted. Naturally, some people come forward and request to remain anonymous. As journalists we have to respect those wishes. Information can be direct, or from a source close to a person."

Skelgill gives a small inclination of his head; perhaps it is a signal to DS Jones that Veronica Smith's role as informer has been dealt with to his satisfaction.

But Percy Tuseling is far from content. His words come quietly, laced with anger and spittle.

"Simeon, I think you'll find that's called hearsay – and weasel words do not stand up in court."

The professor raises a hand to his chin.

"Well that's not something we need to worry about, is it, Percy?

We're not the judge and jury here. Our job is to clear up as many queries as we can." His manner, though at once avuncular and patronising, again hints at a neutral stance. But any such impression is quickly dispelled. "Such as, around about that time, you were trying to pass on an unusual bag – a distinctive carpet bag, of the type that had been fashionable in the 1960s – and that bag contained antiques. You can see the questions this might raise?"

"I cannot."

Percy Tuseling seems to be running low on ammunition; as he hunkers down, the professor redoubles his bombardment.

"Percy, you could have called at Caldblow Farm. It was usually left unlocked. If the owner Lady Fitzrovia had returned early from exercising her horse, you would have just said you were looking for her – or doing some task for Mr Bell-Gibson, and that you'd popped in to ask for a drink of water.

"She wasn't there – so you walked in and helped yourself not to tap water, but to a handy bag which you began to fill with antiques, ornaments, crystal. The police found the glass stopper of a decanter in bushes by the side gate.

"You worked together with your brother-in-law. A good little number. You had access to large old properties throughout the area.

"You called at such places to mend television sets.

"You were able to garner something here, something there."

Hitherto bereft of a counter argument, Percy Tuseling finally interjects.

"For your information, Simeon, I did used to garner something here, something there. Obtained legally and paid for. From little antique shops and market stalls. Sometimes, at a house, I would make an offer, ask if a person was interested in selling. Then they might tell me about things they wanted to throw out. I would pass them on to Harry and he would sell them and take his cut. It was all above board."

The professor does not dwell upon his success in winkling out Percy Tuseling's admission; instead he keeps the conversation moving.

"Did you ever keep items for yourself?"

"Perhaps I did, the occasional sculpture – I was always interested in that. I was building up a small collection in alabaster and bronze and suchlike."

"What became of the collection?"

'Hah!" He turns to look directly at the camera – the move that has been witnessed several times now. His expression is a manic grimace that reveals rows of small, almost childlike teeth. "Veronica had one of her funnies."

"Her *funnies?"*

The professor casts a brief glance at the camera, as though there is some particular significance in the moment, that a narrator will in due course elucidate.

"She threw them out, Simeon – or I don't know what she did with them. Some of them – not all of them – were naked figures. That's what sculpture often is. Classical sculpture. She accused me of them being something to do with debauchery."

"What, on your part?"

"I don't know what she meant. That would be ridiculous."

The professor ponders; he leans forward and rests his jaw upon the back of his hand, aping the pose of Rodin's *The Thinker.* He gazes away past the camera, and speaks abstractedly.

"Of course – your claim is that your attitude would be the exact opposite – and that's why you reacted with such vehemence. And that would be logical – if your wife Veronica was offended by your collection, you would anticipate correctly that she would find Mr Bell-Gibson's salacious proposal abhorrent."

Percy Tuseling is regarding the professor with some confusion: the point is even-handed, arguably erring in his favour. It seems to prompt him to backtrack on what was his previous denial.

"I often had small quantities of antiques and second-hand goods in my car."

Without compunction, the professor seizes upon up the admission.

'So you *did* try to give your brother-in-law a carpet bag of goods. Why would he refuse to accept them, Percy?"

Percy Tuseling's indignation is revived.

"Is it Veronica? Have you found her? You know you couldn't

ever believe a word she said. She was a fantasist. She was paranoid. She injured herself running through hedgerows from Belltower Farm and blamed it all on me."

It seems he has few qualms in turning upon those erstwhile companions who fail to corroborate his version of events. But, as he doubles down, there is an inherent contradiction in his illuminating denials.

"How much are you paying her? *Hah!* For ten pounds she'd probably tell you that I came home covered in blood toting a shotgun – and that I buried a sack in the garden. Let her make these accusations in public – and I'll be the one suing – for defamation!" He stares with menace down the lens of the camera. 'Do you hear that, Veronica?"

Speaking softly, the professor repeats the man's words.

"You came home covered in blood toting a shotgun. So that would be a lie?"

"Of course it would be a lie – you've been taken in – she was always a money-grabber, a gold-digger."

Simeon Freud does not answer; he merely regards Percy Tuseling with an expression of exaggerated disbelief – plainly for the benefit of the audience. Indeed, after what becomes a heavily pregnant pause, he reaches to tap Percy Tuseling on the shoulder – a kind of rubbing salt in the wounds, that he has taken the bait, swallowed the lot. Without a word of commiseration he rises, smirking, and ambles out of shot past the camera. His lapel mike is still live.

"Ange, *darling* – what chance of getting this infernal woman on the record? Surely with *your* powers of persuasion – I would be eternally in your debt – just name your price, *mmm?"*

The man's voice is oily and obsequious, and the tone of veiled complicity has Skelgill instantly bristling. DS Jones continues to look at the screen, though she makes a brief face that might suggest discomfort. The sequence ends and the picture goes blank. She turns to her colleagues.

'That was all we usefully got. Obviously they're keen to interview Veronica Smith. There's a production meeting tonight. I told Jen I would discuss it with you. I said you'd want to see Percy

Tuseling's reaction before coming to a decision.'

'What about Freud?' It is Skelgill's question.

'Well – you heard – he thinks it's the missing link.'

But she misunderstands Skelgill's point.

'Will he be there?'

'At the meeting? Well – yes, I expect so.'

Skelgill folds his arms. His subordinates might accurately read motives ranging from procedural through competitive to proprietorial. DS Leyton quickly clears his throat, and somewhat ostentatiously displays his wristwatch.

'Guv – I'm supposed to attend a first-aid refresher at ten. Perhaps I can just fill you both in on the burglary report?'

DS Jones seems unilaterally to approve this suggestion, for she slides the laptop along to her colleague.

Skelgill, however, does not object, and with a couple of clicks DS Leyton has a table of figures projected onto the big screen.

'It's simpler than it looks, Guv. These are just the raw data. If I go to the next page, you'll see.'

Skelgill's scowl softens as the new slide displays a map of the West Cumbria Coastal Plain.

'The red dots are farm or country house burglaries to the south of Whitehaven. The blue dots are the same, to the north of Workington. The idea is that the red dots would be on Percy Tuseling's patch, and the blue ones represent the area that would have been covered by the Workington branch of Radio Rentals – so that would have been a different engineer.'

DS Leyton clicks again and an inset box appears.

'Between 1975 and 1977 there were eighteen burglaries on Percy Tuseling's patch and eleven on the Workington patch – sixty-four percent more. The boffins reckon it's too small a sample to be statistically significant – but it's in the right direction.'

Skelgill is perhaps nodding; maths came a close second to English in the fierce competition to be bottom of his grades.

'But I reckon here's the interesting thing, Guv. I got them to analyse the lists of stolen property. Out of the eleven Workington burglaries, five of them included TVs. There were no TVs stolen on Percy Tuseling's patch.'

The light in the room might be changing, but Skelgill's eyes seem a greener shade than a few moments before.

'What about sculptures?'

DS Leyton is not a man for excuses.

'I'll need to look into that, Guv – I thought my TV idea would do the trick. But obviously after what we've just heard – yeah, sculpture.'

DS Jones chips in, supportively.

'I don't think that will be so clear. A TV is unequivocally a TV. Whether an ornament would be described as a sculpture is much more uncertain.'

But DS Leyton does not respond. He has absently turned the cover of the manila file left by DC Watson, and is staring open-mouthed at the single sheet of paper it contains.

'Leyton.'

It takes him a couple of seconds to look up at Skelgill.

'Guv – she's only gone an' found it!'

He turns in his seat to look at where DC Watson had been sifting through the documents at the corner table beneath the windows. Of course, he knows she has gone – that she left without interrupting their flow. He brandishes the page at his colleagues.

'It's the flamin' inventory – the list of items stolen from Caldblow Farm.'

He holds the report two-handed, at arm's length, as if he cannot quite believe what he is seeing. He reads aloud.

'13th August 1976. Stone the crows! There's glasses and a decanter. Waterford crystal. It even says the stopper of the decanter was recovered.'

Skelgill gives a sharp rap on the table.

'What about wine?'

There is a short pause before – sure enough – DS Leyton locates the entry.

'How about three bottles of Chateau Mouton Rothschild, 1966. Reckon that was red wine?'

Skelgill seems momentarily troubled.

DS Jones is working fast with her mobile phone.

'Red Bordeaux. You can still find it. It's selling for nearly a thousand pounds a bottle.'

DS Leyton exclaims.

But Skelgill remains focused.

'Carpet bag. Leyton?'

'Oh – yeah. Hold on – *yeah!* It's there, Guv – at least, I reckon so. It says, Mary Quant Gladstone bag.'

Now he quickly runs his index finger down the entire list. He looks up with glee.

'And no TV!'

Skelgill grimaces – and now he reaches for the list.

'Hardly likely, in a carpet bag, Leyton.'

'Right enough, Guv.'

Skelgill narrows his eyes. The type is small and, like DS Leyton he extends his arm, trying to find a practical medium between distance and sharpness. The inventory is in no particular order, and inconsistent in its detail. It includes "vintage French brass carriage clock", "Ferguson cassette recorder", "crystal vase", "silverware: plates & cutlery", "small ornaments: silver, brass, cut-glass and china" (Skelgill hesitates over this entry), "Casio electronic calculator", and "figurine: golden pearl Aphrodite" (now he stops in his tracks entirely).

After a few moments he lowers the page, but when he opines it is of another aspect.

'There's no jewellery.' He passes the sheet to DS Jones, and rises and strolls across to look out of the window. 'All that – it's belongings that would be kept downstairs.'

After a moment, DS Leyton responds.

'Maybe he'd just gone upstairs when he was disturbed, Guv. Heard the lad come in. Ends up shooting him. Makes himself scarce. There's not many burglars as would carry on after that. Even a vicious cove like Tuseling.'

Skelgill is plainly distracted – and not necessarily by the scenario his colleague conjures.

'There's no mention of a purse, either.'

DS Leyton takes note.

'Maybe the Fitzrovia woman took it with her, Guv?'

'On a horse ride round her farm?'

DS Leyton gives a shrug of his shoulders.

'Perhaps it was kept out of sight – upstairs – locked away somewhere.'

Skelgill seems unconvinced.

DS Jones, perusing the inventory, has noticed the itemised figurine. She is curious, and searches on her phone. She leans to show the result to DS Leyton and then rises to cross to Skelgill.

'Here's what a classical sculpture of Aphrodite looks like.'

The figure is largely naked. While Skelgill merely stares at the image somewhat censoriously, it is DS Leyton that offers an observation.

'That'd be right up Tuseling's street, Guv.'

But Skelgill remains ambivalent. They have apprised DS Jones of the main finding of their after-dark mission to Blindkirk (if not the bungling escapade itself). However, that it potentially derails one line of speculation is still to be properly debated. Indeed, Skelgill has absorbed the fact of the 'sculpture class' without jumping to a premature conclusion.

DS Leyton is wise to the argument. He runs the fingers of one hand through his tousle of dark hair.

'I was thinking just as a collector, Guv. Going by what he's got in his garden. It looks much the same.'

DS Jones has another take on the matter. She picks up the inventory from the boardroom table.

'There's witness evidence of the wine, and the glasses – and the carpet bag – but if we could connect Percy Tuseling definitively to any other of these items …'

She leaves the suggestion hanging.

DS Leyton completes the equation.

'The Aphrodite? After all these years?'

DS Jones grins wryly.

'I don't suppose it would be any more of a long shot than some of the coincidences thus far. Families keep ornaments for generations. This one sounds like it was quite distinctive.'

Skelgill is watching her closely. A decade their junior, she often demonstrates a worldliness beyond her years. Now she takes the floor between her male colleagues; he feels a sudden urge to approach her – she might almost be modelling the figure-hugging navy sleeveless business dress; her bare arms and calves are tanned, and sculpted themselves by gym work; was Aphrodite such a Hellenic blonde?

'Guv?'

For a second time, topping and tailing their meeting, she has to shake him down from another plane.

'Aye?'

'The final interview with Percy Tuseling. We'll be discussing it at the meeting tonight. But I know the broad idea is to conduct it back at his bungalow, to bring his story full circle. I could suggest that we make more of his interest in sculpture. It would provide the opportunity to look the place over.'

Skelgill digs his hands into his trouser pockets and turns to gaze out of the window. The fair weather persists, unseasonably dry now for a fortnight, and small flocks of woodpigeons are visiting the River Eamont to drink. When he remains silent, DS Jones takes a couple of steps towards him.

'I'm actually a little worried, Guv. I think Simeon Freud is possibly about to jump the gun.'

Skelgill appears to follow the trajectory of a couple of passing crows.

'In what way?'

'Turnpike have a limited time to complete the project – they're running low on budget. Jen told me that Sim has something up his sleeve – he won't say what it is. He referred to it as his secret weapon. He's thinking of unleashing it on Percy Tuseling – catching him unawares – in the hope that he'll crack … and confess to Will Featherston's murder.'

DS Leyton now interjects, plainly indignant.

'How can Freud know something we don't? The geezer's got to be bluffing.'

DS Jones is nodding.

'I know. But I think it might be more of a psychological technique than some damming evidence. It's obvious he believes Percy Tuseling is guilty. And if Veronica Smith won't testify in person – it might prompt him to revert to other means. And if it goes wrong, and Percy Tuseling ceases to cooperate, that could block our progress for good – just when we're getting closer to the truth.'

Skelgill now turns to face DS Jones.

'The Aphrodite – it's a long shot. What chance it would have survived his time in jail? If it wasn't already disposed of by his wife.'

He extends a palm, requesting that she pass him the inventory. He peers once more at the list; it seems a painful exercise to him – but he stares for a few moments before handing it back.

'Can't do any harm.' He reaches to touch lightly the neckline of her dress. 'What say you wear a camera?'

19. OLD NEWS

Mountain Café, Keswick – 11.00 a.m. Saturday 7 August

'Are you okay, Inspector?'

'Why wouldn't I be?'

'No – no – I merely meant – er, I thought perhaps – that you might be feeling a little under the weather. There's a nasty summer cold going about, so they say.'

Kendall Minto's gaze shifts from the seated Skelgill to the two empty and one half-empty coffee mugs on the café table.

The coffee is being consumed black – or 'Americano' as stated on the menu, a descriptor which Skelgill refuses to follow the herd and use. There is also an empty foil blister pack.

'Can I get you a refill?'

Skelgill points to the pine settle opposite.

'She's just bringing summat.'

'Ah, righto.'

Kendall Minto has a trendy satchel slung around his neck. Outside, it is shaping up to be another hot day and he is without his trademark leather jacket. He wears a thin black polo-neck wool sweater and black jeans; with his long hair swept back he has something of a youthful Roger Moore *Bond* look about him.

He brings the satchel around onto his knees as he sits.

He senses Skelgill's scrutiny and hurriedly offers an explanation.

'I left my phone at the Gazette office. I had to go in anyway.' He pats the bag illustratively. 'This material is not meant to leave the archive – but there's no one about for another hour – so I can 'borrow' and replace it without getting my knuckles rapped.'

A waitress arrives. She puts down what is a fourth black coffee for Skelgill and a more elaborate-looking layered milky affair in a glass for Kendall Minto, and two Cumberland sausage rolls on a side plate.

'Oh, thanks – I've actually had breakfast – but –'

'They're mine.'

'Ah, of course – don't let me hold you up.'

Skelgill is already taking a large bite; over the rim of the bread bun he conveys that he won't.

Kendall Minto is for a moment uncharacteristically tongue-tied.

'Shall I, er – cut to the chase?'

Skelgill gives a curt nod.

The younger man delves into his satchel.

Skelgill's favoured table overlooking the balcony and approach by stair is a six-seater, and there is plenty of free space. Kendall Minto produces his illicit haul and carefully lays it out. It comprises several original editions of the Westmorland Gazette, of a 1970s vintage, although in good condition, the wood pulp only slightly yellowed. The newspapers are large – the old broadsheet format – and pre-date colour printing, and their front pages feature densely typeset columns of classified ads.

Perhaps a half-dozen fluorescent pink highlighter stickers protrude from the right-hand margins.

'You wanted to know about the Chief of Police at the time of the 1970s farm murders.'

Skelgill continues eating, his stare beady. The boy has stated the obvious.

'To be sure, I had to do a bit of historical research. This was all long before my time – and yours, of course, Inspector.' He clears his throat a little nervously; Skelgill's silence is disconcerting. 'Modern-day Cumbria was constituted under the Local Government Act of 1972. It seems that – as in many parts of Britain where changes were imposed and traditional county structures dismantled – it took time for civic organisations to catch up. The police were no exception. There was no overall regional command established or overseeing chief officer appointed until towards the end of the decade. In the interim there were autonomous heads of the six newly combined boroughs. Whitehaven, of course, fell within Copeland.'

Skelgill grunts that it did.

'In Copeland the temporary role was filled between 1975 and

1978 by an officer drafted in from one of the disbanded northern Lancashire districts. He was called John Bromilow, also known as Jack.'

'The superintendent who was in charge of the Caldblow Farm inquiry?'

'That's correct. It appears he personally oversaw the case.'

'What was the district he came from?'

'Oh, er –' Kendall Minto is not expecting the question. 'Let me see, now.'

He turns to the first marker, handling the brittle newspaper with considerable reverence.

'Here we are.'

He indicates an article that includes a man's portrait.

The headline reads: "Lancashire's 'Jack the Lad' gets top Copeland police post".

He sees that Skelgill is scowling.

'I'll read it. It says: Copeland Borough Council have announced the appointment of Chief Superintendent John 'Jack' Bromilow, 53, as Acting Head of Police; a stand-in role pending county-wide consolidation of resources. Seconded from West Pennines Constabulary, Chief Superintendent Bromilow comes with a reputation for getting things done – and the nickname 'Jack The Lad', for his often unconventional and no-nonsense approach to policing. A spokesman for the Police Appointments Subcommittee stated, "We have no doubt John Bromilow will take a firm hold of the tiller, and chart a course through the uncertain waters of the reorganisation, during these stormy times of rising unemployment and social dissolution." *Hmm* – I wonder – *dissolution* sounds a little Dickensian, don't you think?'

Skelgill regards Kendall Minto as if he does not think.

He swallows down some coffee and leans over the periodical.

The photograph draws his eye.

Though it is just a head-and-shoulders shot, the impression is of a large man, thickset, with prominent features that might be attractive were they symmetrical. There is a bad haircut – almost a basin type – and dark eyes stare out ominously from beneath a heavy brow. There is no smile; just the hint of a knowing grin. A person not to be trifled with.

Skelgill does not speak. He leans back and takes up his second sausage sandwich.

Kendall Minto understands he should continue.

'Now, it seems to me that, despite his reputation, he kept a low profile – at least, as far as matters of public order were concerned. I began by going through the crime report pages – other than around the time of the Caldblow Farm murder, I could find no mention of him. Indeed, he left no epitaph. I located an article dated in late 1978 announcing the appointment of the new overall chief of the entire unitary authority – but it makes no reference either to John Bromilow or his five counterparts, all of whom were simultaneously replaced by a candidate from the Lincolnshire police. Read into that what you may.'

Grim-faced, Skelgill is looking disinclined to read anything into it, or into anything.

The reporter soldiers on.

'I have to say, I was a little surprised. John Bromilow came with something of a swashbuckling reputation and a penchant for publicity. I would have thought he'd have taken every opportunity to blow his own trumpet, knowing he was in contention for the top job.'

Skelgill does not indicate agreement; Kendall Minto puts on a burst of enthusiasm.

'But I was determined to find something for you, Inspector.'

He slips the first newspaper to the bottom of the pile and, smiling engagingly, lifts the marked tab of the next, newly exposed. However, on the point of making a great reveal, he seems to suffer a pang of doubt, and holds the page only half-open.

'It, er – it struck me that there is a traditional association between the police and the, er – the freemasons.'

He inhales sharply in self-reproach, an overt show of treading on eggshells.

But if Skelgill returns a look of malcontent, it does not appear to concern the cub reporter's trespassing upon forbidden territory; more likely that he disapproves of any such association. Or it might just be last night's Jennings ale.

Kendall Minto therefore takes a tentative step further.

'The organisation is known for its secrecy, but they do of course have regular charity dinners, ladies' nights – that kind of thing. And the Gazette has always reported such. Our readers like to know what the county set are up to. Who is hobnobbing with whom – even today, it's the most-read page on our website.'

Now he opens fully the double-page spread. The top half of the left-hand page, closest to Skelgill, is dedicated to photographs of groups of people at what looks like a dinner dance – the men are wearing black tie and the ladies ballgowns.

'And – hey presto!' He points triumphantly. 'Whitehaven Lodge, Ladies' Night, October 1975. And … here he is.'

Skelgill narrows his eyes. John Bromilow is seated at a table, raising a pint beer glass that looks more like a half in his great ham of a mitt; a woman, much younger, is beside him. The legend gives his name and title – but most intriguingly the female is merely described with the words "and partner".

Kendall Minto deems he should keep up his momentum. He closes the newspaper and slips it to the bottom of the pile. Now he opens the third.

'I then looked ahead to the following year – and sure enough – here he is again. But look – a different female. Closer to his age.' He is beginning to sound a little breathless. 'She's a striking woman – expensively bejewelled, by the look of that tiara. I was just beginning to think – 'Jack the Lad' – maybe it had another origin – until I read the caption …'

He slides his finger to the legend and holds it there until Skelgill leans closer.

Skelgill must take in instantly the significance of the tiny eight-point type, but he allows his gaze to linger over the composition. There are six diners in the shot, two males on the left, two females on the right. None of their four names means anything to him. Not so, however, for the man in the centre: Acting Head of Police, Chief Superintendent John Bromilow. And, beside him … *Lady Fitzrovia of Caldblow Farm estate.'*

That Skelgill does not react perhaps disappoints the young hack.

'I mean – there's no definitive statement that she is his partner –

even for the night – and I realise the consecutive seating plan of three males and three females might suggest otherwise – but – well, naturally, when I saw her name it rather jumped off the page.'

'When was this?'

Skelgill is squinting at the date printed at the top corner of the page.

'The edition was published on Friday 29th October, 1976. It was two months after the death of Will Featherston.'

Skelgill remains inscrutable. The journalist, unfamiliar with such habits, feels obliged to fill the silence.

'Of course – it struck me – that could be how they became acquainted. Even if he didn't handle the investigation personally, he spoke at daily press conferences. We have plenty of reports of that. Undoubtedly he would have visited the crime scene at Caldblow Farm. Surely he would have met Lady Fitzrovia. She was a widow. He was ostensibly single. Moreover –' Now Kendall Minto pauses for dramatic effect. '*I found another.*'

More hurriedly now, he closes the third newspaper and brings a fourth to the top of the deck.

'While I couldn't find any other masonic dinners – I thought, maybe there were other society events. And – *dah-daah* –'

With a flourish he opens the newspaper.

This time, the entire left-hand page is given over to a great gallery of photographs.

'It's the Copeland Hunt Ball, held at Muncaster Hall in June, 1977.'

Kendall Minto first draws Skelgill's attention to a section of larger shots in the upper section. At a glance it can be gleaned that John Bromilow was the guest of honour, for he presents awards – trophies of varying size and perhaps import – to a succession of winners.

'Now, look – here he is – and Lady Fitzrovia.'

Mid-page, a sticker marks a specific photograph. He peels it away so that Skelgill can see more clearly.

'This is rather like the precursor to the selfie – and he appears with several groups like this. But – well – see for yourself, Inspector.'

Skelgill, glowering somewhat, leans as close as he may.

There are four people – standing, displaying cocktails, responding in varying degrees to the camera. On the extreme right, the unmistakeable hulking figure of John Bromilow. Dinner suited, he towers menacingly, his heavy features casting their own dark shadows.

There is no caption, but if the woman in the earlier photograph was Lady Fitzrovia, then without doubt it is she to his right, her opera-gloved hand resting against his upper arm. There is a metropolitan sophistication about her attire, coiffure and make-up. And she is possessed of an exotic allure. Long, straight black hair, fine curved brows and prominent cheekbones, large dark eyes and a wide, full-lipped mouth. An hour-glass figure narrows preposterously at the waist and blooms to fill the low-cut satin gown.

Yet it is the supreme self-confidence that most strikes Skelgill. All of the rays of the photographer's flash might have refracted towards her being, rendering her in three dimensions while her companions languish in two.

It takes him a moment to move on to the man close at her other side. Short, middle-aged, by comparison he seems positively uncouth. Though he wears the regulation tuxedo, it is ill-tailored and shabby; his features are weaselly and his hair lank and lacking basic grooming. A salacious grin reveals uneven teeth and seems not unconnected with the fact that, most unpalatably of all, he has opportunistically hooked an arm around the woman's midriff, to the extent that he cups her bosom.

The last of the quartet, on the extreme left as viewed, stands just slightly detached. A young girl – questionably old enough to be wielding the cocktail – she conveys at once awkwardness and rebellion. Awkwardness, in that the dress is just a little too large for her youthful and somewhat flat-chested form; rebellion, in that her hair is bleached blond and spiked, and extravagant mascara, liner and eyeshadow speak volumes.

Kendall Minto watches anxiously while Skelgill's countenance slowly shifts through its subconscious repertoire. A little kaleidoscope of emotions, there might be enmity, desire, distaste and approbation.

Eventually, he can no longer contain himself.

'What do you make of it, Inspector?'

Skelgill does not answer – but the question causes him to pull away from the group photograph.

He pushes back his chair and stands, better to lean over the large spread of the newspaper. He rests the heels of his two hands upon the publication, and now reviews the upper section of images.

Still without a word he straightens, and closes the newspaper, and picks it up, folding it by its natural crease to half-size. Then, as Kendall Minto makes to protest, he folds it again, and once again – and then he gives a short, sharp whistle – and bends to feed the conveniently folded baton horizontally into the mouth of his dog, Cleopatra, as she appears blinking from beneath the settle.

Kendall Minto gasps with alarm.

'But –'

Instinctively, he reaches as though to retrieve the precious artefact – however, a baleful glare from the Bullboxer has him recoiling just as quickly.

Already, Skelgill is leaving the scene.

'Inspector – I – I'll be crucified – nothing is ever meant to leave the archive – it's a sacking offence.'

'You'll get your paper back. And you'll get your story.'

Rounding the banister at the head of the open staircase, he casts a hand at the table.

'And you can get the bill – I reckon it's your round.'

*

'A fine dog you have there, Inspector.'

Skelgill looks doubtfully at Cleopatra, who seems to understand she is receiving praise.

'Aye, she has her moments.'

'Is she specially trained to detect a certain criminal residue or illicit substance?'

Skelgill thinks for a moment.

'Scones?'

The woman winks heartily.

'Then you have come to the right place. Not that we're not doggy friendly, of course – although we have a compound for our hounds – they can be highly strung – they pick it up from the horses and sometimes can be a bit of a handful.'

Skelgill nods understandingly.

'Aye, it's no mean feat, whipping in. The fell pack's tapped enough – I should think when you chuck horses into the mix it's bedlam.'

The wide-ranging Copeland Hunt, like many of its ilk, is a disparate organisation, peripatetic in manifestation and with no proper headquarters. But judicious enquiries among his contacts have directed Skelgill to a large country house on the outskirts of the old iron-mining town of Egremont, little over a half hour's drive from his parking spot in Keswick.

The elegantly dilapidated Georgian mansion, set in chestnut-dappled parkland, with its working stables and dusty Coniston green Land Rovers, is home to a rather well-spoken and pukka forty-something Englishwoman, a sturdy tweed-clad stereotype of the 1920s mystery novel. By the name of Arabella Henson, and the latest in her line to fill the post, she is present incumbent in the office of Honorary Hunt Archivist.

And though Skelgill feels in his bones a growing sense of urgency (though nothing more tangible than that), he has been persuaded to partake of tea and lemon buns in the great traditional-style kitchen, with its high ceiling and Belfast sinks, and row of bells labelled with the likes of 'Drawing Room' and 'Study' and 'Tradesman Door'. He can picture mob-capped maids scurrying back and forth, a plump perspiring cook toiling over a great steaming cauldron, and an overseeing butler, supercilious at the door jamb. Those days are past now, and in the past they must remain. More recent events, however, are to be re-imagined.

He spreads out his newspaper. He tries to be careful, but notes that he leaves a greasy thumbprint conspicuously close to the masthead. He opens it to the marked page.

Immediately, Arabella Henson is enthralled.

'Oh, this is wonderful! I had no idea such photographs existed.

I could use some of these for the next newsletter. It's 1977, did you say? There might even be survivors from the actual event.'

Skelgill regards her earnestly.

'That's exactly what I'm hoping, madam. In particular, the winners of the awards.'

He indicates the upper section of the page.

Arabella Henson rises from her oak carver chair, the better to see.

On bootlaces she has reading glasses, and now she dons these and peers closely at the upper gallery of grainy images.

'Well, I recognise the trophies. As far as I can tell, they are the same seven prizes as to this very day.'

'Would they be engraved with the winners' names?'

She looks up over the rim of the spectacles and gives a small shake of the head.

'I am afraid not, young man.' But she raises an index finger in a somewhat reproachful manner. 'However, if my Great Aunt Tryphena did her job, we might just be in luck.'

The woman straightens up and backs away from the table, a purposeful expression taking hold of her ruddy and reliable countenance.

'Inspector, give me a moment. Help yourself to another lemon bun – and for the delightful Cleopatra – maybe just a half?'

'Happen she'll manage a whole.'

When Arabella Henson returns after a couple of minutes she bears a heavy-looking black box file that she drops with a relieved sigh upon the table; dust rises. Skelgill can see that the label on the spine is marked, "Events 1950 – 1999".

'This contains the programmes.'

She makes an educated guess, removing about half of the contents, and misses only by a couple of years. A little more sifting, and she gives a triumphant yelp and flourishes a small pamphlet.

Immediately, she begins a short presentation.

'The front – the introduction. Inside left – the running order. On the right – the menu. And the reverse – hey presto! – speeches and prize-giving. Let me see, now.'

Skelgill has been sitting obediently, but now he rises, and from their respective sides of the table they lean over the newspaper. Skelgill now deposits a full set of lemony fingerprints from his left hand.

'The photographs are out of order – but no matter. I recognise the trophies. So – first we have *Best Turned Out.*' She peers at the pamphlet. 'Mrs Kenneth Barrington-Smithe. Commended for exceptional style. *Hmm.*'

She hesitates, her gaze hovering over the photograph. She does not explain her small exclamation of dubiety. Skelgill sees a woman in her late forties, perhaps, but no cause for concern.

'Next – that one is called *Fence Builders.* And – we have joint winners – youngsters – George and Gertie Higson. A special mention for their cross-poles.'

She glances briefly at Skelgill.

'The Higsons have long farmed over at Nether Wasdale.'

Skelgill nods but remains silent. His pulse is rising, but his calm outward demeanour belies inner turmoil.

'Number three. *The John Peel Memorial Cup.* Main award of the year, of course. And the winner is – yes, Colonel Archibald Bulstrode, DSO – it states he was a veteran of the Battle of Arnhem. Fine stock, the Bulstrodes. One of our legends. He was killed a few years later. Broke his neck trying to jump a beck in spate. Mount refused.'

Skelgill makes an expression of sympathy, but the woman seems unperturbed by such an occupational hazard.

'Four. Aha – the leaping hunter – that is the trophy for *Most Daring.*' The woman jabs a finger at the photograph before cross-referencing it with the pamphlet. 'Yes – a slip of a girl. Plucky. And she's getting a kiss for it, too. Her name, Inspector – Susan Bell-Gibson. A special commendation – the first junior winner – an upper-sixth pupil at St Bees. Well, there's a thing – my own alma mater, don't you know?'

Arabella Henson pauses to take a sip of what must by now be cold tea, but she seems to need the liquid to facilitate the remainder of her presentation.

She proceeds to relate the titles and winners of the remaining three awards: *Fastest Eight Furlongs*, Mr Roger Bannister; *Hip Flask*

Fanatic, Mr Ernest Morecambe; and *Best Fall*, (surely no coincidence) also Mr Ernest Morecambe. Indeed, that she expresses some mirth at this latter duopoly causes Skelgill to start – for, despite that matters have confirmed his expectations (or, at least, his intuition), since hearing the account of *Most Daring* he has been entirely deaf to proceedings. He can think only of the peroxide princess, the punk Cinderella of the hunt ball.

'What do you think, Inspector?'

'Aye – aye – definitely.'

The woman eyes him suspiciously. He senses he has answered incorrectly. But it is time to dispense with diplomacy. He begins to close up the newspaper.

'Madam – that's been very helpful – but I've trespassed enough on your time.'

Now she looks surprised – and possibly just a little offended that he appears to be leaving so peremptorily. She is just getting into her stride.

'But – er – do you want to take a copy – a photograph with your mobile telephone?'

Skelgill taps the rolled-up newspaper against his temple.

'I've got a good memory.'

Perhaps she harrumphs.

Skelgill knows he is exiting with less decorum than her hospitality merits. And, not least, he has provided scant explanation of the basis for his enquiry.

'If I stay any longer, I'll be bursting at the seams. Your lemon buns are the best I've tasted. And I've never seen the dog eat more than one.'

She seems a little mollified.

'Oh. Well, then – you must take the last of them.'

Skelgill makes as if to protest – but his objection when voiced is half-hearted at best.

'I suppose in my line of work – you can't always stop for proper meals.'

'Oh – I was rather thinking of a doggy bag.'

Skelgill grins a little sheepishly; but he is thinking it is all the same to him.

20. TWO PLUS TWO

St Bees School – 1.00 p.m. Saturday 8 August

'Are you asking me to break the rules of GDPR, Inspector?'

'Madam, do I look like someone who would ask you to break the rules?'

'If the truth be told, yes.'

'Then perhaps it's just as well I don't know what they are.'

The woman across the broad oak desk murmurs, throatily, it seems to Skelgill.

'The General Data Protection Regulation. It restricts the transfer of private data. It became EU law in 2018.'

Skelgill tilts his head to one side.

'That's alright then.'

Now she plies him with a well-practised look that says, nice try.

'It remains on the UK statute book.'

'Can you not make an exception?'

'The trustees would have me hung, drawn and quartered.'

Skelgill grimaces; it is a day for hearing of medieval punishments and mishaps.

The woman continues.

'I would need there to be a warrant – or a sealed order of the court. You cannot imagine the strictures under which schools must operate. We are guardians of the naïve and the vulnerable.'

'Not when they're in their sixties.'

The woman folds her arms and leans back in her reclining chair. She is entirely amenable – to Skelgill's mind she is enjoying the exchange – indeed, unless he is mistaken, she is almost flirtatious.

His gaze falls again upon the desktop nameplate. *Miss Joanna Deedes, Head Teacher.* She seems young to occupy the august post; about his own age – and in looks as about as far from the stereotypical *Trunchbull* battleaxe as he can imagine. Directed from reception, he had anticipated a brooding matriarch – and upon entering her airy, spacious study, thought he was being greeted by a glamorous personal assistant with flowing auburn tresses and manicured nails to match. A light floral fragrance replaced the smell of polished wood.

Now, barely perceptibly, she seems to soften.

'Whom do you want to find out about?'

'A Susan Bell-Gibson. She was a sixth-former in 1977.'

She glances at Skelgill's calling card, placed on the surface between them. It appears she has no difficulty in reading at some distance. She might be double-checking his name – that he is no relation.

Then she tips herself forward and draws towards her an open laptop.

Deftly, she types.

She scrutinises what she sees, and then types some more.

Skelgill falls prey to one of his own tricks.

'I thought you might have an old – what would you call it – old boys, old girls club?'

'An association of alumni?'

'Or that, aye.'

She smiles, quite engagingly. Immaculate white teeth complement her model looks.

'We do. It's called the Old St Beghians.' She seems amused by Skelgill's reaction to the name. 'The school was founded in 1583 – we retain many archaic descriptors and traditions. Hogwarts is not so detached from reality, wizardry aside.'

Skelgill could swear she wrinkles her nose – but it might just be the act of concentration – now that what she seeks has apparently appeared upon her screen.

This time, he holds his tongue.

'Yes. We have her. Just an email address. We send her the electronic version of the termly magazine. Let me see. Yes, she opens them all. She was alive at least until two weeks ago.'

Skelgill can feel the hair on the back of his neck beginning to prickle – and he glances a little anxiously at the backs of his hands, as if concerned that a matching reaction will betray his excitement.

The Head lets out a small sigh, as though she has been inadvertently holding her breath – but she continues to peruse whatever protected data are before her eyes.

Skelgill is thinking, if only she would excuse herself – as she could so easily do – a comfort break, to fetch glasses of water from the cooler in the passage, to hail a passing janitor. It would take him ten seconds to spin the laptop, read the address and be sitting apparently unmoved on her return. He wills hard for such an outcome – but the magic fails.

The woman again scrutinises his calling card – and returns her attention to the laptop, touch typing rapidly, looking at the screen and not the keyboard.

She signs off with a flourish.

She plies Skelgill with a look of intrigue – as if she reads his thoughts and half approves of the mischief therein.

'I have sent her an email. She has your phone number. The ball is in her court. Without a warrant, that is the best I can do.'

Skelgill, too, has been holding his breath. Now he exhales, revealing something of his hand – but it is relief mixed with frustration. Since Kendall Minto unwittingly put him on the scent of the peroxide princess he has been champing at the bit. And if Professor Simeon Freud suspects the police are stealing up on the rails, he will surely throw everything he has got at Percy Tuseling – even if it means taking them all down.

Skelgill nods, a little defeatedly, perhaps – but showing some appreciation for the woman's cooperation.

She smiles, sympathetically it seems.

'Perhaps we'll meet again.' She folds shut the laptop and slips it into a drawer, which she locks. 'But now, if you will excuse me, I must change to referee a game of quidditch.'

*

Skelgill is thinking, what is it about redheads?

There is no quidditch – *of course* there's no quidditch – there are no pupils; it is another month before autumn term begins at

England's misleadingly named public schools. Perfectly 'public' if your annual salary is roughly four times the national average.

At such expense come facilities the likes of which the state school student could only dream. Skelgill is seated on a graffiti-free bench in the sun, beside pristine nets on the edge of an immaculately mown oval. His station is just over the boundary at deep square leg, for the right-hander receiving from Skelgill's left as he views.

The click of leather upon willow has attracted him from the perusal of an ancient quadrangle.

There might be no school – but a bunch of what looks like local kids, perhaps in company with children of live-in staff, are playing cricket to improvised rules – only one batter instead of pairs, and all hands fielding – but better than no game at all. He has thoughts of Will Featherston; an unrealised talent.

Shading his eyes, Skelgill hopes for the ball to come his way.

There ensues a little daydream, in which he is called upon to play – but he can't go out there and skittle this poor lot. That was how Percy Tuseling played – flaying the bowling no matter how young or inexperienced the opponent; a flat-track bully, they call that. He'd like to have taken on Percy Tuseling – flat track or not, he'd give him some chin music.

He gets quite carried away with this fantasy – a codified form of combat, skewed heavily in favour of the bowler, who can legitimately aim the ball at the batter's head – while to reciprocate is not in the rules.

Adrenaline runs in Skelgill's veins.

Uninvited, his hangover, hitherto artificially subdued, reveals itself still to be lurking.

For a moment his head thumps.

He clamps his hands over his ears but it makes no difference.

He feels momentarily nauseous and fastens a palm over his mouth.

Then dizziness assails him, and he covers his eyes.

Instinctively he lowers his head, almost to between his knees, allowing unwilling blood to gain the benefit of gravity.

He holds the pose; equilibrium is slowly restored.

He feels a tap against his left instep.

He removes one hand to see: it is a cricket ball.

He picks it up – momentarily puzzled by the materialisation – but when he looks up he sees a girl in her early teens is running towards him – she has obviously given up the chase to prevent the boundary – but still comes at a fair lick.

Impulsively he flicks the ball towards her – bouncing it just short. It turns prodigiously with the finger-spin he applies – but her reflexes are up to it and she adjusts to take the delivery cleanly, one-handed, low at her side.

'Owzat?'

Skelgill grins; she has spirit.

'That's out.'

He gives the umpire's signal.

Her momentum has carried her on close to him.

She is looking critically at his mobile phone, beside him on the slatted bench.

She points.

'You've got a call. You're on silent.'

She turns and jogs away.

Skelgill picks up his handset.

The number is withheld – but DS Jones for good reason has occasion to do such a thing, and may not have switched back on her identifier.

'Jones?'

'Detective Inspector Skelgill?'

It is not her, but an older female voice.

'Aye?'

There is now a pause – although there might also be a delay on the line.

'What took you so long to find me?'

'Who's speaking?'

'Susan Bell-Gibson.'

For a moment speechless, Skelgill finds himself on the defensive.

'We've only been going four weeks.'

'My father was murdered more than four decades ago.'

He sets aside thoughts that he should be checking the woman's credentials; though her accent is curious – could there be a Scots burr?

'Can I come and talk to you about it?'

'Sure.'

'Where do you live?'

'Perth.'

It accounts for the accent. He does his sums. An hour to Carlisle. Another one-and-three-quarters to Edinburgh. Forty-five minutes to Perth.

'I could be with you in under four hours.'

'Then you have a form of transport that has not yet been invented.'

'Come again?'

A sudden sound in the background seems designed to answer. A haunting laugh. *A kookaburra?*

'Are you in Australia?'

The woman chuckles, familiar it seems with the misapprehension.

'I should have said Freemantle – it's just that, only people interested in cricket have heard of it. So I'm in the habit of saying Perth. It's easy to forget the original is in Scotland. I've been here most of my life.'

Skelgill looks at his wristwatch.

'What time is it there?'

'Approaching six p.m. The sun is just setting. We're the equivalent latitude of New Orleans – except the other side of the equator.'

From Cumbria, the other side of the world.

But there is something she has said that he must revisit.

'What made you say it was about time we contacted you?'

'Last week a friend – she knows I'm from Cumbria. We've been gripped by the *Teacher's Pet* podcast – and she brought my attention to *Murder on the Farm*. I binge-listened – or whatever is the expression. I have been wondering whom to contact – somehow I expected the appropriate person to approach me first.'

'Consider it done.'

'Then I am at your service.'

Skelgill does not dwell over the offer.

'You've been in Australia for what – more than forty years?'

'Since I was eighteen.'

'When you left school?'

'You obviously know I attended St Bees. I won an equestrian scholarship to the University of Woolamaloo. It was due to begin at the end of October 1977.'

'Your father died at the start of the month.'

'That's right. It perhaps sounds a little heartless now. But my mother passed away when I was a small child. I attended boarding school from the age of eleven. I didn't know my father well. And then I was an orphan. My guardians at the school advised me to see out my plans. I should say they were correct – I would have been entirely ill-equipped to remain alone at Belltower Farm.'

'You didn't come back – after your degree?'

'The trustees sold the farm. When I came of age I inherited the capital. I used it to start an equestrian business out here. I still have the land and stables and livery to this day. It's what I do. I'm not ready to retire. I love it out here in the country.'

Skelgill tries to picture the scene – he strains to hear more sounds, the clunk and whinny of horses in their boxes, night birds, frogs and crickets. The land down under, of deadly spiders and snakes, and of great white sharks and saltwater crocodiles that must severely restrict the market for fishing waders.

'The police at the time – they didn't want you to attend the trial?'

'They were content with a written statement. Percy Tuseling had pleaded guilty. In fact they said their case would be stronger if I were not subject to cross-examination.'

'Did they say why?'

'Only that my account would be disputed – that, given my age, my reliability as a witness would be challenged. And I suppose I would naturally be viewed as hostile to Percy Tuseling. The police said that if he changed his plea they'd pay for me to come home. He didn't, there was no need.'

Skelgill ponders this point. Despite his misgivings, it is accurate to say that the Prosecution's strategy was successful.

'Can I ask you first – about the night your father was killed. I've seen your statement. Not long before – roughly a fortnight – the Hares had been convicted and jailed for the murder of Will Featherston. Did that come up in conversation?'

'Yes.'

Her response is unequivocal. For a moment Skelgill is caught off guard.

'Did it cause any controversy?'

She takes longer to answer this question.

'No more than it *was* controversial. They were pleading innocence – which proved right, yes?'

'You could call that a moot point. The acquittal was based on a forged confession. The actual evidence was never retested, nor any new evidence brought.'

'Which is where the podcast comes in?'

Skelgill finds himself wishing to object to the suggestion. But it is not the woman's fault if that is the public perception. Besides, it means he is satisfying his clandestine brief.

Notwithstanding, he inserts a correction.

'Well, they're not the police – they have no official jurisdiction.'

The woman murmurs a little ironically.

'They – well, he – the professor – seems to be acting like judge and jury.'

Skelgill is nodding in grim agreement. But however much he would be happy to bemoan the approach taken by Simeon Freud, he senses he must press on.

'Madam, you've heard the podcasts. There's the suggestion that your father might have known something – that Percy Tuseling had a hand in the murder of Will Featherston – that he challenged Percy Tuseling. What do you think about that?'

'It's not impossible. Whether he knew something – I don't know – but that wouldn't have stopped him. He was cantankerous and an agent provocateur. He might have just said it because he'd had too much to drink and let fly for no real reason other than devilment.'

Skelgill wants to understand a contradiction.

'Percy Tuseling described your father as a best friend – like a father to him.'

There is sufficient inflexion in his statement to prompt a response.

'He may have believed that – but my father's relationships were transactional.'

She offers no more – perhaps she is sidetracked by memories that her answer rekindles. Skelgill waits for a moment before returning to the main point.

'Okay. What did you think of Percy Tuseling's new explanation?'

'The Special Cocktails?'

'Aye.'

Again, she takes her time to answer.

'I don't know. It could have been an innocent turn of phrase.'

'You were what – seventeen, eighteen then?'

'Eighteen. But I was a public schoolgirl, a boarder, at that. You can knock off a few years on the maturity scale.'

It takes Skelgill a moment to find the right words.

'Did Percy Tuseling ever show any interest in you in that way – make any unwanted advances? Suggestive remarks?'

'If he did, I was too naïve to notice. Even to imagine the idea of an older man. And I'm sure my father would have railed against it – it was bad enough that I knew Will Featherston.'

'And what about –' Skelgill checks himself mid-question. Has he just heard correctly? 'You knew Will Featherston?'

Susan Bell-Gibson must detect alarm in Skelgill's voice, for she seems to row back a little.

'Not well, Inspector. But I knew who he was. We were the same age. I had girlfriends from junior school – from before I went to St Bees – they ended up in the same year at high school as Will Featherston and his mates. Sometimes a few of us from St Bees would sneak into town in the evenings – the train took under ten minutes. There was a live-music bar near the station that would serve under-age kids. The punk rock movement was just beginning – it was the cool thing to do.'

Skelgill nods as he pictures the photographs of the hunt ball –

the peroxide princess.

But he is not entirely satisfied.

'So, why would your father disapprove?'

She chuckles.

'I'm sure that like most adults at the time, he despised punk rock and all it stood for – I mean, the public image was designed to shock – safety pins in the ear, ripped clothing, pogoing, spitting. *Anarchy in the UK.*'

'But why Will Featherston, in particular?'

'He saw me speaking to him – on a couple of occasions.'

'Where was this?'

'At the farm – during the school holidays.'

'Will Featherston came to your farm – to Belltower Farm?'

'Oh, no – Caldblow Farm – he had the delivery job – you know, of course.'

'Aye.'

'I used to hack across the land of both farms. Sometimes with Lady Fitzrovia – so I would call for her. We had a loose arrangement for Fridays – and that was Will Featherston's delivery day.'

Skelgill is striving to understand what might have taken place.

'So, what – your father thought you were meeting him?'

'I just think he put two and two together and made five. To look at, Will was a pretty heavy-duty punk – I suppose if he saw me chatting with him – he probably automatically blamed him for my own unsatisfactory appearance.'

'So, he disapproved.'

She laughs ironically.

'I think he sent poor Will away with a flea in his ear. He held firm ideas that I should not mix beneath my station. Indeed – that I should marry well above it – that there were eligible sons of the wealthy at St Bees whom I should be cultivating. We were far from landed gentry – to be frank, my father was an uncouth farmer – but he aspired to what he saw as higher society. Paying to send me to St Bees was part of that. And I suppose his arrangement with Lady Fitzrovia gave a boost to his status. He used to hold shoots for influential contacts that he made through the freemasons and the rotary club and the hunt. When I reflect, looking back I'm not sure he was ever accepted – but, like I say, it was all transactional to him.'

Skelgill is beginning to understand that this principle extended to Colin Bell-Gibson's relationship with his daughter. That he would pack her away to board at a school just a few miles from their home. It seems unlikely a mother would have done such a thing. But his thoughts return to Will Featherston. He is still a little stunned by the revelation that she was acquainted with the boy. No such reference has been turned up in their records.

'When Will Featherston was killed, were you interviewed?'

'No – I was away with the school riding club. We were at a gymkhana in Wales – I think from the Thursday morning until the Sunday night. Obviously in those days there was little communication. I found out when I returned.'

'But you say you weren't interviewed, afterwards?'

'No. I was never approached. But I don't know what I could have added. There must have been plenty of Will's contemporaries that knew him much better than I.'

'Other than the farm connection.'

She hesitates before she responds.

'I see that now – and am reminded of such by the podcasts. But at the time – you have to remember how it seemed. Armed robbers had got away with murder the next farm. I returned to a rural community that felt under siege. My father was on constant guard – until the Hares were arrested, I guess. It must have been nerve-wracking for Lady Fitzrovia.'

Now Skelgill is given pause for thought. From the perspective of the police, powerful and on the offensive, it is easy to overlook how the populace at large might be terrorised. Lady Fitzrovia – living alone and something of a city fish out of water – may have felt particularly vulnerable, all circumstances considered.

'How well did you know her?'

'Only as well as a teenager can know an adult neighbour. I suppose I was just getting old enough for there to be the beginnings of some common connection. But, on the whole, I was company to ride round with – someone from whom she could get tips. She wasn't too good on horseback – she wasn't a country person – she had no interest in the farm – though she didn't mind riding. I think the idea appealed to her – and the society aspect of hunting.' She murmurs, perhaps it is a laugh. 'But age-wise – and worldly wise – we were some distance apart. She humoured me – though I think she approved of my rebellious streak. Veronica Fitzrovia was a bit of a rebel herself.'

Skelgill wonders if for a moment he has misheard.

'She was called Veronica?'

'Bearer of victory.'

'Come again?'

'It's what she told me – the original meaning – it always stuck in my mind. When you're a Susan you often yearn for something more exotic.'

Skelgill has put his phone onto speaker, and is tapping and scrolling, scowling darkly. But he continues to speak.

'Did you ever go into Caldblow Farm – into her farmhouse?'

'On occasion – on a hot day – for a lemonade after a hack, perhaps.'

'What do you remember of it?'

Again there is something of a pause before Susan Bell-Gibson replies.

'It's funny – because it was a little exotic, too. It's hard to put a finger on it – there was an aroma – maybe incense? Essential oils – I don't know. It certainly didn't smell of wet dogs and old boots like our place. And it was expensively furnished. It was shadowy – there were heavy velvet curtains.'

Skelgill falls silent for a few moments as he wrestles with technology. Then he exhales, as it appears he succeeds.

'I've got a screen shot of something – an ornament. Can I try texting it to you?'

'Sure.'

He mutters, and curses under his breath; for a few seconds he is all fingers and thumbs; give him a snarl of near-invisible fishing line, any day of the week.

'Good onya.'

She knows before he does that he has managed to transmit

successfully.

Skelgill is still prodding in frustration at the screen. He halts and stares at the image.

'Did she have anything like this?'

'Yes, she did – several – quite a collection, in fact. Now you mention it, I think she said something like they were given to her by admirers – that struck me as curious. They were scattered about the place – it was a bit of a theme. Various styles and different materials. All comparatively small. Although I remember now a large one facing down from the half-landing on the main staircase. It was a little disconcerting.'

There is a *thwack*.

Instinctively, Skelgill raises his eyes towards the sound. The cricket ball is skimming at speed across the short turf in his direction.

But when he might gleefully field and return the ball, demonstrating the prowess of his left arm, it is as if he does not see it at all. He stares down the line of its oncoming trajectory, but he does not blink, nor move a muscle as it glides between his feet and beyond the bench.

'Hey up, Mister!'

A cry exhorts him to step in for weary limbs.

He seems not to hear it.

'Inspector? Can you still hear me?'

But neither does Susan Bell-Gibson's entreaty rouse him.

A hand falls lightly upon his shoulder.

Now he starts and turns.

Offering the cricket ball – slender bronze-tipped fingers – his gaze traces the arm to the lithe figure of Miss Joanna Deedes, clad in sports kit, her distinctive locks drawn back by a band.

'How's that?'

*

Skelgill grimaces and pulls down the visor above his windscreen. It is not like him to be bothered by the sun, but he must still be dehydrated and his hangover has one last sting in its tail. His Kelly kettle is out of water; he could go back into the school – but that feels awkward – besides, he has a growing sense that time is slipping through his fingers like fine dry desert sand – an image that makes him feel all the more parched, and his tongue reminds him of a desiccated fish he might find on a dried-up river bed.

His mobile rings.

Emmalene.

No doubt about the caller this time.

'Jones.'

'Guv?'

She sounds to Skelgill apprehensive.

His speaking tackle is tangled and she follows up before he can respond.

'I tried you last night – your phone seemed to be off – it kept diverting to voicemail.'

Skelgill makes an incoherent growl in his throat.

'I was with the lads from darts. What time did you ring?'

'A few times – around nine. The production meeting wrapped up earlier than expected. They were badgering me to go for something to eat – so I went with them in the end. I figured the more I could find out about Sim's intentions, the better.'

Uncharacteristically, she yawns. It seems to Skelgill a note of greater significance than its merit. His expression becomes somewhat more pained. He does not, however, reply, and it is left to DS Jones to make the running.

She, too, seems a little reticent.

'I got a cryptic text message from Kendall Minto.'

'Aye?'

Skelgill is further discomfited.

'Yes. It said for the sake of his career my assistance would be appreciated in ensuring the safe return of a valuable artefact. And that this would probably make sense in due course. What do you think he meant, Guv – I mean, what artefact?'

Skelgill is appraising the reporter's request, as now relayed. On the whole, it seems he has not broken any confidences, and must be more troubled by the loss than Skelgill had realised.

'I've been putting two and two together.'

His rejoinder does not make a great deal of sense to his colleague.

'Today, you mean?'

'Aye.'

'Have you made any headway?'

Skelgill takes a time to answer.

'Possibly. Probably.'

DS Jones's mind ticks over more quickly.

'Where are you?'

'St Bees School – parked up.'

'Ah.'

'I've just spoken to Susan Bell-Gibson.'

'What – at the school?'

'Nay – she's in Perth.'

'Scotland?'

'Australia.'

DS Jones hesitates. She senses that Skelgill is on the cusp of something that he either doesn't understand – or perhaps quite yet believe. At such times he is not a money-box that responds well to being tipped upside down and rattled, knife-assisted or otherwise.

'Do you want to go for cuppa, or something?'

Another pause.

'I'll pick thee up.'

'Or I could meet you, if it's easier?'

'Nay – I'll swing by – you're on the way.'

'The way?'

'Carlisle.'

DS Jones would have been less surprised had Skelgill's destination been Bass Lake or Haystacks.

'Okay. Is that part of putting two and two together – to make five?'

'In my case, call it three.'

21. EPISODE 5: LIVE

Blindkirk – 2.15 p.m. Monday 9 August

'So, Percy, I've been watching you.'

'And I've been watching you, Simeon.'

The perspective is that of DS Jones, from the back of the sitting room. For once – for this last time – the crew is visible to Skelgill and DS Leyton – what the TV audience never sees, albeit a restricted, lower-resolution image, its quality further compromised by the inherent instability of the camera wearer's movements. The protagonists on the sofa. To one side, angled in, a camera on a tripod directed at Professor Simeon Freud. Videographer Kate prowling with a second camera. From a corner, out of shot and holding the long boom mike, audiographer Mel. In the foreground on her haunches with a clipboard, producer Jen. And, finally, seated near the door upon a dining chair moved in for the purpose, Percy Tuseling's second wife Maria, a silent observer, stiff and upright, beehive hairdo piled high, unmoving and regal like Nefertiti among other statuettes.

Percy Tuseling seems to sense that something is heading down the tracks. The rails are humming and an arc of steam is visible over the horizon. The sound in his head of pistons is getting louder.

His voice has started out at its elevated falsetto; there is not much headroom should he desire to convey greater discontent. But all the threat emanates from the professor, suave and ominous at the opposite end of the sofa.

Indeed, this is the impression made upon DS Leyton.

'Sounds like he's going straight in for the kill, Guv.'

Skelgill does not answer but scowls severely at the small screen balanced on the dashboard of the car, a laptop connected wirelessly via DS Leyton's mobile telephone to the live feed from their female colleague's body-worn camera.

DS Leyton remarks further.

'And Tuseling looks like he knows what's coming.'

Skelgill nods. Percy Tuseling might not be the most analytical of men – low cunning being his obvious attribute – but he cannot have failed to feel which way the prevailing wind has blown during the course of his encounters with the great criminologist. Under the guise of sweeping away the years of debris, the professor has relentlessly pursued a single-minded agenda, to expose the buried half-truths that will wither upon exposure to the disinfection of daylight.

Now he ignores Percy Tuseling's petulant rejoinder.

'Much hinges, Percy, on your alibi on the afternoon that Will Featherston was murdered.'

'Ye-es.' Agreement is uninvited, and thick with impatience.

'Joan Arkwright understood you were at work. You had communication with her. You took her to St Bees Head. But she wasn't overseeing your every move. And by your own account you spent time away from your workshop, ill disposed. And let's not forget those conveniently missing timesheets.'

Through limited detail, the fly-on-the-wall audience can detect increasing discomfort and tension in Percy Tuseling.

'It was ten minutes' drive from Radio Rentals in Whitehaven to Caldblow Farm. And your alibi – it has holes – it is not cast-iron – it … well, frankly, it disappears, Percy.'

'I accept what you're saying. I don't have now a cast-iron alibi. Do you have any evidence that I killed Will Featherston? If you do, sir, bring it forward. If you don't, shut your mouth. Okay – you've now annoyed me.'

Percy Tuseling has uttered these terse phrases – a somewhat incoherent sentence structure – with bitter ire. His lips are compressed to the point of being gone. His face is flushed. His small eyes are unblinking.

'You get annoyed by me fairly regularly, Percy – and you threaten me quite a lot.'

'It's not threatening, it's me talking straight.'

The professor, however, is disconcerted. He crosses his legs and leans back.

'We've had it on good authority that the subject of Will Featherston was mentioned that night at Belltower Farm – when you shot your friend Colin Bell-Gibson.'

This much, and other limited findings, have been conveyed to the production team by DS Jones.

'Well, if it was, I wasn't in the room at that time. *I* didn't mention it.'

'We also have information that there was a hotspot of farmhouse robberies that corresponded to your territory as a repairman. And of course you supplied antiques and second-hand goods to your brother-in-law, Harry Robertson. Perhaps Mr Bell-Gibson also had some knowledge of that. Did you discuss robberies and antiques with Mr Bell-Gibson?'

'I did no such thing.'

The professor reaches out to producer Jen and is passed some items.

'Let me show you these, Percy.'

Percy Tuseling's keen eyes are alert to danger.

'These are very distressing, Percy. The crime scene photographs of Will Featherston's murder.'

Taking the enlarged prints, and plainly feeling under pressure to react in a conventional manner, Percy Tuseling looks like he is double-guessing just what that convention should be.

'These are the crime scene, are they?'

His complexion is becoming crimson and his head seems to be bursting out of the too-tight waistcoat and jacket and tie that he has donned to be smart for his final interview. And there is deflection in the way he repeats the statement as a superfluous question.

A little too quickly, it seems, he hands back the photographs and reaches for a glass of water on a side table. He struggles to drink, as though his mouth is dry beyond redemption.

If the professor's intention is to shock, to disorient, his tactic seems to have met with success.

'You did go to Caldblow Farm, didn't you, Percy?'

'No, I did not.'

The professor plies his victim with a long look, inviting him to change his mind.

Now, like the magician he likes to portray himself as, Simeon Freud receives a clipboard.

His demeanour is patronising, condescending – self-satisfied, smug.

DS Leyton glances anxiously at Skelgill. Is this it – the so-called secret weapon?

Skelgill's eyes stare out lake-grey from a pained countenance. He looks like he would wish to intervene, were he able.

The professor allows the tension to build further, until he finally pronounces.

'Percy, based upon our interviews I have done a P-Scan on you.'

'What's that?'

'It's a psychopathy scan – a tool of the qualified psychologist. This isn't a clinical diagnosis – but a way that I can gain some insight into the person that I'm talking to. There are ninety criteria and the total score for you was in the high range.'

He raises his clipboard in order to quote aloud.

' "A total score that falls in the high range should be a cause for serious concern. It suggests that the person of interest may have many or most of the features that define psychopathy. Such a person is likely to be egocentric, callous, cold-blooded, predatory, impulsive, irresponsible, dominant, deceptive, manipulative and lacking in empathy, guilt or genuine remorse for socially deviant or criminal acts." '

He pauses.

'And that fits you to a T.'

'It also fits you, *you bastard* – some of the things you've said. *To a T.*'

The professor ignores the retort – and the warning signs of emphasis.

'This is you Percy. You are somebody that I regard as a –'

'A psychopath, yes –'

'As a liar, Percy – as somebody that has bent the truth – as manipulative – as conning – not this kindly old fellow' (he gestures towards the older man). 'That's your performance, Percy – and I see through it. And all I can say to you is in the absence of you having any alibi –'

'I'm not going to *say* let me get a word in – *I am* going to get a word in, Simeon – I think *you* need to see a psychiatrist – you are wrong – *so very wrong* – you're egoistic – all Mr Important – *what the hell does it matter what you think?* There's not a scrap of hard evidence. You'll have to prove that. Go ahead. Do what you want' (he jabs a finger at the clipboard) 'But I think *you* need psychiatric treatment, son. There's something wrong with the way you think. *You're a ******* nutcase.'* He employs an oath that will certainly be bleeped from the final production.

'I think, Percy, that now it's for other people to make their decision on these kinds of things, because all I can do is tell you what I felt – and I will raise this elsewhere. There will be trouble –'

'I'll give you trouble –'

Perhaps in the absence of close-ups that have revealed in fine detail the several times that Percy Tuseling has neared boiling point but somehow managed to keep the lid on the pressure cooker, Skelgill and DS Leyton watching on are caught unawares when he lurches across the settee and grabs Professor Simeon Freud two-handed by the throat.

But they do not wait to watch events unfold – only as they each eject from their respective car doors does Skelgill get an impression of DS Jones's camera approaching the melee.

Thirty seconds later they are inside the bungalow and in ten more Skelgill hurtles into the sitting room where first filming and now a fight is taking place.

Simeon Freud cowers in a corner, keening plaintively and grasping his windpipe.

On the floor before the settee DS Jones straddles a screaming and spitting Percy Tuseling.

Audiographer Mel jabs him on the head with her boom microphone – and in a further effort to subdue him producer Jen kneels across his shins. Camera operator Kate – with interesting presence of mind – is continuing to film and at the same time she blocks the access of Percy Tuseling's wife Maria, who is clutching an Oscar-sized statuette in perhaps a half-hearted attempt to intervene on behalf of her spouse.

Percy Tuseling might be in his seventies but he is sturdy and there is the legacy of his years of prison body-building. And, he is infuriated.

Skelgill bellows an instruction for the females to move clear.

He and DS Leyton swoop.

They haul the man to his feet and now Skelgill gets him in an armlock.

Percy Tuseling slavers and snorts and swears blue murder, flinging curses at the cringing academic, threatening to sue him for his two-faced double-crossing, and calling an end to their agreement.

Skelgill casts a disparaging glance at Professor Simeon Freud – a man in his early forties and more than half the bulk again of the lionesses who came to his rescue. Then he hisses an aside to his colleague.

'Leyton – make sure everyone's alreet.'

He begins to frogmarch Percy Tuseling out of the room.

Anticipating a question, he calls over his shoulder.

'We're having a little sculpture class.'

There ensues the sound of an external door opening and closing.

It appears Skelgill has taken his charge into the back garden.

*

By the time Skelgill returns, order is restored.

DS Leyton regards him questioningly.

'Where is he, Guv?'

'Handcuffed to a statue.'

Skelgill is casually tossing some small item in his left hand.

He ignores the professor. The man is still snivelling, touching his throat gingerly. One of the girls ministers to him reluctantly. She raises her eyebrows to Skelgill.

He turns to producer Jen.

'You three might want to come and record this.'

'Oh, really – why?'

'Just get your skates on, lass – before he changes his mind again.'

The three – video, audio, production – grab their gear and fly.

The professor is left alone.

Last out of the garden door, DS Leyton, intrigued, tugs Skelgill by the sleeve.

'Guv – shouldn't we look for the flamin' golden pearl Aphrodite?'

Skelgill presents his closed fist.

'Leyton, it's not Aphrodite we're looking for.'

He unfurls his long fisherman's fingers to reveal the little brass sculpture of the Three Wise Monkeys.

22. STOP PRESS

GAZETTE EXCLUSIVE – YOU READ IT HERE FIRST
CUMBRIA FARM MURDER EXPOSÉ
By Kendall Minto

ONE GIANT LEAP FOR THE GAZETTE! We proudly bring you in today's edition an exclusive interview with the man who has cracked the Caldblow Farm murder – a case that has languished unsolved for the last half century.

Nowhere else can you read or hear or see this story. If you have been following the *Murder on the Farm* podcast, produced by our partner Turnpike Media, the final episode has been delayed for a week. It is hoped that the TV documentary will be premiered at next year's Cannes film festival.

Working behind the scenes, a team of detectives led by Inspector Daniel Skelgill of Cumbria CID has finally achieved what their predecessors, the courts, the probation services, social services, investigative journalists – and even the legendary criminologist Professor Simeon Freud have failed to do: to get to the bottom of the mystery.

We print below the verbatim transcript of our reporter (yours truly) Kendall Minto's exclusive interview with the modest and retiring Inspector Skelgill – a man rarely seen and less often heard – and we take this opportunity to claim a tiny slice of the glory for the Gazette, for our own small part in this famous success.

Without further ado, herewith the interview:

MINTO: Inspector, the sixty-four-thousand-dollar question – who killed Will Featherston? That's what every Gazette reader wants to know.

SKELGILL: Happen we should leave that to the end.

MINTO: Do you mean it is still inconclusive?

SKELGILL: I mean if there were a trial there would be a conviction.

MINTO: How cryptic of you, Inspector. In our opening article, we stated our aim was to give Will Featherston justice. Has that justice been served?

SKELGILL: That depends on your definition of justice.

MINTO: *Ahem.* I understand you obtained a confession from Percy Tuseling?

SKELGILL: Let's say he provided two missing pieces of the jigsaw.

MINTO: Can you share these – without compromising the legal position?

SKELGILL: I can present you with the evidence that he's now prepared to state publicly – then you can make up your own mind.

MINTO: I am all ears, Inspector.

SKELGILL: You need to remind yourself that Percy Tuseling had a sideline as a small-time crook and wheeler-dealer. He had a record of petty crime that included burglary – and a reputation of a violent temper. He occasionally supplied antiques and second-hand goods to his brother-in-law, a market trader. Their origin may not always have been legitimate.

MINTO: He was an unsavoury character, shall we say?

SKELGILL: Except he held down a skilled job, he was in a stable marriage, he was making his way in the world. He was developing an interest in sculpture. He played for a cricket team to a good standard.

MINTO: Ah, yes, the cricket – that was how he knew Will Featherston, right? They were neighbours, and the men used to join in with the local boys after work.

SKELGILL: He may not have known Will Featherston.

MINTO: Really? I thought that was the whole basis for suspicion. The accepted scenario. Percy Tuseling realised he had been recognised by Will Featherston in the act of burgling Caldblow Farm – and shot him.

SKELGILL: You've seen the videos of Percy Tuseling.

MINTO: Er, yes?

SKELGILL: Percy Tuseling quite likely paid no heed to the bairns. They were cannon fodder to him. He was just there to get free practice. By the time Will Featherston got shot, he'd grown up, changed – and he dressed as a punk rocker. Even his former friends didn't recognise him.

MINTO: Well, okay. Then I digress, Inspector. You say there are two new pieces of evidence?

SKELGILL: On the afternoon of Friday 13th August, 1976, Percy Tuseling received a phone call at his workshop in Whitehaven. It was a message to go to Caldblow Farm. He was to collect a bag of unwanted bric-a-brac. The bag would be in bushes by the side gate. He was told it would be of interest to him.

MINTO: Oh, my. Several questions crowd my lips! This bag – it must be the carpet bag of which we have heard mention in the podcasts?

SKELGILL: Aye.

MINTO: The bag of antiques that became "too hot to handle" – one might say?

SKELGILL: Aye.

MINTO: So, let me get this right. Percy Tuseling has admitted to being at Caldblow Farm on the afternoon of Will Featherston's murder?

SKELGILL: At, aye.

MINTO: By that, you mean not in the farmhouse?

SKELGILL: He drove up. He saw the fishmonger's van parked. He took the bag and left. He was away from his workshop for less than half an hour.

MINTO: So – the corollary, if I am understanding correctly – he still maintains he played no part in the murder of Will Featherston?

SKELGILL: He's consistently denied it.

MINTO: Right. In that case, did he know – could he have known – that Will Featherston was killed?

SKELGILL: Balance of probabilities – not at the time.

MINTO: So – what did he think he was doing – in taking the bag of antiques? Wasn't he a bit suspicious? People don't normally throw out such valuables.

SKELGILL: Like I say – he was a small-time crook and it suited his sideline. That's about all you need to know.

MINTO: Ask no questions, be told no lies?

SKELGILL: Aye.

MINTO: But – it could not have been long before he found out about the murder? It was plastered all over the media.

SKELGILL: As soon as he got home, he heard it on the radio. Caldblow Farm had been burgled and a kid whose name he knew had been shot dead. It made him ill.

MINTO: And, presumably … not least because it dawned upon him that he had just ostensibly committed the burglary?

SKELGILL: Aye.

MINTO: Did he not think of contacting the police – of coming clean? He hadn't actually done anything wrong, had he?

SKELGILL: Try putting yourself in his shoes.

MINTO: You mean, because the police in due course framed the Hares – and he foresaw in advance a similar fate, given his background and connections to the farm?

SKELGILL: Plus he'd worked out he had a watertight alibi. And he had the valuables.

MINTO: So it was a tad more than self-preservation. There was self-interest at play.

SKELGILL: You've seen what he's like. His warped personality. He believed he'd get away with it. Brass it out. He said as much to his wife, Veronica.

MINTO: Okay – let me get this right – the phone call – to collect the valuables. So, if it wasn't a robbery – was it – I mean, Inspector

– was he set up?

SKELGILL: You could call it that.

MINTO: Help me here, Inspector. Was it – wait – was it the Hares? No – it couldn't be. They would have taken the booty. I'm confused, I must confess.

SKELGILL: Consider the evidence. What happened next to Percy Tuseling?

MINTO: *Ahem.* I'm sure I'm supposed to be doing this interview – but I shall humour you, Inspector. Well – what happened to Percy Tuseling was that over the course of the next few weeks he became a suspect. Indeed – the evidence that has been assembled for *Murder on the Farm* comprises so many unlikely coincidences that it approaches the incontrovertible. And he didn't help himself by his efforts to throw the authorities off the scent.

SKELGILL: Some might say, well beyond the standard of proof required, beyond reasonable doubt.

MINTO: Exactly, Inspector.

SKELGILL: So, what happened to him?

MINTO: Well – I mean – *ah* – I see. Nothing happened to him, did it?

SKELGILL: Nay. Nowt.

MINTO: You are looking at me as though I should be joining the dots.

SKELGILL: It's you that's got the degree in joining dots.

MINTO: *Ahem.* I scraped a 2.2 on re-sit – a Desmond, as the saying goes. And not the most prestigious college.

SKELGILL: Park that. What happened to him next?

MINTO: You mean, after the Hares had been sent down?

SKELGILL: Aye.

MINTO: Well – of course – the significant thing that happened is that he shot Colin Bell-Gibson and was found guilty of his murder. He never revealed the motive – until a couple of weeks ago – the tale of the Special Cocktail.

SKELGILL: And do you buy that?

MINTO: *Aha!* I would – but you say you have two new pieces of jigsaw. Is this the second?

SKELGILL: Try blackmail.

MINTO: *Blackmail?* Over what?

SKELGILL: It's been touched upon plenty.

MINTO: Are you talking about the suggestion that Colin Bell-Gibson accused him of some involvement in the death of Will Featherston?

SKELGILL: That wouldn't exactly be blackmail. But you're halfway there. I'll put you out of your misery.

MINTO: Please do.

SKELGILL: Colin Bell-Gibson announced that he intended to bed Percy Tuseling's wife. If Tuseling didn't agree, Bell-Gibson would let it be known that Tuseling took the antiques from Caldblow Farm.

MINTO: Did he know that? Wait – did *he* make the phone call?

SKELGILL: Leave out the phone call. Just accept that he received it – and that on the night of the second murder, at Belltower Farm, Colin Bell-Gibson convinced him he did know about the antiques.

MINTO: But, again – Percy Tuseling could have come clean – or he could simply have denied it. It was just Colin Bell-Gibson's word against his.

SKELGILL: Not when there were two other witnesses.

MINTO: You mean, the witnesses who identified his red Ford Corsair?

SKELGILL: I mean witnesses he considered far more powerful than that.

MINTO: But who?

SKELGILL: I won't say who – Percy Tuseling is not presently saying who – just like he's not saying who made the phone call. But look what happened next.

MINTO: Well – he admitted to the killing – hoped to get off with the lesser charge of manslaughter on the grounds of temporary psychosis.

SKELGILL: He covered up his true motive. Even for these podcasts – he's been covering up his motive.

MINTO: Until you twisted his arm.

SKELGILL: Who told you that?

MINTO: Oh – I speak figuratively. I mean – you found

secondary evidence that proved persuasive. I think that's where I lent a small helping hand?

SKELGILL: Aye – I'll give you that. Even if it started out as the blind leading the blind.

MINTO: I suspect that's a backhanded compliment. But I'll take it … if it has led to the solution of this confounded mystery. The true killer of Will Featherston.

SKELGILL: You must know that after the thick end of half a century, the key actors are all deceased.

MINTO: But you said if there were a trial there would be a conviction?

SKELGILL: I stick by that. If there'd been a trial there'd have been a conviction. That's still open to the Coroner today. A jury can still hear the evidence and find the truth – your true killer.

MINTO: And whom do you think they would convict?

SKELGILL: Far be it from me to double-guess a jury.

MINTO: Yet you say you are confident there would be a conviction.

SKELGILL: There was a murder. At the very least there would be a finding of manslaughter. There were accessories. There was a cover-up. There would be a finding of obstruction. There was probably perjury. Take your pick.

MINTO: But we can only speculate who might have pulled the trigger?

SKELGILL. I've got a few middle names – some of them unprintable – but one's not speculation.

MINTO: Which is why you said it might be a disappointment?

SKELGILL: There's still some road to travel.

MINTO: Can I hold out hope for a further interview?

SKELGILL: You can hope.

MINTO: But one thing you are certain of – that Percy Tuseling did not shoot Will Featherston?

SKELGILL: Let's just say I've got a nose for the truth.

AND SO, DEAR READER, there it is. Reading between the lines, the police do not believe that Percy Tuseling was the killer of Will Featherston. And we must wait a little longer – but hopefully not too long – to find out who are the 'deceased actors' in this long-standing mystery. Inspector Skelgill holds out hope of there being more news forthcoming. What we can conclude from our own researches and the findings of *Murder on the Farm* to date, is that if the key actors are dead, then we can exclude from the list of suspects the likes of Joan Arkwright, Veronica Smith (formerly Tuseling), Susan Bell-Gibson and – perhaps most significantly – the Hare twins (whom we have tracked down to a farm near the Ulster border town of Warrenpoint). You might begin to draw your own conclusions from names that have appeared in the Gazette's articles hitherto and which do not appear in this list. If not … then watch this space! In fact, why not sign up for a subscription!

23. WISE AFTER THE EVENT

St Bees Head – 3.45 p.m. Friday 13th August

'So, there's no chance of Freud stealing our thunder?'

'I swear, Guv – Jen says he's resigned from the project – retreated with his tail between his legs. That's why they want us to film this piece – just an informal discussion that pulls together the loose ends.'

'It's like what they call the denouement in those detective stories, Guv. That little French geezer.'

Skelgill glares at DS Leyton for what he considers reprehensible connivance with DS Jones. He transfers the glare back to her.

'Are you filming now?'

'Yes – it's just set to run – in the background – so we forget it's there.'

'And a phone's good enough?'

'It's pretty high definition – and besides – Jen says a sort of casual quality is perfect. As if we were just making a recording of a meeting instead of taking notes.'

Skelgill shakes his head.

'I can't believe the Chief's agreed to this.'

DS Jones gestures with open palms.

'She'll be doing her own piece to camera. An official statement – an apology for historical failings.'

Now DS Leyton chips in.

'She ain't half taking it seriously. I overheard George saying she's booked a hair-and-make-up artist and a personal stylist.'

'She's waiting for our final report. I just need your input, Guv.' DS Jones regards Skelgill questioningly.

'Aye – aye – I'll read it. I'll take it out on Bass Lake on Sunday.'

DS Leyton splutters.

Simultaneously, the Kelly kettle begins to erupt and gives Skelgill the excuse of a diversion.

DS Jones gets up and on tiptoes cranes to check her phone, set on the lighthouse boundary wall behind their impromptu picnic spot. The picture is dramatically composed. In the foreground the participants are ranged around the smoking kettle on the short, dry clifftop turf; beyond the vast expanse of the Irish Sea, shimmering in the angled sunlight, the Isle of Man the long ship on the horizon that has made no headway since Skelgill's last visit. The video is running and the battery displays satisfactory charge. She returns to her fold-out foam sit-mat, one of three produced from Skelgill's capacious army surplus rucksack.

Their environs are silent but for occasional cries of seabirds and now the regular tinkle of a spoon. A faint salt breeze drifts from the west and stirs the pleasant aromatic scent of wild thyme they have crushed underfoot. It is a precious balmy afternoon – weather that is becoming dangerously familiar in what is shaping up to be one of the best summers of the millennium, if no match for 1976.

Skelgill doles out teas in tin mugs and DS Leyton is again the provider of vittles – more of his neighbour's Borrowdale chocolate shortcake that Skelgill insisted he would not like.

He takes a bite and waves his piece at Skelgill.

They have not rehearsed, but neither have Skelgill's subordinates yet extracted from him the full story of the unexpected 'turning' of Percy Tuseling.

DS Leyton addresses the crux.

'So what made him come clean, Guv?'

Skelgill seems for a moment camera-shy, and reverts to his trusty recipe for such situations, that mixes a measure of evasiveness with a pinch of recalcitrance.

'I wouldn't say he did come clean – not completely.'

DS Jones anticipates the need to oil the cogs of such caprice.

'Without your intervention we'd have been back at square one – he was all set to retract everything and cancel the contract.'

Skelgill might now just play up to the camera, the praise being too much for him to resist entirely. He gives a slow nonchalant shrug. But he contrives still to play down his accomplishment.

'Happen Veronica Smith was right when she said she thought he knew more than he was admitting to.'

Now DS Leyton joins in.

'Surely it wasn't just that, Guv? I mean, you didn't say, tell us what your ex-wife reckons you know – and he just spilled the beans.'

Skelgill shakes his head.

'I mentioned it though – but there was a bigger picture … and this …'

He rolls half to one side and produces from his trouser pocket a small item that he now displays in an open palm.

It is the bronze ornament, the Three Wise Monkeys still on loan from Veronica Smith. He glances at the camera.

'Thought I'd better bring it.'

He hands it to DS Jones.

'Look at the bottom.'

She turns it over.

It is engraved in just-legible script.

'To Veronica.' She inhales sharply. 'Ah – I see.'

DS Leyton strains to look.

'What is it?'

DS Jones rises and takes the ornament to present it before the lens. She explains what she has deduced.

'Lady Fitzrovia – she was also Veronica.' She looks at Skelgill. 'This is originally from Caldblow Farm, isn't it?'

Skelgill nods; he is decidedly now trying not to look overtly smug.

'It was her trademark. She had a collection – from admirers. Oath of secrecy, you might say.'

DS Jones goes further.

'He couldn't resist keeping it – when he disposed of the rest of the haul. A gift for his wife.'

Skelgill clicks his tongue against the roof of his mouth.

'Bang on.'

Now DS Leyton reaches for the item, and examines it,

frowning.

'Surely this alone didn't make him confess, though, Guv?'

Skelgill now gives a sideways glance at the camera, as if he could be suspicious of its motive. He relents, and replies, perhaps a hint sheepishly.

'It's amazing what a couple of white lies can do, Leyton. Folk'll believe owt if you mention the word DNA.'

DS Leyton seems unperturbed. He weighs the item in his palm; it is a reaction provoked in most holders by its unusual density.

'Fact is, Guv – DNA or no DNA – this ties him to the burglary, right?'

Skelgill is nodding.

'And – don't overlook this – Tuseling wanted out. He wanted all this over. He was desperate to prove his case. He just needed the right encouragement. The prof made a balls-up of things – but he gave Tuseling a rough time – softened him up. Brought back the trauma – the prospect of more jail time. Tuseling was on the verge of chucking in the towel. When I put to him what I believe happened – he was ready to meet us halfway.'

DS Jones has the morning newspaper that carries Skelgill's 'exclusive' interview.

'Speaking to Kendall Minto, you say he took the antiques on the strength of a phone call. And that subsequently he was threatened with blackmail. That these are the two significant new admissions.'

Skelgill understands the story is far from told.

'If you look at his history – apart from the obvious, like claiming he weren't at Caldblow Farm – he doesn't tell a lot of lies. He just avoids certain parts of the truth. It pains him to lie. I don't reckon he's a psychopath. In that interview I stuck to the facts. I reckoned I owed Minto a favour – without him, I couldn't have made headway – even if he couldn't see the wood for the trees.'

Skelgill suddenly reaches to dig into his rucksack – but it seems to no avail. His colleagues wait for some explanation.

'He lent us an old paper from their archive. I promised I'd get it back to him. I had it in the car. I'm wondering what I just used to light the Kelly.'

DS Jones, having received the reporter's somewhat desperate entreaty to restore the artefact to his possession, raises her eyebrows. But DS Leyton is unaware of the minor side-drama, and he is eager to hear more of the main event.

'So, behind these facts … is what? The true story – or just what you think happened?'

Skelgill responds with a wry grin. He gestures loosely with his mug towards today's copy of the journal.

'Like I said – there doesn't have to be any difference, Leyton.'

'But you ain't one for speculation, Guv.'

'Leyton, there's speculation and there's gut feel.' He pauses to eat and drink. Then he leans to look to see what is left in the cake tin. 'Who was it who said – when you're down to your last explanation?'

DS Jones, the English graduate, supplies the solution.

'Are you referring to Sir Arthur Conan Doyle? He put the words into the mouth of Sherlock Holmes. *When you have eliminated the impossible, whatever remains, however improbable, must be the truth.*'

Skelgill motions with his cake.

'Proof of the pudding, Leyton.'

'But, Guv – he's a made-up character.'

Skelgill seems unperturbed.

'Leyton. Look at what we know. There's no debate about a miscarriage of justice – the Hares' false confessions. That officer was from West Pennines, same as Bromilow – no prizes for working that one out. Bromilow – a maverick who wanted to make his mark. Ambitious. Got his eye on the top job when the six district forces finally merged. Then along comes a golden opportunity. The biggest case in decades. It's all over the media – a cakewalk to national fame.'

'Right. I get all that.'

So why didn't he nail Tuseling?

There is a long silence.

Skelgill looks pointedly at each colleague in turn.

'It's the question that answers the case.'

His sergeants lean in from their sitting positions, as if drawn by a magnetic force. Both nod slowly – as if, despite the grammatical conundrum, curiously his words begin to make perfect sense.

It is DS Jones that first responds, her own words tentative.

'It would have been counterproductive to his ambition – that it would have put him in some jeopardy.'

Skelgill regards her sternly.

'Go back a few steps. Colin Bell-Gibson was a social climber. He was in the masons and moved in county circles – like the Copeland Hunt. He hosted shoots for local bigwigs. Inveigled himself into their company. He was also interested in – let's call it – the seedier side of life. That Special Cocktails ruse he told Tuseling about was true. And in that department he had a nice little asset – in the shape of Lady Veronica Fitzrovia.'

He pauses to take a gulp of tea, and to allow his audience to absorb the tranche of information.

'By the look of her, she was doing very nicely, despite having been bankrupted, and her only obvious income being the lease of her land. But say she had a lucrative sideline. Let's not put too fine a point on it – she'd worked as a high-class courtesan in Knightsbridge. A highly portable business that came with her to Caldblow Farm. Colin Bell-Gibson introduced her to influential clients – the sort of men who could be trusted to keep their own counsel. It's clear from the record – photographs of dinner dances – that she was well acquainted with John Bromilow.'

'Jack the flippin' Lad.'

Skelgill nods at DS Leyton's apt rider.

Indeed, DS Leyton expounds upon his line of thought.

'Something like that was taking place on the day Will Featherston was murdered? Will Featherston didn't walk in on a burglary – it was something more compromising that was in progress. Lady Fitzrovia … and … the Acting Chief of Police. And Colin Bell-Gibson?'

Skelgill has listened closely.

'Mid-afternoon, the two males had slipped away from the race meet for their own preferred entertainment. A spot of shooting at

Belltower Farm – hip-flasks charged – and made their way cross country to Caldblow Farm. They were getting up to whatever they were getting up to – drinking their way through half a case of vintage claret – and they were rudely interrupted.'

DS Jones completes the account.

'And Will Featherston was shot. By whom?'

But Skelgill waves away her question.

'Now look at what happened. What we already knew – and what Tuseling has now added.'

But DS Leyton has arrived at a caveat.

'Okay – so Tuseling responded to a phone call and came and picked up a bag of antiques. Why wasn't he more suspicious? That it was straight knock-off?'

Skelgill looks pointedly at DS Jones.

And she has the answer.

'Because the call was made by the owner of the antiques?'

Skelgill nods grimly.

'I don't know why Tuseling doesn't want to admit it. Pride, maybe. But – aye – that's got to be it. The lady of the manor. A woman to whom he doffed his cap – a woman he probably coveted – an attractive woman who'd've had him wrapped round her little finger, if he could have afforded her fee. So, there's nowt much suspicious when she says I'm having a clear out – come and help yourself before the rag-and-bone man turns up.'

DS Jones presses the tips of her fingers together.

'It would have been suspicious – as a theft – had one of the males phoned. Yet, wouldn't that have needed to be Colin Bell-Gibson?'

Skelgill holds up a palm, understanding that she has identified a small wrinkle.

'Aye – but you're touching on another key point of logic. In the heat of the moment – only a seasoned copper would have thought of the plan. It needed to look like a robbery gone wrong. And that's exactly what the investigators fell for. The kid had stumbled across armed intruders.'

He allows the words to sink in before he speaks again.

'They might have discussed one of them taking away the loot –

but that would have been very risky. Then Colin Bell-Gibson had the brainwave that ruined the rest of Percy Tuseling's life. Percy's at my beck and call – let's phone him – he won't look a gift horse in the mouth – antiques are right up his street.'

DS Leyton is regarding Skelgill a little wide-eyed, clearly perplexed.

'But, Guv – if they made Tuseling the patsy, there and then – but – what you said about not nailing him?'

'Leyton, when you're up the creek with no paddle, a broken paddle's an attractive option. Tuseling solved their immediate problem. I'm not saying they thought of framing him. And Bell-Gibson would have been right in his choice – so far as knowing that Tuseling would come like a shot, and also that he'd keep his trap shut once it dawned on him he could be in the frame. So Lady Fitzrovia pulls together a bag of swag that looks like it's been swiped in a hurry – not her purse or personal jewellery, note – stuff that's to hand, including the half case of wine they've not drunk. Only her prints would have been on the items. Then she makes the call. Tuseling's only too happy to oblige.'

Skelgill inhales and takes a draught of tea, exhaling after he has safely swallowed the hot liquid.

'The two men melt away, taking their guns with them. Back to Belltower – and away by car – back to the race day at Cartmel. Right?'

DS Leyton is nodding.

'Struth, they'd have the perfect alibi, Guv. Who keeps track of folk at a race day? You're talking hundreds of acres, a couple of miles of track, hospitality tents and bars, the bookies' stalls, the grandstands, great milling crowds. Some racegoers wander off round the town – for a drink, lunch, sightseeing. Once you're there, it's easy to lose touch with your group – you might not see your mates until you meet up after the last race.'

Skelgill seems satisfied with his colleague's informed contribution.

'Now Lady Fitzrovia phones 999 to say she's returned from horse riding to find the farmhouse burgled – and a body.'

A longer silence unfolds. A lesser black-backed gull lands on the wall and eyes them apprehensively. Skelgill reaches to slide the lid over the cake tin.

DS Jones finally ends the hiatus.

'And the real proof of this is because Percy Tuseling was not apprehended and charged.'

Skelgill grimaces.

'Think about it – he were a sitting duck. They had his head on a plate. We've identified that. Freud identified that. The ordinary cops at the time identified that. There was more than enough rope to hang him, and he put the noose round his neck with incompetent efforts like the card message.'

'Whatever remains, must be the truth.'

Skelgill regards DS Jones pensively.

'It's not like Bromilow was averse to stitching up an innocent crook. It was his MO in the West Pennines force – look at the number of cases that were overturned when the whistleblower shopped Officer Y. Look at what he eventually did to the Hares. There's only one possible explanation for the organised chaos that surrounded the investigation into Tuseling – *because it was organised.'*

DS Leyton is nodding.

'Those poor old Hares couldn't come along fast enough for Bromilow, eh, Guv? Then they came down on them like a ton of bricks.'

Skelgill scowls briefly.

'Go easy with the poor old Hares, Leyton – but – aye – a ton of bricks. The spotlight's off Tuseling – and the risk of it all unravelling goes away. The involved parties keep their heads down – and Tuseling's too terrified to rattle any cages.'

'Until the night at Belltower Farm.'

It is DS Jones that makes the statement.

Skelgill regards her intently as she continues.

'Until a drunk and debauched Colin Bell-Gibson couldn't contain his urges and opened his big mouth.'

DS Leyton makes an ironic growl.

'Just when they think they've got away with it – the Hares sent down – and all's hunky dory – normal service can be resumed. Then – *ka-boom!'*

DS Jones is nodding.

'Colin Bell-Gibson dies – but the corollary was renewed jeopardy for John Bromilow. All of a sudden the Hares case might unravel. The coincidences were too powerful to ignore.'

Skelgill, having let his colleagues run with the scenario, now interjects.

'Aye – except he pulled it off again. Managed to condense the investigation into Percy Tuseling to the bare minimum – same for the trial. Suppressed any witnesses or evidence that might have set off alarm bells. And Tuseling had no choice but to play along.'

More silent reflection ensues.

Again, it is DS Jones that next speaks.

'Do we know – was there ever any come-uppance for John Bromilow?'

Skelgill shrugs.

'I reckon there's stuff in sealed archives. The Chief might reveal some of that in her statement. But what we do know is he never got the top job. He returned to West Pennines. And he'd have been retired by the time the Hares were acquitted. A lower-ranking copper was the scapegoat – rightly so, for his part – but the verdict was mistrial – not about evidence. So they were always able to hide behind the argument that the Hares *were* the culprits. No need to go looking for anyone else, or for some other explanation – let alone look under our own carpet.'

DS Jones is pensively twisting a lock of hair around an index finger.

'Until now.'

Her remark elicits only nods, and it is half a minute until DS Leyton hands round the tin; they share the last three slices of Borrowdale chocolate shortbread.

Skelgill breaks off a piece of his and tosses it up into the air. The seagull is primed for launch and catches it mid-flight, disappearing before its fellows discern its good fortune.

DS Jones wipes crumbs from her lips.

'We've still not dealt with the pulling of the trigger.'

They turn expectantly to Skelgill.

'Don't look at me. I'm no wiser than you pair.'

DS Leyton is the more overtly exasperated.

'But you must have a theory, Guv? I mean – to get so close – it's nail-biting.'

'You'll have to bite your nails, Leyton. Aye – we're close – but that's on the basis of every other suspect being eliminated, and what's left. But when we're down to the final three inside the farmhouse – it's pot luck.'

'But what about motive?' DS Leyton is scratching his head; it may be midges.

'Who says there has to be a motive?'

Skelgill's retort prompts more silent reflection.

DS Jones now responds.

'Can you elaborate, Guv?'

Skelgill twists his shoulders, as if the mental discomfort manifests itself.

'Look – I can give you motives. Bromilow – aye – a lot to lose if he were caught with his trousers down and it ended up in the papers. He was distinctive looking – he would have been recognisable – his picture had been in the press. Add to that, he was a ruthless operator, completely unscrupulous – and he knew how to use a gun.'

Skelgill pauses.

'Bell-Gibson – same story. He had a nice little number going with Lady Fitzrovia. You scratch my back, I'll scratch yours. He wouldn't want that to come out. And Will Featherston would definitely have known who he was. Chuck in the fact that he didn't approve of the lad's interest in his daughter. Nasty piece of work – always out for himself – transactional, his daughter called him. And he too was handy with a shotgun and most weeks probably killed things with it.'

The gull returns; it lands on the wall and regales them with its hungry lament. Skelgill eyes it knowingly.

'Then Lady Fitzrovia. You might say the same for her – about publicity – but, I'm not so sure about that. What do they say, no publicity's bad publicity? As for guns – she'd probably never picked one up in her life. According to Susan Bell-Gibson she hardly knew one end of a horse from the other. I doubt she'd know a safety catch if it bit her on the finger.'

He picks up a fragment of stone and casts it into the air, just as he had done with the piece of shortbread – but the gull does not move; it is not fooled.

DS Jones, too, has paid close attention.

'Wait. It was an accident? Bravado? Teasing?'

Skelgill regards her phlegmatically.

'Two loaded shotguns, both safety catches probably left off. Three folk who've had too much to drink and high on who knows what. Next time there's guns about – you watch where I stand.'

Skelgill gives a shake of the head and swivels around to face out to sea. He leans forward wrapping his right arm round his knee and grasping with his left hand the stubble of his chin. He stares out across the ocean, squinting into the setting sun.

His colleagues follow suit, and settle to gaze meditatively westwards.

Were Turnpike Media's hired drone camera to be pressed into service for a parting shot, gliding in like an inquisitive seabird, as their three forms on the clifftop took shape, huddled close in a row, they might almost be mistaken for a human rendition of the Three Wise Monkeys.

EPILOGUE

CLIPPING FROM WESTMORLAND GAZETTE

Court Reports

THURSDAY. CARLISLE CORONER'S COURT. At the re-opened inquest of the 1976 death of teenager Will Featherston at Caldblow Farm, Copeland Borough, the Cumbria Coroner has recorded a narrative verdict as follows. "The Court finds that Will Featherston died in the presence of three persons. First, Colin Bell-Gibson of Belltower Farm, deceased 1977, following a shooting incident. Second, John Bromilow, formerly of West Pennines Constabulary, deceased 1989; overdose of prescription medicine. Third, Lady Veronica Fitzrovia, deceased 1982, at a benefactor's villa, South of France; cause of death not established. The cause of Will Featherston's death is held by the required standard of the balance of probabilities to be unlawful killing by a person whose identity is unknown."

***

NEXT IN THE SERIES

THERE'S NO PLACE LIKE HOME

Drifting absently in *The Doghouse* on Bassenthwaite Lake, Skelgill has a feeling that he is being watched. From a wheelchair in the adjoining grounds of Duck Hall Nursing Home an elderly man looks on. They exchange a wave; it becomes a regular occurrence. And when later Skelgill engages with his bankside supporter he learns of his tragic circumstances. The helpless man has fallen prey to unscrupulous next of kin. As Father Time looms, there ensues a race against the clock, and the realisation that this may not be their first victim.

'Murder at Home' by Bruce Beckham will be released in January 2024.

FREE BOOKS, NEW RELEASES, THE BEAUTIFUL LAKES ... AND MOUNTAINS OF CAKES

Sign up for Bruce Beckham's author newsletter

Thank you for getting this far!

If you have enjoyed your encounter with DI Skelgill there's a growing series of whodunits set in England's rugged and beautiful Lake District to get your teeth into.

My newsletter often features one of the back catalogue to download for free, along with details of new releases and special offers.

No Skelgill mystery would be complete without a café stop or two, and each month there's a traditional Cumbrian recipe – tried and tested by yours truly (aka *Bruce Bake 'em*).

To sign up, this is the link:

https://mailchi.mp/acd032704a3f/newsletter-sign-up

Your email address will be safely stored in the USA by Mailchimp, and will be used for no other purpose. You can unsubscribe at any time simply by clicking the link at the foot of the newsletter.

Thank you, again – best wishes and happy reading!

Bruce Beckham

Printed in Great Britain
by Amazon

32936515R00169